Scratched
An Algy Temple Mystery by
J.J. Partridge

ISBN 978-1-940192-72-7

Published by
 köehlerbooks™

210 60th Street
Virginia Beach, VA 23451
212-574-7939
www.koehlerbooks.com

to Pat
Good reading
Happy Holiday

[signature]

18/7/11

Scratched

AN ALGY TEMPLE MYSTERY BY

J.J. Partridge

VIRGINIA BEACH
CAPE CHARLES

1. Scratch: *skrach*: to scrape as with claws or nails; in pool, the act of shooting the cue ball into a pocket, either intentionally or unintentionally, and forfeiting a turn

2. Scratch: *skrach*: money or cash

3. Scratched: in athletic contests, terminated or withdrawn, to lose

1   WaterFire

Whenever Esmeralda Gonzalez recollected that night, her thumb and index finger went to her lips and she signed a Cross.

◦ ◯ ◦

Luis Gonzalez found a parking place on College Hill and led his family down the steep incline to South Main Street. The family was dressed for a warm, humid August night's *fiesta*; Luis with pressed jeans, white short-sleeve shirt, and new Nikes, his wife Esmeralda in a white blouse with red lacing and flowing black skirt that showed off her trim figure, and Laurienda, their five year old *niña*, in flip flops, shorts, and her favorite Mickey Mouse tee. This was the immigrant family's first evening venture into downtown Providence; they were nervously excited and ready to encounter what neighbors had promised would be an adventure: the exotic, mystical, wonderous WaterFire.

Earlier arrivals sprawled on blankets on the worn summer grass of Verrazzano Park or crowded railings along the Providence River to watch black-garbed fire keepers in work boats load splits of hardwood into mushroom shaped braziers. Others lined up at food trucks and stalls conducting a brisk business in sausage rolls, tacos, bulgogi, empanadas, pizza slices, lamb kabobs, and Rhode Island–style fried calamari with hot peppers. Braving a rush of Latino teenage boys in shorts, numbered T-shirts, and angled baseball caps followed by a possee of giggling girls, Luis bought chicken empanadas and cans of Coke for the family and found a bench along a busy brick walkway for their meal. A troupe garbed as ferocious gargoyles across the walkway got their startled attention; shy Laurienda hid her face in her mother's skirt until cajoled into peeping out at two Anglo girls her age dropping coins into outstretched cups and posing for photographs.

They finished their food, Luis stuffed their plates, cans, and napkins in a trash bin, and crossed a grassy expanse past marble memorials to veterans of wars barely familiar to Luis. They paused before shiny aluminum sheaths formed into towering rings, rusted-for-effect twisted metal crosses, an ominous obelisk adorned with parts of cap pistols and real guns. *"Que es todo esto?"* Luis, his shoulders in a shrug, asked his wife.

Choral music from speakers hidden within the shadowy corridors between river embankments accompanied the family as they joined a throng of noisy celebrants down to a cobbled path at river level where jugglers and mimes performed. Laurienda, her fingers secure in her parents' hands, became wide-eyed for glo-toys, whirligigs, and balloons on sticks sold by roving vendors. As they reached the shimmering pool of the Ellipse in WaterPlace Park, a setting red-orange sun made a blinding appearance through a bank of vermillion clouds; a partying couple in a water taxi held up wine glasses in a toast to spectators. The Gonzalezes joined in the appreciative applause.

As dusk gave way to night, WaterFire transformed the river and park. Braziers became saucers of crackling orange, yellow, and blue flames creating undulating stained glass effects on the surface of the inky water. Gregorian chants provided a melodic background for huge, tethered LED-illuminated dragonflies circling above their heads, a fire-baton twirler entertained an enthralled audience from a bridge parapet, drifting wood smoke added an ethereal quality. Across the river, one side of a granite and green glass office building became a five-story screen displaying a live video of excited, happy children; Luis hoped the roving camera would capture the image of his pretty Laurienda.

They found seats on granite steps leading to the river and watched tongues of fire lick the night and sparks snap skyward. Esmeralda pointed to a mist forming on the river's surface; Luis, an avid fisherman when his job with overtime at a busy Alex and Ani jewelry factory in Cranston allowed him a few hours of free time, explained that cooler water must be flowing from Narragansett Bay on a rising tide.

As a gondola glided by, its boatman in a striped shirt and straw hat with ribbon tail, his single oar propelling the craft toward South Water Street's promenade, Laurienda found a stick from a discarded toy, took a step closer to the water, and swirled it beneath its surface, creating bubbles and foam. As the music changed to a friendly Latin beat, Luis and Esmeralda experienced a sense of comity with the strangers sitting nearby, with those in their *paseo* around the Ellipse; all were absorbed in an other-worldly ritual of light, color, sound, scent, and shadow that was the essence of WaterFire.

A swirl of Laurienda's stick was impeded beneath the reflective surface of the water. She poked at something vaguely white that had moved into the Ellipse with the tide. "Papa, Papa," she exclaimed, turning to her father who raised his chin in response. Laurienda called again, a child's demand creeping into her voice. "Papa! Come here!"

"What, Laurienda?" he replied, in English, as his daughter thrashed the water with her stick. "Laurienda, what have you got? A big fish?" He laughed and nudged Esmeralda. "A whale?" He laughed again as he stood.

"Let Papa see."

Am I stabbed? Is blood rushing out of my belly? Is this how I die? The impact is not so much pain as paralysis. An acid taste of vomit gorges in my mouth, the tape slapped over my lips prevents my gag, another covers my eyes leaving flashing spirals in blackness, as though my head is spinning. Maybe it is. Tape circles my wrists, a cord loops my neck and thighs, I'm lifted with grunts and swearing, and dropped backside first into the Charger's trunk.

Only then does my stomach relax enough for me to snort air into my lungs. I am not going to die … . Yet.

2 Monday

A CONVERSATION WITH BENNO Bacigalupi was like shaving with a dull razor.

I put my mug of coffee on the table where the ex–state police detective hovered over the remains of breakfast. He was garbed in his work uniform, a narrow lapel suit, white shirt, and nondescript tie; his throat bobbed with a swallow of coffee as he raised his narrow face to me.

"So …?" I sat across from him.

We were in a rear booth at Costa's, a classic Providence greasy spoon on Thayer Street, a hangout for the campus cops, and maintenance and grounds crews essential to Carter University's operations. I had been summoned by his terse message left last night on my home phone—not exactly a command but close—to meet him here at seven thirty. Benno wouldn't call me on a Sunday night to meet for less than something consequential; he conducted all important business in person because, as he once explained, "never just hear a voice when you can see a face."

"Italo Palagi." The lip of his mug remained at eye level. "Interested?"

I was. Immediately. And surprised, and circumspect. Benno was, after all, these days a detective for hire. "In what?"

Benno responded impatiently. "How he died, of course."

I *thought* I was already well informed. The body of Italo Palagi, the Director Emeritus of Carter University's Institute for Italian Studies, had been discovered weeks earlier in the Ellipse during a summer WaterFire, causing a huge commotion. An accidental death according to the preliminary report of the medical examiner who found a massive overdose of OxyCodone in Palagi's corpse. As Carter University general counsel, Palagi's death, although *not* the manner of his death, was of professional interest because the Institute was the beneficiary of a multimillion-dollar bequest from his estate. Only last week, a demand letter had arrived from a lawyer in Rome and co-counsel in New York challenging the bequest on behalf of one Vittorio Ruggieri who claimed to be Palagi's son and heir.

"Sure," I responded, cautiously, as the tempting smells of fried eggs, grilled onions, hash browns, and bacon began to weaken my resolve to avoid a high caloric breakfast.

Benno's stubby fingers grabbed the table's saltshaker and sugar dispenser and lined them up in front of me. A Moleskine notebook came from his inside jacket pocket; he flipped it open like cops did in *noir* movies, laid it flat, his eyes focused on its tiny handwriting.

"Palagi owned a condo at Corliss Landing on South Water Street near the river," he began in his raspy lisp. His index finger touched the sugar dispenser, which became a proxy for the condo. "Came home from his office that Wednesday night at five by cab." His finger moved to the saltshaker that now represented Palagi.

"Security guard noticed he carried a valise. Like most nights, had his dinners delivered from Al Forno, that fancy restaurant practically next door, a featured pasta of the day, garden salad with a balsamic vinaigrette, a couple of rolls, delivered at seven o'clock. At eight thirty-seven, he called his longtime secretary on a landline. She lives in the same condo complex. Conversation lasted less than two minutes. She told the detectives that Palagi said not to come in on Thursday or Friday. She wasn't surprised because he had been moody, sickly, not a lot of work for her. On Thursday afternoon, she called his condo to check on him. No answer. Again, on Friday, no answer at home or the office. She went to his condo, she's got a key, and he wasn't there. So, she called 911. He surfaced Saturday night and Monday, after he was identified, cops did a pass at his condo. The delivery box from Al Forno was in the trash, his plate, utensils, and a wine glass in the dishwasher, and get this, his pajamas were laid out on his bed." Benno picked up the saltshaker. "So give him an hour for dinner, time to clean up, call the secretary, lay out his pajamas, and then sometime between nine and early the next morning, that's the medical examiner's best guess, he's in the river."

The saltshaker advanced down the table toward a napkin holder, vinegar cruet, and ketchup bottle that had to represent buildings along the river. "Hard to tell exactly with him in the river for a couple of days."

I hid a grimace with my mug at my lips. Hadn't thought of the effect of seventy-two hours in the summer temperature of the Providence River on the old man's body. Or tidal currents bruising the body on river rocks as it scraped along its bottom or against the petrified wharf pilings near Point Street. Then, unexpectedly, from an unsettled place in my psyche, came an unwanted echo of a horrific combination of rasp, snore, and gurgle, a death rattle. Years ago, during President Reagan's ill-fated intervention in Lebanon, I was among hundreds of Marines trapped under the twisted steel and broken concrete of our crumpled Beirut barracks, unable to move, covered in debris and grit, a steel beam creaking inches above my head. In the long hours before I was rescued, helpless, I suffered through my comrades' forlorn, muffled, heart-rending cries, their blood and dust blocked breaths, and finally, their death rattles—sounds once heard, never forgotten—and now always associated by me with death. Was there something like a death rattle in a drowning? Water in place of blood and phlegm? I shivered involuntarily and lost my appetite.

"You okay?" Benno asked evenly. The ghosts vanished from my thoughts, I nodded, and he continued. "Now," he said, "here's an old guy, not good on his feet, used a walking stick to get around, aches and pains at that age, right? It was steamy all day and a stay-in night that the Weather Bureau said ended up in one of those pea soup fogs they get down by the harbor. He locked his condo, left his building through a rear door that's got a deadbolt, crossed South Water Street to the river. Somehow, somewhere along there, he got down to the river's edge, popped his pills, fell, conked his head on a rock or something on his way in, gulped river water," he snapped his fingers, "heart went." The saltshaker toddled past the cruet, ketchup bottle and napkin holder and was tipped on a side.

"Okay, suicide," I said. Perhaps the medical examiner's conclusion of accidental death was a less judgmental, less intrusive, way of categorizing Palagi's demise.

Benno's chin jutted out at me in a challenge. "So, if you're not coming back, why lay out your pajamas? Why lock your apartment?"

Reasonable questions. "Force of habit?"

"Guess what was in his pockets?"

"His keys?"

Benno blinked. I had been paying attention. "Good guess, but not on him when he was found." His eyes gleamed with anticipation. "What else?"

"Shit, I don't know," I answered impatiently.

"A Beretta!"

"A what?"

"Beretta. Single action, semi-automatic, an Italian army officer's side weapon. Carbon steel and plastic grips. Carries eight rounds of .32 caliber in a magazine. Stopped making this model, an M1935, at the end of Mussolini's era. Looks like this," and from his shirt pocket, he unfolded a page ripped from a gun magazine displaying a sleek looking, metallic-gray pistol. "Compact enough to put in a trouser pocket. Managed to stay inside his."

An eighty-two-year-old retired university professor packing OxyCodone and a pistol? "Which tells you what, exactly?"

"Nothing I can figure right now. According to the investigation report, the pistol wasn't registered and maybe never fired, one cartridge in the chamber, not even sure it was still live ammo. If there were fingerprints, the salt in the river water took care of them." The torn page was refolded and slid into his notebook.

I said, "Maybe he had a meal, a glass of wine, put out his pajamas, called his secretary, and then decided to do it? Went to the river, took his pills and the gun because he hadn't made up his mind how ...?"

"So," Benno interrupted, leaning into me, his voice becoming contentious in his harsh whisper, "if it was suicide, where's the friggin' note? Average suicide, probably not. But a professor? Man who wrote all his life? C'mon, there's got to be a note. He's got to explain."

I wouldn't accept that. "You said the secretary had a key. Maybe she tidied up and took the note when she went into his apartment?"

Benno frowned. "Why?"

"It was too personal ...?"

He shook his head, refusing to acknowledge my conjecture wasn't farfetched. "Even with no note, why go down to the river to swallow pills? Why not take the pills in bed with a glass of vino after asking somebody, the secretary for instance, to come over the next day? And what's with the Beretta? The guy was ... clean ... you know what I mean? Clean. That kinda guy doesn't stick a gun in his mouth and pull the trigger, his brains spattered everywhere. That kind of guy doesn't want to end up in the Providence River, bleached out, bloated, crabs eating his face ...."

I remembered Palagi as fastidious, even prissy in dress and manners despite age rendering him stoop-shouldered, his eyes myopic behind stylish rimless glasses, his ring of white hair always in place.

"Why are you into this, Benno?"

"Did some work for him a few months ago."

"What kind of work?"

"You know better than to ask," he said tersely. "His obit said he had been a big giver to the University so I figured you might want to know what I know." Benno straightened his shoulders from their hunch and pushed the table's accouterments back against the wall. "Here's the thing," he said, his voice rising in sharpness, "the detective squad did a crappy job. When the prelim found the junk in his gut, they went for the easy answer of prescription overdose suicide because cops move on, there's always another file. After they spoke to his secretary and gave the condo a once-over, they didn't treat it as a suspicious death. Didn't try to find where he went in. Didn't know he used a walking stick. What happened to that?"

Benno, ever the statie, would despise a shoddy investigation.

"You got to *ask*!" Benno's hand pounded the table, sloshing coffee out of my mug. "Use some shoe leather. Okay, maybe the margarita drinkers at the bars over there and the coked-up hookers patrolling Hard Core"—a particularly vile, garish strip club on South Water Street—"wouldn't have noticed Santa Claus at the river. Still, you got to ask. Like those little guys ... Asians ... fishing off the walkways all kinds of hours even if it would be a waste of time because them Asians never talk to cops. But a kid, first Cambode we took in the state police, did me a favor, checked them out with me last week. One remembered an old man with a cane on a foggy night a couple of weeks ago. Thought he banged the cane on a car window and got in." Benno shook his head. "Probably not Palagi. Doesn't fit. Likely some old doofus coming out of Hard Core."

I asked, "Why are you so sure he went in the river off South Water Street?"

"Had to be inside the Hurricane Barrier," he replied. "No way a body gets up river from the Bay through those narrow tainter gates in the Barrier. And why walk far if you live a couple of hundred feet from the water."

"So, what do *you* think happened?"

Benno wiggled out of the booth and slid his notebook back inside his jacket pocket. "They kept the case open after I got a look at the file because I asked questions, like what's with the gun in his pocket. Got them a little pissed. But they'll close it today, tomorrow, soon, without something else." Then, pointedly, he added, "If you need me, you got the number."

"But..."

His breakfast tab was left for me as though it was already an expense of an investigation.

o O o

George, the gap-toothed morning counterman, grinned broadly as he took my twenty at the register, ready with a wisecrack for any familiar face from College Hall. "Hey, Mr. Temple, what do you get when the Godfather becomes a Carter professor?"

"Jeez, George, I don't know."

"Somebody who makes an offer you can't understand."

Heh, heh, heh.

3

THE GREEN, THE PHYSICAL and cultural center of Carter University's historic main campus, was crowded with barely awake, earbudded kids toting backpacks and holding cell phones and Starbucks cups on their way to classes or the dining hall. As I paused for the passage of a phalanx of cyclists and four black-caped Goths on skateboards, my cell phone vibrated with a text from the Provost, the University's chief administrative officer, asking that I join him in his conference room in College Hall. I found him holding a newspaper, his bushy white hair and brows, long nose, craggy jaw, and slate gray eyes projecting a biblical anger.

"Palagi's financial advisor is caught in Sugarman's fraud!" The Provost's voice struggled to contain his exasperation.

The *Wall Street Journal* that he thrust at me was folded to a headline that read *Ravensford Capital Clients in Sugarman Ponzi*. The article reported hundreds of the Ravensford's investment accounts were in jeopardy, the SEC and FinRA were investigating, as was the US District Attorney. As I finished the grim news, he handed me a monthly statement from Ravensford Capital listing the number of units the Italo Palagi Trust owned in the Select Investment Fund, the dollar value per unit, and a total value of six million five thousand and twenty-one dollars as of August 31. "The Bursar says nothing in our files contains any mention of Palagi's assets being invested with Sugarman."

Unspoken was our mutual awareness of Bernard Sugarman and his infamous Ponzi scheme, dubbed by New York tabloids as *Bernie's Follies*. Posing as one of New York's and Palm Beach's cagiest investment managers, Sugarman had taken in billions into his investment company by promising moderate but steady returns through his *proprietary* option and stock index strategy. Employing dozens of *feeders*—investment advisors, hedge funds, and money managers—including, apparently, Ravensford Capital, Sugarman kept his cash machine rolling for decades by craftily creating an image of exclusivity, giving investors, including significant donors to the University, the warmth of positive returns even in a down market, allowing them to indulge in the sweet pleasure of financial ignorance.

"Under his trust's provisions," the Provost continued, "Palagi kept control of the investments during his lifetime. Started off at Smith Barney and then went over to Ravensford maybe ten years ago. The Bursar is sending over his files. If there's anything left, get it out of there. You've got the helm." The Provost, a graduate of Annapolis, was addicted to Navy vernacular.

Open-ended, *you're the lawyer*, questions were thrown my way every day. "Let me get up to speed," I responded and as quickly recollected a scheduled ten-thirty meeting. "I have an appointment this morning with Brunotti to discuss Palagi's son's claim to the estate. Should I tell him?"

The Provost blinked and tugged at his Churchillian blue with white polka dot bow tie. He never disguised his disdain for *Direttore* Cosimo Brunotti, Palagi's successor at the Institute. "*You* have to keep a relationship with him," he replied slowly as though he had decided that he didn't. "We'll inform him when we have a plan of action. Otherwise, he will go off half-cocked."

I agreed. Brunotti was pompous, temperamental, and notoriously oblivious to budgetary constraints. As between us, we had reached a level of polite animosity in our dealings.

"The Bursar also said since Palagi's death, we haven't received a nickel from the Italian bank that administers Palagi's royalty account." Long before he arrived at Carter, Palagi wrote, anonymously, a series of thrillers wildly popular in Italy with an Italian James Bond-like hero. Royalties, along with license fees from movies, television, games, and clothing lines, had made Palagi wealthy and even today produced a stream of income that he generously shared with the Institute. "Something else we have to look into."

I thought of Benno Bacigalupi's suspicions as to Palagi's death but decided the Provost had enough to digest this morning. Instead,

I offered, "Outside of his trust, Palagi had other assets, his condo for instance, and whatever bank accounts and personal property he might have. After some specific bequests, the balance goes to the University. His two apartments in Italy are also in his trust, so there will be something left."

"The Institute has four sources of annual funding," the Provost rejoined, ticking them off his raised fingers, "its endowment income, annual donations, our portion of Palagi's royalties and license fees, and general budgetary support from the University. Endowment income is down, donor support both from here and Italy has slumped, and his royalties and fees are miniscule compared to what we once received. Part of our budget expectation for the Institute's continued viability was receipt of Palagi's trust assets. Without those funds ..."

4

"HOUSTON, WE HAVE A problem," I whispered to Marcie Barrett, my longtime legal assistant and friend, as I entered the third-floor suite of the Office of University Counsel. She was on the phone, tasked with double duty with our shared secretary out for a week of vacation, and held up a wait-one-minute finger in reply. I went into my cramped, file-strewn office and sat behind a multidrawered yellow oak desk, a family heirloom from behind which my great-grandfather ran Temple Bank, Providence's largest at the time.

"What happened?" Marcie asked expectantly as she entered, her washed out, greenish eyes apprehensive.

As I explained the decimation of Palagi's trust, astonishment flushed her face. I instructed her to make it a priority to go through the expected files from the Bursar and flag information on any person or persons handling the account at Ravensford Capital and anything else she thought pertinent. "And call Champlin & Burrill"—our principal outside counsel—"for a teleconference this afternoon. I need securities and bankruptcy lawyers."

"Six million dollars! Gone like that," and she snapped her fingers. Then, she said, "And I thought *this* would be the top of our agenda."

She handed me a United States District Court civil action complaint entitled *GLBT Campus Action Coalition v. Carter University* with a summons directed to the Office of the University Counsel, Alger M. Temple, Esq. "Served this morning." I skimmed through the twenty-page complaint. The Coalition, together with the Student Council, with an ACLU lawyer, claimed a violation of student First Amendment free speech rights because campus police had removed flyers—copies attached—posted on dorm and classroom walls and bulletin boards, as well as utility poles, trash containers, and benches on Thayer and Waterman Streets, depicting graphic lesbian lovemaking in a promotion for a campus feminist discussion panel on female sex at various ages and levels of maturity.

I sat back, frustrated; the University is constantly hauled into court or administrative hearings because of a perceived violation of student or faculty rights. After ten years as University Counsel, I should be inured to the sound and fury of an Ivy League campus with its significant population of cultural war militants whose throbbing moral certainties exhibited little concern for the sensibilities of others. But I was not. I hated the manufactured crises, the passionate outcries that led to demonstrations and sit-ins, even more the daily pettiness that arrived at our office. That part of being University Counsel was like being Attorney General in a mini-state inhabited by the opinionated, the insensitive, and the stubborn, surrounded by antagonists ready to rub each others' faces in the *merde*.

I handed the complaint back to Marcie, telling her to send it on to Champlin & Burrill for review and comment. She ran her fingers through her prematurely white curly hair, grimaced, and left my office. I snapped on the iMac on my credenza to search for information on Palagi's investment advisor, Ravensford Capital. My screensaver was a last year's vacation image of Nadie Winokur, my fiancée, under a red umbrella on the patio of Osteria Pazanzo in Chianti, her eyes shining and expectant, her lips pressed to blow a kiss. It made me feel better. Nadie, the *wunderkind* of the Department of Psychology, was beautiful and vivacious, self-assured, passionate about life and her causes. Her happy image soothed my angst; we would be married weekend after next followed by a week in Rome and another on the Amalfi Coast. Just had to pace myself until then, not get too deeply involved in anything, not let campus mean-spiritedness get to me.

o O o

Ravensford Capital's elaborate website invited inquiries from *qualified investors* to consult with the firm's team of *experienced advisors.* Its pages stressed the firm's adherence to high ethical standards and fidelity to client interests, and a pledge of *client focus*; one of many graphs depicted growth in assets under management to over nine hundred million since it began operations in 1986. The site pop-ups touted various domestic and international investment vehicles and listed the names of a dozen or so partners and managing directors, giving a general impression that Ravensford Capital—the name seemed so very WASPish considering the ethnicity of its partners—was an aggressive money manager and not exactly Morgan Stanley. How much had it lost to Sugarman?

For some practical guidance and financial community intelligence, I telephoned my older brother Nick, a partner at the venerable international investment house of Brown Brothers, Harriman. "They're going down, Algy. Started out on Long Island, came into mid-town eight or nine years ago. Some of the money maybe is ... or was ... warmer than most. But that's a rumor, I hasten to say."

"What's likely to happen?"

"In days, a week at most, bankruptcy. Probably, the principals have already liquidated everything they could, gotten their money out—they always do. If your professor had his trust funds there, you're not going to see very much except something from SIPC insurance, maybe not."

"Any chance of getting anything out now?"

"Not on your life," he replied soberly.

o O o

Near to ten thirty, I entered Marcie's office where she was working through two cartons of Redweld files. "Years of monthly statements from the Bursar," she said as she looked up . "Shouldn't you be leaving for the Institute?"

"Yeah," I replied sourly and continued out of the office and down the hall to the men's room. A splash of cold water on my face refreshed me; I wiped dry, caught my reflection in the mirror over the sink, and thought of Nadie as captured in the screensaver. When she looked at me, did our twenty-plus years difference in age creep into her mind? To be honest, nobody was going to confuse me with George Clooney. The image I saw was comprised of bold features: a large, square head, a long, straight nose over a full-lipped mouth, ears that protruded from wiry, salt and pepper hair, and the Temple family's formidable jaw: the family portraits in Temple House's library evidenced that jaw had been in our genes for decades. I took a step back and let my hands slide to my hips. All in all, not bad; I was trim, tall, broad shouldered and under my shirt there was a body kept in reasonable shape from daily exercise. Right now, I could carry off my years well enough but I wondered when or if age would eventually give her pause.

I leaned in to the mirror. My blue-gray eyes, Nadie said, gave me a defining *look*, what she called "self-possession" which I flattered myself meant a calming seriousness of purpose. With the preening Cosimo Brunotti next on my plate, I would need self-possession super-sized.

5

THE INSTITUTE FOR ITALIAN Studies was located off campus in a three-story, ecru colored Italianate house on Benefit Street, only a block away from Temple House, my family's historic Federalist-style mansion. As I awaited admission at the entrance off its John Street parking lot, I recalled, upon my return to Providence to practice law at Champlin & Burrill, my mother's dismay over the building's deterioration into a neighborhood eyesore when savaged into Class C office space, with *For Rent* signs sprouting on ragged lawns. As the doyen of East Side society, the matriarch of a family with a two hundred year history in Providence, and as a Trustee of Carter University, she fostered its eventual purchase and renovation by the University with anonymous and substantial financial assistance from Temple family's trusts. Her gift fulfilled two lifelong interests; not only was she an ardent preservationist, she was also an Italophile who relished the idea of a center of Italian culture at the University. To her surprise and chagrin, the building's designation as the home of the Institute was not without protests from some Carter faculty who ridiculed the restored mansion as a "jewel box" for a program of studies derided as "a mere cultural ornament" and "expensive monument to Western elitism."

Wounds were opened within the liberal arts departments that two decades later were still healing.

○ ◯ ○

"*Buon giorno*, Signor Temple," Brunotti's attractive secretary smiled and escorted me to a second-floor room, ducal in its rich furnishings of heavy brocade curtains, eggplant-colored walls, parquet floors, and thick red rugs under an elaborate ceiling medallion supporting a chandelier sparkling with Murano glass. "*Direttore* Brunotti will be with you momentarily," she said and left me to sit in a stiff back chair before an ornately carved, marble-framed desk centered in the room, its surface bare except for a remote control device. A wall-mounted plasma screen behind the desk displayed a computerized map of Italy, which with the click of a remote allowed Brunotti to zoom in on the smallest Italian city and call up names, parties, politicians, reporters, economic data, and history, even the latest political gossip.

A door opened behind me. "Alger. Good. You are prompt," was weightedly spoken in a vaguely Euro-smoothie accent.

I acknowledged Cosimo Brunotti with a barely audible "*Direttore*" as he strode across the room toward me, his demeanor, his bullet head with black hair combed straight back, and formidable chin daring disagreement. He was dressed in a well-cut, dark blue, double-breasted suit with pleated trousers pressed razor sharp, a white shirt with collar pin holding in place a red Pucci 'key' tie, and a matching red pocket square, clothes, I thought, meant to distinguish him from the Institute's academics, or an administrative functionary like me. I shook his delicate hand which was withdrawn quickly as he passed me on his way to the desk in a billow of cologne. Despite his demeanor and attire, he failed to achieve the effortless *la bella figura* that he too obviously sought. He was, to put it bluntly, overdone, a Milanese bling.

"This Palagi business..." Brunotti leaned in toward me, his fingers splayed on the desktop, his face fixed in a frown as though gathering thoughts from far more important matters, and proceeded to enumerate the many inconveniences and annoyances resulting from Italo Palagi's death, all of this business clearly irritating and beneath his status as *Direttore*. His air of self-importance made me wonder, again, how the Institute's Leadership Council, a group of its largest donors sprinkled with Italian governmental officials, got it *so* wrong when it recommended Brunotti to succeed Palagi.

A beep from speakers below the plasma screen interrupted his complaints and a name flashed over Verona. Brunotti eyed the screen as two more beeps registered and he touched buttons on the remote to transfer the incoming call or e-mail elsewhere. "Over the summer, he became exceedingly unpleasant and difficult."

Brunotti paused for my reaction to his dismissive comments, probably because my mother's good will toward Palagi had not been transferred to his successor whom she found to be a pretentious ass. Not getting any response, he made a very Italian dismissive hand gesture of one in authority to someone not attentive to his needs.

I swallowed hard and addressed the subject of our conference. When Brunotti had been informed of the putative son's legal challenge to Palagi's estate, he pressed me to immediately settle, even after I emphasized that we had been given no records to support a claim of paternity and that the old man might have been duped. "Strike now!" he said, his hand hammering his desk. "Negotiate! See what you can get away with. Don't let this fester into a media circus."

As I again made my case for patience, Brunotti rolled his eyes. He thrust his hands dramatically into the pockets of his suit jacket, striking a pose of a posturing Italian politician last seen in a Fellini movie. "The situation will be an embarrassment. Mark my words, Alger, the Italian public will expect that a son would receive a rightful share of his father's estate, no matter what Palagi's estate plan may have directed." He went through a litany of Italian notables and politicians and Leadership Council members likely to be offended if the University was obstinate, and how the Italian media would delight in a messy dispute involving the estate of a well-known thriller writer and scholar. "And now, there are local lawyers." He reached into a desk drawer and handed me an oversized business card that shouted "Lucca & Lucca, Attorneys at Law."

Their names rang as many bells as an Easter Sunday in Rome. Former state senator Rudolph 'Rudy' Lucca, known in Providence politics as *Il Mazziere*, the card player, was a shrewd pol from Federal Hill; the other Lucca was his son, City Councilman Robert 'Bobby Flowers' Lucca, the leader of a cabal of politicos that vied for control of city government with Providence's newly elected and reforming mayor, my oldest and closest friend, Tony Tramonti. My immediate and overriding concern, however, was Brunotti's apparent blatant breach of the University's absolute ban on communication with lawyers representing real or potential claimants against the University. No exceptions. Not even for *il Direttore*.

"What could I do?" he exclaimed in reaction to my scowl.

"Senator Lucca is the Italian consul in Providence. He demanded a meeting. An *official* visit to the Institute on behalf of the Republic! He'll be here on Friday at eleven."

"He's not coming for espresso and cantucci," I responded sharply. Was it not clear to Brunotti that Rudy Lucca would use and confuse his status as a consular representative to press his legal representation of Palagi's alleged son? My comment to that effect was met with a flit of a dismissive eye. "So, will you be here?"

A light blinked on the plasma screen over someplace in the Piedmont where it must be late afternoon, followed by a string of beeps. Brunotti made no move to respond. I stood to leave, knowing I had to make clear who was in charge. "This will be *my* meeting, Cosimo. I am the only University officer authorized to deal with the Palagi estate. You can participate as host but you will not offer comments or answer any questions unless I direct you to do so. And, I repeat, the University's position is that *all* of Palagi's assets under his will and trust come to the Institute."

"You want *me* to be a party to such a rigid position, one that is a disaster for the Institute?" he retorted as he sucked in a breath for what surely would be a speech. "Just so *you* know, we ... I ... the Institute ... cannot afford negative publicity, here or in Italy, in these times of economic distress. A fight over Palagi's assets would demean us. Our prestige is at stake. You understand this? Palagi was a member of the Roman Academy, one of Italy's men of distinction, an author, a scholar. Only last year, the President of the Republic presented Palagi with Italy's highest civil honor, the Cross of Savoy. His son must be ... accommodated!"

My response was interrupted by another string of beeps and blinking lights, this time over Rome, which got Brunotti's attention. "I must take this call," he said coolly and opened a desk drawer and removed a cell phone.

I felt his stare drill my back as I left.

6

THE CRYSTALLINE NOONTIME SUNLIGHT did nothing to alleviate my *agita*. I left the Institute and turned south on the narrow brick and slate sidewalks of Benefit Street toward Fox Point, navigating overflowing bins and recycle boxes of a refuse pick-up day. Yellowed ginkgo and plane tree leaves drifted to the ground, bikes and cars shot by, historic houses painted in authentic blues and yellows brightened the street, a nice distraction, if only for a few seconds, as I ruminated over Brunotti's egotism and likely perfidy.

Jimmy's, my destination and widely recognized as the best Portuguese-American restaurant in the area, had been newly renovated, sheathed in natural shingles that covered worn clapboards and a mansard roof with double-sized windows that allowed daylight into the second floor Billiard Club. A flame-red canopy with a cursive white *Jimmy's* went from the curb on Wickenden Street to the entrance; this being artsy Fox Point, the utility pole by the canopy also served as a stanchion for one of designer Madolin Maxey's street installations, a prancing wooden stallion constructed by artist Norma Anderson.

Bells jingled from above the door, sounds that harkened back to the Jimmy's of the past. In contrast, its new interior shouted *upscale* in its earth tone colors, well-crafted landscapes, displays of Portuguese faience crockery, subdued lighting, white tablecloths, and cushioned booths.

I chose a stool at the stainless steel counter in front of an open kitchen that gave diners a view of bustling cooks at ranges, ovens, and prep tables. Spicy aromas, particularly cumin, sharpened my appetite—no breakfast, not even a donut all morning—and I opened a multi-page menu that had replaced a daily insertion in a plastic sheet. Today's lunch specials included several of the restaurant's featured fusion dishes. "Portuguese *fusion*?" I asked Nadie at the restaurant's grand reopening in April. "Yes," she replied. "Smile. Get with it."

Chef Jao, in whites with a red bandana around his neck, saw me and came to the counter. I was about to order a Goan shrimp salad when I heard "How ya doin'?" followed by Young Jimmy Hannigan's hand on my shoulder. "The scallop risotto," the co-owner barked to Jao. I raised an eyebrow and nodded in acceptance.

Young Jimmy took the stool to my right. His long fingers began to drum the counter. "How's business?" I asked.

"Business sucks," he muttered and lapsed into silence. "Restaurant's down twenty percent. The function room doesn't draw squat during the week."

I spun on my stool to face him. A white polo shirt covered an upper body so skinny that as a kid he rarely doffed his shirt out of embarrassment. His elongated face had features that were somehow out of place, or the wrong size, as though mixed up at birth, his sallow complexion contrasted poorly with longish, wavy hair and eyebrows likely touched-up with Grecian Formula. That didn't matter much because his widely spaced, stunningly blue eyes grabbed instant attention, eyes that I have always believed were his edge in shooting pool.

"The Club is *way* down," Young Jimmy continued. The Billiard Club was the plush private pool club on the second floor, successor to Hannigan's Billiards and Tap, his father's—Old Jimmy's—pool hall *cum* bookie. I have been a Club member since it opened.

The risotto arrived in a bowl accompanied by a fork and soup-spoon. Jao waited for me to taste. "Fusion?" I asked, with a wry smile, spoon in hand.

"Yeah," he snickered without looking at Young Jimmy. "Stonington fusion! Bomster flash frozen scallops. The best you can get." I had a spoonful of the risotto and let Jao know with a smile of satisfaction that I appreciated his efforts before he left us.

"Even the Saturdays," Young Jimmy lamented, slamming his right hand palm down on the counter. On Saturday nights, the Club's sporting members backed their hunches on exhibition matches between touring pros arranged by Young Jimmy who took a hefty house cut from the betting pools he managed. I skipped Saturdays in recent months because my weekend schedule that now included Nadie.

"We overdid it," he said and to make his point, turned to the nearly empty dining room. "We thought it was time to renovate, make the investment." Then, he brightened. "I gotta tell you, though, the Shoot-Out will be a life saver." He lowered his voice. "A fuckin' lollapalooza for us with my host gig and exhibitions at the Dunk, plus what we expect from here and ..." he shrugged, "... upstairs."

I was well aware of Young Jimmy's expectations. The Shoot-Out Tournament was advertised as the largest nine-ball amateur and pro pool tournament ever held east of Chicago, with huge pots of prize money. The event, to be played mostly at the Dunkin' Donuts Civic Center, known locally as the Dunk, was expected to attract thousands of pool players and fans to Providence, a bonanza for the city's hotels, restaurants, bars, and clubs. Young Jimmy had said he expected to coin it, especially in the Club where looking-for-action road players, railbirds, pool junkies, and hustlers would gather like ants at a picnic. He was so confident that he closed the Club to its regular membership over the Shoot-Out's two weekends and had scored short-term *event* liquor licenses from the Providence License Board. That was, in his word, "huge" since the License Board, reliably deep in the pocket of politicians, was frugal with liquor licenses unless some vigorish passed through member's hands.

"Hey, so you took the Mayor's appointment to the Commission!" He slapped my back with exuberance. "That's great! That's great!" and he enumerated the perks I could expect as a member of the Shoot-Out Tournament Commission created by the city and state last fall and nominally in charge of hosting the tournament. I smiled amicably even though the perks—like good tickets for events—meant little to me; I had accepted the appointment the previous Friday afternoon because our mutual friend Mayor Tony Tramonti called and asked me. The Mayor grew up with Young Jimmy and me, and was a longtime pool player; he recognized that the Commission was where Providence's well-earned reputation for political shenanigans and toleration of skanky business would surely meld with the crimped ethics of the world of pool. Tony cajoled me, saying that a "new face" on the Commission that was controlled by political hacks and hangers-on appointed by his predecessor might tamp down rampant conflicts of interest and outright sleaziness that could embarrass Providence once again.

Young Jimmy continued. "And how about the Gala?" That was the Shoot-Out's opening dinner reception on Wednesday night when Young Jimmy was to be honored as Providence's premier pool player.

"Yeah," I said, and meaning to give him a friendly dis, I continued, "the resurrection of the Fox Point Kid?"

He jerked his head back at my snarky wisecrack.

"You know," he grumbled back to life, "you can be a downer. In addition to the Gala, just for being a greeter at the Dunk, a Mr. Hospitality like Vinnie Paz or Ernie D at Foxwoods, I get three grand a weekend! Plus I play an exhibition each night, old pro versus new, you know that shtick, each for another grand!" His eyes expected approval.

I quickly added up Young Jimmy's payday: six grand a weekend. "Not bad," I commented.

"Not bad?" he hooted. "Not bad? And with what we will do here?"

Maria Catarina, his wife, co-owner, and dining room hostess, was suddenly behind him. She gave him a meaningful rap on a shoulder and said, "Algy, you got to talk to him."

Young Jimmy turned to her and lowered his voice as a customer sat at the end of the counter. "I keep telling you it's not like when I was on the road. I get paid just for being there, smiling, being a good guy, and play exhibitions, win or lose makes no difference. For Christsakes, stop worrying, Algy's going to be on the Commission, one of the watch dogs!" It was now apparent to me that Maria Catarina's concern accounted for much of Young Jimmy's enthusiasm for my appointment to the Commission. He raised his eyebrows to me. "See you later," he said and left in full retreat.

Maria Catarina immediately sat on the vacated stool, her red skirt pulled around her legs. Maria Catarina's shiny black hair was drawn straight back and held by a silver clasp. In her mid-forties, she retained the exotic Iberian beauty that took Young Jimmy off the road. Usually, she flashed her huge dark eyes and a smile that was welcoming. Today, her face showed concern.

"What did he tell you?" She didn't let me answer. "The hospitality stuff downtown, okay. The exhibitions too. Things are tight now, we can use the money, but he can't go back to *that*."

That meant his days on the road as a pool hustler and later the private big money matches that he played up and down the East Coast and out to Chicago, before meeting Maria Catarina and marriage, before her family's restaurant moved down Wickenden Street to become Jimmy's, and his reinvention of his father's pool parlor into the elegantly appointed and private Billiard Club.

"People tell him playing again is great publicity for the restaurant, for the Club. Your buddy the Mayor said it will give us a boost." She threw back her head. "A 'boost'? All we need is customers! Tony should have some of his times here."

In Rhode Island, a political fundraiser is known as a 'time.'

Jao approached the counter, checking my progress with the risotto. "Want some heat?" he asked, looked at Maria Catarina, then back at me, took my bowl, and returned to his ranges.

"Algy, he respects you. Talk to him. We've got a good thing here. Maybe we shouldn't have expanded, remodeled, done the party room, but we'll be fine. I'm not going to lose it." Then, she whispered, "What he does upstairs, that's okay. He's just a ... manager. But, if he went back to playing, to the life, I don't know what will happen to us."

"I'll do what I can."

She threw up her hands and left me.

7

MARCIE TEXTED ME THAT she had scheduled a telephone conference with the Champlin & Burrill lawyers for two o'clock, giving me an hour or so before I had to return. I climbed the interior staircase to the second floor, expecting to be alone in the Club this early in the afternoon, but there was Young Jimmy bent low, cue poised for a shot, at the brilliantly lit center table, a Gabriel with electric-blue felt known as *Jimmy's Table* because its blue matched his eyes. The table was set up for nine-ball.

Young Jimmy moved quickly through the rack, pocketing balls in sequence with shots that were sweet and true, like they were guided by laser. There were bursts of power in his play, consistency in his stance, strength in the finger bridge for the cue. His forearm seemed like it was on a hinge, over, under, back and forth. With the table cleared, he stood to face me. "Twenty racks so far today, drills every day for the past few weeks."

That sounded like his practice routine of years ago as a road player and sometimes hustler, when he could come home to Providence with a roll of fifties and hundreds bigger than your fist, or so broke, he slept on a sofa in my Benefit Street bachelor apartment. Backed by dodgy sponsors known as *sweaters*—guys with lots of cash who didn't bother with tax ID's or memberships in the Chamber of Commerce—Young Jimmy Hannigan played big money matches with the best in the East and became a master at setting up and relieving a mark of available cash. He also bore the scars of a hustler's life: a disgruntled loser broke a cue over his back in Baltimore; in Albany, punks took him on in a parking lot and closed a door on his left hand, which required two operations. After that, his sweaters provided on-the-road protection.

He reracked and demonstrated a sharpened skill with cute shots like a double carom and a shot off the rail that could have been on a wire. I watched, thinking of the competition he would face in the Shoot-Out exhibitions. Were the smooth mechanics, the muscle memory, the legendary hand-eye coordination, really in place? He was obviously comfortable on his own table, in his own venue, but play in public against today's felt artists?

"Gotta go," he said, "got stuff to do," and unscrewed the pieces of his Predator cue, which he slid into a black leather case and zipped it closed. "Algy, twelve grand just for showing up, shaking a few hands, a couple of matches. Plus, what we do here. Pretty god-damn good, if you ask me."

I didn't ask because his eyes held the steady confidence, the swagger, of a rejuvenated Fox Point Kid. "Don't worry, man," he said. "It's all under control."

o O o

After he left, I removed one of my three cues from the members' wall rack, set up on Jimmy's Table for nine-ball, and made a decent break. *All under control* stirred a memory. What was it?

I rarely played nine-ball; I was a straight pool and eight-ball player. In straight pool and eight-ball, you decide which ball to pocket, call your shot, and execute. Nine-ball, however, is a rotation game, meaning the cue ball must first strike the lowest numbered ball on the table on every shot. The winner is the player who pockets the nine-ball after striking the lowest ball on the table. That meant a player could pocket the one ball through the eight ball, miss the nine ball shot, only to have the opponent pocket the nine-ball and win the game. Nine-ball matches are played quickly, ideal for the popular ESPN television matches from Las Vegas; most often they are a 'run to seven' which means the first player to win seven games wins the match. That was how the Shoot-Out Tournament planned to get through hundreds of qualifying players in three days: runs to seven until the semis when the matches would be runs to nine.

Another reason for nine-ball's popularity is that it is a good gambling game. Players easily handicapped themselves by nego-tiating with an opponent to 'give up the break' or letting the game end by pocketing a designated ball lower than the nine. Negotiating the 'play' was a key to nine-ball wagering.

I made two more shots and then missed a double bank shot. The Fox Point Kid would have made the shot. It was always that way, going back to when Tony Tramonti and me and Young Jimmy as kids played here when it was still Hannigan's. Of the three of us, remaining friends despite the divergent paths we took, only Young Jimmy—and I'm probably the only one who still thinks of him as *Young* Jimmy—still related to the idioms, customs, and culture of pool.

I left myself a difficult shot with the cue ball within a cluster of three balls. As a kid, Young Jimmy would practice a shot like that for hours until he had it down pat. Pool didn't care about his plain face or his hand-me-down clothes or bad acne. Only skill mattered. For him, every spread of balls was a puzzle to solve, every shot a makeable challenge.

I flubbed the shot but cleared out the cue ball, allowing me to make the five ball, then make a decent shot at the six. I chalked the cue, surveyed the table, and proceeded to clear seven through nine. Satisfied, I put away my stick and grabbed a Poland Spring bottle from the refrigerator behind the long mahogany bring-your-own bar near the outside entrance for my walk back to the office. *All under control?* And it came to me, that misbegotten weekend I became Young Jimmy's sweater.

A month before the end of my first semester in my third year at Harvard Law, I was running low on the cash I earned as a summer bartender at the Black Dog Tavern on Martha's Vineyard.

Being stubbornly independent even then, I was intent on paying my own way through my third year. First semester tuition had been paid and I had banked the necessary for living expenses but was way short on both for second semester, in part because I shared an apartment in Cambridge with Tony Tramonti, whose family owned a growing construction firm, who wasn't on much of a budget.

I saw myself weekend bartending all second semester until one night, as I watched a visiting Young Jimmy on a hustle in a dingy Cambridge pool hall near Porter Square, I got an idea. By then, Young Jimmy was known in Rhode Island and parts of Connecticut, but not so much in Massachusetts. His play that night was not at all flashy, making easy shots and winning most—but not all short money matches—which he claimed was luck, hoping to attract a bigger fish. In the haze of too many beers, I calculated that in a weekend being *his* sweater, and some decent action, I could double or triple the twenty-five hundred I had left, more than enough for second semester tuition and expenses without all that bartending. Young Jimmy enthusiastically agreed, we would split winnings fifty-fifty, and he said he had a place in mind.

The play was in Everett, a blue-collar town north of Boston, and the venue was Falvey's Billiard Parlor, a strip-center pool hall with decent tables that attracted upper tier players on weekends. On a Friday night, we checked into a Holiday Inn off Route 28, and reconnoitered after eight. My cash and another five hundred from Young Jimmy gave us three thousand to stake against players who occasionally frequented Falvey's, the likes of 'Boston Shortie,' Jimmy 'Varnish' Vacca, Roland 'One Eye' Miller, Leo 'the Saint' Cardillo, 'Slim' Atkins, 'Big Bob' Halsey, and Freddie 'Dinner Pail' Moscato. Pool guys love nicknames.

That first night, Young Jimmy lined up ten-dollar, twenty-dollar matches, flashing cash, haggling about points, playing one-pocket and nine-ball, and not very well. I also played and lost a few bucks to give the impression that my pal was as amateurish as me. The hustle was on. Young Jimmy sipped orange juice—the rail birds probably thought he was downing screwdrivers—and he got louder as the night progressed, saying he was looking for action.

The next day, we arrived at Falvey's in the early afternoon, Young Jimmy again sipping orange juice, chatting up players who drifted in, from whom he determined to concentrate on local attorney Harry Blatt, an okay player who liked and could afford action. Word was he would be in that evening. We left, spent the rest of the afternoon watching a Paul Newman movie on a crappy TV in the motel and returned to Falvey's about six. More shooters showed up and Young Jimmy played a few twenty dollar nine-ball games, winning some and losing some, showing no spark of brilliance, but flashing his roll, saying he needed a *real* game. It was, of course, more hustle.

We went out for dinner and came back around ten thirty. By then, players would be talking about this braggart, long on talk and short on ability, and it wasn't long before he had a match set up with Harry Blatt.

Harry Blatt looked like his name sounded. Almost bald, sallow skinned, black goatee, wide shoulders, a gut, a greenish dress shirt that tailed out of his trousers, and a hip swivel in his gait. He had an exotic shot that somehow seemed to work for him but would never work for anyone else, like a Jack Furyk golf swing. The bet was two hundred dollars, the game was nine-ball, our cash matched his on top of the table's lamp shade, and Harry got spotted the eight ball, which meant that if Harry made the eight ball, he didn't have to pocket the nine to win. They played to seven games and it was close, but Young Jimmy lost. More hustle. They played again, same bet, and this time Young Jimmy won by one game. The attorney swallowed the con and raised the third match to five hundred dollars. He started off great, winning three games but soon faded and Young Jimmy began his move. Nothing he did was brilliant, playing not for show but for game, and won seven-five. The crowd of rail birds grew and whatever else was going on at Falvey's paled.

We were up five hundred and I was getting excited, thinking how much we would win. Harry, clearly a sore loser, called for another match at five hundred. He won two games, then began to lose it. After every shot, he started talking trash, muttered or screamed, as the case may be, "fuckin' this," "fuckin' that," "motherfuckin' balls," "the lights in here are terrible…" Young Jimmy didn't say much, just sipped orange juice. After Young Jimmy coaxed Harry along so as to beat him only by a game, Harry gave it another try for five hundred, got the break and the eight ball and won four straight games. It didn't look good for Young Jimmy and then the roof fell in on Harry. Once again Young Jimmy managed to keep Harry in the game, but the result was certain. So, by one in the morning, we were up fifteen hundred—for me that was seven-fifty—and more to come.

After Harry quit, Big Bob Halsey, who had come in during the last match, approached Young Jimmy at the bar. In a size fifty sport coat over a gray tee and baggy trousers that fell from his gut, he was as advertised. His round head reminded me of a pumpkin because of a cowlick of thick brown hair that sprouted out of his head like a stem. He said simply, "Thousand a game. Even." Young Jimmy told the whole bar, including Big Bob, that he was tired but maybe he would play on Sunday night. That wasn't part of our game plan, but I figured Young Jimmy was ahead of me. We left but not before agreeing to a match at nine o'clock on Sunday.

Later, Young Jimmy talked about playing Big Bob. The pool wisdom of the time was that heavyset players, on their feet for hours, tired early, their feet would hurt, and they would lose concentration. I liked the thought, easily putting out of mind that there was a world class player known as Minnesota Fats. Young Jimmy said Big Bob, by reputation, was good, but not a top ranker. Since we were up by fifteen hundred plus our stake of three thousand, he figured this was an opportunity to score big, especially if he could finagle the eight spot in the wager. We were charged up and forgot a rule: never play someone for high stakes you haven't seen play. Especially on tables in a venue you don't know well.

On Sunday evening, we arrived at eight. Big Bob was at a snooker table shooting balls, wearing the same jacket and pants. As a crowd of rail birds gathered, Young Jimmy ordered an orange juice and practiced at an adjoining table, occasionally taking a break to watch Big Bob's shots.

After give and take, they ended up playing even; the bet was a thousand which went into escrow on the lampshade. News of a money match quickly spread and the sports crowded the table, their antics nothing short of commodity traders in their pits as they laid down bets. After two matches, the same cash remained on the light fixture, each player having won a match. The rail birds were still expectant; as for me, I watched the play, waiting for that Fox Point Kid flash of brilliance that hadn't yet come. Still in a hustle? I knew Young Jimmy had the uncanny ability to ignore distractions, that he poured on his game when he had to, so I remained confident.

The next match was raised by Big Bob to fifteen hundred and Young Jimmy lost seven to five and paid the bet. Dance over? We were still five hundred up. Young Jimmy assured me, "I can beat him. Got to catch a roll." He went for another match at fifteen hundred and lost again and suddenly we were into our stake by a thousand. I took Young Jimmy aside. He looked pale and uncomfortable. "What's happening?"

"I don't know. It isn't like I'm just not playing well, I'm just not playing great and he's a steady Eddie if there ever was one."

"What do you think we should do?" My stomach was churning.

"I think we should go for two big ones." That was all we had left. "I can take him."

"You don't look good. Maybe we should quit. Tell 'em you're

not feeling well."

"No, it's all under control." He wanted to play so badly, I didn't insist.

Throughout the match, Young Jimmy remained a consistent game behind, missing shots by an extra spin or a spot more English. I was beginning to wonder about the orange juice; was a drop or two of something added at the bar? Young Jimmy lost seven-five after a flourish of great shots by Big Bob. He collected his winnings, offered to buy us drinks, which we declined. One loud mouth rail bird who won his bet muttered "sucker." I felt my fists harden, thinking Young Jimmy had been somehow hustled. When a couple of sore losers glowered menacingly, I got Young Jimmy out of there, into the parking lot behind the pool hall where we had parked my car, where Young Jimmy heaved. *Heaved!*

As we drove back to Cambridge, I insisted that the orange juice was spiked. He said, "No."

"So what went wrong?"

"Nothing went wrong. It's just the way it goes. Some days you have it, some weeks you have it. You win when you're not supposed to, so you lose when you're not supposed to. You can have months when you have it, and then it's gone." He shrugged. "I just hit a gone."

So ended my career as a sweater; ahead of me were months of second-semester bartending for tuition and expenses. A hard and good lesson for me; never bet on pool. A walk in the park for Young Jimmy.

As I recover from the sucker punch, my breath returning, my heartbeat pounding less in my head, I concentrate on nose breathing—never had to think about that before. Except during that long day in Beirut. Then, a siren blares. A police siren. Coming closer. We slow, and for a moment, hope is alive. Benno! And the siren shuts off abruptly somewhere behind us.

Another bad jolt and oh, my knees! My knees? I remember being grabbed from behind, my arms in a body lock. Marine training had locked in with a head-butt that missed, but getting my thigh into a crotch and an elbow into a gut loosened the hold. "Fuck," he groaned, and that's when a fist pushed my stomach into my backbone. I went to my knees, breaking my fall, sliding forward to be face down in the greasy smell of wet asphalt.

With effort, I flatten my back on the floor to brace my shoes against a side of the trunk. Then I sense the car gain speed without jolts, has to be on a highway ramp on to either I-95 or the I-295 ring road around Providence. In the minutes of relative smoothness, I discover that the hastily wound tape around my wrists also covers the cuffs of my slicker, giving a little wiggle room underneath. I work my wrists, I yank, I twist, feel some give, but not enough. Anyway, just what the hell am I going to do if somehow I got loose? Use my cell phone? It's in the pocket of my jacket on the rear goddamn seat!

8

THE CONSENSUS OF THE Champlin & Burrill lawyers, most of them in the New York office, was that Ravensford Capital wouldn't survive the weekend. For what it might be worth, I authorized drafting a court complaint seeking a restraining order against any disbursements by the investment firm until things were sorted out. We also agreed to meet in their Midtown office in the late morning for a strategy session. The timing worked for me because I could look forward to Nadie's company on Amtrak; she didn't have classes on Tuesdays and planned to be in the City tomorrow for a final gown fitting at Vera Wang and a last visit with her widowed mother in Brooklyn before the wedding. Mrs. Zelda Winokur was a nervous Nellie about our wedding, even at this late date, with frequent cautions and suggestions and dependence on her daughter, even for simple matters like transportation to Providence and appropriate mother-of-the-bride clothes.

After the conference call, Marcie informed me that Eustace Pine, a senior partner at Champlin & Burrill and Italo Palagi's estate lawyer, had telephoned. "Wanted you to call back as soon as you can. Sounded anxious."

I was aware that Pine, a crusty practitioner of the arcane art of probate law, was frustrated. He had to wait weeks for an autopsy report before filing a petition to probate Palagi's will. The unexpected challenge from the putative son was another cross to bear. Had something else triggered his chronic irritability when carefully laid plans for a smooth estate administration went awry? He was still sputtering when he said, "After all this time, Palagi's secretary, Claudia Cioffi, his nominated executor, just refused to sign the probate petition! Or serve as the executor!" An executor is the individual that the deceased nominates in a will to administer the provisions of an estate plan under court supervision and sees to the payment of taxes and bequests. Not a difficult task, especially when counseled by an experienced attorney such as Pine.

"Why?" I asked.

"Wouldn't give a reason. Hung up on me," Pine said, dismay in his Yankee twang. "His bequest to her is two hundred thousand and she won't serve? Can you imagine? As a precaution, I called the nominated alternate, Father Pi-e-tro Sac-chi"—the syllables in each name were elongated—"a professor at Providence College. He's the beneficiary of a fifty thousand dollar bequest. And, *he* turned me down! Can't believe it! There's even another complication. He said Palagi gave him an envelope to be opened in my presence, and *yours*, Algy, thirty days after Palagi's death. That's today. Wants to meet immediately. What's this all about?"

"Damned if I know."

Pine continued, *sotto voce*, as though unfriendly ears might overhear. "I fear some sort of will amendment. These Italians are so damn murky." He pronounced it *eye-talians* as East Siders of a certain pedigree and age tended to do.

I interrupted his take on *eye-talians* to inform him of the probable loss of Palagi's trust assets in the Sugarman debacle—he was aghast—and that Lucca & Lucca had surfaced. "Contingency lawyers," he grumbled, "just like the lawyers the son retained in New York ... ah..." he was likely searching a file strewn desk for the lawyers' names, "...Guc-ci, Mon-te-cal-vo and Ot-ta-vani. All they do is hold up an estate administration to force a settlement. And their Roman counterpart is likely much the same."

"You've had time to check out the claim. What's their legal theory?" I asked.

"They argue that Palagi died an Italian citizen so the estate laws of Italy apply, which would favor a son. Completely specious, of course," he said firmly. "Under Italian law, if Palagi had domicile in Rhode Island—which he did—only Rhode Island law applies to his estate and any inheritance in the United States. In any event, Palagi had ample time since the date of his alleged acknowledgement of his son in April to change his will in favor of the son, which he didn't. In addition, two clauses in Palagi's will negate their position."

A rustle of papers preceded his reading, *"My failure to make any provision herein for any heir at law, known or unknown, whether living or hereafter born, is intentional and not occasioned by accident or mistake."*

"And here is the other, an *in terrorem* clause: *It is my intent, to the fullest extent permitted by law, that any person who commences or joins in any litigation opposing the probate of my will or any of its provisions shall be totally disinherited by me and shall take no share in my estate."*

"Sounds like out on both counts," I said.

"Of course," Pine continued, perhaps smugly, "those paragraphs apply only to his estate assets. We don't know what his estate consists until we can gain access to his records. As to trust assets ... as to whatever is left in the trust ... the son, assuming he *is* a son, has no right whatsoever under Rhode Island law to assets long ago placed in trust."

"Doesn't sound quite fair, somehow," I rejoined. "If he didn't know he had a son, planned his estate accordingly, and..."

My hesitation appalled Pine. "Algy, the law encompasses important principles and assumes rationality and presumes he knew of the provisions of his will and trust and failed to change his estate plan to favor his son. He had time but didn't. The burden is on the plaintiff to produce uncontradicted, clear, and convincing evidence that the will should be put aside. Can't make things up after the fact."

Despite Pine's certainty, years as a litigator at his firm before I became University Counsel taught me that in a court battle, the literal reading of the documents and applicable law, fairness, right and wrong, fell away to skill, gamesmanship, and craftiness. Intention, virtue, truth, or good guys did not always prevail.

He continued, "There is urgency to our meeting with the *padre*. He is leaving for Italy on Sunday. For a year!"

"See what you can arrange, Eustace. I'm in New York tomorrow, so try Wednesday."

"Algy, he's very insistent it must be today."

"Today?"

"Very insistent. And I want to convince him to act as executor. It's more than a little out of the ordinary to have both the nominated executor and the alternate refuse to serve. Gives the probate judge, Judge Cremasoli, the right to appoint a crony as administrator. And you know how expensive and time-consuming that could be."

And might well favor the politically entrenched Luccas. I checked my watch. It was three-ten. "Can't do it until after four ... try for four thirty."

"He said he would be free all afternoon." What followed was a series of throat-clearing gasps ending in a chortle. "Wait until the Luccas find out that the trust may be practically worthless." He barely repressed another chortle when he likely remembered that, the University was the real loser.

9

AT FOUR, MARCIE ENTERED my office and handed me a copy of a letter from Ravensford Capital to Palagi acknowledging that when it took over management of the trust account from Smith Barney, it inadvertently placed an investment "in your other account."

"What other account?" Did Palagi's estate hold an asset we knew nothing about?

"Let's hope it wasn't with Sugarman!" she replied, and as she turned to leave, she added, "His trust account never had a down month. Not one. Even during recessions. Shouldn't someone have noticed?"

"Ya think?"

I thanked her for her efforts and reminded her I would be in Manhattan tomorrow. "I was curious about Professor Palagi," she said, "so I Googled him. Had no idea of the impact of his thrillers in Italy. When you saw him hobbling around the campus, you'd never guess he wrote anything other than scholarly tracts with footnotes and bibliography."

With my curiosity piqued, I went online and found a Wikipedia entry on Palagi's thrillers. Decades ago, from Trieste to Palermo, an audience of enthusiastic readers, largely teenagers and young singles, devoured his books and adopted his hero Caesare Forza's svelte, macho image or mimicked the style of his girlfriend, the sexy and sassy Allessandra Greco. Augmenting the buzz at the time was the author's mysterious identification as *L*, a contrivance, according to the essayist, designed to protect Palagi's academic status and reputation, and compatible with his publisher's likely rationalization that the professor of the history of philosophy at Bologna was no dashing Ian Fleming. Such anonymity also provided the opportunity for the publisher to drop specious hints at one time or other that *L* was a cabinet minister, an eminent member of the Vatican's curia, a scion of Roman aristocracy, a Milanese designer, the heir to the fortune of a Turino automobile manufacturer, and, for a while, Sophia Loren. "L," I said aloud and remembered that Palagi once joked to me *L* stood for *lira*.

Like Marcie, I was also surprised by cultural controversies spawned by Palagi's creations, that *forzaissmo* had been coined to describe a distinct, youthful swagger, that Caesare Forza had been denounced by the political left as a crypto-fascist and pro-Vatican dupe while extravagantly praised by the political right as a patriotic Italian hero. Clicking through various other sites, many in Italian, a language I absorbed during a year in Florence as an undergraduate and frequent Tuscan vacations, I discovered Forza comic books, stills from Forza movies and a television series, a limited edition supercharged Forza Fiat convertible, clothing lines, and board and electronic games.

I logged off. Italo Palagi's visits to Temple House for espresso and Italian pastries helped my mother retain her fluent Italian. She found Palagi to be congenial and never quite understood my own antipathy toward her 'Italian gentleman.' That, Nadie, ever the psychologist, later explained to me, was because I had made a snap judgment of Palagi's character, resulting in a "spontaneous trait reference." Jargon free, that meant a single, powerful, impression coupled with the human tendency to generalize from a single perception, created a halo-effect that would be all positive or all negative.

Palagi's *halo* came early in his directorship when I accompanied my mother to a welcoming reception at the Institute for a celebrated Italian film director, a Cannes prize winner for a scathing exposé of corrupt Italian politics. The event was lavish, catered with Italian delicacies, choice wines, peopled by Italian *glitterati* and New York's filmmakers, the kind of event designed to give luster to the new Institute's reputation. Palagi was a genial host, clad in an elegantly cut suit tailored to slim his plump body, coordinated with a pale yellow, mock turtleneck shirt; his dark brown eyes were luminous, his lips pink, as he used his walking stick for occasional emphasis in conversation. My mother, among the founding board members of the Institute, was given appropriate attention by our host, which initially pleased me.

The stark moment of negativity came after his welcoming speech. Palagi, in English, had been effusive in his praise of the director's film, his courage, his sensibility, his art, and expressed a seeming solidarity with the director's political views. Only a few minutes later, I overheard Palagi speaking to an apparent confidant in Italian, which he had no reason to know I understood. He criticized the film, describing the filmmaker as naïve, a dilettante, a "poseur," and a "propagandist of the left." With this shoddy duplicity, his small mouth became tight and mean, his smile pouty.

His halo had been set. And in our not infrequent encounters in at Temple House, despite effort to the contrary, I probably betrayed my attitude toward Palagi. Whenever we met in the course of the Institute's legal matters, his body language toward me indicated he was similarly disaffected.

10

THE CITYSCAPE THROUGH THE twentieth-floor reception area windows of Champlin & Burrill's downtown office was a stark, black-and-white topographic map, the winding Woonasquatucket River a gray snake with its tail ending in the Ellipse in front of the marble-domed State House on Capitol Hill.

I was a few minutes early for our meeting with Father Sacchi and used the time to text Nadie, telling her I would be home close to seven and that I would join her on an early train to New York City. The receptionist then allowed me the use a guest computer in a cubicle area, where I quickly located an image of Pietro Sacchi, OP on Providence College's website. A white-robed, tonsured, distinguished-looking man with a narrow face, ears pressed to his head, he had a thin nose, trim academic beard, was maybe in his sixties. Born in Parma, he attended the University of Rome, entered the Dominican House of Studies in Florence, received his doctorate in philosophy at the University of St. Thomas, the *Angelicum*, in Rome, then to the University of Bologna for another doctorate. A long list of his publications in mostly European academic journals indicated a concentration in Greek philosophy and Thomistic thought. Since 1998, he had been a member of the college's philosophy department and a lecturer in its Liberal Arts Honors Program, with terms as a visiting professor at Columbia, Georgetown, and St. Louis. Among his non-academic interests were the opera, Italian soccer, and chess.

His smile seemed both serious and kindly; maybe his eyes gave up a touch of whimsy.

o O o

Rather informally for him, Eustace Pine sat on the edge of his office desk to face me. The lawyer's age showed in thinning hair combed over a summer's tanned scalp, hollows in his cheeks, and the beginning of a turkey neck. A gold chain with a Phi Beta Kappa key flashed on the vest of his dark suit. I asked if the priest had arrived.

"In my conference room," he answered and smacked his right hand into the palm of his left. "I can't understand why neither Claudia Cioffi nor the priest will serve as Palagi's executor. I need one to change his or her mind.

I informed Pine of the reference to 'another account' of Palagi's in the letter from Ravensford Capital found by Marcie. Pine replied with a shake of his head, "Without appointment of an executor, we can't gain access to his condominium or office or bank records or any of his accounts." His eyes dropped to his watch. "Ready?"

Pine led me along a hallway. "By the way, our counsel in Rome has given me more insight to Italian inheritance law. The Italians don't have a probate system like here. It's all *it is what it is* and fight about it. Absurd, isn't it?" he sniffed.

"What about the paternity claim?"

"Interesting." He stopped to answer me. "Apparently, there is something called the *uf-fi-cio ano-gra-fe*. Go into this governmental agency, sign an acknowledgement of paternity before a notary, and the child is recognized. I don't know as yet if that's what happened in Palagi's case or whether there was a judicial determination. Our counsel is investigating." Then he added, "No need to upset the priest with this Ponzi-scheme business. I want him to accept the executorship."

He opened the frosted-glass door to the conference room. Father Sacchi, in a black suit with a clerical collar, awaited us by a window. He appeared older than in his online likeness although his face evidenced the same benign intelligence. His charmingly accented voice was cordial during my introduction by Pine. As we sat, he invited us to address him as Father Pietro. Pine winced at such intimacy but made an effort. "Father Pi-e-tro," he said, "we are meeting at your request. Would you repeat to Mr. Temple what you told me as to your instructions from Signor Palagi."

"Yes, most certainly. Italo directed me to deliver this envelope to Mr. Pine thirty days after his death. Today is the thirtieth day." He touched a cream-colored envelope on the table.

"And the envelope has not been opened by you?"

"That is correct."

"His will provides a bequest to you."

"That will go to the Order. I have taken a vow of poverty."

"...and his will so provides," Pine interrupted, self-satisfied that he foresaw such a possibility. "Since Ms. Cioffi refuses to act as executor, you are the nominated successor."

Father Pietro lowered his eyes. "As I informed you, I cannot act in such a capacity. Among other reasons, I leave on Sunday for Rome for research in the Vatican Library for the better part of a year."

Pine drew in his chin in disapproval. "Distance is not a problem, Father. You can appoint a local agent to act in your stead, although all important decisions would still be yours."

"I am sorry if I disappoint you," Father Pietro responded with calm determination. "It is in any event inappropriate for a priest." Pine frowned off rejection, suggesting to me that the topic would be discussed again. "I have known Italo since our days as students," the priest continued, directing his comments to me. "We renewed our friendship when chance brought us together in Providence. May I say, Mr. Temple, I know that he was pleased to have your family's acquaintance."

Given my disdain for his friend, I was evasive when I said, "He was often a visitor to my mother's home."

Pine picked up the envelope and let a dry throat clearing underscore his impatience to proceed.

The priest ignored Pine. "Do you know of his writings? Not those Forza books, although it is interesting that he could also write popular fiction. I am referring to his philosophical studies. His *Essays on Pessimism*, for instance, a seminal work tracing the concept of morbidity of spirit in the writings of Greek philosophers, the Fathers of the Church, the medievalists, the Renaissance writers. A brilliant if dour assessment of mankind's search for the reasons for its communal bouts of pervasive spiritual darkness. Something which also afflicted him, I am sad to say. I particularly thought insightful his essay on Italian culture and society as portrayed in di Lampedusa's *The Leopard*, a book he much admired. Surely, you know the novel?"

I was saved from confessing that I had not read the greatest Italian novel of the twentieth century, although I had enjoyed the Visconti film based on the book with Burt Lancaster as the Prince and Claudia Cardinale as the ambitious Angelica, when the priest asked, "You know of Italo's son?"

"He never mentioned a son to anyone at the University," I replied.

"Nor to me," he shrugged, "until ..."

"We should begin, Father," Pine interrupted with ill-disguised annoyance at our continued conversation and slid the envelope toward the priest.

Father Pietro nodded but continued. "The weekend before he died, Italo asked me to meet him at Café Rossini, our favorite café on Federal Hill. We had not met recently, as he had been in Italy, so I was surprised at his appearance. He was disheveled, his hair uncombed, his beard untrimmed, his face drawn, jaundiced, his eyes rimmed in red as though he had not slept for days. He told me he had fallen ill while in Rome, had sought treatment for an illness he did not name. He then told me of his son and handed me this envelope, gave me instructions as to its delivery, said it was my duty to him, as a friend, to carry out his wishes. Although I recognized an overwhelming sadness in him, I refused, twice, but because my refusals pained him, I eventually accepted." His hands rose, evocative of regret, then he opened the envelope and placed what appeared to be a handwritten letter on the table., He smoothed its crease, removed an eyeglasses case from inside his jacket pocket, and put on reading glasses. He read the letter to himself, his lips moving with his eyes, a growing guardedness in his face, as though he was rapidly assembling facts, contemplating duty. His dour expression led me to assume the letter might well be Palagi's attempt at a will amendment, awarding the estate to his son; Pine's face betrayed similar anxiety.

"The letter is in English. Handwritten. I shall read it aloud," the priest said.

"Dear good friend Pietro,

Thank you for taking on this obligation. There is no one I trust more than you. The revelation of the existence of a son might be expected to change my ideas as to my estate. I have given it much thought."

Father Pietro's eyes moved to each of us in turn before he continued.

"I want to relieve any uncertainty. I hereby confirm my existing will and trust in all respects. I do not amend my will or my trust, and confirm in all respects the documents that I have executed and in Mr. Pine's possession. He would have drafted this in a more professional manner, I am sure, but I cannot believe the laws of Rhode Island are meant to confound my wishes.

I'm sure Mr. Pine will follow through with the appropriate legal actions to effectuate my intent.

Thank you, my friend."

Father Pietro re-read the letter in silence before he said, deliberately, "It is signed, *Italo Palagi* and dated August twenty-seventh of this year. It is also notarized."

He handed the letter to me. The handwriting was crab-like, barely legible, written in ball pen and signed above a typed standard Rhode Island notary clause. The notary had signed her name, dated the document, and sealed her notarization with a circular embossment of authority. Likely, I thought, the notary had typed in the notarial clause upon presentation of the letter by Palagi at a convenient bank branch.

Pine, who should have been relieved at the letter's confirmation of Palagi's estate plan, nevertheless allowed fussiness to leak into his voice. "I don't know why he didn't see me to do this properly, thereby avoiding a potential challenge to authenticity."

The priest protested, "I have kept the sealed envelope in my room at the Priory at the College until now. If you need my sworn statement to that effect, you certainly can have it."

I handed the letter to Pine who examined it as though searching for an error in form or substance. Finding none, he said, more brusquely than necessary, "I need the envelope, too." Father Pietro handed it to him. Pine put the letter back into the envelope. "I will put both in our office safe so we can trace custody from this moment on."

I reacted to Pine's brusqueness. "Clearly, the letter is strong evidence of Palagi's intent to disown the son, and it is notarized."

Pine glowered as though I had trod on his role as estate counsel. "Authenticity and custody of the letter will be issues since Father is a beneficiary, or rather the Order is a beneficiary, and where it was kept, in his room, at the College was..."

"I assure you it was kept in a safe place," the priest said with sincerity.

Pine ignored the response. "Father, I assure *you* the son's lawyers will challenge you on both. You will be subject to a deposition and giving evidence in the probate court. Perhaps you will now reconsider..."

"No."

Pine shook his head with meaningful regret and rose to call his secretary to make copies of the letter for us. Father Pietro appeared crestfallen, so I stood and thanked him for his efforts on behalf of an old friend. He replied without rising. "Mr. Temple, would you spend a few more minutes with me?"

Pine, at the doorway, took a step back into the conference room. "If there is anything else I should know as attorney for the estate?"

"No, Mr. Pine. It is something personal."

11

THE PRIEST APPEARED TO relax with the lawyer out of the room. As I regained my chair, he said, "I will conduct a private memorial service for Italo this Friday at two o'clock at the chapel at Swan Point Cemetery. Are you familiar with this place?" I was. "His body is to be cremated, according to his wishes, and his ashes will be secured there until a final depository is established. His son has assented, according to Signor Lucca, the Italian consul, who contacted me and will represent the son and the Republic." He added, "Italo was not a believer but I think he would approve. I wanted you to know, to perhaps attend? And your mother, of course."

My cell-phone calendar listed only my meeting with Lucca & Lucca at eleven on Friday morning so I agreed. "As for my mother, I'm sure she would attend, if possible."

"I hesitate to ask this on our short acquaintance but would it be possible for you to provide me with a ride to the cemetery. My eyes are poor and so I must arrange assistance at the College for transportation. Not always convenient."

I agreed to meet him at the Dominican Priory on the Providence College campus and thinking we were through, I was surprised when the priest reached inside his jacket and removed a metallic Sony mini-recorder, holding it gingerly as though it was hazardous. "When I agreed to accept Palagi's envelope, I was also given this device and instructed to listen to its recording after the same time-span and before I delivered the envelope to Mr. Pine and you. But only *if* Italo's death was not *witnessed* as it would be in a hospice or hospital. If it was so, I was to erase the recording without listening. Under the circumstances of his death, I listened to it this morning and discovered that I am to share it with you. He speaks in English. No doubt, you will recognize his voice." He thumbed a switch, there was a click, then static, followed by the distinct voice of Italo Palagi.

Pietro ...

Another twist? I raised a hand in protest and he stopped the recording. "Should Pine be here?" I asked.

The priest replied softly but firmly. "My instructions were to listen to it and then play it for you. Not lawyer Pine."

In the silence that followed, my curiosity surged. Was this recording the suicide note Benno sought? I nodded acceptance and he placed the device on the table. The recording continued.

... my dear friend, how often have you instructed me as to the sacrament of confession. How it could wipe away my sins. And how often have I disputed you, saying that confession is an artifice designed to make one subservient to those to whom you confess, and that some sins cannot be forgiven.

The priest lifted his eyes to mine in a suggestion that he remembered this colloquy.

We will never agree on the power of the sacrament. You are a good man, Pietro, and I know that there are not many good men. Most of us are selfish, maybe not evil, but at least sinful, as you would say.

There was a long pause before Palagi continued.

If you are listening to this recording, my death was not witnessed and I ask you to share my words with Alger Temple. He is an honorable man from a distinguished family, a lawyer. I leave it to you and him to make such judgments as are appropriate with respect to these matters. And what, if anything, should be done. Importantly, whatever appearances might be, I tell you that I did not die by my own hand.

There was another pause, perhaps a sip of liquid before he resumed.

You know me, my family, my circumstances, Pietro. For Alger, I must explain. My father was a professional naval officer, a hero who died of wounds while saving dozens of lives during a British air attack on the Italian fleet at Taranto in 1943. Mussolini awarded him Italy's highest military award for valor. My mother was from the local aristocracy of Romanga. Both confused their patriotism with Fascism.

Even after Mussolini's death in 1945, there were those in Italy who faulted him only because of his weakness in joining Hitler. They styled themselves nationalists. One of those was my uncle, my mother's brother, who managed to become respectable as a supporter of the early Christian Democrat government.

As a young man, I was in Rome, a graduate student, poor, struggling, with a mother not reconciled to her lost status, and shunned by many as the son of a Fascist hero. I was restless and unfocused and I yearned for what I could not afford.

My uncle, by then an important politician, invited me to a meeting of these nationalists. They needed a writer to take their scattered memories and lies, turn them into something readable, although very far from the truth, defending, justifying, pleading. I was apolitical, a patient listener, and a passable writer, and soon came into demand as their ghost writer, someone to whom they confessed their truths even as they tried to change history. For this, I was richly rewarded. No longer did I worry about money, or my studies, even my thesis; all I had to do was write for them, and everything was arranged for me. In truth, I began my life in academia as a fraud.

Father Pietro eyes found mine, his face in a sorrowful frown. He was clearly affected by Palagi's story.

Soon, I had a Fiat, an apartment on the Via Veneto, money to spend, to gamble. I was introduced to the illicit, to your mind, pleasure of the affection of other young men. And parties. It is difficult to remember any one as they were all the same—drinks, drugs, sex of all kinds—but on such an occasion, Claudia Cioffi was introduced to me. She was from Modena, from a wealthy family, attractive, a degree in literature, she smoked and drank and drove an Alfa Romeo. After we became lovers, I foolishly shared with her my role with the nationalists. Like me, she didn't care.

My knowledge of post-war Italy was from Fellini and De Sica films. I found his depiction of la dolce vita compelling.

This was during an era of civil unrest, Red Brigade bombings, political assassinations, the rule of law and Parliament jokes, the South ruled by criminals, the government corrupt, and even worse, lazy. People were living in despair, a propitious time for conspiracy among those still believing the fiction of a prosperous, strong, united Italy under Il Duce. One evening, I was invited to the home of a rightist senator from the Piedmont. I expected little more than a dinner, some reminiscing, a request for my services. But, it was more than that. Even now, when they are all dead, I would not identify those in attendance because I fear retribution. They were conspirators in a conspiracy or the beginning of a conspiracy or the hope of a conspiracy to overthrow the Republic. The cabal had a name, La Lega dell' Amici d'Italia, or La Lega. All present assumed that I was one of them in mind and heart, with no idea that I loathed them for their disloyalty to Italy, their arrogance, for the ruin they had brought our country. But for their money, I became a center of communication among the cells of their traitorous organization.

The hierarchy of La Lega included a ranking Army general, a senior commander of the Carabinari, an industrialist from Torino, a banker from Milan, a columnist with a national newspaper, a priest with vague connections to the Vatican, an important land owner in Calabria, and lastly, its leader, a minister of state, the conspirator-in-chief, a ruthless politician, unscrupulous, with criminal ties, and who, to my certain knowledge, ordered at least one political murder. He was to find a face from among the military to be our new Duce. He was to foster national disunity, blame and crack down on the Socialists and Communists, incite violence, and finally lead a coup d'etat.

I began a life of clandestine meetings with the cells of La Lega and those in sympathy or in their pay, including elements of the Mafia in Sicily, the Camorra in Naples, and particularly, the 'Ndrangheta who controlled Calabria and Basilicata. The worst, the most vicious of them, was the 'Ndrangheta. As I could pay for a secretary, Claudia came into my employ.

For two years, as the conspiracy ate into our crumbling state, I travelled throughout Italy, and, I say now with pride, I succeeded in causing confusion among the traitors. Then, the conspiracy was uncovered by the SDI. The minister, about to be arrested for treason, destroyed all records and committed suicide. Only powerful influences, of which such a cabal had many, kept the conspiracy from becoming a national scandal.

My income immediately stopped. Claudia disappeared. I used my fraudulent degree, with assistance from sympathizers, to secure a position on the philosophy faculty at Bologna. Once again, I was desperately poor, in debt from my gambling, miserable, more so since I had tasted the good life. It was then that I created Caesare Forza and sold the idea to a publisher. The nonsense I authored in only a few weeks became my fortune. My identity was concealed by the publisher because of his fear of our past associations, and my anonymity worked well in terms of media attention. My new wealth was explained to friends and colleagues as an inheritance. After two decades of serious scholarship and writings, I left Bologna, coming to Carter. I believed I was far away from my former illicit associations.

Again a pause. Perhaps getting his thoughts together. Did he have notes in front of him?

Chance brought us together, Claudia and I, in New York at the Italian Consulate. We had dinner and she revealed a meticulous memory of La Lega. She mentioned that she needed employment to stay in America. Fearful, I wanted her close by and she became my secretary at the Institute. When my identity as Forza's creator was later revealed, and I suffered notoriety in Italy and here, I felt compelled to do certain things for Claudia to protect myself from her implicit threats of exposure. A sordid bargain. I made provision for her in my will, did other things for her silence, never explicitly saying why, although she knew.

And she was not alone. Shortly thereafter, the New

York cell of the 'Ndrangheta threatened me with exposure, forced me to open an investment account in my name for their use at a brokerage in New York. It remains to this day. I know nothing about the account except that I have been told it has done exceedingly well. It is handled by a manager who invests their money and pays any taxes. I make no claim to that account. Just know, my name was used because of duress.

I raised my hand and Father Pietro stopped the recording. The coerced investment account he referred to must be Palagi's 'other account' at Ravensford Capital. "Are you alright?" the priest asked solicitously. Right then, I should have called in Pine, but, in deference to Father Pietro, I did not.

Claudia early on came to despise me for my forbidden affection, adding another dimension to the rasp that is our relationship. Recently, her mania has become more manifest, her condemnations louder, always with her face in her Dante, reading aloud the cantos from the Inferno, making allusions to me as a conspirator and my sins of avarice, cupidity, and pederasty. She gains financially from my death. I am afraid what she might do in her hatred of me, in her lust for money. I ask you to judge if she had a hand, a gnarled, Harpy's claw, in my death.

The priest abruptly snapped off the recorder. He removed his glasses and rubbed tired eyes with his thumbs. "I find it difficult to listen to this ... a second time. Never did he speak to me of these issues." In the silence, I attempted to absorb what I had heard. The back of my neck tingled with the thought of Palagi's accusations. Then, Father Pietro replaced his glasses and clicked on the device.

I want you to know why I do not change my will as to my son.

Last April, I received a letter from a lawyer in Rome on behalf of Vittorio Ruggieri. It said his mother was Maria Ruggieri, a woman I lived with in Rome for a short time. A nurse, older than me, from the South, a strange woman, dark eyed, beautiful, very emotional, very independent, stubborn, wild in her own way, like a ... gypsy? One day, she disappeared. I didn't know she was pregnant.

Palagi's voice lowered, perhaps in regret?

Enclosed with his letter were copies of a birth cer-

tificate, which stated his client's birth date as being nine months from our liaison and contained his mother's name, her birth place in Basilicata, a village called Gianosa d'Acri, a certificate from an orphanage attached to a Catholic hospital in Rome where the baby was left to be cared for, his baptismal certificate. I was not named as the father, but the boy was given my father's first name by the mother. According to the lawyer, Maria had long since emigrated to New York and had recently died there. My name as the father was revealed by Maria only shortly before her death.

Within weeks, we met at the lawyer's office in Rome. It was worse than I could have anticipated. Vittorio was ungroomed, a face like a hawk ready to peck apart his prey. He said no more than a few words, did not embrace me or shake my hand when offered, stared straight ahead as his lawyer talked, not a spark of love or even curiosity in his eyes. I became numb, unable to answer the lawyer's questions as to what I would do for my son. Despite the rough encounter, I knew in my heart it was not a hoax. There was something about Vittorio, his face, that engendered a memory of Maria, maybe even of myself. I considered a medical test to verify paternity but I dared not mention it in that surrounding.

The day after, coming to the conclusion that I had expected too much at our meeting, I hired a car and we were driven into the Tiburtina hills for lunch at a small restaurant in Tivoli where we could shake off the dust of Rome and perhaps have a real conversation. We sat in a leafy arbor, ordered wine and antipasti, and I tried to engage his interest but elicited only dark smirks and cynicism. It was then that he spoke about his reluctance to let the world know of his abandonment by his famous father. Abandonment? As Claudia's extortion victim, I was acutely aware that I should take those words as a threat. Still, my guilt at his orphan's life overcame my common sense and I promised that I would make amends. He pressed me for cash, and weakly, I gave him what euros I had with me and promised a modest monthly stipend. Even then, he was unsatisfied.

Palagi's voice, which had been strong, now wavered.

It was then I decided to investigate Vittorio. It was not difficult to arrange through old contacts. Within days, I learned Vittorio had a criminal record going back to his teenage years, petty crimes, an imprisonment for stolen cars, arrests for selling stolen goods, extortion, suspicion of running with cells of the 'Ndrangheta. I was aghast. One morning, I met him in a gloomy, smelly bar near his apartment, a place where men of his kind seemed to congregate. He was hungover, I'm sure, hadn't bothered to shave in disrespect to me. He doused his espresso with grappa, and was soon drunk. I asked him questions about his mother, which he shrugged off, and he complained I was demanding, which was true since I wasn't tactful. Then, he told me that he had recently visited Maria's family's village in Basilicata, and through a cousin still living there, had learned of a blood oath taken against me by her father, a capo in the local 'Ndranghea, to avenge Maria's disgrace. He said I would not long survive unless I made peace with the family.

I was, at first, incredulous. This oath was from fifty years ago. He laughed, saying in the South, such things have no age. Then, he said that for two hundred thousand euros he would arrange for the debt of honor to be paid to the family, sparing my life. I was shaken. How could a son participate in such a scheme? Before I left Italy, I wrote his lawyer, telling him I recanted the monthly stipend.

Shortly after my return, I received a plain envelope mailed from New York City, my name typed on it, no return address, and inside a copy of both sides of a prayer card. Alger, for your benefit, a prayer card is a card of remembrance, provided by funeral homes and found at entry ways to Catholic wakes. On one side was a sentimental image of the Blessed Virgin of Loreto, on the other, "In loving memory of" on one line, the name "Maria Ruggieri" on the next, and a prayer.

The 'Ndrangheta cell in New York, of course, sent it to me, only it would know that Vittorio made me aware of the threat to my life.

Knowing how vicious the 'Ndrangheta could be, I then

undertook measures to protect myself. First, I satisfied myself through an investigation that Maria had indeed died before I informed Vittorio that I would pay the family. Then, I used my bargaining chip so I would not be threatened again. I let it be known to the New York 'Ndrangheta that harm to me would disrupt their investment scheme. Confident of my protection, in July, I negotiated and paid this debt of honor to the New York 'Ndrangheta who in turn would pay the family in Basilicata. Then, just a week ago, as I was leaving Rome, Vittorio contacted me, pleaded with me that he would be harmed if payment was not immediately made to the family in Basilicata. I was shaken. Had it not been paid? Had the New York 'Ndrangheta siphoned off the funds, leaving nothing for the family? Would the family harm Vittorio, would it hunt me down as twice offended?

The recording was silent for a few seconds and then a bitter, angry voice startled me.

Listen a few more moments, please. I'm scandalized by Cosimo Brunotti's mediocrity and personal corruption. I accuse him of fraud on the Institute, a gross misuse of funds for his own enjoyment, to spend on mistresses, lavish parties. He knows of my investigation, that I remain at the Institute to irritate him. He hates me, fears I will bring him down. If death intervenes and I cannot complete my investigation, I will leave that to you, Alger. The task will be yours, without harming the Institute.

There, you have it all. If my death is not witnessed, is suspicious, each of them, Claudia, the 'Ndrangheta, Brunotti, has motive. One is responsible.

I have made many mistakes during my life. Sins have been abundant. I have, however, kept my bargain with the University and hold my head high that my gift to the Institute from years ago, that which is in my trust, has risen greatly in value. That is my legacy. On this one thing, I have done well. I leave the Institute fiscally sound despite Brunotti's fraud.

Pietro, as I record my ... confession, I wish your promise of forgiveness could be mine. But, it cannot be. Your 'salvation' eludes me. You never did convince me.

12

STATIC SIGNALED THE END of the recording. Father Pietro snapped off the recorder, his face pale, his eyes moist. "I am affected, Mr. Temple, by his despair and his accusations."

"I'm not sure what to make of it, to be truthful."

"You may ask why a recording? I believe I know. While in his late sixties, Italo was a victim of Guillain-Barré Syndrome, a rare disease which attacks the body's immune system by producing antibodies that attack nerves in the extremities, the hands, the feet, leaving him impaired. Hence, his difficulty in walking and extreme weakness in his hands and fingers. He could barely hold a pen. For his work, his correspondence, he dictated to Claudia Cioffi or used voice recognition software. I suggest he used the software to create his draft which would have been imperfect and then read it into this device. He could not have used a keyboard or written out so long a piece without correction or collaboration with someone else. And who did he have? Certainly not Claudia who he accuses!"

I recalled the virtually illegible handwriting in Palagi's letter and that his handshake was a mere touch of fingers and my mother saying something years ago about Palagi's ailment.

Before leaving the conference room, we agreed that I would secure the recorder in my office safe and that we would discuss our obligations, legal and moral, if any, after Friday's memorial service.

Then, the priest shook my hand, holding it seconds more than necessary. "Death," the priest continued, "is the most expected thing that can happen, yet most of us can't quite believe it will happen to us. Apparently, Italo did. From the grave, he presents his views of himself, asks questions, points his finger." His apt comment resonated with me. "You now understand why I could never be his executor." He sighed, "Italo's personal life was never … transparent."

o O o

It was near to eight when I unlocked the door to our home halfway up College Hill on Congdon Street, a classic neo-Grecian house
from the 1830s that I had completely renovated and redesigned and
made its interior functional. The recorder was in my office safe and
I had dictated a memo to Marcie as to its importance. A quickening
wind accompanied me during my five block walk; the downtown
was bathed in a smudgy orange light fading into a stark, Prussian
blue horizon. I remained conflicted as to Palagi's motives. To persuade Father Pietro, or me, as to his basic decency? To excuse a life
of duplicity? To accuse all who failed him with crime?

I didn't get past the drinks cabinet in the dining room. With a
splash of Jameson in an Old Fashioned glass, I went upstairs to the
loft, a combination work space, library, and bedroom that took up
most of the second floor. I snapped on my iMac at my end of our
shared work table, pushed back in my comfortable Alerion chair,
and Googled 'Ndrangheta.

The crime family had hundreds of links, mostly in Italian, from
newspapers and sites specializing in organized crime. Once again,
Wikipedia was helpful. "Ndrangheta," I learned, was derived from
the Greek word *andragathia* meaning courage or loyalty. The gang,
based in Calabria and dominant in Basilicata, consisted of almost
two hundred cells with as many as six thousand members throughout Italy engaged in labor racketeering, loan sharking, illegal immigration, toxic waste dumping, kidnapping, extortion, and drug
trafficking. Each cell was closely knit, based on blood relationships
and marriages. While not as widely known in the United States as
the Mafia or Camorra, the 'Ndrangheta had become the most powerful crime syndicate in Italy by the late 1990s and early 2000s and
was thought to be responsible for up to eighty percent of the cocaine traffic in Europe. Cells were also active in New York City and
Florida. The latest update noted that Pope Francis had condemned
the wanton cruelty, the viciousness, the greed of the 'Ndrangheta in
a vigorous, courageous speech in the gang's heartland in the Boot.

I logged off, sat back, and considered Palagi's situation before his death. These were very bad guys who had Italo Palagi by the balls.

I finished the Jameson, then went downstairs to the kitchen, microwaved a bowl of turkey-and-barley soup prepared during the day by our housekeeper, cut two slices from an Olga's Crusty Loaf, and took my supper out to the table in the den off the kitchen. I had a spoon in hand when I heard the front door unlock, followed by marching steps clicking down the central hall. The swinging door opened and Nadie breezed into the kitchen, was quickly down three steps to the den, and plumped her trim bottom on the divan. She looked like an academic in a comfortable looking Eileen Fisher ensemble of blouse, long cardigan, and slacks in varied gray shades. She shook her head vigorously, loosening raven tresses that emphasized her regally long neck, and turned her head to face me, her large, emerald eyes and natural pink lips contrasted with her Mediterranean complexion. She took a deep breath. "I have something to tell you that you won't like."

I readied for another last minute change in wedding plans.

"The faculty senate voted tonight to change the University calendar and rename Columbus Day. It's now Native American Day. And the weekend is now Fall Weekend instead of Columbus Day Weekend."

My spoon dropped with a clatter. I was speechless. I stood slowly to gain composure and returned to the drinks cabinet for more Jameson. Renaming Columbus Day was a campus cause so long in the tooth that College Hall had relegated it to the bottom of a very long list. Only true believers, those ready as always to impose their views on the rest of the feckless world, kept the idea alive. And where better than the Carter University faculty senate, where campus causes go for ignition, where righteous indignation can become viral in a nano-second. I returned to the den, glass in hand, as Nadie said with a touch of satisfaction, "Packed the room with supporters, and bing, bam, bong, done."

"You were there?" As a progressive activist, she had to have been briefed, if not a participant.

She stood, her eyes widening, and approached me, hands on hips, going into defensive mode. My waif-like fiancée, open-hearted, loving, caring, a defender of the poor and downtrodden wherever, became hard-nosed and rigid in defense of any progressive cause was marshaling her arguments as she did twenty years ago as a champion debater at Brooklyn's Benjamin Cardozo High School.

"In deference to *you*, I was *not* there..."

I tried mightily to avoid confrontation. Maybe I would have but exasperation grew when Nadie mounted a spiel, likely rehearsed, of what she knew I would consider sanctimonious clap-trap: "Columbus is a symbol to millions of indigenous people of European brutality and destruction of their cultures ... We should be apologizing to them for their centuries of agony, the tragic death of civilizations instead of giving him a holiday.... He was a gold-seeking slaver, bringing with him an epidemic of syphilis and small pox.... *We* know what evils he did, never mind those who came after him ...!"

I interrupted her. "Why now, why just before Columbus Day?"

A morally certain Nadie responded not with an answer but with her list of persecutors, a cast of horribles that includes conquistadores, missionaries, Puritans in New England, Andrew Jackson, Kit Carson, right up to Wounded Knee. I was half listening; such a proclamation by a university somewhere else might only be a blip of news but in Providence, Rhode Island? A city populated by thousands of Italo-Americans? Where, Columbus Day Weekend on Federal Hill, the epicenter of Italian culture in Rhode Island, would be celebrated a *molto importante festa, ricca di tradizione* that competes with *festas* in Manhattan's Little Italy, the North End of Boston, and San Francisco's North Beach. Over a hundred thousand visitors would eat, shop, and participate in three days and nights of weekend festivities—at which, the faculty senate of Carter University in its wisdom was giving a middle finger Rhode Island salute. Nadie was still going strong when I again interrupted. "Even if you are correct in everything you say—and you're not—the ramifications..."

"Ramifications?" she exclaimed, her hands stretching toward me for an explanation.

"Half the City Council is Italo-American..."

"What's that got to do with anything?"

I decided it would be pointless to explain how Italo-Americans would react to the trashing of Columbus, especially just before Columbus Day, what it would do to frayed 'town-and-gown' relations between City Hall and the University. Nadie had a head of steam and my arguments would be heard as a litany of excuses. Her response would be a deconstructive *You judge the entire world by your experience, as if there is no other measure of human behavior.* Summarized: *Algy, get with it!*

The Charger bounces one more time and I hear a scrape of its muffler on the road surface as it slows to a stop. A door opens and slams as a second car, something with a straining four cylinders, brakes noisily nearby.

The driver whacks the lid of the trunk. "How you doin' in there, eh? Eh?" *His laugh is a donkey's 'hee-haw-ay.' He whacks the lid again. Harder.* "Listen, afta awhile, somebody calls somebody, they come and letcha out." *I refuse to be trunk music.* "Look, fuck-off, you shouldn't have taken a whack at me." *Pause.* "Take a nap. You know what I'm saying? Relax."

'Relax?' I've been sucker punched, stuffed into my car's trunk, thighs pressed against my chest, hands tied behind my back, tape over my eyes and mouth, cheeks sporting carpet burn, something poking into my rear end. 'Relax?'

"Oh," *he adds,* "don't bother looking for that little gizmo, that release thing. I cut it off." *Hee-haw-ay.*

"Fuck 'im!" *another voice, almost falsetto.*

"Nice car," *the first voice bellows as he bangs the trunk lid one more time.* "Love the sound of that fuckin' Hemi!" *He walks away; I hear the crunch of heavy feet on gravel.* "Where'd ya get this piece of shit?" *he complains loudly as car doors creak open.*

"You breakin' my balls? Broad Street. Some greaser's shit-mobile. Nobody's gonna report it. Where's the keys to his car?"

"Front seat. Don't fuckin' worry, I wiped everythin' down including the keys." *Don't forget to stop at Caserta's for take-out. I'm fuckin' starving."*

Doors slammed, tires screeched, an engine whine trailed away into silence.

13 Tuesday

NADIE AND I BOARDED the seven-ten Acela within the wa-ter-seeping cavern beneath the Amtrak station, the gloomiest, chilliest place in all of Providence. Only the stalactites were missing. Fitting for our frosty co-existence since last night. We did manage to agree not to discuss Columbus Day for twenty-four hours. *Could we?*

I hadn't slept well, and it had nothing to do with Columbus Day. The dream that had dogged me for years after Beirut returned: I'm in a dark, compressed place, immobile with dust carpeting me, filling my mouth, my nose, smothering me, my lungs refusing to clear, hacking coughs in fits. I resist the urge to gulp in air for fear of more dust, and from close by, comes the first death rattle ... . I awoke in a sweat to be restless through early morning hours.

The train's quiet car had been packed by Boston passengers and we settled for cross-aisle seats in the following business class car. I had my laptop and this month's *Car and Driver* and *Automobile*; Nadie had a Vera Bradley carryall filled by her iPad and books. We were barely out of the station when she began to send and receive texts and tweets that resulted in occasional *aha's* and even giggles.

I logged on, e-mailed Marcie to be watchful for the expected Columbus Day fallout, and read her e-mail to me to check this morning's *Political Notes* on *ProJo.com*. Under the heading *Changes at the Shoot-Out Commission,* I was astonished by a ten year old photo of myself under *In,* next to a singularly unflattering photograph of Francisco 'Frannie' Zito, a cigarette stuck in the side of his mouth emphasizing a sneer across his darkly handsome face, under

Out. Apparently, I was replacing Zito, an appointee of our mendacious former mayor Angelo "Sonny" Russo. Zito resigned after a complaint from Mayor Tramonti that Zito had failed to report a decades old assault arrest, with a baseball bat no less, on his required state Ethics Form. The article went on to note that "flamboyant" Zito, the President of Heritage Finance Company on the Hill, had been tagged as the "Bentley Banker" because he was chauffeured nightly in a Bentley sedan around town to restaurants, bars, and clubs he financed. I winced; had my buddy the Mayor *forgotten* to tell me the circumstance of my appointment? Would it have made a difference? "Geezus," I murmured, loud enough to get Nadie's attention, which led me to show her the screen.

She had been irritated when I took the appointment, not being enamored by what she had seen and heard about the sleazy aspects of pool tournaments, but particularly because the tournament's second weekend—the pro event—would coincide with our wedding; now she was wide-eyed and had real concern in her voice when she said, "You're replacing a Mafia guy?"

"I don't know that ..."

"Well, he looks the part," and he did. She said, "Can't you get out of it? Didn't Tony tell you who he was?"

"No, wasn't relevant, I guess. Anyway, it's too late." Was it? Probably. "Don't worry. I'm a big boy."

Unfortunately, that drew out further apprehension that dissolved into her take on the nastiness and Byzantine ways of Providence politics, its *nudge-nudge* baseline of governance. At least, we were off Columbus Day.

Her receipt of a text took her back to messaging and I found the file holding Palagi's estate plan documents which I had loaded on my lap top to review before today's conference. His will consisted of seven pages, executed with due formality, his signature a scrawl, with two of Pine's assistants acting as witness and notary, replete with stilted *provisos* and *whereas's* and *grants*, with the Institute as a residuary beneficiary. His trust, a more complicated document of thirty pages with the same signature, same two witnesses, designated Palagi as a lifetime trustee; upon his death, the assets in the trust also went to the Institute. The last document was a Royalty and License Fee Sharing Agreement which assigned one-half of the income from Palagi's royalties and licenses to the Institute during his lifetime, all coming to the Institute upon his death.

Scanning the documents, I recalled the Provost's explanation of their origin. Palagi was outed as the author of the Forza thrillers a year or two after he arrived at Carter University, allowing campus enmities as to the Institute to be rehashed and questions raised as to Palagi's credentials, apparently, an academic writing thrillers was no more respectable in democratic America than in tradition-bound Italy. That reaction triggered Palagi's well-publicized gift to the Institute of an income stream from royalties and license fees from his thrillers and an estate plan that bequeathed substantial assets upon his death to the Institute, quieting and out-maneuvering his Pecksniff critics. His generosity was likely not unalloyed; it was, it now seemed to me, to be an expensive attempt to tamp down any interest in his past life.

I logged off, and yawned, and gave into drowsiness brought on by a lack of sleep, the legalese of the documents, the muted clackety-clack of the rails, the gentle sway of the car, and a comfortable seat. Somewhere past Bridgeport, Nadie touched my shoulder and brought me back to consciousness. "I don't ... suppose ... that you'd have time to come out to Brooklyn with me? I was going to ask you last night but ... ." Nadie always used her widowed mother's given name for reasons inexplicable to me.

"Nadie..."

"For moral support. You know she wears me down."

The intimate Providence ceremony we planned months ago with a few close friends and relatives hadn't survived pushbacks from Zelda Winokur along the lines of 'I've only got one daughter,' 'your father, he'd want,' 'well, I don't know,' 'I *suppose* we could,' 'but don't you think that,' and 'we'll just have to see.' Eventually, we compromised, the ceremony became more formal and, surprise, surprise, Nadie had become enamored with wedding details and froufrou she previously dismissed.

"Please ...?" she said softly and reached across the aisle to take my hand in hers. Her engagement ring, a large, yellow diamond chosen from among my mother's jewelry, flashed in the overhead lights.

Sensing the opportunity to thaw our relationship, I said, "If I'm through in time with the lawyers, I'll call you." That was not completely honest; I was already thinking how to stretch out my appointment to avoid more wedding planning.

14

IT WAS RAINING AS a cab left me at Champlin & Burrill's midtown address; Nadie stayed in the cab for the remaining few blocks on Madison Avenue to Vera Wang. The receptionist ushered me into a small conference room set up with vacuum dispensers of coffee, bone china cups and saucers, and pastries. A securities litigation partner, a smartly dressed woman, joined me and said there had been a positive development: another Champlin & Burrill partner had been approached the prior week by a recently dismissed stock trader at Ravensford Capital to handle his wrongful termination and whistleblower suit.

"Since the firm only represents employers in HR matters, the partner referred him to a boutique plaintiff litigation firm. Late yesterday, after our partner became aware of the University's interest in Ravensford Capital, he called the referred firm and inquired if its new client might talk to us."

"This morning they called back and we've got a meeting set up with the trader, one Joseph P. Civittolo," she said. "One o'clock, in his lawyer's office. I looked him up," she continued. "He's got all of the securities licenses you need for a place like Ravensford. Lives out in Hempstead on the Island, St. John's graduate, worked out there for fifteen years, then came into the city. Can't for the life of me figure why he's willing to talk unless he's just bitter. But there's an issue."

"What's that?"

"We were told an hour ago that the deal is that only *you* will be permitted to interview him."

"What? I'm the client!" The University pays Champlin & Burrill over a million a year.

"We've already made and lost the argument. It's up to you. Go or no go."

"Of course, I'll go. Have to," I said, extremely annoyed to be placed in such a role.

○ ◯ ○

After being thoroughly briefed on questions I should ask Civittolo and a sandwich lunch, I walked to the nearby Park Avenue office of Civittolo's counsel. Its sleekly modern reception area was the domain of a young woman whose makeup, hair, and smile would not be out of place on *Jewelry TV*. She took my name, made a call, and pointed to a couch. The firm must be doing well if I could measure success in terms of thickness of carpeting.

I sat and read the morning's *Times* until I sensed, more than heard, someone approach. I looked up and saw, in this order, black high heel shoes, good legs, a black skirt, a black silky jacket opened to a red silky blouse, and the fabulous face ... of my ex-wife.

"Algy," Jocelyn said in a voice combining liquid chocolate with a hint of huskiness. "It is so-o-o good to see you."

I took in a beautiful face that exuded intelligence and seemed not to have aged except for a character line or two at the corners of her brown eyes. She remained a thin, tapering, California girl with a wide smile showing perfect teeth. So, what was the protocol for an ex-husband taken unawares by an ex-wife he hadn't seen in six or seven years? Shake the ex's hand, or give her a quick buss on the cheek? Tell her she looked great, or say something non-committal?

"I hope this isn't too much of a shock," Jocelyn said, obviously relishing that it was.

"A nice surprise," I lied and stood, bringing us close to eye level because she was five-eleven in her expensive heels. I immediately recalled her need for spatial domination over clients, colleagues, and, especially, female associates, opponents, and competitors.

"When the request came in from Champlin & Burrill and you were mentioned as sitting in as counsel to the University, I thought it best, under the circumstances, if it was just you who interviewed our client. Reduces some knowing looks. Do you mind?"

"Not at all," I said with some false warmth because I knew Jocelyn had to have planned this ambush when the serendipitous opportunity arose, reminding me of moments in our marriage when she sought to gain an edge with surprise.

She sat, as did I, responding to my questions as to her recent career, while I recalled a marriage with more ups and downs than the Appalachian Trail, a nightly scrum in SoHo, mistaking lust for love. We had met and married after I left the Marines when I joined the Manhattan District Attorney's office, hoping to learn the ropes and become a good government, public integrity prosecutor. Instead, I was mired in the trenches as a lowly night court assistant DA learning a life lesson or two, while she was the gifted, always available Stanford Law Review litigation associate at Cadwalader Wickersham & Taft. Within months, our disparate work schedule created a cavern of lonely nights and wasted weekends. Our communication became loaded with innuendoes and hurt feelings. It might have gone on longer but in moments of uncommon good sense, we recognized it would have been emotionally draining and futile. Since our divorce, she had remarried and divorced again, became a player in Democratic Party and an intimate of Hillary Clinton.

"Cadwalader was great but I like being plaintiff's counsel. And this firm has a great reputation and a client list that is top shelf. I've found my niche." She paused. "You're getting married!" she exclaimed, her voice giving away a touch of insinuation that I might be getting too old to be tethered.

I felt coerced to recite Nadie's resume: Radcliffe, research fellowship at Johns Hopkins, University of Pennsylvania for a doctorate in psychology, through which Jocelyn's knowing smile gave away that she had previously researched my fiancée.

"A psychologist! No place to hide, Algy. She'll have your number," she said with a voice that suggested *poor Algy*.

Our initial skirmish concluded, I was guided to a small, plainly furnished conference room. Seated across a polished oval table, Joseph P. Civittolo was a slim figure in a dark suit, white shirt, loose red tie in an unbuttoned collar. His black curly hair was too long to be fashionable, his eyes so dark their pupils were lost, a prominent nose held thick, black framed eyeglasses. The full lips and a weak, square chin reminded me of the sneering nephew on *The Sopranos*.

Jocelyn introduced me and said her client had been a senior vice president of Ravensford Capital until two weeks ago. "I ran the equity trading desk," Civittolo said, his accent very New Yorkese, his tired, unsympathetic eyes taking me in. "Domestic stocks only. No bonds, no international, not the hedge fund investments. Plain vanilla trading."

Jocelyn interrupted him. "Not that it is relevant, but I've explained to Joe that you and I have had a ... prior relationship. I've also explained that he's under no compulsion to talk to you or to describe the way Ravensford Capital ran its business or anything that might relate to your client's investment. Joe, will you confirm that?"

"Yeah, you two were married?" His tired face tried a smile but didn't make it past a sneer. "How about that."

I sat at the table facing him and took a yellow pad with my briefing notes out of my valise. Jocelyn sat at his right, her expression told me she was going to grade my performance. "Those bastards took me. I gave them twenty plus years, had over three million locked up there, what they owe me on bonuses, my severance arrangements, my deferred comp. The sons of bitches ... ."

Jocelyn touched her client's wrist as his fingers clenched into fists. She said, "My client became suspicious when the partners—there are four, including one based in Garden City—held an emergency meeting. With the turmoil in the markets, stocks taking a dive, bonds down, investors getting antsy, some clients were making demands for funds. The next day, a lot of money was shuffled around, some accounts were liquidated, money moved offshore. The partners cashed out, leaving just statutorily required working capital, and the only reason Joe found out was that he is ... *friendly* ... with one of the administrative assistants to a partner who, supposedly, was Joe's long-time buddy. At first, Joe got a line, then was offered a bonus to keep quiet, then was told that if he didn't, he'd be fired, threatened as well, with a hint that certain clients would be very upset if he complained. He confided in a friend who had a friend at Champlin & Burrill and the referral came here. Joe's status is as a statutory whistle blower for fraud, violation of SEC and FinRA regulations. We've sued the firm and its principals. Joe is also talking to the SEC and with the US Attorney."

"I know the account your guy had. I should say *accounts*." His fingers slid away from his lawyer's touch. "The first one was an A-4 account, the other was like an A-4 account but wasn't."

"A-4? What does that stand for?"

"Nothing I know of. Just how accounts for connected people were set up."

Being from Providence, I knew the connotation of *connected*.

"A-4 accounts were worked differently. Only partners ran them. They needed special handling, access to liquidity, online to accounts in Europe, a few to Hong Kong. An A-4 might balloon overnight in investments from overseas or right here; an A-4 might get closed quickly. That's why all A-4s were invested with Sugarman. No waits with Bernie. Bernie paid out on a phone call. Funds available same day on the wire. Didn't matter when the ticket went in, Bernie paid off. We called him *Bernie T-bill* because redemptions were so easy. Ideal for an A-4 account."

"Could you be more precise?" I asked. "Before his trust account arrived at Ravensford from Smith Barney, Palagi had another account?"

Civittolo became impatient. "Yeah, as I said, an A-4 account. Look, this is how it went down. Your professor had two accounts. Both out of Hempstead on the Island, where the firm started. A lot of Italo-Americans on the South Shore, like the partners. Your guy must have had some *connection* there because that's how and where his first account came in, as an A-4. Was there almost as long as me. At least a couple of bricks—millions—in the account, all with Bernie. Sometimes, there was more but every so often some got cleaned out, just like the other A-4s. Later, his trust account came over from Smith Barney, a plain vanilla, my kind of account. I wanted the trades but it stayed with the partner, and was run like an A-4, right into Bernie's shop. Everything's fine until the rumors on Bernie began."

His voice caught and rose in pitch. His eyes left me and stared out of a window. "Having two accounts with the same name was a problem. I remember a screw up about some money going into the first A-4 account when it should have gone into the second, and Palagi is furious, calling the partner on the account who went ape shit. On the Smith Barney account, the second account, we sent monthly statements. On A-4 accounts like the first, we didn't."

"When did the A-4 accounts get liquidated?"

He grunted. "Right after the partner meeting on Sugarman, wired out, mostly to Italy. Cash came from Bernie. The second account, your account, didn't get liquidated because it wasn't a *real* A-4. It got stuck at Bernie's like all the rest. If your client asked for it to be liquidated, it was too late. Frozen. Sugarman wasn't redeeming anymore."

Jocelyn, no longer smiling, lawyerly summarized her client's description of Palagi's involvement with Ravensford Capital. "Both accounts were invested with Sugarman. The first account was an A-4 account that got liquidated, funds wired to Italy or wherever, when rumors began. The other, the second account, your trust account, invested like an A-4 account but not one, that account didn't get liquidated before the firm closed."

Civittolo interrupted her, his voice and face angry, impatient, and unsympathetic. "All I'm telling you is that one of your guy's accounts, the one from Smith Barney, didn't make the cut. Your guy got screwed!"

o O o

As I walked back to Champlin & Burrill in a blustery raw wind, I considered the disgruntled Mr. Civittolo. Jocelyn will earn her fee in representing this guy. Then, more about Jocelyn. Outside the reception area, Jocelyn brushed my cheek with a kiss and asked me if I was in town long enough for a drink after work at Clover's Lounge on East 34th Street, our long ago *special* place. I declined. But her invitation triggered memories. Her classy lawyer image was replaced by one of her barefoot in the sand at the South Hampton beach where we first met, gorgeous in a pink sundress billowing in the breeze, her hair swept back from her tan face, her eyes cool, her smile dazzling.

I shook my head to get rid of her image. Back to Mr. Civittolo. Bizarre interview but why would he lie? Nothing in it for him. And I could place the timing of when Palagi knew the trust account was in trouble. *If* before meeting Father Pietro on the Saturday before his death, he would have said so or it would have been on his recording. *If* he found out about the Ponzi after, it had to be between that Saturday morning and the following Wednesday evening. *It could have been an impetus to suicide.*

Upon my return to Champlin & Burrill, I was informed that Ravensford Capital would file for liquidation in the morning, any attempt at injunctions or attachments would be ineffective, the principals of the firm had scattered, and tomorrow a trustee was likely to be appointed by the court to sort out the mess. In other words, as Civittolo well said, Italo Palagi, and now Carter University, was screwed.

15

IT WAS TWO FORTY-FIVE and I thought Nadie must be in Brooklyn by now. I texted her that I was out of my meeting, sorry it was so late, and to my surprise she replied she was at Bloomies only a few blocks away. There was nothing for it and I was soon in the back seat of the black Lincoln limo provided to Champlin & Burrill clients. A doorman held a huge umbrella over her as she dashed into the limo loaded with shopping bags. She wore a new lipstick color, darker, almost purple, and maybe a blush. "Success," she exclaimed as she settled in. Her wedding dress fittings were over, Vera Wang personnel were wonderful, she purchased a jacket and pants at the Celine boutique, had a facial and a makeup treatment after lunch with a college roommate who had organized Nadie's bachelorette weekend in Manhattan beginning on Friday. She expressed no curiosity about my meeting other than a casual "How did it go?"

"Okay. Lots to do," I said and thought maybe the best course of action was not to mention my ex-wife.

○ ◯ ○

On the ride down Broadway and into Chinatown, across the Brooklyn Bridge, on to Flatbush Avenue, Pashto music leaked from the ear buds of our turbaned, head bobbing Afghani driver who ignored his passengers complaints as he navigated the congested traffic. Horns blared at the Kabul kamikaze's lane shifts in what had become a windswept, steady rain. Nadie was busy texting when not glaring at the back of the driver's turban. In between, she said, "Zelda called me to make sure I'm coming. Not like her."

"If it's another change ..."

"I won't let that happen."

Which I had reason to doubt. Zelda Winokur's snits and demands also had the unfortunate effect of focusing Nadie's interest in my prior marriage. Her questions about Jocelyn came at odd times, like when we were having dinner. "Did Jocelyn cook?"—or in bed—no need to be precise here. It peaked when weeks ago, I brought up a prenuptial agreement.

Nadie's reaction to a prenup urged by my brother Nick and common in our family was that she was being treated as a bartered bride and aggravated the issue of our families' disparate wealth and, as Nadie saw it, social class differences, an early impediment in our relationship, even more problematic than our poles-apart political and social views. Eventually, begrudgingly, rationally, she agreed. We exchanged list of assets—mine took six typed pages and hers fit on a single sheet—and she ignored my request to have the agreement reviewed for her by a lawyer at my expense. "Did Jocelyn sign one?"

"No. The whole thing was accidental. No planning, a quick trip to Maryland, a justice of the peace ..."

"She could have cleaned your clock if she wanted to. She must have had her own reasons not to. You were lucky. That's what this is about."

No explanation of family responsibilities inherent in the protection of generational wealth would quiet the nerve I struck.

o O o

Our driver found curb space in front of a brick façade, a fiftyish apartment building on Ocean Avenue. We interrupted his music with shoulder taps, emphasizing in near shouts that he was to wait for us. That took several tellings. We left him, unsure if he would be there, and took a cranky elevator to the fourth floor. Nadie used her key, called out "Zelda" and we were immediately assaulted by wails from beyond the hallway. Nadie's mother rushed to the door and in astonishment threw her arms around ... *me*. "Algy! It's you! Look, Ida, look! It's Algy!"

"Ida ...?" Nadie eyes widened. Ida was Aunt Ida Gershowitz, her mother's sister and always a speck in Nadie's eye.

Mrs. Winokur herded us through to the kitchen, the place of mourning. Aunt Ida, neither made up nor coiffured, in a faded housedress, slumped at a dinette table. Her reddened eyes brimmed with tears. "Mortie's money is gone!" she shrieked. "Same for the homes'! It's ... *gone!*"

Through heaving sighs and outbursts of anger, her story emerged. Mortie, her late husband, the founder and operator of the nine Gershowitz Funeral Homes in Brooklyn and Queens, had deeply ensnared the family in Bernie Sugarman's ever widening Ponzi scheme. As she finished, Mrs. Winokur soothed, "Ida, Ida," and grasped her sister's trembling hands, "it'll be alright. You have the boys."

That set off a screech that tinkled pendants on the chandelier over the dining room table. "Mortie, *Mortie*, you died not knowing." Aunt Ida's hands were unleashed to stretch to heaven in supplication. "You left us penniless. You trusted that, that ..."

"For a Jew to do this to Jews," Mrs. Winokur complained to me. "In the old country, they'd take off his clothes, throw him out of the village, say *shiva* for him like he was dead."

Nadie and Mrs. Winokur sat next to Aunt Ida at the dinette table. I pulled out a chair by Nadie's side.

"*Everybody* we know had *something* with Bernie." Aunt Ida, having quickly recovered, ignored the peeved look on her niece's face and directed her complaints to me. "*Everybody* knows that Mortie knew Bernie. *I* know Bernie. I play cards with his sister Rachel in Palm Beach. For years, Mortie played golf with him. His father was buried by Mortie. And Mortie gave him *everything* to invest. Even the burial trust." I must have looked quizzical at *burial trust* because she explained, "People pre-pay for their funerals; we invest it in a trust and provide the service they contract for when they die. Bernie had that money, too. Suppose people ask for an accounting? Or their money back? How are we going to do that?" Her solid body began to sway as her fists pounded the table. "What will we do, Zelda?" and the sisters rocked back and forth in an embrace.

It was quite a show, so different than my first encounter with Aunt Ida last spring, a formal meet-the-family in her over-furnished, wall-space-covered penthouse apartment in a Brooklyn high rise next to one of the largest Gershowitz funeral homes. From a parlor sofa under an original or good copy of a Chagall, her hair carefully colored and piled high, in an expensive blue dress with a pearl choker that could keep Mikimoto's polishers busy for a week, she deigned to grant me occasional smiles while her sons, Arnie, the business son, and Simon, the face of the funeral homes in the community, both dressed in dark 'undertaker' suits, were friendly to the point of unctuousness. Somehow Nadie and I got through two hours of too much information about the funeral home business and dry tea cakes.

I asked Aunt Ida if she had consulted her lawyer. Aghast, she spat out, "Jack Rabinowitz? I have to tell Jack Rabinowitz what we lost? I can't do that," she explained, "you can't trust lawyers." Nadie winced. "His clients are our clients. What's he going to do? He'll tell them," and her hand swept the table. "When they finally think of it, those with money in the burial trust, they're gonna want to know." Her eyes went blank as she confronted the ungrateful hoards of Gershowitz Funeral Home clients. "They'll ask cute questions, then make gossip, then 'Ida, how's my money I gave to Mortie?', 'Ida, can I be in peace?', 'Ida, you didn't invest *my* money with Bernie, did you?' Everybody's going to want their money back." Then, to her sister, "We're ruined, Zelda, ruined!"

"Surely," I said, "the homes can get a loan."

"A bank?" Aunt Ida stopped pounding the Formica long enough to focus her glare at me. "They would have to *know*, right?" Why was I, the rich *goyim*, so dumb? "Look, here it is. Our business is all reputation. It's rabbis and families, and ... Oy vey!" She wiped her eyes with the back of her hand. "Not even our best friends, could we tell. Yes, we would say we had a loss. We did! But they got to think Mortie mostly got out a long time ago, kept some in for old times' sake. If he didn't leave *some* in, they'd think he knew something and didn't tell them! But all?" She shrugged away from her sister's fingers kneading her shoulders. "Zelda, how can we hold our heads high?" This from someone Nadie once remarked was chauffeured across the street. "The business will be gone, the boys ruined, I'll have to put the apartment on the market, sell Palm Beach. I'll never go back. And you, my sister, if you go south, where are you going to stay? In some miserable room in Hollywood?"

Mrs. Winokur's sorrowful face went from her sister to Nadie, and finally, to me. "What can we do?"

The *we* in her question hung for a few seconds too many. Nadie's hand pressed my knee, her expression perplexed. Unless the

Gershowitz family was righted, our wedding would have the gaiety of a morgue. Mrs. Winokur added plaintively, "What a disgrace. And you, Algy, coming into the *family*."

Aunt Ida's eyes rose abruptly to mine. They cleared and I got the drift. I was being asked to do something. *For the family*. The Winokur-Gershowitz, nee Zuckerman, sisters were nobody's fools. What did they want? A discrete attorney who could handle the claims against Sugarman without tipping off New York's Jewish community? *No*, I concluded, more than that. In the face of calamity, I was expected to be a *mensch*.

"Maybe my brother could look into the possibility of a private loan," I began, "to carry the business and the trust until things straightened out, to tide you over."

Aunt Ida dabbed her eyes, which widened considerably; Mrs. Winokur smiled and embraced me, and revealed the plot. "See, Ida, I told you. Algy would find a way."

Aunt Ida continued to act wide-eyed surprised at my offer as she reached into a pocket of her house dress and handed me her son Arnie's business card. "Arnie knows how much ..."

16

WE MADE THE SEVEN-TEN Amtrak Regional at Penn Station with a few minutes to spare and found adjoining seats. Nadie, loaded with bags she refused to relinquish, fussed with passenger debris left on her seat, and complained about the air conditioning and lack of space in the overhead bin. She fiddled with the contents of her carry-on, opened a paperback and then closed it angrily when the overhead lights dimmed as the train approached the East River. Since Ocean Avenue, her cell phone's buzzings had been ignored. My attempts at conversation had not penetrated her funk. Only when the train screeched and swayed its way into Queens did she open up.

"Ida had the scheme worked out. Calls Zelda, asks her to put the bite on me, in person, to talk to you, I cajole you into coming, and you arrive to save the day! I was the perfect foil."

"Listen," I replied, "Ida, her family, took a real hit. Any loan that Nick might arrange will be for the business, not the family, and will depend on the homes' finances, its cash flow. Nick will be sympathetic, but he is a banker."

Nadie's cheek was pressed to the rain streaked window. Graffitied, dilapidated factory buildings and weed-strewn lots with piles of discarded tires, garbage trees, industrial trash, and junked cars sped by, an urban wasteland, a desert of shame, that shocked anyone on a first train trip to Boston. Then, even less agreeably she said, "Ida must be desperate. If Ida loses her stature in Brooklyn, she'd take to her bed, with Zelda waiting on her hand and foot." Nadie has long complained her mother lived in the shadows of her older sister. "My mother is such a patsy!"

Seconds later, Nadie shook my knee. "There's another thing that concerns me. About the loan, I mean. Arnie and Simon may not understand that the loan is a business deal. Arnie, I don't trust, and Simon is as smart as a sack of rocks. Maybe it won't be like, 'Thank you, thank you, for saving us'; it could be more like 'Is that all?'"

o O o

After reading several texts from Marcie on the evolving story of *Carter University v. Christopher Columbus and the Italo-Americans of Providence,* with links to the local media pouncing on the juicy story, I began a Lee Child thriller picked up in Penn Station. That got me through to Old Saybrook where Jocelyn snuck back into my mind. I remembered her hair spread on a pillow, framing her face, a single sun-blond curl playing peekaboo, her slim, ripe body, her tan highlighting alabaster body parts that needed my hands.

Nadie slapped her book close. From the corner of my eye, I saw her staring out at the dusky marshlands of Long Island Sound whizzing by. "Do you ever think of Jocelyn?" she asked.

ESP? Telepathy?

"Only when you bring her up."

I gave myself a pass on my white lie.

o O o

When we arrived home, Nadie went upstairs to the loft while I punched in numbers on the telephone in the den for messages. Two awaited recall. The first, from this morning, was a man's hard-edged, breathy voice crackling with anger. "Fuck off, who do ya t'ink ya are? Yer shit don't smell? Well, fuck you, butt plug." Click.

Huh? What the hell was that all about? A blowback from this morning's *Journal* article? I listened to the message again, more carefully. The voice was rough, like a longtime smoker's, slurred, and muffled as though spoken through a handkerchief, with a Providence accent and cadence, the words evenly spaced.

Next call had come a half hour later. Same voice, "Fuckin' WASP blow job. *Figlio, a bocchino, testa di cazza.*" Click.

Some goomba of Frannie Zito letting off steam? Who else would take the time to so elegantly describe me? Was it just the unpalatable idea of a *fuckin' WASP* replacing a somebody from the Hill?

A robotic voice insisted I had to save or delete the messages. What were my options? Ignore? A phone trace that would surely get Nadie involved? A call to the cops? I decided not overreact, and hoped that I wasn't letting my ego, my Yankee stubbornness, get in the way of good judgment. I pushed 'seven' on the keypad to delete the calls and tapped in my brother's speed dial number.

"More on Ravensford?" Nick asked, surprised by the late evening call to his West Seventies condo. I updated him on what Joe Civittolo had revealed. "All I can tell you is that if I was going to launder money, I'd use a hedge fund. You can move large sums of money without supervision and you don't have to reveal who your clients are. That's my bet. The money is long gone."

"Thanks and no thanks," I replied and briefly got into the financial perils facing Gershowitz Funeral Homes, the likely effects on Nadie, her mother, and importantly, the wedding, and the need of a quickly arranged loan.

"Funeral homes?" he interjected more than once. Money and finance, which ran in my family's DNA, have strangely skipped me while Nick, like my father, had taken on investment of our family's multi-generational fortune and augmented it several times over.

"I doubt the firm would fund a loan to a string of funeral homes," Nick said very calmly, very bankerly. "That's not the kind of situation in which we risk partnership money, let alone investors' money, even if the interest rate is attractive, plenty of security, and positive cash flow." There was a long pause. "Of course, we've got to take care of Nadie." Another pause. "We could put them in touch with some work-out lenders outside the city or, if you feel it necessary, tap the TF?"

The TF, our shorthand for the Temple Fund, would be a last resort. The Temple Fund, managed by Nick, consisted of highly liquid, super-safe investments reserved for unanticipated needs of Nick's family, me, and our mother, and from the investment portfolio he invested for our extended family and charitable foundations. Since Nick and I live within our earned income, and our mother had both family investments and income from trusts my father left her, the TF had grown considerably over the years and, although accessible, was rarely invaded.

Before we reached out to third-party lenders or used the TF, I suggested some due diligence on the funeral homes' books. "I don't want either of us to be embarrassed. There's something slick about Arnie. Just to make sure ... "

He replied that he would have a credit analyst call Arnie Gershowitz in the morning—I gave him the telephone number from Arnie's business card—to determine if the funeral homes were bankable.

o O o

I went up to the loft, Nadie was already in bed. I realized I wasn't ready for sleep, told her so, kissed her forehead. I probably should have gone online for more Columbus Day reactions, but I decided that could wait for the morning when I would be clear-headed and ready to deal with the challenge. Instead, I went downstairs into the basement's exercise area and my pool room.

A touch of a remote of the Bose CD player produced the first notes of Keith Jarrett's *Koln Concert* and I picked up my cue from the restored 1928 Brunswick-Balke-Callender pool table. It had a pristine, traditional green, Simonis cloth surface, classic leather basket pockets, and in-laid mother-of-pearl diamond spots along its nine foot rails. The balls on the table were in a triangle rack and I broke to a decent spread, missed a cut shot at the rail, then missed a carom shot as I played too quickly, leaving the cue ball boxed. I tried to squeeze it out with a shot loaded with English and missed again. *And missed again.*

I backed away and stared at the positions of the balls, cue cradled in my arm. Seconds passed; I let my breathing slow as the piano music became hypnotic. Something I just read in a pool magazine came to mind, that an MIT geek was designing a pool robot that trained laser sensors on the table, instantly calculated all of the possibilities in any shot—cue tip placement on cue ball, angle of approach, speed, and spin—and executed every shot with absolute precision. I shared the writer's reaction that while pool looked like it was all geometry, angles and shots on a wire, its essence was beyond mechanics. At its best, pool was mental agility married to physical prowess within the psychological arena of competition, it all came together when a player reached the shooter's *zone,* the *dead stroke*, when skill, training, and experience were like fluids mixing in a bottle.

I made two shots and took a deep breath. I thought the Zen of pool and its physical, geometric mechanics would be evidenced in brilliant play over the course of the Shoot-Out but in a hundred matches in big money games in back rooms and pool pits all over Providence such qualities would be augmented by guile, hustle, stamina and the grease of gambling. Because that was the reality of pool.

It isn't as though I don't have a clue where they had abandoned me. The driver had been one side of cell phone chatter over the static of a police radio that he must keep handy. He complained that he missed supper, and laughed when told somebody's in 'deep shit' for 'banging Chickie's camorata. "She's ripe 'cause his dick is piccololini," he responded Electrifying. Then, he said, "Next exit for the dump."

In Rhode Island, the dump is the Central Landfill, Mount Trashmore, highest elevation in the state's glacial plain, decades of garbage and junk covered by impenetrable plastic and tons of earth, the feeding ground for every lazy seagull within thirty miles of Narragansett Bay.

As I begin to assess my situation, I straighten to reposition myself every few minutes to keep circulation flowing. My brain is clearing, less buzz and murk. Who is the 'somebody' who calls 'somebody' to get me out? Would the second 'somebody' be a cop or worse, a reporter? Think of the notoriety! Damn!

A rotten egg odor seeps into the trunk, confirming I must be on the western side of Trashmore, off Shun Pike, where methane gas is extracted for electric generation from the decomposing garbage. Which makes me wonder how much air is in this trunk? I seem to remember sixteen cubic feet of cargo space. How much space do I take up? How much air do I need? My breaths suddenly became shorter, the air seems staler. There must be airholes some place in the frame because I can smell the stench. Right?

The specter of claustrophobia seeps into my brain.

17 Wednesday

I AWOKE WITH SWEATY sheets wrapped tightly around me, after a night of scattered, confused, all too familiar dreams. Nadie's side of the bed was empty. I put on a robe, went downstairs, and found her note on the breakfast counter: *Gone to the gym, and I forgot to tell you, I have dinner and an early movie date tonight with Kate and Louise. Wedding present. Love and kisses and 'Goodbye, Columbus!'*

Well, better than a brooding silence at breakfast.

With my coffee, I read the *Journal's* coverage of the Columbus Day mess. *Columbus Day Banned at Carter* was the banner headline, the story replete with vitriolic quotes from city council members, the President of the Sons of Italy, the Commander of Italo-American War Veterans post, and a Knights of Columbus spokesman. Strident proponents from among our faculty fired back, joined by the President of the Third World Students Association, and the sachem of the Narragansett Indian tribe. Buried in the last paragraph at the end of the second column, inside page was a statement from the University's Public Information Office, a bland "studying the situation" equivalent of "no comment."

After a shower, and in consideration of both my first Shoot-Out Tournament Commission meeting at noon and the Shoot-Out Gala tonight, I dressed in full lawyer mufti: a light gray suit, blue tattersall shirt, blue tie, and polished black shoes. Because of an overcast, I took a Burberry raincoat and headed to our garage around the corner and down the hill on East Street. I unlocked its side door and snapped on overhead lights. "Algy's Autorama," was

Nadie's disapproving description for my garage full of cars. Nadie, who usually walks or bikes and handles a steering wheel like a tricycle's handlebar, cannot understand the attraction. 'Who needs four cars?' she asked early on in our relationship.

I did. I'm a car buff. A Mini Cooper, our jointly used city car, was almost hidden between my muscle car, a sleek, midnight blue Dodge Charger with a big-mouthed grill, a rear spoiler, and a fuel injected 6.4 liter, Hemi V-8, and a black, aluminum trimmed Range Rover, our comfortable travel car. Under a dustcover in the fourth bay was my trophy car, a Maserati Gran Turismo convertible that deserved driving gloves, only the best of weather, and the open road.

If you are what you drive, what does that say about me? I have had a love affair with cars beginning with an ancient Ford pickup driven on the rutted roads around my family's retreat on Fishers' Island. In high school, I owned a souped-up V-8 Plymouth Barracuda, then a Chevy Camaro while in college and law school. I rebuilt carburetors and refinished scratches or dents, did most of my own repairs. I handled trucks during summer jobs at Tramonti Construction and a deuce-and-a-half in the Marines before Officer Candidate School. Later, at Thompson Speedway and Lime Rock's natural terrain track, I had driven everything that could be driven there, from ancient Austin Healeys and Shelbys to muscle cars, in time trials and races. Like pool, track driving concentrates the mind.

Within minutes, I was behind the wheel of the Mini on Waterman Street turning the AM dial and finding the expected snorts and snarls of talk radio jocks decrying *elitist* Carter, *freeloading* Carter, *insulting* Carter. One got into the rumored negotiations between Mayor Tramonti and Carter University President Charles Danby on a treaty providing for a payment from the University to the City in lieu of taxes on its exempt real estate. Such a treaty was known as the 'third rail' of Providence politics: whatever would be agreed to would never be enough for critics. As University Counsel, I knew that Tramonti and Danby were close to resolution; Danby had made a public offer to sign such a treaty if the amount paid was "reasonable," and if the city worked cooperatively on issues like policing near campus, zoning, and campus expansion. That opportunity, I thought, was now in a swirl of a toilet flush.

The rain, fitful during my drive, began in earnest as I left the protection of the administration parking garage. Say one thing for a good soak, the boisterous rally I might have expected on The Green was reduced to a paltry dozen kids and faculty in hoodies, slickers and rain gear bouncing wet, hastily made anti-Columbus Day signs and placards for the benefit of the cameras of Channel 11 and our campus station WCAR-TV. Off to one side, a solitary student in a knee-length yellow slicker enthusiastically waved a sign that read *Young Republicans—Italo-Americans—Proud of Chris!*

Inside College Hall, I shook off the wet like a field dog, walked the length of the building, and climbed two flights of stairs to our office suite. Marcie immediately flagged me down. "Claudia Cioffi is in your office," she whispered. "She was pacing around my desk, mumbling, wouldn't sit in the library, there was nowhere else ..."

"Just what I needed!"

"And you have a conference call with the President and Provost at ten. About Columbus Day. The President is still in California." I took off the Burberry and knocked perfunctorily on my office door and understood why Claudia Cioffi had been moved here. The chair in front of my desk was occupied by a muddle of sweaters, scarves, a red knit cap pulled down to eyebrows, a non-descript brown skirt hovering above scuffed laced boots. The pile of musty smelling clothing stirred at my entry, enough to allow a pale, angular face, with perhaps a trace of what was once prettiness if not beauty, to appear.

I introduced myself, asked her not to rise, but she did and gave off a shiver of damp. She was taller than I might have expected, perhaps five-eight or so, her shoulders wide, although affected by curvature of the spine. Her stare was unnerving; one eye was milky, maybe with a cataract. My offer of coffee was ignored as she lowered herself into the chair and loudly announced, in a heavily accented, almost masculine voice, "Brunotti fired me!" She thrust what I assumed was her termination notice at me. "Because I refuse his demand that I act at Palagi's executor."

As I moved to behind my desk, I read a one paragraph termination on Institute stationery signed by *Direttore* Brunotti. Even before I finished, I considered that at her age, she would be ineligible for any federal or state protected employment status and that since her employment was at will, Brunotti, her boss, had the authority to dismiss her. Being terminated for not acting as a pliable executor, however, was neither appropriate nor honorable and probably constituted two or three violations of the University's Employment Handbook. If she pressed her case, the University had a problem.

"Hah," she shouted, as only someone going deaf might, "Executor? Keeping me responsible for his estate? Me? Executor?" A laugh ended in a hiss. "Let the priest pick up after him."

Her head began to move from side to side with the regularity of a metronome. "Suicide confirms his cowardice. Dante's *Inferno*, *canto tredicesimo*. There, self-murderers ... suicides ... become eternally stunted trees, gnarled, warped, their fruit is poison. The Harpies gather, eat their fruit, and tear apart the trees. For eternity. You know of the Harpies?"

I nodded that I did, recalling Palagi's description of his secretary.

"So fitting that one who flees life should become rooted in eternal pain," she said and added, "Brunotti will suffer for his sins. Who is ... was ... worse? The day before Palagi died, they argued."

"What about?"

"Back and forth. I could hear them," she said sullenly as the milky eye narrowed and her voice lowered to a hoarse whisper, *"frode, ingannotore, rapinatore."* Loosely translated, these were accusations of fraud and criminality.

"Brunotti searched our files while Italo was in Italy. He was not careful. He left files out of order. When I told Italo on his return, he was outraged. Later that day, they had their argument." Her fingers found a lock of errant hair and twisted it like a shy little girl. "How can I be sure it was him? That cologne he soaks on himself!"

"You said *frode* ..."

Even though my office's room temperature was set at seventy, her hands clasped her elbows as though she was freezing. "Brunotti insisted on seeing him after five o'clock, when everyone would be gone. I remained in my office across the hall with the door closed so they thought I had left. I heard their shouts."

"Palagi alleged fraud?" I asked again. "Or was it Brunotti?"

"Italo Palagi lived a life of fraud ..." Her voice withered away.

Damn it, I needed her to address allegations of fraud! "Palagi accused Brunotti of fraud? Vice versa?"

Her head straightened, her expression questioning my single-mindedness. "Everyone knows Brunotti overspends, has no interest in research, in academics, the work of the Institute, only in the show, the prestige of his position, to gain a reputation with donors, to pay for his women. Italo said Brunotti was a *sciocco*, a fool and thief and that he had evidence that would get that puffed-up *portiere* dismissed."

"Maybe, it was more of the same? Do you know of anything specific?"

Her milky eye was unnerving in a blank stare that lasted thirty seconds. "I do know how Palagi lived—in a mirror. He saw what was behind him and he didn't like it." As a characterization of Palagi, it struck me as stark but penetrating, but didn't help as to accusations against Cosimo Brunotti.

She blinked, apparently remembering another thought. One hand went to a jacket pocket, which produced a plastic swipe card and a metal key on a ring. "This," she brandished the key, "is for the apartment. The card is for the gate. His apartment number is on the key." She tossed them on my desk and abruptly grabbed her termination notice, stood, wheeled around my desk, and swept out of my office. "He will pay!" she declared in disgust and left me in a trail of damp.

I followed her into our tiny reception area where Marcie stared as the old woman trudged by her and slammed the door. I confirmed she had heard the accusations and asked her to contact the Institute for a copy of the termination notice. I returned to my desk trying to make sense of her rant. Harpies? Palagi also used that metaphor?

I went online in a search for a depiction and quickly found several including an etching by the French artist Gustave Doré. His Harpies were the personification of agents of punishment, hideous, vicious creatures, half woman, half monster, scratching at their victim's vitals with terrible claws, inflicting unimaginable, unrelenting pain.

Each of Italo Palagi and Cosimo Brunotti had their very own Harpy.

18

THE PROVOST RAISED HIS eyes at my late entry and continued to complain to the speakerphone on his conference room table. "Not one faculty senate member had enough guts or common sense to argue that something so sensitive needed consultation before it was rammed through."

I took my seat quietly, focusing on the room's single window and the foliage of The Green beyond. Did any of those present—the Provost, his assistant who normally deals with the vagaries of the faculty senate, the public information officer, or the vice president for community relations—suspect Nadie Winokur as a participant, or worse, in the Columbus Day coup?

The Provost whipped on reading glasses, and said, "From today's *Crier* editorial, quote, 'Columbus Day is a colonizer's holiday. Should we celebrate European hegemony, violence, oppression, and brutality? Should we honor a racist whose hands are blood-stained?' How's that for nuance?"

President Charles Danby's distant, soft, and unruffled voice responded. "I need advice, not recriminations. I've got to return Tramonti's call."

The Public Information Officer, the PIO, a relative newbie to the arcane world of university public relations, hunched forward toward the speakerphone. "We have drafted a media release for your approval," she said. "I'll e-mail it to you. Very simply, it says that the President has not as yet reviewed the faculty senate resolution. When considered, the President will then discuss its implications with senior staff and faculty representatives."

While short and sweet, it was a kick-the-can-down-the-road cop out that confused a naïve hope with a nasty reality. The Provost rejected it. "Too late for that," he said gruffly; the ruffled feathers of the PIO could be sensed if not heard. "Charlie, it's national news," he continued. "Public Information has been called by the *Times*, Fox News and CNN ... so far. Chris Mathews demanded a University spokesman tonight, said he had proponents and opponents lined up. So did Bill O'Reilly. Sean Hannity's already making us look like crass bigots. The Italian press office in New York is all over us. The Institute must be deluged with calls ..."

Danby muttered, "Brunotti," which silenced all participants. When he continued, his voice had turned steely. "The timing couldn't be worse with Columbus Day coming up, with the negotiations on the tax treaty getting close to agreement. I can't lose this opportunity to resolve the tax issue because of what is seen as a provocation."

Despite my intuition that the tax treaty was history, we had to fight on. "I have a thought," I said. Before I left Congdon Street, I had conjured up some ideas that would be characterized by Nadie as "lawyer's tricks."

"Release a statement without attribution to the President, stressing the faculty senate's failure to give notice, or to encourage debate, before voting on a sensitive issue. Don't agree or disagree, just don't embrace it. And here's the substantive kicker. While the faculty senate sets the *academic* calendar year, there's no precedent that gives the faculty senate the right to *rename* holidays. Besides, the calendar for this academic year is already printed as the Columbus Day holiday. So, nothing changes this year, our campus calendar remains as is, and the whole issue is in the under-advisement category. Maybe the Trustees would like input on the issue? Maybe it's a holiday with no day off? If asked, the PIO's position is whatever our faculty and students do individually is up to them but, officially, it's still Columbus Day at Carter University."

The Public Information Officer coughed at the responsibility. Others audibly exhaled relief.

"I don't know," Danby said thoughtfully. "The cat's already cleaning her whiskers, as my mother would say. When someone's hero is denigrated, victimization explodes and it's an excuse to act out. But we just can't hunker down." As the first African-American President of an Ivy, he was no stranger to controversies, insults, and reactions.

I heard his reluctance but continued, "There must be someone in the faculty senate who's a stickler about Robert's Rules of Order, we let him or her know that objections have been raised as to lack of notice on such an important issue, suggest reputations for probity and correctness are at risk, convince him or her to file a notice for reconsideration so that the vote is transparent. Everybody loves transparency. That puts it back on the faculty senate agenda, which means it gets assigned to a committee for review. That's at least six months of lead time. Right into graduation."

All heads around the table, including mine, turned to the Provost who, to my surprise, cracked a grim smile as Danby, with a chuckle barely hidden in his voice, was heard to say, "Slick ... and passes the sniff test, for now. That means no interviews and a press release that plays the controversy down, respectful of all points of view, Columbus Day is in on the calendar for this year, faculty senate should review its procedures. Make it clear that the University is not and will not insult any one's ethnic background, we appreciate the achievements of all peoples, etc. I'll return the call from the Mayor, otherwise, I'm not going to respond. I repeat, no interviews by anyone in the administration, only the press release. Community Relations should be reaching out to our friends in the city with the same message. And prepare something for the Institute along similar lines. And the donors. And make sure the message gets to Brunotti!"

"He's in Italy," the Provost said with exasperation.

Italy? Not here tomorrow when Pine and I grapple with Lucca & Lucca? The no-good son of a bitch!

"Reach him," Danby thundered. "Send him the press statement, speak to him personally and caution him. He can be somewhat defensive, downplay it with the media in Italy and donors, but he must be supportive of the statement, with no major deviation from our position, and no, I repeat, *no* interviews. When he returns, we will sort things out."

"By now, he could be with the Italian press."

Danby responded coolly. "As I said, make sure he knows my position."

As the conference room emptied, I asked Danby to remain on the line. I summarized events in Palagi's estate: Palagi's affirmation of his estate plan, the mysterious A-4 account at Ravensford Capital, the recording's accusations of fraud against Brunotti, Claudia Cioffi's confused account of an argument between Palagi and Brunotti about fraud the day before Palagi's death, and her termination by Brunotti. In deference to Father Pietro, I did not reveal further details of Palagi's confession.

The Provost correctly observed that public airing of Palagi's recording would be a public relations disaster for the Institute. "And what is there left to fight about if the investments are lost?" I reminded him of Palagi's condominium in Providence, his apartments in Italy, his royalty and license fee arrangements, and whatever else Palagi might have owned at his death. The Provost muttered, "In comparison, small potatoes."

Danby, who had been briefed by the Provost as to the decimation of Palagi's trust assets, said, "The Institute's finances are a problem. But right now, frankly, I'm more concerned over allegations of Brunotti's fraud. Who else knows?"

"The priest, of course, Claudia Cioffi, but it's difficult to understand what she thinks."

"Whatever you need," Danby replied. "Move quickly. If Brunotti took a nickel or if he wrongly fired her for personal reasons, he's out. Algy, am I obligated to inform the Trustees?" I replied it would be premature. He agreed, said he had to leave for the airport, and we heard him click off.

The Provost took off his glasses and pinched the bridge of his nose, "Timing. It's all timing. An audit of the Institute is something we were going to get to this year. Its Italian financial operations are handled internally by someone Brunotti hired over there. The Bursar is responsible for checking the books *after* the cash arrives in the University's account but we don't match Italian donors with donations or royalties with the payors, or the actual amounts collected in Italy at the collection bank to the amounts deposited in our account. That's done in Rome. Leaves us vulnerable!"

He smacked his right hand into his left palm. "Damn! Brunotti could do it!"

19

THE CONVENTION CENTER'S PARKING garage was a labyrinth designed by a diabolic engineer who used Escher's *Ramps* as an inspiration: once you got in, it was damn hard to get out.

A ticket was spit out by a machine at the entrance, I drove up, then down, five levels looking for a space without result, and tried to exit only to be stymied by a monosyllabic attendant who demanded a minimum charge of two dollars for the privilege of wasting my time. After a heated discussion accompanied by impatient horn sounding from cars behind me, the barrier finally lifted and I drove around the corner to the valet at the adjoining Omni Hotel. From there, it was another five minutes to reach the Convention Center Authority's second floor conference room. I was now ten minutes late for my first meeting as a member of the Shoot-Out Commission.

My belated entrance and apology for tardiness elicited grumpy muttering from my fellow commissioners. I was handed a three ring binder marked *Commissioner Temple* and directed to a chair at a large oval conference table. The chair next to me was unoccupied but designated by a seating plaque for *Legal Counsel.*

My impression of the four Commission members present from Providence, all appointees of our ex-mayor, the morally bankrupt Angelo 'Sonny' Russo, was that eligibility requirements included bad haircuts, double chins, florid complexions, suspicious eyes, and frowns. They were two men and two women, whose names and occupations were in the binder—a club manager from Olneyville, a state representative who worked for the City, the owner of a taxi company, and the owner of a downtown messenger service next to City Hall—were clearly from Sonny Russo's core constituencies. Their resentful impressions of me came not only from the source of my appointment but were likely grounded in the ingrained prejudices of Providence ethnic families to anyone with my lineage and wealth: *Another East Side asshole to judge us.* They grew up rarely hearing *Yankee* without *goddamn* before and *bastard* after.

The Commission chair, retired Superior Court Judge J. Francis Sanders, stood, gavel in hand. Sanders was a red-faced old pol known as *Hap* for happy or hapless depending on your experience with him. On the bench, he was hostile to lawyers he didn't like, like me, representing establishment and institutional clients. He banged the gavel sharply and introduced me as Mayor Tramonti's replacement for Mr. Zito who had 'resigned,' noted I was employed by "good old Carter University," and that I wore neither "a white hat nor crusader tights." His jibes prompted Commissioner Calvino, the Providence bar owner, to offer a single, echoing clap, as they say in Woonsocket, while others inspected the room's interesting acoustic tile ceiling, blew noses, or picked lint from lapels.

Sanders then began what turned out to be a lengthy and glowing report on this week's amateur portion of the Shoot-Out, the full house hotel occupancy numbers, the efficient distribution of scrip to players, the status and growing numbers of national and local sponsorships, and finally, arrangements for tonight's Gala. While he droned on, I reflected on the tournament's checkered connections with Sonny Russo and his reelection gambit that brought the Shoot-Out to Providence.

During the last months of Sonny Russo's unsuccessful reelection campaign, the Shoot-Out promoters, Las Vegas guys, came to town looking for a host city. They had signed up national sponsorships and hundreds of eager pool halls, taverns, and sports bars to run weekly nine-ball elimination events to be followed by regional and super-regional tournaments designed to winnow contestants down to five hundred slots for a mega-tournament—somewhere. Each contestant slot would be worth scrip to be spent in local hotels, restaurants, and clubs, and an opportunity to win cash for each match won through the brackets of play. The total prize money for the amateurs was an unheard of one hundred and fifty grand with a fifty grand first prize, and another two-fifty in prize money for a pro tournament the following weekend and all the promoters needed to pull it off was a hefty, up-front subsidy from a city in return for delivery of thousands of players and fans to spend, spend, spend.

Sonny Russo didn't see the tournament as an opportunity to show off his city, but a chance to cash in politically and revive his campaign. Cupidity, Providence's rampant civic vice, also came into play. In record time, the General Assembly passed Sonny's heavily lobbied legislation to create the Shoot-Out Commission to *operate* the tournament and allow sports betting run by the Lotto Commission on the Shoot-Out's pro matches, with a fifty percent rake off of the betting profit for the promoters. That largess was, in effect, a guarantee of a goodly part of the promotional costs, scrips, and prize money, thereby obviating the need for a direct subsidy from cash starved Providence. A home run for Sonny, his supporters, the city's gamblers and club owners, and all those panting to be at the trough of patronage. It was almost enough to get him another term as mayor.

o O o

"Always like to work with the *good* guys" whispered in my ear roused me to attention. The legal counsel's chair had been filled by Leon 'Puppy Dog' Goldbloom, Sonny Russo's City Solicitor, his legal lackey and my nemesis in city-university relations during Russo's reign. Every machination of the Russo regime went through his office. Hard to believe! Puppy Dog Goldbloom as my legal counsel? Sonny Russo's scheme had been realized: this Commission was simply lipstick on a pig for the tawdry business of politics.

Somehow, I managed a tight smile. Life out of City Hall seemed to agree with Puppy Dog. His blue blazer and tan trousers looked new, his comb-over hair was no longer an inky black, more of a yellowish gray, his complexion wasn't as sallow and his nose not so carrot colored. His small, squinty eyes, however, retained the familiar rat-catcher quality and I knew he would be up to his neck in every crooked deal that came within the purview of the Commission.

The conference room cleared rapidly when the meeting quickly adjourned after Sanders' report. I closed my binder, ready to leave when confronted by Sanders, who handed me a green folder. "All the information, schedules, whatever, you're gonna need," he said. "And your badge. You know that you got Zito's position with the refs, right?"

I didn't.

"Every Commissioner has a specific coordination and oversight role," he explained with a smirk at my surprise. "Hotels are with the Commissioners close to the hotels, restaurants and clubs are monitored by owner members, you get it? Frannie Zito had the refs." A Federal Hill bad guy assigned to *officiating*? I could hear Nadie saying "Only in Rhode Island."

"First meeting of the refs is seven thirty tomorrow morning in a room next door. Like to have you there. Shows we care. Kind of appreciate it if you'd, ya know, hit a few of the matches, too. They're volunteers, from lots of places, and they've been vetted, but you never know. By the way, the Commissioners didn't like the Mayor's idea about having the refs' names run through the BCI"—Bureau of Criminal Investigation—"for criminal records."

I didn't take ownership of the idea, which in fact was mine.

"You got a computer PIN in the folder so you can navigate the Shoot-Out website for Commission-only info. Oh, I almost forgot. Heard you play pool, understand the rules, so I also put your name in as a ref supervisor in case you're needed somewhere during the first round tomorrow. Just in case ..."

Sanders gave me a patronizing smile, patted me on the back, and left me feeling as useless as Don Quixote with a pool cue as my lance.

20

"HOW DO YOU GUYS do it?"

I was on the overpass from the Convention Center over West Exchange Street to the Omni, walking briskly past the riotous colors and shapes of artist Joseph Norman's huge mural *Vision of Providence*.

"What were you thinking?" Puppy Dog, breathless, a worn and heavy valise in hand, was catching up to me. "Half the people in that room are Italo-American. Columbus Day's part of their DNA. And you thumb your noses at them? I just heard some bozo on the radio comparing Columbus to Hitler!" Then, his voice lowered as he grabbed for my elbow at the top of the escalator. "Thought I should tell you so you won't be surprised on Friday. I got hired as local counsel for the son in the Palagi estate case. The Luccas will represent Italy. But we'll work as co-counsel."

He got his desired reaction: my jaw dropped. But he didn't see it because he was two steps behind me in our glide to the lobby.

"So, this old man finds out he fathered a kid fifty years ago, after he's left his millions to you guys?"

"Bad timing," I said over my shoulder.

"How well do you know Judge Cremasoli?" The Providence probate judge. Didn't know him at all but guessed that Puppy Dog had participated, as Sonny Russo's legal beagle, in the politics of the City Council's annual reappointment of the probate judge. "He's old school, a family guy. He's not going to allow Carter to benefit from an injustice."

Puppy Dog pursued me through the lobby's bustle of arrivals

and departures, bellmen and hospitality aids. "Tramonti's suddenly got a tin ear. He's got a city council full of Italo-Americans who will gag at his appointing Carter University's lawyer to the Commission with all this Columbus Day stuff." Then, he added, smugly, "Bad timing."

He followed me through the slow spin of the revolving door to the hotel's porte-cochère where a valet took my parking ticket and disappeared. "Bobby Lucca *owns* the popular side of this. You guys are fucked on the tax treaty."

The Mini appeared, I tipped the valet and got in; Puppy Dog stooped to peer through the passenger side window, smiled, and waved.

o O o

Marcie glumly reported she had watched the *News at Noon* on Channel 11 and it was rough on Carter; it probably didn't help that its popular male anchor was Italo-American. Sonny Russo was interviewed and spewed vituperative nonsense. I asked for her appraisal of the situation. Marcie, practical and focused, lived and breathed Common Cause idealism and NPR liberalism that often prodded me into reflection. Unlike Nadie.

"If it was up to me, we wouldn't have any day-off holidays named for a single individual, including Columbus. That's what got us into trouble."

"Great idea! Get rid of Columbus Day and the only named day-off holiday would be Martin Luther King Day. We'll change that to *Minorities Day*."

She wagged a finger at me.

o O o

I closed my office door and tackled a lease for the Medical School in the reborn Jewelry District across the Providence River from the main campus, occasionally checking media websites for painful Columbus Day updates. At four-thirty, I entered Marcie's office as she was about to leave. As she put on her rain coat, she said, "Why can't it be like St. Patrick's Day. It's fun, everyone is Irish, drinks beer, has some corn beef and cabbage, great parades."

She always was trying to figure out why the rest of the population didn't share her worldview.

"Marcie, can you imagine insulting the Kennedys in Southie on St. Patrick's Day?"

"No."

"That's what we just did to Federal Hill, half the City Council, twenty percent of the population of Providence. Retribution is coming."

21

IT WAS AFTER FIVE when I stepped out of College Hall on to the trimmed lawns of The Green on my way to the parking garage. The sky had cleared during the afternoon; the smell of air cleansed by rain—*petrichor* I remembered from a *Sunday Times* crossword—was refreshing.

A bench in the shade of majestic elms invited me to stop; I put my valise at my feet, took off my jacket, loosened my tie, and stretched my arms heavenward, my head circling my shoulders, releasing audible creaks. Above me, the canopy of leaves had taken on the rich intensity of early autumn. In another two months, the trees would be stripped for winter, their limbs becoming a pattern of intricate lines against the prevailing high winter clouds. Bleak days were coming, as bleak as the outlook for a tax treaty with the city.

I shook my head and replaced the Columbus Day debacle with a question: Why did Italo Palagi include me in his end-of-life disclosures, his allegations of faithlessness, his suggestion of murder?

The answer was not felicitous. A conversation with me, Nadie once said, could be like an interrogation. Years of depositions and witness examinations had not honed conversational skills. If he thought of me as a resolute inquirer, Palagi might assume an inclination to investigate his allegations. What he might not have expected was that I would also feel compelled to probe his confession.

o O o

With two hours to kill before the Shoot-Out Gala, I was drawn to where Benno suspected Palagi went into the Providence River.

Before it was officially dubbed the Old Harbor District by a well-meaning urban planner, the warren of warehouses, factories, wharves, taverns, whore houses, and rooming houses along the Providence River and into India Point had not changed much since its days as a center of the rum, slaves, and molasses trade. The sixties and seventies brought the Hurricane Barrier to the river and the incursion of Route 195, but even then, the area took another thirty years to be reinvented by boutiques, galleries, antique stores, expensive condos, upscale restaurants, trendy bars, and a marina. Only Hard Core, the strip club pimped up in a garish orange stucco and lit by twenty-four hour neon, the oldest continuing business on the riverfront, and some adjoining bars, survived gentrification.

I parked the Mini in the late afternoon shadows of the Corliss Landing condominium where Palagi had lived. Once, its thick red brick walls housed Corliss Steam Engine Works, manufacturer of the world's most powerful steam engines, a sprawling factory where iron and steel were noisily formed into machines designed to govern nature, shorten distances, and reduce time. A thoughtful renovation retained the building's architectural integrity, its perfect sequences of granite sills under multi-paned windows, its ornamental masonry, and even a fifty-foot brick chimney, all of which evoked the practical engineering skills and brilliant mechanics once employed there.

I peered through an ornate iron entrance gate lined with vertical spear point rods into an interior courtyard paved with cobblestones, a carefully tended lawn, a spouting fountain, and two unoccupied tables under open striped umbrellas. A portly, ginger-haired security guard in gray uniform, badge on his chest, radio at his wide belt, waddled toward me. He screwed up a freckled face and said, "Can I help ya?"

I stammered out, "A friend of mine from the University, Italo Palagi, lived here."

His "Yeah?" invited a further response.

"Said it was a safe place, security tight."

The guard's shoulders snapped back. "Never had a break-in since I've been here. Can't get in through here," he clutched the gate's bars, "and the windows on the first floor are nine feet off the ground. And if you did get in, with all of the security stuff, we'd still get you. That's how I seen you. Camera up there." He pointed above the gate and let his gray eyes drop to my toes and range back up to my face. "You interested in his unit?"

"Walking by and thought of him. Terrible that he drowned."

"Yeah," the guard agreed, letting a hand run through gray bristled hair. "Can't understand the crime-scene tape at his apartment. Finally came down today after the owners complained." The guard tugged at his belt that held up trousers slipping below his gut. "Nice old guy. Never any trouble. I was on duty that night. Must have gone out through the rear exit to South Water because I never seen him."

"So, that'll be on video?"

"Nah, not back there. That's only an emergency exit, although some owners use it for convenience if they want to go in or out to South Water. He ..." He abruptly stopped, realizing I had been nosy.

I smiled and said, "Have a good night," and walked away. I heard the clink of the gate latch as it was opened so he could watch my leaving.

The sidewalk led me past the rear of Al Forno, Providence's most renowned restaurant, where kitchen exhaust fans gave hints of its menu, and down to South Water Street to the rear exit of Corliss Landing. From there, I crossed the street and cut through Hard Core's mostly empty parking lot to the pedestrian walk along the river bank. A chest-high metal rail with vertical metal slats six inches apart protected the drunks from Hard Core from a fall of ten feet or more to chunks of sharp edged granite, meaning that Palagi's point of final departure had to be either up river off one of the marina docks, or down river closer to the Hurricane Barrier.

Walking north to the marina, I kept pace with the putt-putt of a small engine pushing a skiff up the river. Benno's Asians, short, brown-skinned men in baseball caps, T-shirts and jeans, stood along the railing every twenty or thirty feet or so, some casting vigorously to where the striped bass and blues hide in the warm water discharge from the Manchester Street Power Plant. Others were in conversation with their poles propped up against the railing next to plastic bait and catch buckets. Judging from their reactions to me, Benno was right; someone would remember a white, old geezer with a cane in their territory on a foggy night.

The Old Harbor District Marina, smaller than its grandiose name suggested, consisted of a half dozen floating docks stretching out to mid-river off identical gangways, serving watercraft from Sea Doos and Whalers to Sea Rays and Bayliners to cigarette boats, houseboats, and cabin cruisers. Each gangway had a gate that required a punched in code to open, making it unlikely Palagi could have gotten out on a dock unless invited or a gate was wedged open for the convenience of guests. There would be activity on an August night, even with a fog, at the party boats tied up for the convenience of booze, music, and food from bars and waterside restaurants and from the houseboats supposedly permanently reserved for the intimates of Hard Core. Not a place for anyone to jump into the river—privately.

I retraced my steps, and continued on, stopping for the moment at a new laminated storyboard detailing the history of the Providence & Fall River Line overnight steamers to New York. The railing ended behind the storyboard; the embankment became guarded by a four-foot-high metal fence, its posts anchored in concrete, with cords of wire about a foot apart, possibly wide enough for the rotund Palagi to slip through, but still at least ten feet above the rocks and river. Not there.

The last fence post was close to the eastern abutment of the mechanically purposeful Hurricane Barrier, leaving a gap of ten feet or so without metal protection, but filled by clutches of red leaf sumac, a thicket of briar bushes, and garbage trees on the steep slope to the water's edge. If Palagi managed to get down there, no one at street level or up river could have seen him.

Following a rough path down the slope—it was easier than I thought it would be—I came to a slab of granite bridging two boulders to form a natural bench; at its base was a high-tide line of green and yellow slime, straw, tangles of fishing line, and trash. A few feet away, a stagnant shallow of viscous-brown water allowed neither the sun's reflection nor a ripple's sparkle. The river's briny smell had become acrid and metallic.

I heard the crunch of footsteps before a blue windbreaker was visible through the brush.

"What are you doing here?" I asked Benno Bacigalupi. He could have, but didn't, ask the same question of me.

"What the detectives should have done. Walking the shoreline.

Recognize these?" he asked. He took two strides toward me and thrust a pair of rimless eyeglasses at me, one lens shattered, the other one perfectly round. "Found them right there," and pointed to the tide line by the slab.

I ran them through my fingers. "Palagi's?"

"And so is this."

In his hand was a brownish plastic prescription vial, its cap missing, its CVS Pharmacy label washed out but still legible, as were the typed words *Palagi*, and *OxyCodone*, a prescription number, and a date, two days before Italo Palagi's death. "Caught in the rocks under that slab. In case you were wondering, that night, high tide was at ten-eleven. Water would be right up against the granite. Fall off and you're in the river."

22

ACROSS THE RIVER, THE power plant's four chimneys were black candles against the sky, its red warning lights glowing wicks. A boat engine at the marina roared to life, muffling the slap of water on the docks. The breeze brought a smell of salt and sea-weed.

We were on a bench, protected from the sun's glare by a bank of purple clouds. Benno twirled Palagi's broken eyeglasses by a stem, his face thoughtful. I said, "On Monday, I heard a recording Palagi made shortly before he died. He said he wouldn't commit suicide."

The spectacles stopped their twirls. "When can I hear it?"

"Give me some context first."

Benno folded Palagi's eyeglasses and slipped them in his jacket's pocket. He leaned back on the bench and began.

"Maybe four, five months ago, Palagi called me. Didn't say where he got my name. I met him here, on the walkway. Wanted information on a woman by the name of Maria Ruggieri. Told me she was born in Basilicata, Italy, her approximate age, that she may have recently died in New York City area. I wasn't looking for work right then and told him so but he insisted he needed the information and didn't have the time himself. So, I gave him my rate and he peeled off five hundred as a retainer. Gave me a phone number for my report.

"Seemed easy enough. I'd check her name online through Vital Statistics in New York and Jersey, phone listings, tax rolls, routine. Turned out to get into their Vital Statistics records, you got to have some information, like a parent's name, date and location of birth or death, etc. Without that, *nada*. So, I traced obits in the newspapers and I came up short for the couple of Maria Ruggieris I found. Wrong birthplace or age, always something. So, I started on the death records for New York City. All five boroughs. I went back six months, then back a year. Then two. Still nothing. Then, I tried Suffolk County, that's Long Island, and I found a Maria Ruggieri, spinster, approximately the right age, from Basilicata. Know where Basilicata is?"

I didn't get a chance to show my geographic knowledge of Italy before he went on, pointing to a mud-caked shoe.

"Basilicata is the instep of the Boot, poorest region in Italy. North of Calabria, south of Naples. Biggest export is people. My people came from Foggia, in Puglia, next region over, so I know. Anyway, this Maria Ruggieri died last April in Babylon Beach out on the Island." His head bobbed up to look at me. "Ever hear of the place?"

"No." Babylon Beach sounded like a Frankie Avalon–Annette Funicello beach blanket movie from the sixties.

"It's on the Sound. Big houses protected by ten-foot fences, watch dogs, and mean-faced guys, the kind of place popular even today with what's left of the Five Families—the Gambinos, the Genoveses, the Bonannos, the Lucheses, and the Columbos. The original gated community."

He pulled out his notebook from his windbreaker and found a place about halfway through. "This woman's death certificate said she died from pneumonia. The address where she died turned out to be a hospice. I called the hospice, faked it like I'm a relative, and got her home address in Babylon Beach. The real estate tax records online showed the place was assessed in the millions, owned by a limited liability company, an LLC. And who owns the LLC according to the New York Secretary of State? Another LLC, this one from Nevada. I know that this is going nowhere so I checked who was listed as the attorney for service of process on the LLC form." Benno referred to his notebook. "Gucci, Montecalvo and Ottavani, attorneys, in Queens."

The names registered. The New York lawyers representing Vittorio Ruggieri. Unlikely a coincidence.

"So, I looked them up, criminal defense lawyers, a partner, one Anthony Cimininni, well-known in certain circles as *consigliore* for the Giambazzi family, the New York cell of the 'Ndrangheta. Ever heard of the 'Ndrangheta?" I didn't respond to his question and my recently acquired knowledge of the powerful gang; anyway Benno was on a roll. "The Mafia is patty-cake compared to them. Not much happens in the Boot without the 'Ndrangheta dipping their beaks. Would kill their mothers for money—and they love their mothers."

"Did you tell Palagi?"

"I called him. I was surprised he took it with no emotion at all, said I was to wait for further instructions. I didn't hear back so I called again in a couple of weeks. He told me to send a bill or to keep what's left of my retainer, said it was all resolved. I got the impression that *resolved* didn't mean happy ending."

"So, after you learned how he died, you ..."

"The connection to the Giambazzis bugged me. Then, three weeks ago, a PI from New York I've known for years called. His client is Assicurazioni Generali, a huge Italian insurance company. Like a Met Life. He needed info on Palagi's death but didn't want to spend a lot of time in Providence. I said I wouldn't mind mucking around."

An insurance policy? "Who's the beneficiary? How much?"

Benno ignored my questions. He had a train of thought and was not getting off.

"Before I got going, he called me again, right after the medical examiner's report was released, and told me that the insurance company ended the investigation, was paying the claim. Kind of abrupt but that was their business." He turned to face me. "So, what's with the recording?"

I paused to consider if I was morally obligated to consult with Father Pietro. Was disclosure left as a joint decision? I decided that Benno was likely to keep pressing his investigation no matter what; better to have him inside our tent. "Benno, can you work for me?"

"You or the University?"

Did the University care how Palagi died? It should, I decided. "The University."

"Usual rates," he replied dryly. "I'll send you a retainer letter. Now, what about the recording?"

I promised he could listen to it but for now, I summarized it. I did a pretty good job of stringing the pieces together, although it was like a bowl of stale spaghetti. When I finished, staring at his shoes, he repeated the gist as though it was in writing in front of him.

"If I got this right, Palagi made the recording and gave it to the priest a few days before he was in the river. Said his secretary hated him, his successor was a fraud, and his criminal son scared him with a fifty-year-old vendetta revived by the 'Ndrangheta. He was once a key player in a conspiracy to overthrow the Italian government and had been for years, against his will, laundering money for the 'Ndrangheta. Got a scare from a copy of a funeral card for Maria Ruggieri mailed from New York, which by the way, he didn't tell me. Thought he bought protection from the vendetta but maybe he hadn't. When he died, someone got an insurance windfall. Not much is left in his estate because of the Ponzi. And you got this son, represented by the *consigliore* of the New York 'Ndrangheta and locally by the Luccas and Puppy Dog, claiming whatever is left." He cleared his throat. "That about right?"

Amazing! "You've got it. Now, who was the beneficiary?"

"Strange deal. You can't get a policy like that in the US. It's a five hundred thousand, second-to-die, policy. Not between husband and wife or other relatives or business partners that's available here because they got what they call an 'insurable interest,' a reason to have insurance on someone else's life. But, in Italy, you can buy a policy on someone unrelated that's more like the medieval idea of a *tontine*. People put their money in a pot and the last one alive collects it all. Lots of motive to be the last man standing. The policy was bought and fully paid up over twenty years ago. Joint owners and beneficiaries were Palagi and his secretary, Claudia Cioffi. One or the other would get a half million, plus the interest earned, just for surviving. She won."

I didn't respond immediately, an apt aphorism came to mind: Palagi and Claudia Cioffi were like scorpions in a bottle, competing unto death.

Benno stood, his back to the railing, his sharp face shadowed from the orange-purple horizon. He said slowly, "Money, hatred, sex, envy, greed, all motives for murder. Okay. But, people die all the time without anybody being there, including people who someone might want to murder. You fall down a flight of stairs, they find you a week later. Accident. You ingest the wrong pills and if nobody's keeping tabs on you, it's the cleaning lady that finds you. Accident. But maybe you were pushed down the stairs or the pills stuffed down your throat. Murder. The difference is a witness. You need someone who can identify somebody with Palagi down by the river. Even if somebody's got motive and opportunity and means and no alibi, you got nothing without a witness."

"So, we don't go there?" I asked.

Benno's fingers created a steeple pointed at his nose. "The complete autopsy report could help. All kinds of stuff in there. Like to get my hands on that ..."

"You're the detective."

He ignored me. "The only way to cut through the bullshit and privacy rules at the ME is if you know somebody. I used to have a snitch but he retired."

Somewhat reluctantly, I admitted I knew a pathologist at the University's medical school who was called in on occasion by the medical examiner. I said it was a long shot but I would give him a call.

"Do that. Meanwhile, I'll check out that homeless camp across the river. Those bums are always down here at night looking for handouts. Maybe one of them saw Palagi."

I told him that I now had access to Palagi's condo through the pass and apartment key given to me by Claudia Cioffi and that the crime scene tape had been removed. He said, "So when do we go in?"

I thought about that. "We have no legal right to be there."

"You're the lawyer," he replied.

Turnabout was fair play. We agreed on Saturday morning for our inspection of Palagi's condo. As to Palagi's office at the Institute, I had no access except through Brunotti and that would tip him off as to my interest.

"And the recording?"

"Saturday, after the condo."

Benno's left hand went to shade his eyes as a shaft of sunlight speared the clouds. His tone became introspective. "Gotta think on this Ruggieri connection, this vendetta. In the Boot, vengeance is the only true justice. If somebody in the 'Ndrangheta took an oath to revenge Maria Ruggieri's family, it would be kept, even decades later, especially if you can add a payday for the trouble. Palagi carried that Beretta because he was afraid he was gonna get whacked. And maybe he did. Without a witness, who knows?"

Benno added, "Poor bastard, he's told he's a target of an old country vendetta and who delivered the message? His son."

23

THE UP ESCALATORS IN the cavernous foyer of the Convention Center were assembly lines of glossy leather jackets with metallic studs, doo rags and big hair, satin jackets over denim jeans, boots and spike heels.

My Commissioner badge got me into a reserved elevator to the second floor reception area where displays of pool tables, elegant custom-made cues, and other pool paraphernalia surrounded ice sculptures of nine-ball racks and pool ball pyramids and mountains of cheese, crackers, and grapes. Placards by three crowded bars advised players that tournament chits were good; all others apparently paid cash. A slew of sponsor banners covered walls; Miller Lite made sure it was the only beer served, ESPN focused on its schedule of pool events from Las Vegas and the finals of the Shoot-Out.

I cut the reception line and was quickly in the din of the Grand Ballroom's tightly packed tables identified by balloons numbered in the style of classic pool balls and anchored by streamers of shiny Mylar. Huge projection screens on either side of the room and behind the podium on a stage flashed flattering images of Providence.

I snaked my way toward the stage, looking for any familiar face, and spotted Joe Laretta, a skilled, tough, criminal defense lawyer and former prosecutor I knew well, conversing with someone seated at a table. In a city where most of the criminal defense bar dressed like their clients, Laretta, tall and slim shouldered, stood out as elegant in his designer suits. His courtroom style and presence were sought after in high-profile cases and his success rate was enviable.

"Hey," he greeted me genially, his handsome, swarthy, chiseled face in a wry grin, "just visiting. Table reserved for you mucky-mucks," he said, pointing to a sign that read *Commissioners and Guests.* "You know Councilman Lucca? Bobby, meet Algy Temple." And Laretta left us with a knowing, mischievous smile.

'Bobby Flowers' Lucca's dark eyes took me in, mine did the same in reverse. He was ruggedly good looking, clean shaven, his curly hair screamed healthy and real; he wore a dark suit, snow white shirt with French cuffs, and subdued tie. He offered me a pliable hand; I shook it, aware that sitting next to him could be a major mistake. In my stubbornness, I pulled out a chair, leaving me cheek-to-jowl with the contingency lawyer and Tony Tramonti's political rival.

Lucca gestured toward the exuberant crowd, his Providence accent belying his urbane appearance. "These guys suck up anything that's free." His eyes sought mine in agreement. "But they'll spend a ton before they're out of here. They ..." A meaty hand smacked his back, he stood and was hugged by well-wishers and back-slappers. A rising pol in Providence wasn't treated like his cologne was Lobster Bait Number 3 and his wasn't; he had been doused with a fragrance only a little less subtle than Brut.

The four other Commission members at the table mostly ignored me, so I busied myself with the glossy *Shoot-Out Inaugural Event* program which included a page on Jimmy Hannigan. I was reading my friend's bio when interrupted by a voice booming from the podium at stage right.

ESPN's "Mr. Pool," B.J. Seifert, the Gala's emcee, resplendent in a white tuxedo, oversized scarlet bow tie, and frilly shirt, his styled reddish hair bobbing, warmed up the crowd. He engagingly mixed wisecracks about Rhode Island politicians in for a free feed with old jokes about pool players—what's the difference between a pool player and a pizza? A pizza can feed a family—throwing in a couple of only-in-Rhode Island lines when he introduced politicians in attendance. Mayor Tramonti earned moderate applause and some isolated boos; Sonny Russo, the "Godfather" of the tournament according to Seifert, garnered sustained applause, appreciative whistles, and You-da-mans.

We regained our seats after a Pledge of Allegiance and white-gloved waitstaff served a choice of red or white wine and cold appetizers, followed by a mini Caesar salad, steak or chicken entrée, with Yukon mashies and green beans. Lucca was frequently pressed by visitors from other tables, a nearby quartet playing something vaguely discotheque-ish made table conversation difficult. As the entrée dishes were cleared, Lucca leaned into me. "Hey, I know this isn't the time, but ..." his lips edged closer to my left ear, "... this Columbus Day stuff ..."

"Still under study," and I rattled off the official line of the University.

"Yeah, yeah," he said and ripped apart a dinner roll, "you try selling that in my ward, on the Hill. And right before Columbus Day Weekend? C'mon ...!"

As dessert was delivered, a fanfare from the quartet returned Seifert to the podium who directed our attention to the projection screens as overhead lights dimmed. What followed was a video, narrated by Seifert, of seventy-five years of billiards and pool in five minutes, captured in newsreels, home movies, promotional materials from table companies and equipment manufacturers, with locales on five continents. Cute ball-boys smiled in a billiard room in Lagos, Nigeria in the thirties and Japanese players bowed to one another at a pre-war Tokyo venue. Next came well-known movie clips of Hollywood stars in pool playing scenes, then old news reel shots of the play of American pool legends Willie Mosconi and Willie Hoppe, quickly followed by a surprise: a casually dressed, relaxed, cue toting, smiling Bill Clinton.

"What y'all are going to hear in the next few minutes is of a proud son of Arkansas," the former president said in his buttery soft, good ol' boy accent. "Your honoree is the *crème de la crème* of pool. He's like me, from Hope, Arkansas and with hope. I'm very pleased that he's to receive the first Shoot-Out Legend Award. Harley, I'm proud of you. Arkansas is proud of you!"

The screen faded into an album of images of Harley Smoot, the Johnny Cash of pool, the first of many shooters to adopt an all black apparel style, an Ozarks boy who made it into the elite ranks of pool players, a living legend whose battles with booze and gambling cost him a year in prison and a couple of ex-wives.

When the lights came on, Smoot was at the podium, long faced, his smile showing dazzling teeth, black hair pulled back in a ponytail, in a black tuxedo, black shirt and white tie, accepting loud applause along with hoots and hollers from the less inhibited. Seifert made a short presenting speech, and then the teary-eyed honoree received a crystal nine-ball on a wooden base that he waved over his head as though he had just won a tournament. Given the mike, in a drawl as Southern as hog-fat biscuits, he disarmed the audience as he thanked Bill Clinton, the Shoot-Out promoters, friends from the pool world, and his family, and made the point that this award also meant a twenty-five thousand dollar donation to his favorite charity, a home for the down and out in Hope, Arkansas. "I've been there, ya know," he added slowly and left the stage to a standing ovation, descending into a sea of well-wishers and huggers.

I admit to being caught up in the moment.

Seifert, arms stretched palms down to tame the clamor, announced a special tribute to Providence pool as the screens displayed Young Jimmy Hannigan in home movies and photographs shooting pool as a teenager at his father's bookie, in an Army uniform, with a John Travolta *Saturday Night Fever* hairdo I recognized from his road days, one from his wedding to Maria Catarina and a recent image in front of his restaurant. The video ended to a loud welcome to Young Jimmy at the podium.

My friend fought back emotion, looked down at his notes, thanked Seifert, and introduced a thrilled Maria Catarina and her family at a table in front of the podium. He spoke of his admiration for Harley Smoot, a "love to play you sometime" got shouts and cheers of approval, and he finished a short, gracious acceptance by saying that he looked forward to lots of great shot-making during the Shoot-Out.

Seifert grabbed the microphone as the applause died and Young Jimmy left the parlor with a plaque. "Tomorrow," Seifert declared, "we begin a new era in pool. Can you imagine? Largest purse ever for amateurs! Would-you-believe-it?" That line was his ESPN trademark and the crowd finished the 'believe-it.' "Players, check our website for where you'll begin the journey. Refs, you gotta be here for our meeting tomorrow at, oh boy, seven-thirty. Mandatory! Players, get a good sleep," ... pause ... and then with a knowing grin, "but there ain't no curfews in Providence!"

o O o

The Gala was over. I intended to immediately congratulate Young Jimmy and his wife but Lucca grabbed my elbow. "On this estate thing, I don't see Judge Cremasoli going out on a limb, not after we present the paternity acknowledgement. Look," he continued, his face in my ear, "with this Columbus Day bull, you don't need Palagi's kid in the papers saying how he's been screwed by the University. Nobody in Italy—or here—will want a son to lose out by mistake. The University needs peace, right? With everything else going on ...?" His dark eyes shined in anticipation of a favorable response.

No insightful genius was necessary: if the University settled with Palagi's son and the contingency lawyers got full measure at the fee trough, maybe the Columbus Day rhetoric would die down, maybe the door reopened to a tax treaty.

I had been offered the *full Providence.*

o O o

Nadie was in pajamas watching *Bones,* her favorite program, on the large screen Sony in the loft. At a commercial break, she smiled, tossed her silky black hair around her neck, and asked me about the Gala. The Columbus Day truce had apparently been extended so, shaking off my loafers to stretch on the bed, I described the successful event, particularly the awards to Harley Smoot and Young Jimmy. She nodded agreeably at Young Jimmy's recognition but was otherwise disinterested. Then, *Bones* returned.

Later in bed, Nadie, a novel propped up before her, raised her reading glasses to her forehead. "You were right about the local reaction," she said evenly. "I watched the news. Some people just want to fight about everything."

She leaned over and kissed my forehead. "Okay, lawyer." She was silent for a moment and then she rolled over to my side and said, "I love you, lawyer. Despite your antediluvian prejudices, make love to me."

"My pleasure," I replied. And it was.

I sweat profusely. But my claustrophobic reaction isn't that bad. Maybe because of the tape over my eyes. Maybe the distant sounds of traffic from Route 295. What time is it? It must be close to ten. Matches at the Convention Center pretty much over? Then, the sound of tires on gravel. A car approaches very slowly, picking up speed as it passes by, its engine barely muffled. I hear it brake, reverse, and creep back. It stops, engine still running, and a door opens. Benno? He'll be cautious in his approach.

"Maybe somebody got out to take a leak or somethin'?" *The voice is of a teenage male.*

The Charger's driver side door opens. A second voice, closer than the first, yells, "Hey, it's not locked! Keys on the seat!"

Time to communicate and I manage to make a sort of "wuuooohhh!" *that stops the conversation. Trunk music.*

"Did you hear that?"

"Yeah."

"Wuuooohhh!"

"There it is again."

"I heard it! It's coming from the trunk."

"Wha! The trunk?"

"Wuuooohhh!" *I bang my heels against the trunk's lid. Thump! Thump!*

"Somebody's in the trunk!"

Silence.

"Some wise guys dumped somebody in there and he's still alive. Like in Good Fellas ...?"

"Wait a second, wait a second ..."

"I'm not waitin'. Get in the car. We're the fuck out of here ..."

"We gotta see if the guy's okay. If they shot him ...?"

"I don't wanna know and I'm not stayin' around to find out."

"Maybe we should call the cops?"

"Are you crazy? What're we gonna say? We just happened to be down here, just drivin' around? We'd have to ditch the stuff we got. C'mon, we're outta here!"

"Wuuooohhh!" *Thump, thump, bang, bang.*

"Christsakes! We can't just ..."

"I'm leavin'." *A car door slams and the engine roars.* "Are you comin' or not?"

"I don't know, Kevin, I ..."

"Wuuooohhh!"

"Now!" *The engine revs again.* "Okay, okay." *A door closes angrily and the car peels off.*

24 Thursday

NADIE HAD OPENED THE blinds before she left for the gym and a muted dawn light filled the loft, buffing up the shelves of mysteries and thrillers on my side of the bed, giving a luster to the black and gold varnished Japanese screens that separated the loft's sleeping area from work and living areas. My hands were folded on my stomach like a knight on a medieval church tomb as I relived her body folded into mine. Slowly, I focused on this morning's schedule; the refs orientation meeting at the Convention Center, followed by a meeting with Tony Tramonti at Tramonti Corporation's apartment at the Residences high rise attached to the Omni Hotel. I had received his text during the Gala but I had failed to read it until I arrived home. Why didn't Tony just seek me out? Too late? My seating next to Bobby Flowers? Had to be about Columbus Day.

o O o

Mornings are not favored by pool players who are habitual night hawks, 'sleep to ten when you can' types. So, I expected and was proved right that the tournament refs would be sleepy looking, sullen, maybe hungover, their loud talk at coffee urns suggesting a fraternity of pool buddies, rail birds, club jocks, and tournament junkies. The age range was from late thirties to fifty; many wore clothes that could have been slept in. My dark suit, white shirt, and plaid tie elicited suspicious 'who's that?' glances.

With a cup of coffee, I found a seat at a rear table where I scanned the contents of a folder handed out at the door: locations of the Shoot-Out's matches, a background piece on *Shoot-Out Pool LLC*, a FAQ with telephone numbers and e-mail addresses, tournament-specific rules, and so on. My reading was interrupted as an over-muscled, overweight, shiny scalp man mountain with earrings in a red Derby City Classic tee shirt brushed by me to envelop a chair at the end of the table. On my other side, a towheaded scarecrow with thick glasses under a shapeless brown sport coat pulled out a chair. I would have taken a nickel bet that one or the other wore motorcycle boots and had a belt buckle larger than my fist.

"Shee-it!" came loudly from the table in front of me as another wide body thumbed through advertisements in the adult insert to the weekly *Providence Phoenix*. "Catch this," he said to the denim-clad ref on his right, "gotta be ten strip joints in town!" For local color, I could have explained that gentlemen's clubs and adult entertainment venues became a growth industry in Providence during the Russo years along with nineteen spa-massage-parlor brothels, on a per capita basis, more numerous than those in New Orleans. "Gotta check *this* out," he said, showing a page of photographs of pasty and G-stringed porno superstars Alexis Texas and Jesse Jane featured tonight at the Amazing Club on Eddy Street. His buddy stretched to check their enhanced topography. "Shee-it!"

Their salivating was interrupted when B.J. Seifert, dressed for the occasion in a lemon yellow suit and frilly, purple, open collar shirt, tapped the podium mike for attention. His bouffant hairdo had been refreshed in its sweep, color, and plumpness. Next to him, in marked contrast, stood square jawed, crew cut, Providence Police Chief Bill Tuttle in a dark blue dress uniform, his service hat with a scrambled egg visor tucked under his arm. He probably considered himself to be there to preach a twelve step anti-gambling program to a room full of deadbeats. Not that he would be wrong.

Seifert opened with, "How ya'll doin'? Not staying up too late, are ya?" The loud response was acknowledged with a mock wide-eyed, open-mouthed laughter as Seifert recognized individuals in the crowd with grins and pointed fingers and shook his head in a what-can-you-do-with-these guys nod to Tuttle.

He introduced Tuttle and asked if Alby Temple from the Tournament Commission was present. Alby? I raised my hand, Seifert acknowledged me, and I smiled back at all the suspicious faces. Seifert then briskly skimmed through the logistics of the tournament schedule, stressing the responsibilities of referees to inspect tables in outlying venues to determine adequacy for play and insure players' practice time, and a list of *no's*: *no* drinking near the tables, *no* toleration of any bumptious behavior by players or fans, and *no* gambling. "Nada, zip, none!" he proclaimed.

"Ain't this Providence?" someone in the front shouted, drawing some cautious snickers.

"If a ref sees *any* gambling, the match could be stopped," Seifert continued.

That brought out unruly jeers and momentarily, he almost lost control. Everyone in the room knew that gaming and pool were inseparable, despite every pool hall's ubiquitous *No Gambling* signs. There was *always* skin in a match, a little side action, a couple of bucks bet here, a few beers there, and not to mention serious money placed on the light fixtures over a table or with a stakeholder. No effort to ban gambling, to clean up pool, even to class it up with upscale pool parlors with bistro menus, had ever worked or been profitable. Pool, played regularly by the estimated eight million amateur players in the United States alone, was and will always be, a one-on-one, win-any-way-you-can sport, and action juiced it up.

Seifert recovered with a couple of call-outs to those present, a joke or two, and he handed Tuttle the microphone, then grabbed it back to wink broadly. "Have a great ... safe ... time!"

A chorus of *yeahs* echoed the room.

Tuttle reached inside his uniform jacket for notes and reading glasses and in short order laid out his rules in a gravelly voice: in Providence, there would be no gaming—"I repeat 'no'"—at the matches. At least one cop would attend every Providence venue, and he expected other cities and towns to do the same. No money on tables, no cash changing hands, no bets being called in or any updates on matches going out by cell phone.

The voice from the front shouted, "Even penny ante?"

Tuttle, putting away his glasses, responded, "Somebody puts down a dollar on a player, that's gambling and that's prohibited. The only prizes here are the official prizes. That's for skill, not odds. If a player or buddy puts up a stake, makes a bet on a Tournament match, as far as I'm concerned, that's a misdemeanor, he gets arrested."

Audible groans and dismissive laughter responded. As Tuttle bristled, Seifert shrugged his shoulders, a 'what can I tell ya' expression on his face, and took back the mike. "Some of you got to skedaddle because," he checked his watch, "you got about ninety minutes to get wherever. Somebody from the Shoot-Out staff is already at every venue. Remember, read the rules, use the website to check postings of match locations and your assignments. All we ask you to do is to show up, do the best you can, and if your shorts get tight, get to the Tournament person assigned to your venue. When play begins, it goes straight through to the finals. See you then."

o O o

As the refs shuffled out with murmurs of annoyance at Tuttle's sermon, I went up to the podium where Tuttle, not surprisingly, had been left alone. He and I were professionally friendly; he was as square as his Irish chin and had won my respect when he reorganized Carter's campus security operations after he left the Providence police force because of run-ins with Sonny Russo over ham-handed political interference in investigations and promotions manipulations. Only months before, he had returned to uniform when Mayor Tramonti needed an experienced, honest cop to replace Russo's corrupt minion as chief.

"These are the refs?" he said with disparagement. "People keep telling me I should loosen up, play it like it's Vegas for ten days. People who should know better. I tell 'em we're not going to become the big sleazy or coddle a bunch of ..." He didn't finish.

"And, you," he said, his eyes boring into mine, "you should watch out for Frannie Zito. Heard is he's very pissed at Tramonti for being thrown off the Commission. Probably you, too. A piece of work, bad temper, huge ego, and he's got mob backing because Heritage Finance cleans its cash. Scuiglie is his goomba."

While Zito had been beneath my radar, not so the infamous Gianvacchino 'Gianni the Brow' Scuiglie, the latest in a long line of Providence crime bosses, less powerful nowadays in the mob's New England hierarchy but still a presence who controlled extortion, gambling, and prostitution rackets, and what was left of the drug trade not taken over by the Latino and Asian gangs. Through fronts, he owned three or four adult clubs of the twelve within city limits, including Hard Core, and extorted payments from the rest. Rumored to be a tough, tough guy willing to give the nod for a hit quicker than a flick of cigar ash.

The Scuiglie connection convinced me to inform Tuttle of the phone threats of Tuesday night. "Sounds like cheap shots," he said, "insulting, not quite a threat, not that they would know the difference. Goes with the territory. Maybe you should have considered who you were replacing. Trace won't work because they use throw away phones. And maybe it has to do with this Columbus Day stuff. But if it happens again or anything else that is threatening, you call me."

I said I would.

"Another thing." He ran his fingers through close-clipped hair beginning to show traces of gray. "You oughta do whatever you can to make sure your buddy Hannigan isn't tempted." Tuttle once ran the precinct that included Fox Point and was aware of the long friendship among myself, Tony Tramonti, and Young Jimmy. "After last night, he's center of attention. Somebody like him can get into situations. Like at his Club. Somebody like that should keep his lawyer's phone number handy."

"I hear you."

25

A ROOM SERVICE WAITER rolled a trolley with cups and saucers, coffee carafes, baskets of rolls with jam and butter into the plainly furnished corporate apartment. Then came a Micheletti espresso machine. That told me Fausto Tramonti, the mayor's brother and chief political operative, would be present. Espresso is Fausto's drug of choice; wherever he spent time, there was always espresso.

I opened glass sliders from the living room to the narrow terrace scooped out of the building's façade. On the twenty-fourth floor above West Exchange Street, I took in a lungful of damp air and edged toward the railing for a spectacular view of Narragansett Bay as far south as the Pell Bridge in Newport. The Bay's surface mirrored this morning's aluminum sky, giving stark dimension to its islands and shorelines. Two dark hulled freighters, cranes poised on their decks, were anchored at the Port of Providence. Fuel barges lined the petroleum depot wharves. At the head of the Bay, the I-Way suspension bridge's columns remained illuminated, its spider web of silvery cables contrasted sharply with the orangey hulk of the Hurricane Barrier, a reminder of where Palagi met his fate.

Voices came from the apartment and I turned as Fausto Tramonti preceded Tony and, to my surprise, Aldo, the oldest Tramonti brother. All wore serious suits and ties. Fausto whacked a newspaper against the back of an upholstered chair and went to the espresso machine, Tony joined me on the terrace.

He said too casually, "Aldo wanted to see you."

Not good news. For years, Aldo Tramonti, the CEO of Tramonti Corporation, an international construction management company with its headquarters on nearby Broadway, had been a generous supporter of the Institute and a member of the Institute's Leadership Council. Had to be here about Columbus Day.

I followed Tony inside, closed the slider, ignored Fausto, and greeted Aldo. Aldo's stature was like his father's, the fireplug as he was known, a day laborer who founded the highly successful construction company, and even expensive tailoring did not hide Aldo's short, barrel-chested physique. He shook my hand without greeting, his black eyes and tight lips set in a stony face, and sat next to Tony on a tan leather sofa across from the chair I had chosen. Fausto didn't acknowledge me until with espresso in hand, he joined his brothers, neither of whom were eating or drinking, on the sofa. Three on one, I thought.

Fausto loosened his tie. Not as handsome as Tony or as well dressed as Aldo, not as trim as Tony or as short as Aldo, he emanated forcefulness, an innate energy of purpose. Clearly, it was Fausto's meeting; he was a lawyer with an office in a restored Victorian mansion across from Tramonti Corporation headquarters on Broadway, who understood how to get things done in Providence, the political whip, the glue pot for his brother who could massage the ethically challenged City Council. Going back to our early days, politically and personally, we did not get along. After I accepted the appointment to the Commission, the Mayor told me that Fausto had forcefully argued for his own candidate and was frustrated that I accepted.

"Algy, we got a situation here," Fausto said and gulped down his espresso. "Did you listen to the talk shows yesterday? On every show, some plant of Sonny's or Lucca's calls in and reads a copy of the press release on your appointment to the Commission and it gets linked with this Columbus Day shit. That's not good for anyone, you know what I mean? It's not good for you, it's not good for Tony, it's not good for ..."

"Who listens to those jerks," I said disparagingly, but knowing the answer.

Fausto's eyes bulged. "A lot of people," he said, turning to his brothers for support. "People that *live* and *vote* in Providence. A lot of 'em work for the city. And they are very sensitive to this kind of thing."

"Nothing is settled about the name change. We have a plan of action ..."

Fausto never heard what he did not want to hear. "You guys can do what you want up there but right now, you're causing a huge pain for Tony. I advised him to distance himself from the University and ..."

Tony interrupted. "Fausto thinks you should resign from the Tournament Commission."

I stared at Fausto. His expression showed expectation, his eyes like two deep black pools, that I would roll over and resign because of my loyalty to his brother. But I wasn't going there. Not yet.

"Look," I began, directing my reply to Tony, "in the first place you pushed me into accepting the appointment. Secondly, since it's known I'm on the Commission, isn't it going to be a cave-in if after two days I take a walk?"

Tony's glance at Fausto signaled these same points had been recently aired. "You just don't get it, Algy. You never do," Fausto grumbled, got off the sofa, poured another cup of energy, and downed it. "*We* gotta deal with *regular* people. All day yesterday, I listened to *regular* people. First thing in the morning, I've got Councilman Ferrucci calling. We need his vote for the budget. I twisted his tail nine ways to get that vote. Now he tells me his ward committee chairman called him because he's really pissed, says the Mayor has to do something to push back against Carter, more than just talk. By the way, I agree! This is a goddamn insult, a goddamn insult!"

"My resignation is a put-back to the University? C'mon, that's a stretch," I replied and noticed Tony had his eyes fixed over my shoulder toward the terrace; his dark face was cupped in his right hand. Fausto, back on the sofa, sensed his brother's indecision so he pressed the loyalty button. "Algy, listen, if you do it now, you don't have to relate it to Columbus Day. On second thought, you've got too much work and you're getting married, right? Or, you're not going to be around that much, or whatever. We deny a connection. Tony makes a suitable replacement, someone who's competent, who gets the good government people and the *Journal* all aquiver." He smiled, snidely, I thought. "You know we got other people like that."

When I didn't immediately respond, he gave up on charm. "What I'm saying is *you* got a big fuckin' target on your forehead and Tony's getting beat up!"

"I ..."

Tony intervened. "Fausto's right about it being dicey," he said coolly. "I've got a budget to get through. Anything that gets in the way of that is playing into Bobby Lucca's hands. For the first time since the inauguration, they'll carve me up."

They would. Providence politics was no-holds-barred, down and dirty. So, because Tony was my best friend, he needed votes to pass a budget, the tax treaty was vital to the University, and because my appointment to the Commission was as useful as another tit on a sow, I fell on my sword. "If you want me to resign, just say it. I'll do it in a second."

Fausto beamed.

"I knew you would," Tony said, got up, stretched and went around the sofa behind Aldo. "You're stand up. And a pool guy. So, that's why I want you to stay on the Commission."

"Fuck!" Fausto exploded out of his seat, his hands rose in exasperation.

"I'm not throwing Algy under the bus. His appointment is already out there, for better or for worse, and I don't see him resigning and not feeling as though I've taken advantage of him."

With that said, I could have, maybe should have, taken everybody off the hook and resigned, making an honorable exit after Tony's declaration, and I would have done so, *except* that Fausto, his body shaking in frustration, thundered, "Jesus Christ, Tony, how can you back the fuckin' East Side when you got seven wards of trouble! I got to deal with the pains in the asses, seven councilmen, half the council, that are calling me on this." He turned to the oldest brother. "Aldo, talk to him!"

Aldo had not changed his dark expression since he sat down. "It's Tony's call."

That's when I got it! Tony Tramonti appointed me to the Commission as a warning to his brother to stay away from Commission shenanigans, even if it gained a vote or two on the City Council. The Mayor was protecting himself. And Aldo knew it.

Fausto's whole body radiated anger, his jaw set like a boxer's, his hands lodged in his arm pits, for him, a speech impediment. "Can I say this?" He walked around the table, stood behind me, and put his right hand firmly on my shoulder. "At the very least, keep a low profile. If you see a problem with anything, come to me. First. I know some of these guys, how to deal with them. Don't go blowing off in the press."

When I didn't immediately respond, Fausto wheeled around my chair and threw his hands up in front of his face. Aldo turned to him, his voice modulated but firm. "You had your piece. It's over." Among the three brothers, that constituted finality. Then, Aldo said to me, "This faculty senate vote. I see it as an attack on Italian heritage, our culture. I've supported the Institute for years, raised a lot of money for it ..."

"Aldo, believe me, the President is very concerned about the reaction of University friends like you. Columbus Day is *not* off the calendar. Perhaps if he called you ..."

He waved his hands dismissively. "The insult from the faculty cannot be taken back. I came here to tell you that. I don't care about the politics. That's for Tony and Fausto. But this stings, personally."

Fausto, seeking to take advantage of Aldo's declaration, said, "This Columbus Day shit is not going away. You'll regret it if he stays on," he said to Tony. When he got no reaction from his brother, he straightened his tie and stormed out of the apartment.

I stood to leave. I was staying on the Commission, for better or worse. Aldo had his cell phone in hand checking messages as Tony came over to me, a wan smile on his face. "Hey, we're going to take some heat on this. Are you going to handle it?"

"I'm wearing my asbestos suit."

"Yeah," he smiled back and moved with me toward the door. "You would have loved Fausto's replacements. Forget his good government bullshit. First and foremost had to be an Italo from the right ward." His chuckle was halfhearted. In the foyer, he added, "Fausto will ease off. He always does. And I need you there." And I considered we had an unspoken understanding as to Fausto. "As to the tax treaty negotiations, it will be a longer haul. Maybe the ante will have to be raised to get any deal done. Get prepared."

26

BACK AT COLLEGE HALL, I took a call from Eustace Pine. Within fifteen minutes of filing Palagi's probate petition this morning, Judge Cremasoli ordered a chamber's conference next Tuesday. Pine, who was, after all, the attorney for Palagi's estate, asked me if I was going to be there to represent the University.

Now, that was a damn good question. I had assumed I would be, but with my knowledge of Palagi's recording, and with Columbus Day now in the mix, I would be tripping all over myself before Judge Cremasoli. I was out. Who should I retain? Pine would do a competent job on all legal issues, but what we needed was a tough lawyer who matched the contacts and political stature of our opponents. Fausto Tramonti? Not after this morning. Who better than Joe Laretta? In the murky intersection of law and Providence politics, I knew I could trust Joe. Once he was locked in, there was no better or more loyal advocate.

I told Pine I would soon have an answer for him and ended the call. I punched in Laretta's cell phone number and he answered from his car on Route 95. I outlined the situation, and as importantly, the players.

"Algy," he replied less than enthused, "I've been in the probate court twice. For relatives. I don't know a damn thing about probate law and never want to."

"Look, Joe, I'm too much of a Tramonti guy and with this Columbus Day ..."

"I know."

"... I need someone to watch our back. I can't think of anyone better than you."

"Thanks. I guess." He touched his car horn. "Listen, I got a huge caseload at the moment, a trial starting Wednesday in federal court. I'm not sure I can give you the time and effort that you need on this."

"Pine will take the lead on the probate procedures and the like. You advise us on a practical level. Besides, you'll want to be there on Tuesday just to see Puppy Dog's face." I emphasized Puppy Dog Goldbloom because Laretta absolutely despised him; if there was an inducement to get Laretta into the case, it was the prospect of whipping Puppy Dog.

"If I do this, it's at a premium. You guys are so cheap up there, that ought to make you gag."

My office is known to keep outside counsel on a tight billing rate leash, but I needed him. "You got it."

He laughed at my quick acceptance. "Okay, e-mail everything you have, a copy of the will, trust, any information on the son, in fact, anything I can read over the weekend. The rest of it I can pick up as I go along. I know Cremasoli. He's a past president of the Italo-American Brotherhood, grew up on the Hill on Spruce Street …"

"Can we get a fair shake?"

"He prefers to keep everybody happy, if he can. By that I mean, he's in every corner when he needs to be. He's also an inquisitive bastard. Laps up gossip like a cat at the milk dish. You should hear him at the Aurora." The Aurora Club was an Italo-American dining club housed in a Queen Anne style mansion on Broadway. Best veal and calamari in Providence, fabulous antipasto. "Member of my table."

I smiled with satisfaction. *My* team was in place.

The Provost informed senior staff at our weekly Thursday meeting that despite messages left at the Institute's campus in Rome and on his cell phone, Cosimo Brunotti, knowingly or not, had crossed the Rubicon with interviews with Italian newspapers, *il Foglio* on the political right, *Il Sole 24 Oro* in the center, and *La Repubblica* on the left, and on camera on RAI television where he was quoted as decrying the faculty senate vote as "an affront to the illustrious character and history of the Italian people." The very angry Provost described Brunotti as a preening, traitorous jerk.

Who knew?

o O o

Carter University was not standing on pride when two hundred years ago it assigned its President a modest first floor office in College Hall, presently consisting of a secretarial desk at the end of the hall, a modest conference room, and a slightly larger office. When Charles Danby saw me leaving the staff meeting, he asked me to join him. The *College Hill Independent*, likely full of pissy rants and rancor on the Columbus Day name change, was on his desk.

"Some difficult discussions coming up at the Trustees' meetings. Columbus Day and the tax treaty will loom over the meetings like a shroud."

I sat across his desk as his eyes searched a cluttered desktop and found stationery with the seal of the City of Providence. "From the Mayor. Not too bad. In fact, one of the few rational ones."

It was formal, addressed to President Danby, and began: *I find it difficult to accept that Carter University, an outstanding educational institution, has erased from its calendar the celebration of a significant moment in history and Italo-American culture for the sake of political correctness.* And so on.

I related the Mayor's comments on the tax treaty negotiations. "About what I expected," Danby responded. "And I don't see this damping down soon. Look at these."

He slid a manila file across the desk that contained printouts from national media, conservative screeds, blogs on Italo-American affairs, e-mails and letters from alumni and politicians, and translations from angry Italian newspapers.

"And these," he said handing me another file of printouts, from *Huffington Post*, liberal blogs, a 'get a life' Keith Olbermann blast at Italo-Americans and right-wing critics, and letters and e-mails from faculty and students coming down hard on the Provost who was seen as carrying the Administration's water on the issue. I returned the files to his desk and he handed me this morning's *Crier* which had the largest print headline I had ever seen in the student newspaper: PRESIDENT PUNTS ON NATIVE AMERICAN DAY. No need to read the rest. "Got it wrong even though I spent a half hour on the phone with the reporter last night."

Changing topics, he said, "Brunotti has had press interviews."

"His ego is as impervious as Carrara marble."

Danby referred to a desk book and punched in numbers into his cell phone and touched the speaker button. Brunotti's secretary answered and informed him that *Signor* Brunotti's calendar indicated he would be in Milan today, meeting with donors. It was now after five o'clock in Milan. Brusquely, Danby said, "I want you to get him my message immediately," he looked at me, "to call the Provost or Mr. Temple. As soon as possible."

How was it I managed to be included?

27

A FTER A LATE LUNCH that consisted of take-out chili from Costa's, I navigated the Shoot-Out's website for details of tonight's events and matches, thinking I would attend Young Jimmy's first exhibition. I also checked the referee schedule page and found that Commissioner Alby Temple was scheduled to super-ref tonight at En Core Sports Bar on South Water Street.

Got to be kidding! Because of the number of players, the first round of amateur play would be at pool halls and sports bars scattered within a thirty mile radius. But I didn't figure on an assignment at En Core, a sports bar adjoining Hard Core, also owned by Scuiglie. Likely, a rub-your-face-in-it challenge that I could not ignore from Hap Sanders or Puppy Dog.

I texted Nadie that I had drawn ref duty and would be home around ten. Later, she texted back that she would be packing for her bachelorette weekend in New York and to "watch out."

o O o

Dressed in casual clothes I kept in the office, I parked in the lot at the rear of Jimmy's next to a dish-festooned satellite transmission truck from Channel 8 at the canopied staircase to the Billiard Club. Chef Jao sat on a back stair smoking a cigarette. His thumb went up. "The Fox Point Kid is being interviewed," and shook his head ruefully.

Beyond the elegant mahogany bar, on the seating platform that overlooked the tables, Young Jimmy, bathed in camera lights, in an open collar, light blue dress shirt, his hair neatly combed, faced the sports reporter for the station. Both were being fitted for lapel mikes. A crowd of pool players, beers in hand, while interested, were audibly cranky about the interruption in their games and had to be quieted by Young Jimmy. I found a spot directly behind the cameraman, so close I saw Young Jimmy's ear-to-ear grin in the camera's view finder. The reporter, adjusting the hardware around his neck, said, "And when we finish, we go down to that table, and you break, and that's it."

"Yeah, yeah," Young Jimmy replied and glanced over to a near-by table illuminated by a bank of lights where a cue lay next to a nine-ball rack.

"Okay," the reporter replied loudly to a question from the cameraman, "sixty seconds." After another voice check, a red light blinked over the view finder, and the reporter broke into a toothy smile.

"You have probably noticed from the billboards and hoopla that Providence is thronged with thousands of pool players and pool fans for the Shoot-Out Tournament. Pool doesn't get a lot of media coverage. It's a game played in sports bars and clubs and rec rooms, not at McCoy Stadium. I'm here in the Billiard Club on Wickenden Street in Providence, owned and operated by Jimmy Hannigan, the best pool player to ever come out of New England, remembered as The Fox Point Kid and who was honored last night by the Shoot-Out Tournament. Thanks for having us, Jimmy."

Young Jimmy smiled broadly. "My pleasure."

"Jimmy, you're involved in the tournament. Tell us a little about your role."

"Well, I'm honored to be part of it. I've been teaching today, giving some pointers, welcoming players and fans to our city. Through Saturday, I also play some exhibition matches."

"How long has it been since you've played professionally?"

"Over twenty years. Now, I've gotta tell you that pool was a lot different in those days. I've played in tournaments for pots that were miniscule compared to what they have now at Mohegan Sun or at Foxwoods or Las Vegas, and nothing like what will be won at the Shoot-Out!"

"Jimmy, this is good for Providence?"

Young Jimmy replied earnestly, "Best thing that could happen to Providence and to pool. All these folks coming into town are going to have a great time, to spend a lot of money enjoying themselves, and play some great matches. I hope everyone comes down to the Convention Center and the Dunk to watch."

"What do you think about the gaming aspects?"

Young Jimmy answered as though he had been scripted. "I know that's a little controversial but it's all legit, being run by the Lotto Commission. And I don't see any reason if there's going to be some gaming, why the state and city can't get a benefit out of it. It's not going to affect the amateur players at all and the pros are here for the prize money."

"So, you're pretty excited about it."

"Very excited. I'm going to enjoy the tournament."

"Suppose you show us some of those legendary skills."

They stepped down from the platform to the table; the video camera followed. Young Jimmy picked up the cue, flexed his fingers, bent low, lined up his shot, drew back, and sent the cue ball zipping across the table to strike between the yellow one ball at the apex of the triangle and the next ball. Three balls disappeared into pockets.

"Whoa! Not bad, Jimmy. A few shots like that and you'll be on the tournament tour!"

Young Jimmy's face broke into a broad smile.

o O o

As the television crew packed up and play resumed at a half dozen tables, Young Jimmy spotted me and came over, still grinning. "You see how this is going? " He mentioned a player's name I did not recognize. "Playin' him tonight in my first exhibition at nine. C'mon down. I'll be shaking hands and slapping backs and giving advice from six-thirty."

I told him I planned to be there after being a super ref at En Core.

"En Core? That dump? Why there?"

I raised my eyebrows in answer to his question, then asked, "Tomorrow?"

"Tomorrow, I teach at the Dunk in the morning, and be Mr. Hospitality, like I told you, in the afternoon. I could play any number of people Friday night. I'm booked for around eight." He pulled a folded paper from his back pocket and scanned it. "If everything works right, on Saturday I check in, smile and walk around, then play a late afternoon exhibition. I might get an interview on ESPN before the finals that night. Wouldn't that be something!" His face was full of enthusiasm and confidence as he leaned in closer to whisper. "I'm tellin' ya, Algy, the restaurant is full, the Club's already jumping, better every night this week. We've got some great action here!"

Time to be lawyer, friend, and killjoy. "Bill Tuttle was at the referees' meeting this morning, made it clear he could be in your face!"

"Nah," he said dismissively, "Tuttle's a good guy. We don't cause any ruckus here and it's just *two* weekends. It reminds me of ..."

He stopped and inspected his shoes. What tournament was he going to mention, Derby City, Big John's in New Orleans, Vegas Nine Ball? The action away from brackets was where shooters like him played serious pool for serious money. He ran fingers through his oily hair and I saw pride and confidence burnished by last night's recognition at the Gala, the respect and acknowledgement of the pool crowd already in town, the media attention.

His demeanor invited my question, "You're not in the action, right?" He didn't reply so I repeated, "You're not in the action?" Maria Catarina's rule had been honored since their marriage: he didn't play for money anywhere and particularly not at the Club.

"Got Ginger Reilly to run the show because I'll get here late." Ginger Reilly, owner of a pool pit in Woonsocket, a mean-faced guy with an uncertain relationship to the law, who knew every player and angle in the local pool scene. "And whether I play somebody tomorrow night depends on who shows up. Who might back me. What the deal might be." The deal was usually fifty-fifty; the player got fifty percent of what was won, the sweater put up the bet and got the other fifty. The player had no cash risk, but any split was subject to negotiation. "Not sure. Nothing definite."

"Don't do it," I urged. "Maria Catarina will ..."

"Like I don't have bills to pay ..."

"Not worth it."

"Easy to say in your situation."

Young Jimmy never before referred to my family's wealth. Never. I opened my mouth to reply when a couple of sporting members made a beeline for Young Jimmy, accompanied by a recognizable pool guy, overweight, punky complexion, bad shave, red-eyed, wrinkled tan sports jacket, open neck shirt, the flash of gold at his neck. All that was missing was a straw fedora with a black band, and a cigar clenched in his teeth. The pool guy slapped a hand on Young Jimmy's shoulder, loudly congratulating him on his award, shifting his weight like a boxer, his head bobbing from side to side.

Young Jimmy smiled and winked at me. I was not to worry. Like it had been years ago in Everett, at Falvey's playing Big Bob Halsey. *All under control.*

28

AFTER DOWNING A BOWL of kale and linguiça soup laced with red wine, I walked the two blocks to En Core, all the way thinking about Young Jimmy.

What do you do if you were once really good, even great, at one thing, your time of greatness had passed, and then suddenly, an opportunity came along to once again kick ass, create a buzz, no longer be a fading memory? The Shoot-Out Tournament was Young Jimmy's chance, probably a last chance for recognition in the pool world, for that moment of respect, and he was willing to risk a successful life, professional and personal.

As I approached the vinyl-sided, three story En Core, Richie Stubbins, the house pro at Classic Billiards in Randall Square, emerged from the alley between my destination and Hard Core. He greeted me with, "Hi ya, Commish!"

Always a flamboyant dresser, Richie wore leather pants and a white tee with a Shoot-Out logo on the left pocket. Years ago, Richie and I played a lot of pool together, before money and talent made him a pro; unlike Young Jimmy, he stayed close to home base, becoming a successful fixture in the Providence pool scene. "Need a butt," he said, flipped open an ancient Zippo lighter and fired up a cigarette. "Been here since eleven."

Richie's assessment of the quality of play was "good," although the players were mostly "hicks" and the refs "good guys." When

Richie said he was the senior referee in charge of En Core's eight tables, I told him that the Shoot-Out website said that was my job. "Some screw up," he shrugged. "You know, it's pretty loose here. Take my two tables. It would give me a break and I got paperwork. Matches resume at seven."

"Why not?" I said, thinking that was about an hour of refereeing, I would be finished by eight-thirty latest, and be downtown fifteen minutes later for Young Jimmy's exhibition.

He took a deep last drag and crushed his cigarette with his heel. "Ready for a look?" and I followed him into the alley and through an emergency exit door held open by a cinder block. We took the stairs two at a time in a dimly lit passage toward the excited, raucous noise of a crowded sports bar: loud voices, bursts of laughter, country and western music, and pool balls clacking. Inside, it was obvious no one paid attention to the fire marshal's posted notice of maximum permitted occupancy. Every square inch of wall space was covered by beer and whiskey ads, cue racks, television screens, and movie posters from *The Color of Money* and *The Hustler*. "It gets calmer when the matches begin," Richie said reading my mind. "Remember, some of these folks have been here since eleven and a couple of beers have disappeared since then."

I barely heard him over the yells and shouts, high-five slaps and clinking long necks in response to a shot at a nearby table. "Even when they lose, they hang around, watch matches, play in between, and eat and drink whatever they got paid for being here. It's absolutely fantastic," Richie said. "Can you believe Sonny Russo could pull off anything like this?"

No comment.

At a rear booth near the bar, Richie found a printed form among a pile of papers on its table. "Fill this out and you're in."

The form was captioned *Officiating* and after personal data, the applicant made a few specific affirmations:

1. I know the rules. (Check this box yes or no). 2. I have no financial or other personal or family interest in the players (Check this box yes or no). 3. I will officiate fairly and in accordance with the rules of the Providence Shoot-Out Tournament and BCA (Check this box yes or no).

I checked *yes* in each box and wondered if I had checked *no*, would anybody notice or care? I returned the form to Richie who reached into a canvas bag and found a black arm band with an

R in a white circle. He gave me a clipboard with sheets identifying my two tables and the players' pool names, their clubs—from Omaha and Louisville, Detroit and French Lick—and local rules: no bathroom breaks, no junk cues, no Masse shots, can't touch a ball after the break. The matches were races to seven, which meant that whichever player first won seven games advanced to the next bracket. Richie checked his watch. "Six thirty. Go over around six fifty, introduce yourself, go through the rules, check the table to make sure nobody's spilled a beer. Okay?"

I left him for a stool at the garishly lit bar. Bottles in tiers shined brilliantly in the ceiling light as did glasses hanging by stems on a frame around the top of the bar. Boisterous drinkers and busy waitresses vied for the attention of two harried bartenders. I ordered a Bud Light, and as my bottle was delivered, noticed two guys at the other side of the bar checking the activity who could have been right off the bus from New Jersey.

Their hooded eyes were surveillance cameras. In nearly identical outfits of tees under leather jackets, with wraparound sunglasses on their foreheads, they were typecast as mob guys even to their paunches. One had curly gray hair, a porcine nose, no visible neck. He acted senior to his buddy whose shaved head bobbed in agreement to everything said to him; his VanDyke beard did his pudgy face no favors, his open mouth was a Three Stooges expression of dumb. As I sometimes do when I see obvious characters, I gave them names: No-Neck and Ditto.

At six fifty, having read the instructions, with my armband in position, I made my way to my assigned tables. The shooters, who had been playing on and off since this morning, had attained the pale, grim look of tired players; since they had advanced to the third bracket of play, they were not ball bangers. I introduced myself, checked their names on the tally sheets, said '*No gambling*' loudly to all concerned and let them continue their practice. At seven, we huddled again and I indicated that if a player had a question or needed a ruling, he should ask before shooting. I wished them well and racked the balls on the tables for their inspection.

Play began. At the table to my left, the break went to a country boy from Omaha, weighing in at least two-fifty with a hundred of that in his gut. When he spread his six-foot frame across the table, his low cut jeans exposed his hairy faultline. His opponent was leather-faced, a Willie Nelson look-alike, from Louisville who didn't stand more than five-six or weigh more than one-thirty, his leather vest festooned with tournament badges. Both used expensive custom cues, didn't speak unless absolutely necessary, and there was no display of temperament or sharking—verbal and body tricks designed to distract an opponent. Louisville, who had some fan support, played a finesse style so that balls barely moved across the table and the cue ball came to rest well placed for his next shot; his opponent's game was all power, and the only ruling I had to make was due to Omaha's Masse shot that sent two balls sailing off the table. That error only hastened his loss as Louisville won the match seven games to two. Omaha muttered, "Shit luck," but stuck out his hand to the victor.

At the other table, a young black player from Detroit was clearly better than the fidgety, tow-headed kid from French Lick whose hair had been shaped in a blender. Both had well-lubricated fans lined up on opposite sides of the table and I had to muscle them to provide room for the players, which was not appreciated. These shooters went at their shots verbally, with *no shot there, easy, easy,* and *give me a break!,* and physically, with body English and cue butt pounding, while their fans comported themselves as though watching pro wrestling. Their match went back and forth to six-a-piece, what is known as *hill-hill* in pool. The final game was a squeaker that either could have won. They traded shots and misses before Detroit sank the nine ball off the seven in a barely makeable carom shot that produced vigorous fist-pumping from the winner, cheers from his mostly black fans, and groans from French Lick's supporters. Detroit was good but not likely going much further; that hand pump stuff had *loser* written all over it.

End of my officiating. I filled out forms that I gave to a tournament rep who tapped the results into her laptop, and found Richie Stubbins in his booth. No-Neck and Ditto remained at the bar, joined in conversation by a third mound of flesh in a Patriots' sweatshirt holding a head as round as a bowling ball, huge ears, a flattened nose that seemed to go in several directions before deciding to drop. Amber sunglasses with white frames were on his forehead and a Bluetooth ear piece framed his left ear. 'Bull' would be a suitable name for him. I asked Richie, "See those guys? The leather models? Ever see them before?"

Richie glanced across the room and went back to his paperwork. "The two in leather been here off and on all day. They tug at their beers, watch the crowd, and then they leave, then they come back. I figure them as bouncers from Hard Core, sent over to make sure nothing goes wrong. Hey," Richie looked up at me, "the other guy asked about you."

"Me?"

"Yeah, the one in the Pats sweatshirt. Saw me talking to you. Asked if *you* was you."

The thought chilled me. I decided I could use more of Richie's company and sat in the booth. Maybe they'll leave.

Richie continued with his paperwork and asked if I was going to see Young Jimmy play at the Dunk. When I answered "Next stop," he went on about our mutual friend. "The Tournament's gonna save his bacon." He lowered his head and said quietly, "I hear he had to go to Frannie Zito—you heard of him, right—for the dough to complete the renovations to his restaurant. Heard Zito gets a cut of the action at the Club so long as he's owed. That's what I hear, but that's only what I hear."

His news gut punched me. It explained, in part, Young Jimmy's determination, after years of abiding by Maria Catarina's rule. But why had he gone to Zito for financing? He knew he could tap me, and probably others. Ashamed to ask? He had to play to pay off Zito, risking Maria Catarina's wrath, and a police raid. I had to corner him after his exhibition, talk some sense into him.

Richie left me for a table where loud, chest thumping fans were in one another's faces. The New Jersey boys remained at the bar watching Richie and a cop defuse trouble. Bull had left their company. *Time for a quick exit*, I thought, and cut through the bottle toting crowd to a flight of stairs that took me out to South Water Street. The night air was cool and reviving after the stuffiness of En Core.

I crossed the street, was in front of the display windows of the Bert Gallery, when a slab of a hand grasped my forearm from the shadows. Bull was a nose guard close up and even more ugly. His voice was like sandpaper. "Mr. Zito needs to see you. You got the time, huh?"

Was that voice familiar?

29

THE DARK GREEN, ALMOST black Bentley Flying Spur, parked in a reserved spot close to the canopied entrance to Hard Core, bore the license plate I-LOAN. As we approached, a rear door of the sleek metal sculpture opened and a shapely leg visible to the thigh found the sidewalk; the rest of the package had red striped short shorts, a full red halter, and shoulder length blonde hair that was peekaboo over glossy eyes. Her red lips puckered in and out as she favored us with a finger wave before she sauntered toward the canopy. Just a working girl–hostess on a professional break.

Bull opened the front passenger door, pushed me down and inside, the door gave off a solid thunk as it closed, and I was enveloped in an interior of brushed walnut and metal trim, hand stitched leather seats, and the smell of something musky. Door locks clicked and heavy breaths came from the rear seat; as I strained to look over a headrest, an iron grip grasped my left shoulder, forcing my hand down between the center console and my seat. Over my head, a hand snapped on the cabin light.

The rearview mirror revealed a square jawed face, eyelids low over gray-green eyes, sleek black hair pulled straight back, a gray, closely trimmed beard, handsome in a seedy way. "Heard you were inside," Frannie Zito said with the huskiness of Chazz Palminteri in *A Bronx Tale*; his breath smelled of cigarettes, alcohol, and something stale. My guess was that he and cutie pie had done a line of cocaine and she had given him lip service back there in their leather cocoon. He slurred, "Thought I'd meet my ... replacement."

"Beautiful car," I offered.

"Only one registered in Rhody." Zito's voice layered pride over menace. "What do you drive?"

I limited my response to the Mini.

"Must take a dozen to make a Bentley," Zito sneered and crammed my left shoulder down another half inch. I felt the pulse beat in my fingertips as they touched something small, metallic, and cylindrical in the plush carpet. Maybe doll face's lipstick. I rolled it in my fingers to keep circulation flowing. "I didn't like getting bounced."

I strained to avoid slipping into locked jaw super WASP inflection. "I can understand that."

"Tramonti made a big fuckin' stink about something that happened a long time ago. And none of his business. He's forgotten where he comes from. Know where that is? Silver Lake. You even know where that is?"

"I do." An Italo-American neighborhood on the Cranston line. "Been there many times."

"Yeah? Yeah?" Zito said without belief. "To make him look good in the goddamn *Journal*, he beats up on another Italian. I told his brother, I'm in business, no better, no worse than anyone else in business, you know what I'm tellin' you? I pay my taxes, know the score. So what if I had a problem a long time ago. Lotta people did. Nobody ever gave me nothin'. No fuckin' golden spoons in *my* neighborhood."

I didn't react to Zito's provocation.

"The fuckin' Shoot-Out's the best thing ever to happen to Providence. It was me that helped bring it here. Me! My idea for the sports betting. Mine!" Made sense to me but he could have been boasting. "Everybody's gettin' action, clubs, bars, restaurants, the hotels are full, taxes rollin' in, biggest out-of-town business we've ever had. But me? What respect do I get? I get a fuckin' shove."

His grip tightened; his fingerprints were now etched into my shoulder, the cylinder rolled away from my touch. "So tell me why do you guys wanna abolish Columbus Day? What is it with you? Prejudiced against Italians?" Not expecting an answer, Zito continued. "You come down here often? Enjoy the nightlife down here? Or are you as self-righteous as your buddy the Mayor?"

His insults made me antsy but I would ride it out.

"You're a buddy of Hannigan too." How would he know? "Shoot-Out's his big opportunity. Believe what I'm tellin' you. Everybody wants Hannigan to do well. You want this to be big for him, right? Nobody should screw it up for him? Especially not a friend?"

I realized then that Zito got Young Jimmy his gig at the Shoot-Out, the liquor licenses for the Club. Zito would be getting a pay down on his loan with his share in the betting action at the Club. He had also inveigled Young Jimmy, who didn't need much of a push, into the Club's action and had somehow learned of our friendship. So, he snookered me to En Core, not only to give himself the opportunity to insult me but also to deliver his *mind your own fuckin business* message.

Zito sat back. I imagined his self-satisfied smile. The Bentley's door locks popped up. "Nice to meet ya," he said in my dismissal.

My cool evaporated. Zito had me pegged as an East Side twit, a snotty wimp he could push around, trembling, wobbly, scared because of threatening phone calls—made by Bull?—being dragooned to his Bentley so I could take his abuse. I had to respond.

I pushed open the car door and got out. Bull, who was standing by Hard Core's canopy, snapped a cigarette butt into the gutter and looked inside for orders as to the manner of my departure. With none heard, he backed away as I took two deep breaths and poked my head inside the open door. "Love to drive it," I said. "Any chance?" My voice suggested I had a case of the vapors over the opportunity, that after getting his message, taking my medicine, I deserved something in return.

He could have tossed off something like 'I'm not a fuckin' dealer' but he didn't. I had read him correctly; the Bentley Banker was a show-off even if suspicious and slightly incredulous that I would ask for a favor. 'Show off' won. "Yeah. Around the block. Knock yourself out."

I walked around the rear of the Bentley to the driver's side, opened its heavy door, and slid behind its leather wrapped steering wheel. Zito chortled out, "Sal,"—Bull had a name now—"man wants to drive a real car. See you inside."

Zito reached over my shoulder, told me to step on the brake as he touched the starter button, not letting me, a Mini owner, into the mysteries of push-button ignition. "Sure you can handle this?" he sniggered.

The walnut dashboard, in the winged shape of the Bentley emblem, displayed illuminated dials and bar gauges; a touch screen provided a rear view; I felt more than heard the huge V-8 engine throb expectantly. My hands went to the steering wheel, I felt in my element, in control and nervy and loose and purposeful, like at the starting line of a track like Thompson's, in command of this elegant, powerful machine. As Zito would discover, I had regained my chops.

I adjusted the steering wheel's tilt, positioned my seat, and snapped on my seatbelt, a sound not echoed from the rear seat. Zito said something about the number of gears and shifting paddles as I eased out of the parking lot into South Water Street. A touch of the accelerator and rear wheels spun street grit into the undercarriage. "Easy, for Christ sakes, easy," he cautioned as we barreled down South Main Street, the tight steering giving me what I expected for control of two-and-a-half tons of metal. "Hey, what's the hurry? Slow down!" I hoped to God no drunk ventured out of a bar. "Christ, what are you doing?" Zito sputtered, "Pull over!"

The new access road to reconfigured Route 195 East was finished by India Point Park but barricades remained because traffic lights hadn't been installed, leaving over a mile of new, empty pavement that the *East Side Monthly* reported had become a drag racing mecca for those inclined to test metal. Like me. Like now.

With Zito pounding my shoulder, I easily slipped the Bentley between orange barrels and cones and sawhorses by the Hurricane Barrier, took a sharp left, felt the strain on the steering wheel and a rear wheel skid, made another quick left, and we were on the straightaway of the access road, testing the advertised zero-to-sixty acceleration in under five seconds. The surge of power tossed Zito back into the seat as I swung into the right lane, heading toward an underpass and upgrade to the open highway.

I didn't need the speedometer or RPM gauge to tell me we were closing in on ninety. A quarter of a mile flashed by, Zito kicking at my seat, screaming at me; we would be on the highway in seconds. I braced myself, braked, felt Zito's body crash into my seat as we careened down a ramp that led to a new road that ran parallel to India Point Park. I yanked a right turn, Zito shouting and beating my shoulder without force, straining his hand toward the ignition button—foolish at this speed—but the yaw of another sharp turn sent him screaming, swearing, to the floor. A few seconds of braking, a deceleration like when an airplane's thrusters reversed on landing, and we approached the tugboat basin by the Hurricane Barrier where a tire-screeching right turn returned us to South Water Street. Zito, now breathless, landed a solid punch on my right shoulder, and fell back as though exhausted. We arrived in the club area at under fifteen miles per hour.

I pulled into the parking space at Hard Core where our adventure began. As a button push turned off the engine, I turned to Zito, crumpled behind my seat, incoherent in his swearing, fumbling with his cell phone, likely calling Sal. I caught some spittle of his rage. "Thanks. Love the car," I said, got out, and slammed the door.

"Son of a bitch!" he yelled back. "I don't forget, asshole!" He scrambled up to lean over the driver's seat and pounded the horn button as I disappeared into the shadows.

30

NADIE WAS STRETCHED OUT on the sofa in the loft, in silky pajamas that made her look comfortably lithe, engrossed in a Richard Russo novel. I described my refereeing debut but not my escapade with Zito; she nodded without great interest. Columbus Day remained *verboten*.

It didn't dawn on me that I hadn't seen her in pajamas for some time until later, as I undressed for bed. She pulled down a sheet, got into bed. She didn't put on her reading glasses or pick a book from the night stand. I joined her from my side of the bed, and after my confrontation with Zito, feeling suddenly randy, ready for foreplay, I nuzzled an ear. She turned away, "Algy, I ..."

As I propped myself up on an elbow for a proper kiss, she continued, "... between now and the wedding, I want to be ... chaste."

"What?"

"I've been thinking about it. We've been together since I gave up my apartment ..."

In a king-size bed for most of two years, we're about to be married, and it was shut-off time?

"The idea is to make our wedding and our wedding night very special."

Must be something from *Bride's* magazine, not *Psychology Today*.

"Lots of couples who have been living together do it. I'm not exactly a traditionalist but the wedding and all ... as it has gotten closer ... I feel different." She turned away from me. "I'm not going to try to explain it. I don't think I have to."

Nadie, not explain?

"And it's not forever, is it? Ten days. It's just a time off."

"A bundling board between us?"

She responded by reaching out and taking my left hand in hers. "It's all very new." She turned to face me with an expression that said I should understand. "The point is ..."

I waited for the professor of psychology to inform me. But instead, she put on her reading light. I decided on a last try. "Let me get you a glass of wine ..."

"I-don't-want-any" was slowly enunciated.

I rolled back to my side of the bed and stared at the ceiling. The blades of the fan revolved without much heart. She said, "I love you. Just ... be patient."

I was not in a mood to be rejected. Hey, I just took down a real bad guy! I huffed in annoyance and slowly got off the bed, donned pajama bottoms that were under my pillow, and went to the bathroom. When I returned, her reading light was off, her eyes were shut. I suddenly had the mental image of us as a married couple, reading novels in bed until we closed our eyes.

Being hog tied, locked in a car's trunk, can focus the mind.

Like what is jabbing my ass?

I get my wrists to the trunk lock and catch where the metal edges seem rough, maybe sharp enough to cut through the tape. I scrape the tape against an edge without success, then work at my wrists under the slicker's sleeves.

I realize that if I can unzip my slicker, get it off a shoulder, a sleeve would loosen, and so would the tape. My teeth eventually find the metal zipper pull and it is like biting ice. With my chin buried in my chest, I work the zipper down its track an inch, then another, it becomes easier further down the track, and the slicker loosens. I rub the slicker against the floor and it grudgingly comes off my shoulder, my fingers edge upward, tips now touching the binding tape, my nails sink into the sleeve, pulling it down as my wrists yank and twist. After minutes of frustration, the tape gives. My left hand is free!

I rip the tape off my mouth. Ohh, I'll never kiss again! Then, off my eyes, leaving eyebrows burned and plucked. When I open eyelids that seem pasted to my face, my eyes sting. I stretch forward and release the loop around my ankles. Free at last!

To do what?

31 Friday

I DROPPED NADIE OFF at the Amtrak Station for her bachelorette weekend, got a very long kiss, and drove up to Federal Hill to Pastiche on Dean Street, a favorite café and bakery, for an espresso and a fig scone. The *Journal* I took from its newspaper rack had a front page feature recapping the Columbus Day controversy, with a sub-headline quote attributed to the faculty senate president: *Columbus does not meet Carter University's standards.* Geezus! The President's letter to the faculty senate raising the procedural issues I had researched, and affirming that this year's calendar remained in place, was buried in the two last paragraphs on an inside page.

I left the Mini parked on Dean Street, and walked through De-Pasquale Square, the cultural center of the Hill, to Atwells Avenue. The Hill, usually gritty, was litter free, spruced up for the coming holiday weekend, decorated with banners, flags, and bunting, with red, green, and white lights strung across streets, red and green stripes newly painted parallel to the existing white stripe down the middle of Atwells. The Italian specialty shops of the Hill would open at nine for early customers avoiding the later rush for pasta at Vendas, veal, quail, snail salad, and Italian cold cuts at Tony's Colonial, fresh chicken and rabbit at Antonelli's, and Italian cookies, zeppoles, ricotta tarts and rice pies prepared by Ronci's or Scialo's. At Antonio's Wines, the windows were full of decorative baskets of wine in plastic wrapping.

I could see my friend Marco Antonio at the register through glass doors. I knocked to get his attention and grim faced, he let me in. "We got a situation," he said in a voice as ominous as that of Robert DeNiro about to punish gang members spending the loot too quickly. I followed him past displays of wines from Alto Adige to Sicily into the tiny nondescript office used for giving valued customers a taste and discrete political gossip. Marco sat in an old-fashioned, oak swivel chair behind a cluttered desk; I leaned against one of the battered filing cabinets, prepared for what I expected to be a dirge of bad news. His forehead wrinkled and he intertwined his fingers tightly on the desk. "The fuckin' faculty. Don't they know that Columbus is more than a name to Italians? So, Columbus, maybe, he had slaves. So, who didn't then. Indians had slaves. I don't hear anything bad about George Washington or Thomas Jefferson because they had slaves, right? C'mon, it's just easier to dump on Italos than on goddamn ..."

"No name change this year. The faculty senate vote is ..."

"Yeah," he acknowledged, "but that means squat, right? I'm past president of the Federal Hill Business Association. They're coming to me and I got to make a statement for the *Gazette*. It isn't gonna be very complimentary. I wanted you to know before. Anyhow, I'm insulted and disgusted! Let us keep our day, the ... freaking ... Indians can have another!"

"I get it, Marco, I do ..."

He put an elbow on the desk top and wagged a finger at me. "Cheap shots like this allies the Russo-Lucca gang with the Brow, gives them a soapbox. Chance for them to look good, attacking somebody who's dissing Italians. Like years ago, when the mob set up fronts to make them look like defenders of our heritage. All part of the act. Frannie Zito, that blowhard, is sponsoring a call out at the Columbus Theatre."

"I ..."

"Everybody's been invited. They got the churches, the Knights, the Sons. Even got that ex-Senator from New York, what's his name. They'd dig up Al Martino or Sinatra or Louie Prima or John Pastore if they could. This isn't good for somebody like me who doesn't buy in. And you might not know this, but Columbus Day is traditionally when the old-timers go in, ask a don like the Brow for favors, and he is duty-bound at least to listen. While lots of that is bullshit, he still does it. Tradition. It gives him some prestige. Especially now."

I recalled the wedding scene in *The Godfather*.

I said, "I wish I could tell you that this is going to go away quickly, but I can't. Danby is doing his best ..."

"Look, this is how it is. You hit a raw nerve. The Hill isn't what it was. It's hollowed out, if you get my meaning. We got tattoo parlors, hookah joints, Chinese take-out, Mexican food. It's all changed. Most of the Italian people are gone. Sure, we got the restaurants, galleries, food stores, Holy Ghost and Mount Carmel, but the people who actually live here are Latino or Asian. We got a Spanish Mass now at Holy Ghost. I go into the Bank of America branch on Atwells and everyone speaks Spanish. The census says we got more Guatemalans than Italians. Guys like me, the Italo-American business owners, we go home every night to Cranston or Johnston or North Providence. Look at me, I'm in Dean Estates!"

His eyes left me for a space on the ceiling. "We live behind a kind of façade nobody talks about, because we think it's shameful. So, everyone on the Hill is into dramatics, including the bad guys. We put on an Italian show once a year, for us, for the other Italians, for the business, we cling to one holiday tradition, and that's Columbus Day Weekend. You come along with this stupid name change, and everybody gets to take out their shame on you ..."

I nodded. What else could I do?

"It's so goddamn complicated," Marco went on, clearly in lecture mode. "We got traditionalists and we got the new guys. We traditionalists stand for something, Italian pride, culture, home. The new guys, even if they got Italian names, it's all about money. They attract the gangbangers who come up here now. A few weekends ago, we had street fights after hours! Never happened before. A Lucca, a Scuiglie, for better or worse, stands with tradition. They'll wrap themselves around old Chris Columbus, provoke a lot of bad feelings against Carter, anything and anybody from the East Side. At the parade, the theme this year is Italo-American Pride. How's that for timing. You'll be getting ready for your wedding when the parade is on when up here, things could get out of hand."

Marco stood and came around his desk, putting a hand on my arm. "That's not all. Fausto Tramonti was in here last night, buying wine for his big party on the weekend." He lowered his voice as though the room walls had ears. "You know, Fausto is not as smooth as his brothers. We got into Columbus Day and Fausto was loud and obnoxious so everyone in the store heard him, so that the Hill knew his stance fifteen minutes later. On purpose, he used me, embarrassed me."

A finger went to the side of Marco's nose. "And another thing, you being on the Commission should know that Fausto's got clients, ward chairs, friends of councilmen with their snouts in this Shoot-Out pie. The limo contract, for instance, vendors like the program printers, the caterers. Just a word to you, okay?"

32

MY DAY DID NOT get any better when a few minutes later as I walked back to my car, Nick called on my cell phone. He was matter-of-fact.

"The funeral home's books were torn apart by our analyst. Nothing was credible, the balance sheet, profit and loss statement, statement of operations, cash flows, trust accounts, all prepared, or I should say, made up, by Arnie. When questioned, Arnie clammed up, like he was surprised anyone would ask, that this wasn't a loan application, more like a ... gift."

I recalled Nadie's prescient admonition.

"There isn't a written trust in place for these prepaid burial arrangements. It's more like a piggy bank. So long as there's not an epidemic of Jewish deaths in the boroughs, it could go on forever, taking money in and investing it like it was their own, providing burial services when it was time. Our analyst also found unexplained deposits and withdrawals in the burial trust accounts. He thinks the Gershowitzs invested for other funeral homes, likely for a fee, because there were checks out to funeral homes together with smaller ones, five percent of the larger ones, to the Gershowitzs. Bottom line, that's illegal. Very illegal."

"How much did he ask for?"

"A million for operations, two for the burial trust. On the operations side, that would be plenty. But another two for the trust? Three million becomes a stretch."

"Sorry, Nick. Damn!"

"Have to say the homes have plenty of collateral, no mortgages on the real estate, and a cash flow no matter how it has been mis-applied or skimmed. They could pay off both loans given time, but no private lender would touch them. So, if you want to tap the TF, I can get the paperwork in place quickly, use a shell lending entity not identified with us."

Nadie would not expect Nick to find a lender if Arnie and Si-mon were cooking the books, but would Nadie be believed by her mother and Aunt Ida when confronted with angry denials from her cousins? What would that do to our wedding? Mrs. Winokur's life? There was no alternative to a loan from the TF.

"Do I call Arnie, or do you?" Nick asked.

"Me. I'm family."

33

AN ENDURING LESSON FROM lawyering classes at Champlin & Burrill was that an early arrival at a meeting with opposing counsel allowed time for a deep breath, a review of notes, and importantly, assuming a confident, even nonchalant pose when the opposition arrived. That explained why I was five minutes early for the meeting with the Luccas in the Institute's ornately decorated conference room. The door to the hall remained slightly ajar; telephones rang, a fax machine chirped, and muted voices came from a distance. Before she left me, Brunotti's officious secretary reminded me that *Il Direttore* remained in Italy in the press of business.

Moments later, Eustace Pine, dressed in a dark suit appropriate for a probate lawyer, placed a battered briefcase on the table across from my chair. His boney nose sniffed. "What's this ruckus about Columbus Day?"

I was saved from a response by Brunotti's secretary. "Senator Lucca," she announced and stepped aside.

A diminutive figure, five two or three at most, with a full head of white, curly hair, in a tight, dark blue, three-piece suit, entered holding a glossy black leather case against his chest. His face was flat as a plate, his eyes widely spaced and perfectly round, his nose hovered above a trim pencil mustache of a kind not seen since Thomas Dewey. His furtive glance around the room signaled his ill-at-ease which likely explained why he barely acknowledged our greetings and chose a chair at the far end of the table. It was left to me to apologize for the absence of Cosimo Brunotti, explaining he had been delayed on Institute business in Italy.

Rudy Lucca's face darkened at the news, no doubt assuming that Brunotti's absence had been purposefully arranged. "I should have been told," he said in a high-pitched voice, like that of a choir boy, as Puppy Dog, in a tan, light weight sports jacket, pink shirt, gray tie, and dark trousers, slinked into the room.

It was Pine's turn to be wide-eyed—damn, I had forgotten to tell him of Puppy Dog's entry into the case—and I quickly explained that the Luccas were representing the Republic of Italy, and Puppy Dog was now local counsel to the claimant Vittorio Ruggieri even as I wondered about the split of fees among counsel. Puppy Dog stretched over the table to shake Pine's reluctant hand and sat next to Lucca and across from Pine. A tiny piece of tissue covering a shaving nick had been forgotten on his chin; Lucca signaled to Puppy Dog by touching his own chin, and Puppy Dog picked it off and stuffed it in his jacket pocket. The adversaries were now in position.

"For the record," Lucca said as he unzipped his case, "Vittorio Ruggieri of Rome, Italy, is the recognized son of Professor Italo Palagi, a citizen of the Republic of Italy. I am here as the Consul of the Republic of Italy in Providence and as a lawyer for the Republic of Italy. Mr. Goldbloom is the attorney for the son, Vittorio Ruggieri. We all know that Signor Palagi only recently learned that he had a son from a ... liaison in Rome many years ago. We also know that Signor Palagi as distinguished scholar and citizen of Italy, when informed of his son's existence, visited him in Rome, and was shown evidence of his paternity. Signor Palagi legally recognized Vittorio as a son and heir in accordance with Italian law." Lucca looked in turn at Pine and me for objection while Puppy Dog inspected his ragged finger nails. "Good. No issue," Lucca intoned and removed a clutch of documents from his case. "These are certified copies of all relevant documents," Lucca said and distributed clipped pages replete with multiple shiny seals and ribbons. "I also have authenticated translations for you," Lucca said as he sent pages across the table.

Pine placed a pair of half glasses on his boney nose and responded stiffly. "Our counsel in Rome will review the official records regarding acknowledgment of paternity."

"No doubt you will learn that in Italy a father may not disown a son," Lucca replied curtly.

"*If* Italian law applies, which is doubtful," Pine said looking over his glasses. "Palagi was for decades, of course, domiciled in

Rhode Island. Section 3 of Article 9 of the Inheritance Laws of Italy makes it clear that domicile is the essential element of any determination as to whether the laws of Italy apply, or not, to a decedent's estate, despite retention of Italian citizenship."

"We'll leave that to Judge Cremasoli," Lucca replied reeking with confidence. "Palagi's will? And the trust? You have our copies?"

Pine dipped into his briefcase, then withdrew his hand with a quizzical expression. "You're not suggesting that there is anything at issue with his trust, are you? Surely you realize your client can have no legal claim against any assets in Italo Palagi's trust which are outside probate court jurisdiction."

Lucca's fingers brushed his moustache. "The trust is part of his estate plan. Signed at the same time as his will, right? If Palagi had then known of Vittorio's existence, no one would believe that he would have ignored his son and placed the bulk of his assets in trust to benefit others." Lucca's voice rose in ascending notes. "Anyway, it is neither here nor there. Italian law applies and Italy will not permit his son to be cheated."

"Cheated?" Pine's voice expressed shock at Lucca's choice of the word.

Lucca turned to me. "I'd like to hear *Direttore* Brunotti on this."

Of course, he would, and very likely had.

"The University," I replied, "expects to retain all assets granted under Professor Palagi's will and trust. Although what you've presented today may be *prima facie* evidence of his acceptance of paternity, Palagi was in his eighties, perhaps easily fooled. There are DNA tests for paternity. We would insist on such tests in the case of a claim by Mr. Goldbloom's client ..."

Lucca's hand and face made unified gestures of irritation and dismissiveness. Puppy Dog, letting Lucca carry the meeting, didn't react. Seemed almost disinterested, twisting a yellow pencil in his fingers.

Pine cleared his throat and distributed sets of documents. "Copies of the probate petition and the will. You will note in particular sections of the will that make it clear that your client's claim, if prosecuted, will result in denial of any part of the estate."

"Boiler plate," Lucca replied.

"The petitioner is the University as beneficiary. We have a chamber's conference with the judge on Tuesday."

"Where's the trust?" Lucca interrupted.

"I'll get back to you." Pine replied.

"We'll get it by subpoena if you don't hand it over."

"That's up to the University's counsel …"

Puppy Dog and Lucca looked at me and I had my opening for my first surprise. "Joe Laretta has been retained as our special counsel."

Puppy Dog blinked. Lucca's lips pursed in surprise. Before they recovered, it was time to carpet bomb the opposition. "We have two other matters," I said. Their faces drained of color as I disclosed that Palagi's trust had been decimated by the Sugarman scandal. Lucca slipped lower into his chair with every revelation as to the status of Ravensford Capital and the loss of assets. When I finished, Lucca's chin was only inches above the table top.

"Why didn't you tell us this before?" he croaked.

"We only learned on Monday that Palagi's investment manager had placed the funds with Sugarman. And that had to be verified."

"Crap!" Lucca exploded, sitting bolt upright, his fingers drawn into a fist to pound the table. "You had us come here to … to… be embarrassed." Lucca's eyes sparked with the imagined insult, his lungs filled with heated air. "As Consul of the Republic of Italy, I am outraged! The man's estate has been dissipated. *You* let this happen! Negligence, breach of fiduciary duty, tortuous interference with an inheritance. This is an infamy to Italy." He stared at Puppy Dog, expecting him to join in the fray; Puppy Dog's fingers were tightening on the pencil, his face becoming florid.

"Hold on," I responded calmly before Puppy Dog met his challenge. "Palagi had the right to invest his own trust money and he did. Not the University. We were not negligent or otherwise culpable. The University has Champlin & Burrill pressing claims against Ravensford Capital. If your client wants to join in the costs of the prosecution …"

Snap! Something flew from Puppy Dog's fingers. He had been applying pressure to both ends of the pencil and it broke, one piece winging its way across the table, nicking Pine on the shoulder before rattling onto the table. "My God!" Pine yelped.

"Sorry." Puppy Dog's tone was unapologetic, even surly.

Pine, recovering from the pencil assault, delivered the *coup de grâce*. "You should read this document." Copies of Palagi's letter to Father Pietro slid across the table. Lucca and Puppy Dog took all of fifteen seconds to go through it, and look at each other.

"What is this? Where did this come from?" Lucca brusquely demanded, thrusting his copy at Pine.

"Hand delivered to my office on Monday by Father Pietro Sacchi of the Philosophy Department of Providence College. The original is in my safe and will be filed with the court on Tuesday. As you can see, Palagi specifically stated that nothing covered by his will and trust was to be affected by the existence of your client. This was months after he may have *acknowledged* your client."

"This … letter … constitutes an amendment of the will. It has to be witnessed," Lucca blustered, waving his copy of the disconcerting letter above his head.

Pine's lips played with a smirk. "If Italian law *were* to prevail, the letter could be a *tes-ta-mento o-lo-grafo*. A holographic will. It is dated and signed and notarized. There is no need of witnesses, or an attestation clause under Italian law."

Another one for Pine!

"But," he continued, "we don't assert it is a will or an amendment. This letter is an affirmation of Professor Palagi's intent." He said that too triumphantly for the situation. "It is simply clear, notarized evidence of his manifest intent to keep his estate plan as it was." He turned his attention to Puppy Dog. "Perhaps, he didn't find your client … congenial? As you may know, under *Chisolm v. Tillinghast*, a nineteen thirty-three decision, when having made a will at a time when the testator is unaware of an heir, a later affirmation of the will by the testator, with knowledge of an heir, must be considered by the court as *prima facie* evidence of his manifest intent to not make any change in the document. I've brought copies of the decision for your easy reference. It is controlling case law in Rhode Island."

Neither lawyer touched the copies of pages taken from a volume of Rhode Island Supreme Court cases that Pine sent their way. Lucca's hands trembled with rage and he went on the attack. "Under what mental duress was Signor Palagi at the time he wrote this? Did the University pressure him? Threaten him?"

"That's not called for," Pine replied, raising his voice in indignation. "You don't trust the University?"

"Trust?" Lucca sneered and reprised Puppy Dog's complaint. "We ask for a copy of his trust and you won't give it to us, even though you must have a copy with you. *Trust?* You insinuate Vittorio Ruggieri is an impersonation, a fraud? *Trust*? You tell us that Palagi's assets are lost and that it is a surprise? *Trust*? You deliver a previously undisclosed and unwitnessed amendment to his will that disinherits our client? *Trust*? We should *trust* you when your client exhibits prejudice against Italians and Italo-Americans?" Seemingly exhausted by his blast, he stood, took a deep breath, heaved his case under his arm and stormed out of the conference room.

Puppy Dog stood to follow. I was blunt. "Leon, as to anything that's in Palagi's estate or trust, you should know that we'll fight forever, here and in Italy. That's institutional policy, even if it's only for the principal. The son may never see a nickel in his lifetime. So, if this is a contingency case ...?"

"Rudy has his orders."

"After payment of legacies, there won't be much left."

His yellowish eyes brightened. "All I can do is urge my client to be practical. Can't see litigating about nothing." Then, he cackled, "You hired Joe Laretta? Getting political after all these years?"

I smiled just the tiniest bit as he left.

34

AT FIVE MINUTES TO one, I was across town in my Range Rover at the security gate at the Eaton Street entrance to Providence College. A warming sun had broken through hazy clouds and stoked up humidity. The security guard put down his newspaper and greeted me with a *how ya doin*, and I said I was to pick up Father Pietro at the Priory. He pointed up a tree-lined way toward an imposing neo-Gothic structure at the top of a slight incline.

I circled the several brick and glass buildings, grassy knolls and playing fields looking for a parking spot, as streams of kids crossed in front of me, as oblivious as any on Carter's Green, some in the company of white-robed Dominicans. Like most native Rhode Islanders, I was very familiar, even proud of the success of the College, administered by the Dominican Order, how when its basketball team, the Friars, became a national power, the small school was transformed from a tiny liberal arts college into a Catholic college of choice for four thousand undergraduates.

I found a vacant parking spot in front of the Priory, where I was cordially greeted by a male receptionist in a white habit who introduced himself as Brother Thomas. Alert to my visit, he used a phone to summon Father Pietro and directed me to a bright, comfortably furnished parlor with three starkly spare oil paintings of the Madonna, the Crucifixion, and Christ's Ascension on its walls. Father Pietro, in a black suit, a white vestment folded over his right arm, soon joined me; the paintings, he said, were by a contemporary French Dominican he knew well and evidentially admired. As we left the Priory, he picked up a pamphlet from the reception desk on the history of the Dominican Order "from our founding by Saint Dominic in 1216 to today's mission. O.P.," he said, "stands for Order of Preachers."

Our fifteen minute drive to Swan Point Cemetery took us past the State House into the edge of downtown, up College Hill on Waterman Street through the Carter campus, then down a long incline to chic Wayland Square and the leafy expanse of the East Side's parkway of new money, Blackstone Boulevard. Father Pietro was engaging in conversation, inquiring about my duties as University Counsel, avoiding any reference to Palagi's recording. I mentioned that Nadie and I were soon to be married and our honeymoon destinations of Rome and the Amalfi Coast.

"You will be in Rome? Wonderful. While there, it would be my pleasure to escort you and your wife on a tour of the Vatican if you have the time." He chuckled. "It will not be what they now call a *Dan Brown* tour, but you would find it of interest."

I replied we would be honored and gave him particulars as to our travel dates. He asked where we were staying in Rome. "The Hassler," I said and felt a touch of embarrassment as he repeated the name slowly in appreciation of its reputation as Rome's finest, most exclusive hotel.

We entered Swan Point Cemetery through massive iron gates softened by gardens of brilliant early fall color and parked in the chapel lot next to my mother's ancient Volvo station wagon. Its low license plate number *24* had instant cultural status in Rhode Island although to her it was just part of being a Temple family member symbolizing nothing else than owning one of the first registered cars. The chapel was a low lying stone building with arched windows, a sharp roofline of slate, and truncated steeple. I remarked to Father Pietro that I expected few of Palagi's colleagues since Carter University's faculty had a long-standing preference for on-campus memorial services months after a colleague's death.

"A difference between our institutions, our communities," Father Pietro replied. "We say farewell to our brother Dominicans with formalities that are centuries old and pray for God's continued providence. These are moments of thanksgiving for a life, allowing us to reflect on our own goals and purposes."

I almost said "Amen."

o O o

Within the cool precincts of the chapel, Father Pietro excused himself and disappeared into a kind of sacristy as I slid into a pew next to my mother and Sylvia Odum, her live-in companion, a self-described African-American lady of a certain age. The two hand-some, spry, nearly octogenarian ladies, dressed appropriately for the service, smiled at me, and resumed their hushed conversation.

We were about fifteen in attendance, including a handful of professors from the Institute. Light filtered through Tiffany glass windows splashed a spectrum of colors across blond oak wall pan-els and two stands of floral arrangements; somber organ music piped in the background. The last to arrive was Senator Rudy Lucca who strode portentously down the center aisle to a front pew. We could begin; the Republic was now present.

At precisely two o'clock, Father Pietro, vested for the service, entered the sanctuary, snapped on a lectern light, asked us all to remember that we were in the presence of God, made the sign of the Cross, and read from Saint Paul and the Gospel of John. His softly accented voice gave depth to the positive characteristics he associated with Palagi, like genial conversation, love of intellectual discussion, generosity, a passion for the opera, and his use of wry anecdotes to make his point. At the end of his gracious, thought-ful talk, he alluded to Palagi's secretive and lifelong battle with the 'demons of pessimism' that reminded us all of a suspected suicide. After final prayers in Italian and English, the priest left the sanctu-ary and we filed out of the chapel. I thought he had acquitted him-self as a member of the Order of Preachers.

In the gravel parking lot, Rudy Lucca drove past me in a shiny black Cadillac sedan without acknowledgement as I chatted with my mother and Sylvia until they left to inspect the formal gardens surrounding our family's nearby crypt. Palagi's colleagues, hover-ing nearby, were now drawn to me, anxious to let me know their positions on Columbus Day—decidedly mixed—unanimous in their complaint that Cosimo Brunotti was not in attendance. Father Pi-etro joined us; they complimented him on his depiction of Palagi and returned to their voluble criticism of their boss as we left them and headed down a cinder path bordered by thick arborvitae.

"A fittingly serene place," the priest said solemnly, "so well-maintained, like an arboretum." Which it was: stands of willows, a few remaining elms, clusters of birch, ash, scattered somber dark beeches, gnarled oaks, acacias, and early autumn colorful maples.

"Claudia Cioffi did not come," the priest began. "I called to invite her to the service. Her excuse was that tomorrow she leaves for Rome. She complained of sickness to be treated there." We came to the cemetery proper and walked past obelisks, urns, mournful statuary mottled with yellow-brown lichen, rows of marble and granite headstones, and neo-Grecian crypts, many with tiny fluttering flags indicating the graves of veterans, then skirted a pond nestled among hillocks where willow branches dipped into dark water and brushed stone benches. "You heard, in Italo's own words, how they grappled, in deepening hostility. Claudia's tragedy is that she has outlived Italo, her protagonist is dead. She has been reduced, in her old age and illness, to live the rest of her life on the sustenance of spite."

We took a sloping path lined in places by cobblestones and fieldstone walls and approached a pond with a spouting fountain edged by swaying brownish reeds. I followed the priest out on an ornamental bridge that spanned the pond; the snouts of hungry golden carp broke the water's surface. He grasped its wooden railing and, looking straight ahead, said, "Mr. Temple ... Alger, if I may ..." his voice steeped in what could only be described as melancholy, "... I have had time to consider why Italo gave me the recording. At first, I thought of it as his confession. But I have concluded, after prayer, it was more. I now believe that his motive was devious."

He left the railing and crossed to the other side of the pond to sit on a low granite bench. I joined him.

"The recording was to remind me that I failed him, that I did not lighten his burden of pessimism and depression, and to spite me for my failure. He had to blame someone other than himself. He long considered himself a victim of fate's thousand cuts. Since I failed to provide him, an unbeliever, any solace he could accept, he mocked my failure, suggested my complicit guilt in the duplicity he found in his life." He sighed. "I forgive him but it is sad, is it not?"

I didn't respond since it seemed likely he would continue.

"Today in my talk, when I recalled that he could be a raconteur, witty, generous of spirit, I did not say it was often defensive in nature. But it was. Di Lampedusa wrote aptly, *He who has the courage to laugh is the master of the world, much like he who is prepared to die.* Was Italo following this dictum?"

We sat in silence, our gazes fixed on the play of light in the spray of the fountain, and I decided the priest should know of the loss of Palagi's assets in the Sugarman fraud. Shocked, he said Palagi would have been devastated.

"Perhaps the trigger to a suicide?" he said. I also told him that in addition to her legacy under Palagi's will, Claudia Cioffi benefitted from an insurance policy, *a tontine*, a policy that might have resulted from his fear of exposure.

He didn't react as I expected. Instead, he was silent as though lost in thoughts. Then, he said, "Tell me, are you familiar with *Aida*? The *libretto*?"

"Vaguely," I said, remembering the stage-filling Zeffirelli production at the Met from twenty years ago, complete with horses and elephants in the Triumphal March of the second act.

"You will recall a final scene when Prince Radames, condemned to death by Pharaoh for disclosing a military secret to the Ethiopians, the people of Aida, had the opportunity to be saved by Pharaoh's daughter who loved Radames despite his treason and his love affair with Aida. All he had to do was embrace Pharaoh's daughter and he would be saved. But instead Radames casts aside his chance to live and utters words that have always chilled me; *It is not death I fear, it is your mercy*. Such words seem so applicable."

To which of Italo or Claudia would these words apply? Or was it both?

35

HAD TWO MATTERS to deal with before leaving Congdon Street for Young Jimmy's exhibition match at the Dunk: seeing what could be done to obtain Palagi's autopsy report and a call to Arnie Gershowitz. I settled in a recliner in the loft, a Jameson within comfortable reach. The first call went smoothly. My contact with the medical examiner's office was a former client, now head of the Department of Pathology at City Hospital and a professor at the Carter University Medical School. I reached him at home, explaining my need, and asked for assistance. He promised he would call the medical examiner and let me know in the morning. Completing the call, I was pleased that I might have something positive to report to Benno.

As for the Gershowitz dilemma, I had a brainstorm that provided an additional benefit for a loan from the TF, had obtained Nick's concurrence by telephone, and had worked out the conditions in my mind. I called Arnie Gershowitz using the phone number from the card given to me by his mother. He was at his home and fortunately, his brother Simon and his family were there for Shabbat dinner. The brothers decided to use a speaker phone in Arnie's home office.

Shock treatment was required to get their full attention. I began with "You guys are crooks."

Gasps. Arnie croaked out, "You are accusing us ...?"

My voice, timely for a change, went into super-WASP mode. "Your financial records are worthless, your books don't balance." A dry cough for emphasis. "The homes' operating account is mixed in with the clients' burial trusts and has provided liquidity and paid operational expenses of the homes. And money was invested in the burial trust by third parties."

I could almost hear the thumps of their heightened pulses before Arnie shouted, "The books are good. I got back up!"

"You're telling me you never tapped the burial trust account for operations? That it is segregated and spent only for required burial purposes?"

Silence. Arnie must have pushed the mute button while he and Simon came up with an explanation. "It's simple," Arnie eventually said, his voice lacking conviction, "we had two accounts with Bernie. *A* was for the operations, *B* was for the burial trust. Somebody dies with a burial trust, we service the burial, we bury them, whatever, Bernie would send us the money from Account B." Simon must have said something I didn't hear because when Arnie continued, his voice had gone up an octave. "Sometimes ... we borrowed from one for the other. If A was short, we would hit B. If B didn't have enough cash, we'd hit A."

"That's fraud against anyone who signed a burial contract. In New York, I'm told that means ten years upstate. At least."

"Fraud! No way! All we tell the family is that we are going to guarantee *x* number of dollars for the funeral. So, Grandpa Stein dies and maybe the family wants something a little fancier for the coffin. There's always discussion, you know, salesmanship, every time somebody dies." *Salesmanship?* "Don't forget our expenses go up, too; some of these accounts were started years ago. The rabbi charges more for the service, the caterer has a higher fee, flowers aren't cheap, Caddies don't go down in cost, the kids want more of everything at the house, who knows? And inflation, right? This is not science, this is death!"

The family's way of doing business was pretty simple: make up the books as you go along, keep cash handy.

"My brother Nick said bringing in other investors is a federal offense, could bring in the FBI, the SEC ..."

Silence. I had been muted again.

"Arnie ...!"

His reply came over too loudly. "Back when the market broke in 2008, all the burial trusts lost money. Except us. We were with Bernie Sugarman. Mortie was the president of the Brooklyn Funeral Directors' Association and couldn't help himself in letting everyone know that we came through okay. After a while, every home in Brooklyn and Queens—out to the Island—was after us. 'How did you do it?' they wanted to know, they wanted in. Mortie knew that Bernie wouldn't take them in as clients because he didn't know them and they didn't have enough to invest. But, collectively? So, Mortie put their money in under our name, in account B, charged five percent to cover his expenses. When they needed funds for a funeral, Mortie would get a pay down from Bernie. He was only doing it for his friends."

"They don't know the money was invested with Bernie Sugarman?"

"No. Mortie made up a name: Charon Private Fund."

Charon, the ferryman of Greek myth who conveyed the souls of the dead across the River Styx? Did that late Mortie Gershowitz have a poetic streak?

"And you didn't tell Nick?"

"I ... didn't think it was important."

"Simon, if you're still listening, talk to your brother. You could be going to jail with him." I heard the intake of collective breaths. "Here's where we are. Your records are worthless, you're caught in a fraud ..." Arnie started to sputter but I kept talking, "... you have a case of the shorts. And ..."

"We'll do anything, Algy." I heard Simon's thin voice for the first time. "Anything!"

"Nick had found a lender, someone that owes our family a favor, before he learned your books had been cooked. Now, to go forward, the loan terms are more stringent."

"Algy, we need the money!" Simon again.

"Alright, this is what Nick will recommend to the lender. The burial trust is first. You deliver every burial contract to an accountant the lender selects, with all the details. And, a complete list of all investors, how much they put in, how much they think they've got in. Send that list of investors to me by e-mail. Tonight." That was only to get the ball rolling; I didn't much care who the investors were.

"But ...!" Arnie was back.

"Everyone. Got it? *Every single one.*"

"Okay, okay, no problem."

"Subject to further due diligence," I continued, "the lender will fund a line of credit for two million for the burial trust, advancing cash for payoffs to investors and obligations under your existing burial trust contracts. Tell the investors that Charon Private Fund has closed, will pay off the investors, one hundred cents on the dollar, plus whatever gains they think they have. Understand?"

"How's *that* going to work? What are we gonna say? How do we figure what is owed. All we did was take Bernie's gross number and apply it across the board."

I didn't respond until Arnie said, with heavy reluctance, "Okay, so they get paid off a hundred percent."

"Anytime you draw down on the trust fund for a funeral or make a payment to an investor, you and your brother will sign an affidavit as to the draw and where the funds are going."

"We can do that," Simon chimed in.

"You pay six percent interest on money advanced and that loan is outstanding for five years. Demand loan."

Arnie squealed, "*Six percent? Five years? Demand loan?* That's squeezing us dry!"

"Meanwhile, you get the burial trust in balance, pay down the debt, anyway you have to, from operations, selling real estate, from wherever, until it balances. Any deviations, Nick says, and his lender will call the loan."

"My mother, she told me ...?"

"Arnie, if you can do better, call me."

Simon jumped in. "Don't worry. We'll do it."

"As for security on the loan, the lender requires only personal guarantees from you both."

Their silence evidenced their surprise. They clearly expected harsher terms for security and waited for the other shoe to drop. Hearing nothing else from me, in a weak voice, Simon ventured, "So, what about the money for operations?"

"The homes will get a line of credit of one million."

Relieved sighs came over clearly.

"The lender wants to be fully secured, mortgages on the real estate, security interests on personal property, plus your guarantees. Interest rate is three over prime. Five year term for the loan, but it can be pulled at any time by the lender, for any or no reason, as a demand obligation. Monthly financial statements signed by both of you going to the accountant. Any screw up, any miscue, and the lender will foreclose." Then, I added the ball breaker. "Your mother will also guarantee the loan."

I heard choking. "What?" Arnie cried. "Ida will never agree. It's too much. It's a hold up!"

"Now, let me have that again: you don't want these loans?"

It must have been Simon who hit the mute button. Thirty seconds later, Arnie was caught telling his brother, "I didn't say that, I didn't say that! It's as hard as a rock, though ..."

"My mother ..." Simon's voice quivered with the thought of approaching Ida. "Does she have to sign ...?"

I paused for dramatic effect. This was my opportunity.

"Maybe I can get her off the guarantee *if* there is a show of appreciation."

"How so?" they chorused.

"Your Aunt Zelda lives very modestly on her teacher's pension and Social Security. Nothing really to spare. From now on, anytime Zelda gets a whim to go out, Ida insists a Cadillac man drives her door to door. If she wants to shop down the block, a Cadillac man waits for her, carries the groceries, whatever. And, it would be nice for Ida to buy her sister an ensemble of clothes for the wedding. And it would be great if this winter your mother takes Zelda to spas, treats her to a vacation in Palm Beach, buys her a fur coat, one that Zelda picks out. Gives Ida the chance to say that for years, she wanted to buy her sister things, take care of her, and now she feels she can because the finances of the homes are secure. And, she's so happy about the marriage!"

"Well, she is, of course, she is. We all are! We're family." They were a duet.

"But," I countered, "our trust in you, the deal, would be diminished if Zelda was not well-treated. A demand loan, remember, can be pulled anytime, for no reason."

"I don't know how Ida's going to react to that," Arnie said, sourly.

"Okay, she signs personally."

Their reactions were gurgles before the mute button was pressed.

"Nadie's in New York this weekend and likely to call her mother. Maybe Zelda will be overwhelmed with Ida's affection and support by the time Nadie calls."

I ignored their groans.

○ ❍ ○

I left a message on Nadie's cell phone to enjoy herself at her bachelorette events, that I would call in the morning, that I missed her, and that I was making progress on the loan to the Gershowitzs. I couldn't help wondering what plans she had for the evening.

At eight thirty, I began to change into more casual clothes for Young Jimmy's exhibition. But, a nagging thought stopped me. I *should* go, I had promised to be there but our discussions on the Zito loan might be time-consuming and require returning with him to the Billiard Club where the betting action would be bubbling like a champagne fountain at a wedding reception. No place for a Commission member. Better to wait until tomorrow, catch him at the Dunk after Benno and I inspected Palagi's condo.

o O o

About half way through *Ripley's Game* on Netflix with John Malkovich as the raffish, reclusive, and murderous Ripley, the loft's fax-printer beeped. I had forgotten my directive to Arnie and Simon to send me the list of investors in Charon Private Fund. I didn't need it for any purpose and was about to toss it into the waste paper basket when among the twenty or so names on the list, I spotted an address in Babylon Beach. Tucci Funeral Home.

I quickly found its website on my iMac. Tucci Funeral Home was a Long Island Tara in brick with white columns; the Tucci family operated a third-generation home, had earned a National Funeral Home Director's Certificate of Approval, and I noted, offered a discrete invitation for inquiries concerning pre-paid funeral services. For those interested, the earthly remains of Joseph Santoro could be viewed in Parlor #1.

Despite the hour, I called Benno who answered after several rings. I asked him what it might give us if we had an 'in' with the funeral home that took care of Maria Ruggieri. He said he might learn more about Maria Ruggieri and the funeral card. "You want a face to face?"

In that moment, I knew that all accused by Italo Palagi in his recording, the University defending Palagi's estate from the putative son, and the inquiry of Brunotti's alleged perfidy deserved boots-on-the-ground, eye-to-eye contact with all the players, in all the locales. Not just Babylon Beach. Italy as well. Was that a crazy idea? For the University, in Rome, I could directly confront Brunotti, question the halt in remittances of Palagi's royalties from the Italian bank that collected them, maybe even confront the son's lawyer in Rome. For me, and this was *so* speculative, a quick trip down into the Boot to confirm Palagi's account of the vendetta. But how and through whom? Had to be Benno with his years of experience in organized crime and background on all things criminal emanating from Southern Italy. A man of many contacts. Benno's interest quickened as I told him more of what was on the recording he would hear tomorrow, my desire to come to resolution as to the manner of Palagi's death, what could I learn if a visit to the family of Maria Ruggieri could be arranged. He didn't respond immediately and I added my ante to his hesitation. "Do you have a passport?"

Then he said almost reluctantly, "Maybe, I know somebody."

So, has Chrysler engineering framed the rear seat of the Charger to prevent pushing through from the trunk?

A shoulder hit doesn't work. All right, how about those legs, those wiry muscular legs of which I am privately proud? Could I brace myself against the trunk lid and push out the back seat? My first try produced only grunts. Second try, only a quiver. Apparently, it is annoyingly well made. Then, a thought! "Brilliant!" I mouth. If I could get my arm through the slot from the back seat to the trunk, where the cross country skis fit through, I'd pull my jacket to me, use the cell phone in its pocket to call Benno, and get the hell out of here.

My fingers scrape for purchase on the edges of the slot, work so hard my wrist bones make clicking sounds. Finally, it opens. I thrust my arm through but can't come up with the goddamn jacket. Too far down the seat? Did it fall on the floor? I'd never reach it there. Was there anything in the trunk I could squeeze through the slot and use to fish around?

What had been jabbing my behind? An emergency auto fix kit. I find the clasp to the kit, flip it up, the top opens, and I feel screwdrivers, wrenches, and heaven help us, a flashlight the size of a cigar. When was the last time I checked its batteries? Ever? I click it on and a tiny, weak beam of light discovers a set of jumper cables still in a plastic casing tucked under the seat partition. With the flashlight in my teeth, using a screwdriver from the kit to punch through the casing, I rip off the packaging, squeeze a jumper close, thread it through the slot, and release it so that the handle could hook my jacket if it remains on the seat.

I whip the jumper around and it bangs off the side of the rear door on to the floor. I pull it in, get it back on the seat, this time it catches on the door handle. I shake it off the handle, retrieve it, get it up on the seat, where it snags on a seat belt. Where's the goddamn jacket! I jiggle it loose, that takes over a minute, and the jumper hits the floor. Once again, I retrieve the cable, whip it around on the seat, and it snares something. Hopefully not a seat belt. Please be the jacket! Can't let the jacket, or its precious cell phone, fall to the floor where I'd never get to it!

36 Saturday

DAWN WAS GRAY, RAINY, and windy. At six, I left Congdon Street. Leaves pasted themselves to the Mini as I drove down tree-lined Hope Street, over the Pawtucket line where Hope Street became East Avenue. The traffic was light but as mean as the weather: a turn signal was ignored by a car in front of mine pulling into a CVS, another blew through a stop sign at Rochambeau Avenue, and I got a horn blast for not moving three milliseconds after a signal change. I recollected a bumper strip I recently spotted that boasted *I'm from Providence and not that nice.* Welcome, pool players!

A mile farther into Pawtucket brought me to the Modern Diner, an authentic road diner with a classic Air Stream lozenge shape, a metal skin painted brown and yellow-cream accented by aluminum striping, and dining car shaped windows. I entered and found Young Jimmy Hannigan slouched at the counter, a spoon exploring his coffee mug.

"Hey, what are you doing here?"

No reply except raised eyes to the mirror facing him. His hair was uncombed, a stubble marred his pale cheeks, purple patches were pockets under his eyes. He said, "Club didn't close until four when we got everybody out and cleaned up." His head tilted toward me as I sat next to him. "Took in more at the restaurant than any night ... ever!"

A guy in a denim jacket and Red Sox cap pulled down over his ears sat at the far end of the counter and began scratching at a pile of Lotto instant game cards. At the curved rear of the diner three guys needing shaves, who might have been boozing all night, were finishing eggs and coffee. "How about breakfast?" I asked. "My treat."

A waitress appeared with a coffee pot and a mug. I waved off the coffee and she refilled Young Jimmy's. "What'll it be?" she asked and Young Jimmy ordered two eggs over easy, bacon, home fries, and wheat toast. I opened a menu that reflected the neighborhood, half up-scale, half blue collar, and I went for a caloric charge with the diner's linguiça, onion, peppers and three scrambled eggs special. "Skip the home fries," I said with reluctance. Our orders were called in through an opening in the wall to the kitchen, forks and knives wrapped in paper napkins were delivered along with glasses of water and an upside down ketchup bottle.

"Went home," Young Jimmy said, "couldn't get to sleep. So, I came down here."

He and Maria Catarina own a large colonial in the nearby elegant Oak Hill section of Pawtucket. I also knew that Young Jimmy could sleep through WWIII.

"Something's up, right?"

"Nothin'," he replied grumpily. His face gave his lie away.

I edged closer. "Are you pissed at me because I wasn't at your exhibition ...?"

His long-fingered hands supported his chin. "I got to tell you. Thursday night, I played so-so but I won. Nothing much. George Mikos. He played like shit. I could have beat him one-handed. But last night, I should have lost to Stevey Romero. You heard of him? Ranked pro. And I beat him! Big crowd, almost as many watching us as the Shoot-Out matches upstairs. He made some good shots but some dumb ones too. It was like ... I don't know ... like he didn't want to win. Couple of times he should have put me away. In the third game, I left him with a hanger, all he had to do is nudge the two ball into the nine and it was over! He looked at it, went around the table to look at it again, looked it over one more time, and screwed it up by scratching. What the hell is going on here?"

"You tell me. What the hell *is* going on here?"

Heaping plates of breakfast arrived with a clatter. Young Jimmy splattered ketchup over his eggs and his fork became a machine while I took my time cutting up the linguiça, spooning the fried onions and peppers and ketchup on my eggs, waiting for him to resume his saga. He used his fingers for the bacon, mopped up yolk with toast, and finally opened up. His voice lowered to almost inaudible.

"What's bothering me is not how I'm playing, but the guys I'm playing against." He balled up his napkin and dropped it on his plate. "Then, I beat Salazar," he said slowly. He stared across the counter, his eyes catching mine in the mirror facing us. "At the Club, I mean."

My face squeezed into a squint. "Geezus, Jimmy ..." Immediately, I felt guilty for not being there last night. Emilio Salazar was a good player, but a first-class shark who could be part of any scheme that fluttered about c-notes. He once hustled me, big time, when I was suckered into a match at the Billiard Club.

Young Jimmy's voice rose, defensively. "Played to nine. Gave me the eight ball. How did I ever get that?"

"Who staked you? Ginger?"

It took fifteen seconds for a *yes* nod.

"How much?"

"Usual fifty-fifty. I got five grand."

"Are you nuts? Tell me something's not going on?"

"I figured the odds are pretty good I'm gonna get knocked out by a name, like a Salazar. I was an underdog against Romero and I won, but against Salazar? Why give me the eight? Had to be his ego, right? He had some decent runs but every time he's got some 'mo,' he died. Lots of noise from him, complaining about the table, the lights, bullshit like that, from him. So how come these guys are playing shitty and ... making bad bets?"

"Did you ask anyone? Ginger?"

"No, too embarrassed."

"So what about tonight?"

"Huh?"

"Are you playing tonight?"

"No." Then, he added less somberly, "Because I get introduced on ESPN. Before the finals. And I stay for the party afterwards. It's a big deal for me. The guys who run ESPN Pool invited me. Could be an opportunity. I hit it off with Seifert, too. Never know, right? Anyway, I'm beat to shit! The Club will be open, Ginger will run it, but I'm not playing." He paused, shaking his fork at my reflection in the mirror. "But here's the thing. Guys are talking about me, how I've been winning, who I beat. If I do good in the interview, there'll be even more buzz. You know how they focus on who you beat." He turned to face me; those blue eyes seemed magnified. "I've been shaking them all up. Me, after all these years. Can you believe it?"

I didn't want to rain on his parade but what are friends for. "What you win, it's going to pay off Zito's loan, right? And he's got a cut of the house action?"

"Who said?"

"Words out." I had to ask, "Why not me?"

"Because I didn't want to owe you."

"All you have to do is ask."

With a shrug, he returned to his coffee. "We just ran out of money when we had to put in all the fire-code upgrades. I told Maria Catarina not to worry, that I had it all covered. But I didn't. She doesn't know how tight it got ... that I had to go to Zito."

"You know he's a bad guy ..."

"A long time ago, Zito worked for one of my sweaters. I knew he knew pool. He's always been all friendly like and when I asked, he said, 'Sure, sure, no problem,' and I signed what the SOB gave me to sign. I was goddamn crazy to do it. Now, he owns me until I pay him off. Ginger's working the house for him." His head moved closer to mine. "I'm into him for two hundred grand, thereabouts." He shook his head wearily, his voice wrapped in despair. "He's got me by the balls. I make the payments to the bank on the first mortgage and then I still have to pay him. Nothing left for Maria Catarina and me. That's why I gotta win big when the pros roll into town next weekend. They'll bring in the whales. I'll get backers by then plus my own cash. What I win, I keep. I play, I pay down Zito, we refinance, we're home free."

Never happen. Not with Zito and his merry band of knee crushers. I didn't say that of course. "If Zito, or Ginger on his behalf, is backing you or lays down money on you, as an underdog, and the other player dumps, he wins twice, on his bets on you and when you pay him down. You're the gift that keeps giving."

"I've gotta do those matches. I'm gonna finish this off."

"Suppose you lose. Suppose Zito wants *you* to dump a match. What do you do?"

"I'm not. Can't."

"If Tuttle finds out, he'll be all over it, and Maria Catarina."

"She doesn't know how deep I'm in or that I played last night. I'm not going to tell her."

"She'll find out."

"I'll cross that bridge when I toss a roll of cash in her lap."

He was wishful and dead wrong. But there was more to his situation than a loan payoff. I saw expectation in his face. I said, "You ... want to play, don't you?"

"After the Gala and who I beat, by the time the pros roll in, the news on me coming back will be everywhere. I'll keep a low profile, practice up, I'll get backers, some fat matches. My last chance, you know what I'm telling ya?"

I persisted. "Even if you want to, you can't back out?"

"Are you crazy? On Zito?"

He swallowed the last of his coffee, stood, found loose bills in his jeans pocket and tossed them on the counter. Breakfast was no longer my treat. He stared at me with eyes that were tired and worried. "Algy, I need you to stay out of this. I mean it."

He left.

He was drowning and didn't know it.

37

I DROVE BACK HOME, thinking this was the day summer became fall, when the wind and wet whittled away at the ash and plane trees on Congdon Street, took down the first of the maple leaves, leaving only the oaks with their browning foliage. I picked the plastic-wrapped *Journal* off the front walk and took it out to the den.

On Saturday mornings, I look forward to *Journal* columnist Bill Reynold's potpourri of wry comments on the week's sport news and jibes at politicians and the famous for being famous. He led off with a zinger aimed at his alma mater. *Hey, Bunky, don't forget, in 1492, Columbus sailed the ocean blue.* Further on, he asked, *Will Carter University sponsor a Native American float in the Columbus Day parade?* and *Is Carter University digging trench lines and fox holes on The Green?* Fair enough.

More Columbus Day noise came in two side-by-side Op Ed pieces, one from a faculty senate member in favor of the name change, the other a rebuttal by the president of the Italo-American Society. The first was condescending babble; the second had the ring of 'falsetti.' The dialogue reminded me of opera, maybe Verdi's 'Sicilian Vespers,' two tenors on either side of the stage engaged in wild gesticulations and high-pitched threats. Our Columbus Day controversy had all the theatrical traits of opera: it was tragic, illogical, and famously emotional.

○ ◯ ○

In the next two hours online in my office in College Hall, I booked travel arrangements on Alitalia to and from Italy and engaged the concierge service in Rome that the Temple family often used for hotel and transportation in Italy. The schedule was tight, leaving Sunday night and returning Thursday night if no hiccups. I rated accomplishing anything significant in Rome as fifty-fifty but worth the effort; as to getting anyone to talk to us in Basilicata, I had to rely on Benno's enthusiastic assurance of last evening that through his relatives—"my family is all over Puglia"—arrangements would be made if at all possible. That was enough encouragement to play Palagi's recording to obtain the name of Maria Ruggieri's village—Gianosa d'Acri—in Basilicata and book a continuing flight from Rome to Bari, the seaport capital of Puglia, which had the closest airport to the village. According to the online *il grande carta stradale d'Italia* published by the Touring Club Italiano, Gianosa d'Acri, a dot on the map, was about forty kilometers over the provincial border.

Then, I e-mailed Brunotti and the senior administrator of the Institute's campus in Rome. I would be there sometime on Tuesday; that if Brunotti could not make himself available to me, there would be consequences. I also directed his office to attempt to make an appointment with Vittorio Ruggieri's lawyer in Rome— Avvocato Maurizio Musumeci, according to the demand letter I had received—on Wednesday or Thursday morning for "discussions." As to the remittance bank in Rome, a call to the Bursar's Office produced the name, Banco di San Paolo; I would need the Provost's assistance to arrange a meeting. If these efforts to meet at the bank and the lawyer failed, I intended to arrive at both unannounced with sufficient self-importance to force interviews. Almost as an afterthought, I e-mailed Father Pietro, by now in Rome, hoping that he had not changed his college e-mail address, and invited him to meet me for a morning coffee on Wednesday at my favorite café near the Piazza Navona.

I felt rather pleased with myself. I was moving forward, and got further encouragement when my friend at the Medical School texted me "Appointment at two pm at ME office. Dr. Fritz Savage. Good guy. Luck."

o O o

Benno waited for me outside Corliss Landing; he carried a valise under his arm as we walked to its archway entrance. A dank southeast wind off the Bay beat against us, carrying a whiff of petroleum from the fuel depots in the harbor. The rain had let up but the sky remained a sullen gray. Proudly, I told Benno I had an appointment at the Medical Examiner's Office that afternoon and asked how he did in shanty town across the river. "Later," he said and I was told, rather self-importantly, that his contact in Bari had proved to be very helpful. Likely, we would be set. He would know for sure tomorrow.

I slid the plastic key card given to me by Claudia Cioffi through a slot, was gratified by a buzz and the snap of the lock, and the iron gate slowly swung open. We climbed the stairwell immediately to our right and Benno pointed to security cameras on the second and third floor landings. Two angled corridors got us to the South Water Street side of the building and the door to Palagi's condo. Benno handed me latex gloves and we each put on a pair. I used the key and followed him into the kitchen where he opened the refrigerator. "Somebody's cleaned up," he said. "Empty." He checked the dishwasher. "Full and clean."

Together, we looked through a serving counter from the kitchen into a dining room–living room. I expected it to be overstuffed with a scholar's hoard of Italian antiques, artifacts, rare books, and artwork; instead, the room had about as much charm and lived-in feel as a model apartment: fake floral arrangements on a table, drawn beige curtains, four chairs set primly in front of place mats and settings at a dining table, Persian design rugs over a yellow pine plank floor, a suite of dark leather couches, a Bose CD player and a rack of CDs in a cabinet holding a large-screen television. Over an enclosed glass fireplace was a reproduction of a Carravaggio masterpiece *Boy with a Bowl of Fruit*. If I remembered my art history, the model was the artist's lover.

"Has to be a study, where he worked," Benno said, and we walked down a hall with three closed doors. The first opened to a spacious bedroom with adjoining bathroom, a double bed neatly made, with the telltale silk pajamas on its spread. Another Carravaggio, a print of the same boy model as Bacchus, was over the bed. A large walk-in closet was set with rows of suits, jackets and trousers, shelves and drawers of neatly arranged socks and underwear, mock turtleneck shirts Palagi fancied, and a rack of slip-on shoes. Benno searched a night table, found nothing of interest, then entered the bathroom and opened a mirrored cabinet filled with the usual bathroom needs, its top shelf of prescription medications in brown and red plastic vials. He inspected the containers, all without caps, reading labels aloud—no obvious opiates among them—and put them back. "All from CVS. Different docs," he said, and closed the cabinet.

The second door was the entry to the bathroom from the hall. The study behind the third door was crowded by a chair by a reading lamp at the window, a plain desk with an oversized computer monitor, a desk chair, a file cabinet, books lining three of the walls from floor to ceiling, and a beat-up leather valise on top of a side table. Only then did I realize there wasn't a trace of family or personal touches in the apartment, no photographs, for instance.

I sat at the desk; Benno went to the file cabinet. The desk top was clear and the right pedestal drawer was empty except for a plastic ziplock bag containing smudgy copies of both sides of a funeral card bearing the name of Maria Ruggieri, either typed or printed, and its envelope. Benno placed the bag in his valise for later inspection. The drawer on the left held pads of lined paper and two spiral notebooks with hard covers in a floral design I would characterize as *Florentine*. Neither had been used. I snapped on his computer and waited for its monitor to brighten.

At the file cabinet, Benno riffled through the top drawer. "Correspondence going back ... years..." and he held up a folder taken from the rear of the drawer. "This one for '07." He closed the drawer and opened the second, where he flipped through files. "Bills. Looks like Palagi has a mortgage on this place. Bank RI. Balance is one sixty-seven. Bank statements," he said as he removed one from the rear of the drawer. "Five years ago, he had almost four hundred thousand in Bank RI in checking and CD's." And then, one in front. "Last June. Bank RI shows direct deposits from Social Security, payroll and pension payments from the University, and a couple of hundred wired from an account at Bank of America. So, maybe eight thousand in total coming in. Get this, a balance of about ten in savings. From four hundred to ten thousand?" He went back into the drawer. "Whoa!"

"What?"

Benno took a folder to the chair by the window. "You're not gonna believe this. It's a copy of a promissory note. From Heritage Finance! Two hundred and fifty grand!"

"When?"

"June 5 of this year."

"Terms?"

"Payments due monthly," he said, reading and talking. "Interest rate is ... fifteen percent. Payable on demand."

"Fifteen percent? Wow!"

Benno gave me the note and returned to the June bank statement. "Whatever he did with the money from the loan, he didn't put it in his Bank RI account."

"Had to be the pay off of the vendetta!"

"The vigorish on two hundred fifty thousand times fifteen percent is ... around thirty-seven grand and change per year divided by twelve is ... about three thousand a month. Almost half his income goes as interest to Heritage?" Benno dug into the drawer and found the August statement for July which included a page of facsimiles of coded checks much reduced in size. "One for three grand and change to Heritage Finance on July 14. So, he was paying on the loan. But where's the proceeds?"

He handed me the statement. The signature on the July check to Heritage Finance, like all the others, was barely legible. "That loan file was just right there, in the front of the drawer. Couldn't be missed. Kinda strange."

His voice drifted away as Windows gonged from a pair of speakers by the monitor. I had come prepared with Palagi's birth date, social security number, and father's and mother's first names, and his birth place. I tried to log on without success with I-T-A-L-O and P-A-L-A-G-I, and then added numbers, and lucked out with I-T-A-L-O with the year of his birth. Icons were arranged in a single row on the screen's left side. I checked his site use history and a list filled the screen. The names were dead giveaways: homosexual pornography sites. Geezus!

I opened a few sites that seem to have been favorites and most involved young men. Benno, over my shoulder, exclaimed, "Look at that shit!" I felt like a voyeur. Further down the list were two gambling sites based in Antigua; each had a sub-site linked into Italian football betting. A separate PIN was needed to gain access.

"So ..." Benno mused, "Palagi's into queer porn and betting on Italian football. What a guy!" he said, his sarcasm mixed with disgust while I focused on our mission. I was thinking: *How did the loan proceeds get to the 'Ndrangheta? By a Heritage Finance check to him endorsed over to some front? A cash payment to the New York cell? A direct payment by Heritage Finance to the 'Ndrangheta account at Ravensford Capital?*

Benno returned to the filing cabinet as I turned off the computer and emptied the contents of Palagi's valise on the desk. Pens, pencils, a pad, and a notebook, like those in the desk drawer, fell out. The notebook's cover evidenced usage with the word *Montecristo* raggedly printed in ball pen. I flattened it out on the desk and opened to lined pages with wobbly columns of numbers left to right across pages, monthly dates beginning six years ago, credits and debits by months, and totals on an annual basis at the bottom of each page, repeated at the top of the next page. The printing was crabbed and shaky, with transpositions, cross outs, and corrections in different inks, even pencil on occasion. The last page of numbers indicated a balance of €1721.06, but no date. The prior page, from a year ago, had a balance of €35,601.70.

"Can you decipher any of this?" I asked.

He took the notebook, thumbed through the remaining pages, and showed me a page with *Brunotti* spelled out in a rough cursive and holes smeared with ballpoint stabbed through the name on the thick paper, like what an angry kid might do with a ball pen. The following pages contained numbers and dates, most within the last two years, in barely legible writing.

"What do you make of it? 'Montecristo'?"

"His record of Brunotti's fraud," Benno answered matter-of-factly. "Brought it home when he learned that Brunotti had been in his files."

Benno's solution was elegant. The timing would be right with the first set of columns of numbers starting just after Brunotti becoming *Direttore*; the meaning of the second, more recent set of numbers less clear.

"Anything else?"

"Nothing. I ..."

His response was interrupted by a loud rap on the condo's door. Then another, louder, more impatient. Benno looked at me, put the notebook, a handful of bank statements, the file containing the copy of the promissory note, and the latest correspondence pack into his valise, which he slipped under his arm. I turned off the computer, closed desk drawers, and with a last look around, we left the office with our latex gloves stuffed into our pockets. I shouted "hold on" as a key from the outside was turned in the lock.

The door opened and I was brushed aside by a uniformed security guard. "What are you guys doing in here? Hey, didn't I see you the other night?"

I identified myself, showing my driver's license and University ID card. Benno opened his wallet to display his PI license. The guard grunted, "So, what's the story? This place is off limits until somebody tells me differently."

"Well, it isn't to us," Benno said confidently. "This condominium is part of Mr. Palagi's estate. The University is his beneficiary. We're doing an inventory on behalf of his estate."

"That cuts nothin' with me." The guard fingered the cell phone on his belt. "Until somebody tells me you're authorized, you're not. I'm gonna take a look around and you're comin' with me."

"Sure," Benno said loudly to the guard's back as we followed him down the hall, "good idea." Benno's expression indicated I was to play along. To me, he said loudly, "As far as I'm concerned, Mr. Temple, the condo and its contents are protected. I don't see any reason why you need any special security here. It appears that *Mr.* Riley"—that was the name on the plaque over the guard's left blouse pocket—"has everything under control." At the door to the office, *Mr.* Riley turned to stare at Benno. "Did you say Bacigalupi? Have I heard of ya?"

"Could be. State police for twenty-five years. Yourself, retired from ...?"

"Providence. Put in my twenty. Sergeant. I'm on disability though. Broke my foot in a chase. Some little bastard ..."

"I bet nobody gave you a medal for that," Benno said sympathetically.

"You're goddamn right!" he replied and turned to me, a civilian, for recognition of his public service. I smiled appreciatively.

Benno said, "As far as I'm concerned, we can go as soon as *Sergeant* Riley checks the place out."

"Yeah," *Sergeant* Riley said, but didn't advance into the office. Instead, with his eyes still suspicious of me—after all, I didn't share the brotherhood of blue—he said, "Next time you guys want to come in, you check with me or who's on duty, right?"

"Right," replied Benno, "but I don't think we'll have to be here again." And he laughed, "Especially on a Saturday. We should get double time for this detail."

Sergeant Riley grinned, "Wouldn't be bad duty. We got air conditioning in the office, nice TV." He gestured down the hall, we left the apartment, I locked up, and he accompanied us down to the courtyard, all the while giving Benno an earful on his career in Providence, his son's lot as a patrolman in Cranston, the pains in the butt that make up the disability board, the threat of a pension reduction because the city was so cash poor. Benno had a new friend.

At the curb by his Taurus, Benno inspected the copies of the funeral card's front and back. "Somebody wanted to throw a scare into Palagi and succeeded. The Giambazzi's *could* do it but it's not like the 'Ndrangheta to be so subtle. From what we know, I put my money on Claudia Cioffi when she learned of the vendetta. Out of spite. I'll go through the rest of the stuff later," he added and used a key to unlock and open the trunk. He leaned in and removed what I immediately recognized as Palagi's distinctive walking stick, its silvery knob covered in plastic. Benno, who allowed himself a smile at my reaction, dryly asked, "Ever been in a shanty town?"

38

THE DEBATE OVER THE future design and infrastructure of Providence created the opportunity for a homeless encampment under the ramp of an abandoned portion of the Route 195–Route 95 bridge intersection. The city could not decide whether to knock it down or use its abutments as the base for a footbridge across the Providence River, to join the 'right' bank anchored in the bio-medical Knowledge District to the trendy 'left' bank on South Water Street. Could be our Pont des Artistes, said Mayor Tramonti's optimistic planners who envisioned a walkable urban span; from one side of empty to the other side of empty countered critics dismayed at the estimated construction cost. During the dithering, the shanties arrived and stayed.

The Taurus jumped a broken curb and parked behind a boxy, rusty VW wagon held together with bumper stickers for various causes. We got out, rain spitting again, Benno with the walking stick, and we plodded across beaten down, rutted, weedy ground to a collection of tents and lean-tos of framed plastic sheeting, plywood, and roofing materials in a ring of Porta Potties and centered on a huge Army surplus tent marked *Office*. The hum of a generator located the power source for lights strung from shanty to tent to shanty. I expected the squat to smell to high heaven but it didn't; in fact, the only odor was that of fried food coming from a tent with a stove pipe piercing its canvas roof. Despite the dismal weather, a pregnant cat cleaned herself under a card table at the entrance of the Office where a bald guy in a sleeveless fleece and jeans, and badly needing skin care, played solitaire. We waited for him to look up but he didn't.

Benno impatiently pulled aside the tent flaps without protest from the sentry and we entered. The furniture on a plywood floor consisted of a metal desk, a couple of flimsy beach chairs, two canvas camp chairs, a cot, a file cabinet, and a table with piles of clothes; a single mega watt bulb hanging from a tent pole lit the interior. A voice from outside shouted, "He's comin'," and seconds later, the tent flaps parted for a thin, ponytailed man in his forties with a black Pancho Villa mustache under a nose like a turnip, greenish eyes in a kindly round face, in a sleeveless sweatshirt over a plaid work shirt, jeans, and thick soled boots. He addressed Benno. "You're back."

"Yeah, like I said. Ray, meet Alger Temple. He's got an interest in this stick your guy found." Benno held up the walking stick like it was a royal mace.

Ray shook my hand. He said, "I picked up Joe this morning. I'll bring him in," and left us.

Benno explained that Joe Riposa had been in detox at General Hospital drying out. He snickered, "Funny name, huh, for a bum. 'Riposa.' Rest ..."

We sat on the camp chairs; I gestured to Benno that I wanted to inspect the walking stick and he passed it to me. Stained hardwood tapered to a half inch diameter and a knob with an intricate design of sharp-edged rosettes and flourishes below the worn features of what could be the head of a lion or leopard. I remembered that Palagi was an admirer of di Lampedusa, the author of *The Leopard*.

Ray returned with a scrawny, wheezened, jaundiced-faced man about fifty with thinning white hair plastered over his scalp, wearing a clean denim shirt, leather vest, jeans, and new white sneakers. "Joe Riposa," Ray said. "Joe, I told you about these folks. They're not after you. But they wanna know about that cane you brought in."

We got up to shake Riposa's gnarled hand. He smiled nervously, revealing pinkish gums holding a few crooked teeth and a space where a bridge would have helped; his rheumy eyes and yellowish skin tone evidenced his life before detox. He lowered himself, arthritically, into a facing beach chair while Ray butted up against the desk. "So, wha' ya wanna know?" Joe asked warily. "I didn' do no'hin'." His *th's*, and *g's* were lost in his lack of front teeth.

Ray, his arms resting across his chest, said patiently, "Just tell them what you told me. Don't worry. It's still your rent."

His ward cleared his throat. I expected a glob of phlegm until he loudly swallowed it.

"So, dis is wha' happened. I was in bad shape, see. I got a habit, ya know? I was strun' out so I can't come here, so I was across da river, over by Hard Core, a crummy night, fog like shit, nobody's out and I couldn't catch no'hin'."

He sniffed, found a handkerchief in a back pocket, and blew his nose before continuing.

"I see dis old guy, he's kinda stooped over, in the fron' row of Hard Core's lot. Has dis cane." He nodded toward the walking stick. "Bangs on a car window. Door opens, he goes in dis car. I figure dere's some kind of meetin' goin' on so I hung around. After a coupla minutes, da horn blows, a big guy comes over from Hard Core, opens da door, and pulls on da old guy. He's strugglin' and t'rows som'em, like pocket change, inside, and runs his cane across da car door. Big guy goes bananas, pushes 'im up against da pole of da canopy, I figure he's gonna get 'im good when som'body in da car shouts som'hem and da big guy hustles da old guy down da sidewalk, keeps right behind 'im, into da fog. I follow 'em down to da Barrier. Da fog lif's for a second or so and I see somebody's at da end of da fence, and then da fog closes up. I was gonna wait..." he stopped and looked at Ray, "...but I was ya know, really sick, needed some s'uff bad, so I headed over ta Shoo'hers. Ya know Shoo'hers?"

"Yes," I said. Shooters was a boarded-up night club at the head of the Bay next to the tugboat basin.

"Figured I'd get some s'uff, and a place to sleep. And I did. So nex' day, I'm walkin' by, gonna bum some change downtown, when I remember da old guy, and I go by da river and dere's dis cane next to a flat rock by da water." He took the walking stick from Benno's hand. "Saw dis shiny knob, looked pretty good, so I figure I could buy in here. Gave it to Ray as an advance but I got pulled in for D 'n' D. Got sent to City. Dat's all."

Like Benno, I believed him. I asked, "Did you see the big guy again? Was it him at the fence?"

"Man, I was slammed. Sick. And da fog. I can't say but som'body bigger den da old man."

Benno asked, "Anything else you remember, Joe?"

"Naw, sorry. Wish I could help youse out." Joe grinned his toothless grin and looked at the sleeves of his shirt. "One t'ing, when you come outta City, you always get new duds."

Ray confirmed Joe Riposa brought the walking stick in for rent on a Thursday morning, was strung out, that it is against the rules to stay at the camp when you're drugged up, so Joe had left it as an advance.

Benno shook his head, signaling we were done with Riposa. He took out his wallet and counted out five twenties which he handed to Ray.

"You gave me Joe's rent yesterday ..."

"Yeah, but now I got resources." He shrugged toward me.

○ O ○

In his car, Benno placed the walking stick tip down, its knob leaning toward the passenger seat, and got in. I joined him as a spatter of rain hit the windshield. I said, "Palagi was under duress right before he went down the embankment."

"Yeah."

"Whomever it was could have ..."

"Yeah."

"... helped him into the river ..."

"Yeah."

"For Christsake, all you can say is 'yeah'!"

"Yeah, and I'll tell you why. You got a Cambodian fisherman who doesn't speak English who saw an old man with a cane go into a car and a stoned homeless guy who thinks he saw somebody hustled down South Water Street. I keep telling you that you don't have a credible witness who actually saw somebody with Palagi at the river."

"But, the car," I argued, "with the connection between Palagi and Zito because of the loan, it had to be Zito's Bentley and his bodyguard that rousted Palagi and pushed him down toward the Barrier. C'mon, Benno ... ." I knew I was right!

I saw a ghost of a smile on Benno's lips. "Remember what I told you about shoe leather?"

"Yeah." My turn to be monosyllabic.

He carefully removed the plastic cover over the knob of the walking stick. "Look close. See anything?"

I turned it slowly. Nothing looked out of the ordinary, then I noticed that two of its elaborate rosettes were filled by spots of a dark color. Grit? Paint? I held the knob up to the window to catch the pale light. The color was black ... or maybe a very dark green? From a Bentley?

"The plastic is only so the paint doesn't come off. Could never get into evidence. Handled by too many people. Any shyster lawyer would have a field day. But there's a guy in East Providence who works on cars. Show him a color, he'll get the formula, tell us from what car, what year. Too bad, he's got a record. I put him away for two years for accessory to grand theft auto, so he's nothing as a witness. He's expensive but good at paint. If he says green from a Bentley, you got something."

"Whatever it takes," I said.

At least we agreed on something.

o O o

Later, in my office, we listened to Palagi's recording. Benno didn't comment until the recording finished. "I'd have liked to have been there. See him. I bet he was reading from something. All down too pat, like it was a script." As I returned the recorder back to the safe, I made a full disclosure as to my run-in with Frannie Zito.

"I always thought you had it together," Benno said sourly. "But I was wrong. You don't. That was nothing short of stupid. You embarrassed Zito by taking that Commission appointment, called him out with that stupid ride. He can't let that go unchallenged. You gotta call Tuttle. He asked you to. You're a Commission member; maybe he'll park a patrol car in front of the house."

"I don't want to alarm my fiancée. I'd have to tell her."

"Then, tell her, for Christsake, before Zito shoves a poker up your behind!"

39

THE MEDICAL EXAMINER'S OFFICE that I imagined as I drove to Randall Square would be in a nondescript building with a loading dock and some delivery doors in the rear. Its examination room would be cluttered by dissection tables, sinks and troughs, chemical hoods, scales, surgical carts and gurneys, shelves full of plastic tubs and shiny metal containers; large amounts of disinfectant would barely cover up corporeal decomposition, a noisy ventilation system of ceiling fans and air filters would be on full blast and leave a trace of carbolic acid. Its walls would be glossy with an easy-to-clean paint treatment, the floor would be tile with strategically placed drains. Hoses would be rolled up on hooks. Probably computers, recording devices, maybe a video system, and refuse bins with plastic liners. The stainless steel 'cooler' would be down the hall.

All of this comes from reading too many Patricia Cornwell thrillers, watching *CSI*, and my one autopsy experience, a visit to the NYPD morgue along with three other fledgling Manhattan DA prosecutors to view an autopsy of a crime victim who sustained 'massive cranial trauma.' What I remember most of that morbid hour were the butch females who squirted testosterone in their morning coffee, the kinky male techies filling the role of white-coated Igors. In the examination room, the sheet over the body was removed to reveal a young, white male, with a skin color that made his hair and eyebrows darker, his genitals tucked away, and filmy eyes open in a skull that had been caved in. I was nauseated with the first Stryker bone-saw application to the scalp and was the second of the four of us to hack my way out.

The Rhode Island Medical Examiner's Office turned out to be an ordinary looking three-story office building, brick with a flat roof, and large parking lot empty on this dreary afternoon except for an SUV with an *ME* license plate, a white delivery van similarly registered, and two or three cars. At least, I got the loading dock and delivery doors right.

A disinterested guard signed me in after checking my name off a list, gave me a badge, and I took the elevator to the second floor as she picked up a phone to announce my arrival. No smells or buzz sounds penetrated here, the walls, clad in gray vinyl, were even bare of a state office's ubiquitous inspirational posters. The receptionist's desk was unoccupied and I waited there until a tall, ruggedly handsome, fiftyish man, receding white hair, tinted glasses, dressed in casual clothes, greeted me. "Mr. Temple?"

"Yes."

"Fritz Savage," he said, extending his hand, which I pumped vigorously. "Sorry for the short notice. Come into my office." I did as bidden and was directed to sit at a small conference table in front of a thick manila folder. Diplomas lined one wall; color photographs of mountains in winter and smiling children in ski regalia were the other principal wall decorations. His tone was neutral, professional. "As I believe you are aware, there is a procedure to obtain our records."

"Yes, I am but ..."

"And you are aware that Mr. Palagi's body has been delivered for burial."

"Yes."

"I understand that you, as University Counsel, were both a colleague and a friend of the deceased."

"Yes." Why the interrogation? Was he making a protective voice recording?

"I also understand that the University is the principal beneficiary under his will. I further understand that you are asking to review our records in your official capacity."

What official capacity? What did my friend say to him?

"You should be filing a written request and I understand you will do so promptly, that this accommodation to a colleague is irregular but under the circumstances seem to be within the broad discretion I have. Until your request is received and approved, I am unable to provide a copy of our records." He pointed to a manila folder. "However, I am leaving it here while I attend to some other duties." He stood. "No notes please. I'll be back in … fifteen minutes?"

I was not sure if I should verbally acknowledge his gesture of goodwill, so I merely nodded as he left the room and sat before the folder. Palagi's name was hand-printed on its front next to a series of boxes that gave choices in the manner of death: natural, homicide, accidental, and undetermined. *Accidental* was checked.

Inside the folder, clips fastened a dozen or so sheets of paper to each side. The cover sheet on the left was marked *Preliminary Report* and was unintelligible in its columns and checked off boxes with codes. The following pages in plastic sheets consisted of color images of Palagi, some taken by an overhead camera, front, back, each side. His skin was bluish, appearing to be drained of blood, with reddish blotches and maybe scrapes, genitals shriveled, a slab of meat with a paunch. The head and face showed bloat in Palagi's distorted features that had wiped out years of wrinkles and creases. His lips were pulled back to yellowish, chipped teeth, a contusion marred his right temple, scrapes streaked his chin, cheeks and jaw with flecks of what might be dry blood. His nose seemed larger than I remembered. Most chilling were his open, milky, opaque eyes.

Behind the images was a transcript of a terse pathologist's narrative of the state of the body recorded during examination, and descriptions of chest incisions, stomach contents, and removal of organs like the liver and pancreas. A note was made to further examine the pancreas.

The top sheets on the right side of the folder contained statistics on Palagi's general physical characteristics, like weight and height, a description of injuries, body temperature as found, swollen hands, and facial bloat. I flipped to a list of what he wore as found: dark trousers, white mock turtleneck shirt, black suspenders, black socks, one saddle loafer, cotton undershirt, and silk boxer shorts. In a pocket, the Beretta, in another, a single cartridge.

The next pages' prose had a disinterested precision. Abrasions to his skin were considered post-mortem as unbloodied, maybe from a bumpy ride on the bottom of the Providence River. The contents of his stomach and analysis of blood were consistent with a pizza dinner, alcohol, and a lethal dose of opioids; the amount of water in his lungs was noted. A gas chromatography test and narcotics screen confirmed the wine and the opiates. Measures of body lividity, flaccid rigor, and decomposition concluded with an estimated time of death within a six hour span on Wednesday night and early Thursday morning; a cardiac examination indicated an infarction, probably in the act of drowning.

The last pages described his organs. Apparently, only the pancreas has been examined critically, with findings of multiple tumors, one identified as an advanced carcinoma.

I sat back. *Pancreatic cancer.* The dreaded cancer that came on quickly, was painful in extreme, and rarely survivable. That could explain the change in Palagi's appearance and demeanor, his possession of painkilling opiates. His horrific cancer reminded me of the Harpy's devouring the organs of their victims.

I reviewed the entire report once more, trying to memorize what I could for Benno's use, before Dr. Savage returned. When he did, he said, "Through?"

"Thank you for your courtesy." I slid the folder across the conference table toward him.

"I don't know, frankly, what you're trying to accomplish."

Truth be told, I wanted to find a homicide. Can't admit to that.

"The cancer. Was it operable?"

"If you mean could it have been surgically removed, possibly, but ill-advised. At his age, it was very likely fatal. We didn't go far enough to test whether it had metastasized, but given the cancer's location and size, it seems likely."

"The OxyCodone. Could Palagi accidently ingest as much as indicated in the report, say in his apartment, then walk to the river, become unconscious, and simply ... fall in?"

"This drug in the amounts ingested would make him lose motor control quickly, and he'd be unconscious within a very short period of time. Perhaps three to five minutes at the outside. He couldn't have walked very far after ingestion. Everything would slowly stop. His heartbeat would be lowered. If he was sitting, he very likely would fall forward. If he fell forward, he could have hit his head and if at the river's edge, rolled in."

"I guess he could have gotten enough of the drug ... legally ... in view of his cancer?"

Dr. Savage's replies became wary, perhaps even exasperated. "Mr. Temple, I know absolutely nothing about the deceased except from reading his obituary, and what little my colleague added. I don't know the source of the drug. Technically, as our report indicated, he didn't die of an overdose. His heart gave out, likely when in asphyxiation. The water in his lungs, even though slight, means his lungs were still working while he was in the water, when and where his heart gave out."

He picked up the folder, shuffled its contents, signaling our interview was over. "Last year," he said, "we had one hundred ninety deaths from overdoses of prescription drugs. More than from car accidents. On a per capita basis, Rhode Island is highest in New England for opiate deaths. We are in an epidemic. Staggering amounts of OxyCodone and hydrocodone—that's in Vicodin—are available from legitimate sources like local pharmacies that fill thousands of dosage units each day. We have seven thousand health care providers licensed to prescribe controlled substances—doctors, dentists, nurses, even veterinarians. Corrupt doctors, negligent retail outlets, and pain centers are also to blame. And then there are stolen drugs. The technical term—it's on our website—is *opioid analgesics*. Death from these far exceed overdose deaths from crack cocaine, heroin, or methamphetamines combined. The victims are often depressed and if you combine antidepressant drugs with prescription opioids, it increases the opioids' effect. As a cancer patient, Mr. Palagi may have been taking an antidepressant as well. The brain accepts them all."

I had a last question. "The contusion?"

"Yes?"

"Did he hit something or did something hit him?"

"Difficult to tell under the circumstances, but not likely life threatening."

"But if he was ..."

"Yes," he answered dryly, "I could speculate on a number of possibilities, none of which are, however, within the facts presented to me."

I left Dr. Savage with thanks and took the elevator to the ground floor where the guard requested my visitor's badge. An ambulance was backing up to the loading dock. A delivery.

I opened the Mini's door, and it was minutes before I put the key in the ignition. The medical examiner was satisfied with accidental overdose, so why shouldn't I be? Because I had heard the recording that rejected suicide, because Palagi carried a Beretta and a vial of OxyCodone, because of his connection to Frannie Zito and his Bentley, because, as Benno had suggested, if he committed suicide, the effete Palagi would do it in a manner consistent with his lifestyle.

Because, I didn't want to.

40

A S I TURNED INTO our garage on East Street, my cell phone vibrated with a call from Nadie. Instead of putting the Mini in the garage, I parked it in front so as not to lose the connection. As I walked into our house, I asked her, "What mischief did you get up to last night?" The other party goers, like her, were mid-thirtyish, one single, two married, one divorced and looking.

"Well," she gushed, "we got together at the hotel—rather too sparse by the way—and what a surprise, thanks for the flowers in the room. You are super! Lots of catching up over drinks at the martini bar downstairs, then dinner—okay—in the Lower East Side, with wine pairings. Got a little drunk at a place near Chinatown called Whiskey, and caught the last Diana Krall show at the Carlyle. Terrific! Got to bed after two."

"No guys buzzing around?"

"Funny you say that. Diane ran into an old flame at dinner and they were a couple when we left the Carlyle. So-o-o-o, *sans* Diane, this morning, we had a very late lunch, and then naps. Tonight, drinks, dinner at the Chelsea Grille and Amy who lives in SoHo says we should go to a place in the Meat Packing District called the Bunker ..."

"Sounds delightful ..."

"But Brenda wants us to go to a tango party, a *milonga*, where tango professionals teach and all the men dress in black. Like a Buenos Aires club, she says. I don't have high heels with me or the right skirt. Might have to splurge," she laughed. "How about you?"

"Exciting! Scintillating! After Palagi's memorial service, I was out on the town to watch the bottom slapping at Providence Roller Derby ..."

"You never ...!"

I explained that I was catching up on movies she wouldn't watch with me and then ventured into no man's, no-win land. "Heard Columbus Day is still on?"

"I suppose this *calendar* idea came from you. It's so like a lawyer." She said that without exasperation, which led me to hope that absence did make the heart grow fonder.

I heard a telephone ring and she said, "Take care, got to run, I'll call you in the morning, love you," and was off the phone. I smiled to myself. Gee, I didn't get the opportunity to tell her about Benno and me at Palagi's condo, or my visits to the homeless camp and the morgue, on this way-too-dull day without you, Nadie.

I smiled again until I thought how and when I would explain my departure for Italy tomorrow night, six days before our wedding.

I finished *Ripley's Game* with a pizza delivered by Pizza Pie-er and remembering Father Pietro's references to Palagi's essay on the novel *The Leopard*, I ordered it online for my e-book reader. If Palagi admired the novel, maybe it would provide insight into his state of mind. Within a few chapters of crisp prose, insightful characterizations and philosophic asides, I began to understand how someone like Palagi born into a highly stratified Italian culture, someone who suffered from psychological isolation or dysfunction, and was a victim of a betrayal of family or societal values, might defend himself and wound his enemies, even to the last breath.

I was about to turn in, I heard an echoing *thunk,* as though something very heavy had been dropped from fifty feet. I almost ignored it; then, another *thunk,* this one with more of a metal-on-metal crunch which caused me to remember that the Mini remained parked in front of the garage on East Street. I ran downstairs, left the house, turned the corner, and stopped cold.

The garage floodlights exposed the black hump of an elephantine refuse truck, headlights off, hydraulics squealing, engine roaring, with its snow plow blade under the Mini, heaving the car on to its side with, this time, a *thud.*

I yelled, "That's my car!" and ran down the incline, waving my arms wildly, reaching the running board on the driver's side of the truck's cab, banging on its door, getting my fingers on its handle. The truck pulled back, its gears grinding in reverse, brakes screeching, and then plunged forward with me clinging to the door handle for dear life, the plow blade tumbling the Mini onto its roof, blowing out its windshield and door windows in a shower of glass, its horn sounding in protest. The jolt loosened my grip, I dropped to the pavement and rolled away to avoid being run over by the behemoth as it backed away from the wreckage.

My mouth gaped, I had no voice, I staggered to my feet, trying in disbelief to get one foot in front of the other. My breath was gone—does your heart's pumping only get louder in your brain?—when with creaking gear shifts and brake squeals, the truck lurched down deserted East Street toward downtown. If the truck's cab or body had any identifying signage, I didn't see it; as for a license plate, it was either missing or unreadable in the dark.

I stared at the ruin of the Mini realizing that its flattened roof meant the car was a total loss. The horn remained on full blast and I felt the scrapes and bruises on my right leg and arm picked up in my fall. Slowly, I grasped the thought that this wasn't some random act of violence. A refuse truck with a lowered snowplow blade running amuck on the streets of Providence in October? This was payback.

I went inside to call 911 and was answered by a recording asking for English or Spanish, stating my call was important, and to stay on the line for the next available dispatcher. It took two minutes. When I got a human being, the incident sounded strange in its telling. After I repeated that I wasn't injured, the dispatcher told me to call the Providence police and gave me a phone number. I followed instructions, twice explained what had happened to the police operator and was told to stay put until a patrol car arrived.

I went back to the wreckage and took photographs with my cell phone camera until a patrol car came down East Street, its strobe lights flashing off houses and stone walls and the wreckage. A muscular looking young cop brandishing both a night stick and a long black flashlight left the cruiser, checked out the flattened Mini from all angles to make sure no one was inside, put his head under the popped hood, yanked at a wire, and shut off the horn. All the while, I urged him to send out a stop-on-sight bulletin for a black refuse truck with a snow blade.

He ignored me and called his dispatcher as neighbors ventured out to view the commotion. A tow truck from East Side Service Center then arrived, its bank of spinning yellow lights adding to the garish show, followed by a second patrol car driven by the precinct patrol sergeant whose chest nameplate read Spinelli. I repeated a demand for a stop-on-sight order and got nowhere. I shouted, "The goddamn truck could be in a garage in Pawtucket by now!" as a larger tow truck with more yellow lights flashing rumbled in off Congdon Street. While Spinelli spoke with the patrol cop, the tow drivers found a way to wrap cables around the Mini's carcass, the truck's winch groaned and screeched as the squashed-like-a-bug car was dragged up steel treads into its bay. Goodbye, Mini.

Spinelli took down my name and address, time of incident, where I was, truck description, noted my Carter University connection—that from the parking sticker on the Mini's bumper—and I answered cop questions like 'you got insurance?', 'you didn't see the face of the driver?' and 'didn't get a license plate?' My answers were noted as I repeated my request for a 'stop on sight' order for the refuse truck. He gave me a 'I know what I'm doin'' look and returned to his cruiser without an answer.

o O o

Benno had been spot on. Frannie Zito had escalated our situation. The Mini was the perfect target since I had called attention to it before the wild ride in the Bentley.

I poured a glass of Jameson, sat in our rarely used living room, and wondered what else I could expect from Zito, coming to grips with issues like Nadie's safety while I was in Italy, when my cell phone buzzed. "What the hell happened?" Chief Tuttle monitored the police radio on weekends.

"A refuse truck, no lights, no name, using its plow, flipped my car over on its roof. A complete loss."

"What's going on?"

"Don't know."

"Bullshit!"

"Really, no idea!" A shameless lie.

"Yeah?" Tuttle replied in a voice that reeked with disbelief. "You get on the wrong side of something? Columbus Day? Shoot-Out?"

"I assume that you've got your guys looking for a refuse truck with a snow plow …"

"It's Saturday night. Normal patrols. If a refuse truck is spotted, we'll stop it."

"Great, I feel so much better."

"Cut the snide remarks. We'll do what we can. Come in and file a complaint."

"I'm not."

"You got to file a complaint."

"Can't.

"Why?"

Had to think about that. "Believe me, it's better this way. An accident. I'll report it to the insurance company."

"Because …?"

"Something personal got out of hand."

"Shoot-Out or Columbus Day?"

"Could I ask you for something?"

"What?"

"Could you stick a patrol car on Congdon Street here for a couple of nights. My fiancée is here alone when I'm away Sunday to Thursday in Italy, and …"

"Not unless you tell me what's going on."

How would the tough cop, the straight arrow, react? With no alternative, I told him of the confrontation in Zito's Bentley, but didn't mention Young Jimmy's connection.

"I warned you about Zito," he said sternly and paused. "Okay, you'll get your surveillance. Better yet, suggest your fiancée spend the nights someplace else. Call Bacigalupi. This time, take his advice."

After anxious minutes, I have my hands on my jacket. The blessed cell phone is in the pocket. I quickly punch in Benno's cell number. He answers with, "Where are you?"

"Where am I? Where the hell are you? You're supposed to keep me covered!"

"You were supposed to wait for me!" he retorts.

"You couldn't follow two cars?"

He let seconds go by.

"I ... got pulled over," he replies sheepishly. "On Allens Avenue. Took five minutes to straighten out."

"I'm at the dump."

"The dump?"

"In the trunk of my car."

"What!"

"How well do you know the area?"

"I grew up in Knightsville two miles away."

"Go down Shun Pike, go over the hill and I'm someplace on the downslope, a dirt side road before the end. Keys are on the front seat."

"Who?"

"Just get here."

"Fifteen minutes. Just hold on for fifteen minutes. I'll be there."

41 Sunday

For me, sleep never solved any problem or answered questions. I woke as angry with myself as when I went to bed. In my stubbornness, I had jerked around a bad guy to the point of revenge. I screwed up. I have to thank my ego and inability to forget an insult. Maybe in addition to the language, I had picked up other Italian traits.

I brewed a double espresso and went to the basement to exercise vigorously on the NordicTrack, determined to puzzle out what to do about Zito, short of raising my arms in surrender.

Benno phoned after I showered and dressed. "I told you."

"I know."

"You hired me for Palagi, not for protection from Zito and Scuiglie."

"I know."

"You could end up in a wooden tuxedo if this goes on."

"I know."

"This is for free. I spent years dealing with the Hill guys. I got to know the 'old fellas,' the guys who had their own code. Used to be I'd go riding by one of their haunts, I'd even get a wave from some of them. Because we knew what we were doing, what our jobs were. They were going to break every law, I'd spend every day trying to catch them. But, these gangbangers? Zito is important to them because he can wash their money by making loans. If it's Zito, and it has to be, he'll stop only if somebody inside and tight tells him that he can't hit on you again."

"Who's that?"

He ignored my question. "This is what I can do. I can get the word out to that somebody that it's over. You forget finding that dump truck, file your insurance claim, concentrate on everything else that's going on, and stay out of Zito's face."

"You mean apologize?"

"No, just keep your yap shut."

In the scale of things, Nadie's safety was paramount. I agreed.

He changed subjects without warning. "Our contact is Gianmarco Barracelli, second cousin on my mother's side. Lives in Bari, in the import-export business, olive oil, wine, cheese, anything, and everything else, that moves. A long time ago, I was able to help out his wife's nephew who got into a scrape in Boston. DA decided that the nephew would do better at home than spending any more time here, if you get my meaning." I did.

"Anyway, Gianmarco's made calls today, located a cousin of Maria Ruggieri, and is getting some approvals. That's the way it has to be, he says, and he should know." Benno also said he had reviewed Palagi's bank statements and found that cash had been flowing out for a decade. "Constantly wiring out to accounts in Italy, three thousand here, twenty-five hundred there. Gambling, boys, what?"

I told him what I learned at the medical examiner's office from Palagi's charts. All he said was, "That's a bad cancer."

I thanked him for his success with his contacts in Italy and he replied, "Do me one favor. Never use the word 'Ndrangheta' when we are in Italy. Friend, *amici*, will do."

o O o

After lunch, I continued to make calls. First, to Arnie. Before I got the chance to explain the reason for my call, he breathily, said, "Algy, I spoke to my mother! Don't worry! You walk with the prophets. Zelda is getting new clothes, they'll be driven up to Providence for the wedding in an Escalade ...!"

I told Arnie what I wanted him to do. Several times, he interrupted with, "I don't get it," which I ignored.

A few minutes later, he returned my call. "I called Joe Tucci.

He wasn't enthusiastic, said that family is, you know ... connected?"

"And?"

"I promised nobody would know he snitched. Okay?"

"Okay."

"Says Maria Ruggieri lived on the Giambazzi family compound where she took care of Luigi Giambazzi's mother until the old lady passed, then was a nurse for his kids, and then grandkids, some of whom still live there. No visiting hours, only a couple of family members at the Mass and internment, 'No surprise,' he said, 'because the Giambazzis are notoriously cheap,' which is something he shouldn't say to too many people. I asked him about funeral cards. Said because there wasn't going to be a wake, he doesn't know if he made them up or not. But anybody could download a copy from the catalogue of any funeral home supplier."

After I contacted Amica Insurance to report the loss of the Mini, I called Marcie at home who overcame her curiosity about an unplanned trip to Italy to agree to make any necessary postponements in the office. The Provost, no surprise, was in his office in College Hall for a few hours of Sunday work without interruption. He quickly concurred with our trip and agreed to call the New York representative office of the remitting bank to set up a meeting. As for Brunotti, the Provost's only regret was that he would not be confronting *il Direttore* himself.

As to the continuing Columbus Day saga,—I hadn't given it any thought since last night—he said that in the intermittent rain of Saturday, Sonny Russo was at Carter Stadium before the Princeton game, leading a drenched chorus of a dozen or so in shouting 'one, two, three, four, Chris forever, as before.' "Poetic," he said.

Lastly, I called my brother who was in his firm's luxury box at Meadowlands watching a promising Giants team play the Colts. Banco di San Paolo, he said, was headquartered in Siena, had a lineage going back to the Renaissance. He warned that Italian bankers were fanatics about client privacy. He would, however, speak to the partner in charge of the firm's European banking operations who had a long-standing relationship with the Italian Ministry of Finance.

Then, he asked, "Was Nadie upset at your trip?"

I confessed I hadn't told her yet.

He sighed, "Are you sure you are ready for married life?"

o O o

Time to make *that* call.

I reached a happy and loquacious Nadie on her cell phone at a late lunch at a noisy restaurant. She left her friends at their table to talk to me, but the background din followed.

"Let me tell you about the Bunker!" And she described a cavernous dance club with high brick barrel ceilings, a crowd that was more disco than hip-hop, a female DJ that blew her away, and hundreds of half-naked strangers body bumping. "It's a wonder I can still hear," she laughed. "I could feel the music coming up through the floor!" She paused and spoke louder through the background clamor. "Yikes, it's already after two. Did Ida get the loan? Something's up. She is taking Zelda shopping tomorrow. A mother-of-the-bride dress, a chauffeured limo to drive them to Providence. Zelda's thrilled ..."

I heard Nadie called back to the table. "Hold on," she said and there was some chatter and the giggle I usually heard only after a second glass of wine.

"Nick has found a lender," I said. "They'll be saved, assuming they don't screw it up."

"Wonderful! Oh, Algy, thank you. Thank Nick. If you ever hear me complain about access to money, shut me up ..."

Fat chance of that but I appreciated the thought. I then told her of Father Pietro's invitation for a Vatican tour. She was surprised and delighted.

On a roll, I laid out the necessity of my quick trip to Rome, and I bombed! Her voice was strained in outrage, only her friends' presence at the table keep her from exploding: "How could you even think of being of away during the week of our wedding? Is Danby insisting?"

"An emergency, otherwise I would never go. The one-on-one with Brunotti has to be now. I can't tell you why but it's very serious. So is the bank meeting." As to Benno coming along, and the side trip to Bari and beyond, I decided these were confusing and unnecessary details.

"Are you sure, are you absolutely sure, you'll be back on Thursday?"

"Home not later than Thursday night! I promise!"

She swallowed hard in reluctant acceptance.

"Why not pack a few things and stay at my mother's while I'm gone. It's wedding central. You're always there these days. And she would love it."

"Not a terrible idea," she replied with some reluctance. "Anything else you want to tell me."

What was left of my secrets? The Mini and Jocelyn.

I couldn't dissemble as to the absence of the Mini but I could avoid Jocelyn. "Something not good and I was going to tell you. A truck broadsided the Mini late last night while it was parked in front of the garage. Hit and run. I should have put it in the garage but I forgot to do it. Had to be towed away. A total loss."

"Hit and run? Awful!" and she proceeded to loudly tell her friends who offered support. What was she going to use for a car before the wedding and if needed? I said she should rent one.

"When will you call me?"

"I land in Rome at seven or so on Monday morning. Six hours ahead of Providence. Not sure when I can call, but depend on it."

"I *am* depending on you."

Like me, depending on Tuttle and Benno to put a lid on my battle with Zito.

42 Monday

W E LEFT LOGAN INTERNATIONAL on Alitalia business class. Airborne, we turned away from the sunset that had transformed the city's skyscrapers into columns of gold. I asked Benno as to his Italian. "Rusty," he said "but I'll get along." That made two of us. Benno, surprisingly to me, enjoyed a half bottle of Barolo with dinner, and by nine o'clock had converted his seat into a recliner, and fell asleep immediately. I was too keyed up to sleep and read more of *The Leopard* and watched the varied offerings of a pop-up video screen, finally getting no more than an hour's rest before awakened for espresso, choice of breakfast rolls, and hot towels.

We landed at Terminal 3 of Rome's Fiumicino Airport in a crimson dawn. Our dazzlingly beautiful hostess, nameplate Rosetta, escorted first and business class passengers off the plane, down a corridor toward two lines of groggy arrivals at Immigration kiosks designated for non-EU arrivals where carabinari and fussy, uniformed inspectors checked passports. Customs inspection was without delay and with our carry-ons and valises in hand, we were soon in a crowded reception area where a young man in white shirt, green tie, and black trousers, wavy black hair and ready smile, held a sign bearing my name.

"Signori," he hailed us and introduced himself as Enzo Morabito, our host in Rome, and hefted our carry-ons. "Please, this way," and we followed him outside to a dark blue Lancia sedan. The uniformed driver snapped to, carry-ons were stored, and we were driven with a fanfare of horn blowing to the airport's Terminal 11 for domestic travel to catch our flight to Bari. I informed Enzo that unless we called him, we planned to return to Rome tonight on the last flight, and meanwhile, he was to deliver the carry-ons to the Grand Hotel de la Minerve in the Piazza della Rotundo. "Of course, Signor."

o O o

The first hiccup.

Terminal 11 was a madhouse. Loud speakers blared incoherently. Tired travelers stood in uncomplaining lines, machine pistol toting guards brusquely approached anyone with dark skin, flights seemed to change gates irrespective of what it might say on the flickering monitors. We checked in, were wanded, found our gate after being bounced from another, washed up and shaved in an unpleasant men's room, and boarded a cramped commuter aircraft for the hour's flight. While waiting for take-off, I read a few pages on Bari and Basilicata that I downloaded and printed before leaving Providence.

Bari, the capital of Puglia, indeed, all of the Boot, was *terra incognita* to me. The city's official website, clearly designed for tourists, featured romantic images of Greek ruins, centuries old castles, cliffs falling into the sea, happy diners and sun worshipers in elegant surroundings. Its inhabitants were described as 'resilient,' with a heritage that included the Greeks, Normans, Saracens, French, Spaniards, and Arabs. Bari's restaurants were 'quaint' and 'charming' featuring Mediterranean and Adriatic cuisine; its harbor was a busy hub for Adriatic commerce and passenger travel to Greece and the Aegean.

So much for official Bari. Other sites were less complimentary, describing a feudal, hard-faced population inured to poverty, a people living in labyrinthine, odorous alleys that coiled around the harbor in endless curves, and a climate that was often too hot or a windy cool, and suffering the sins of seaports worldwide. In 1943, the Luftwaffe managed a surprise air raid on Bari and blew up Allied ships in the harbor loaded with mustard gases, creating a Hades on earth for the civilian population, killing or forever mutilating thousands. Recently, destitute Albanians from across the Adriatic had flooded the city and became tough competition for low-wage jobs and in the drug and smuggling trades. As for food, one local delicacy stood out, *braciole di asino*, a roll of donkey meat in ragout and quail!

As to Basilicata, it was described as "remote and wild," a "shattered lunarscape," sparsely populated by a tough as nails, marginalized people culturally more attune to Sicily than mainland Italy. Named after Basilican monks fleeing from Byzantine lands invaded by Arabic and Turkish armies, its barren landscape of mountains and valleys kept change at bay. Much of the interior region lacked modern highways; one was as likely to see flocks of sheep as a Fiat or a county bus on its lonely tracks. No tourism to speak of because Greek ruins, medieval abbeys, and Norman castles had been long ago plundered. Altogether, a dour place, poor and unattractive.

Seemed about right considering our mission.

It was drizzling as our plane took off, Benno cramped in a seat behind me, and we headed south through squalls and dark clouds with occasional severe turbulence. I was relieved to see the clouds break as we approached Bari, its semi-circle harbor an angry gray of ruffled waves with wharves sticking out into the harbor like spikes. A scratchy intercom voice, which I assumed reminded us of seat belts fastened for landing, turned out, according to Benno, to be announcing that Bari's airport was closed due to thunderstorms. We were going to circle until it was cleared.

Clouds, streaked black and gray, thickened, and a violent, wind-driven rain buffeted the plane as its twin prop engines whined in a fight for altitude. In the seat in front of me, a frightened young girl began to wail, not listening to her mother's cross aisle soothing or demands, and then abruptly, my stomach falling, we dove through the clouds. I braced myself, fearing the worst. The child screamed right through a bump on landing, then through several more, eliciting audible complaints from passengers, which got only louder at the snail speed of taxiing to the terminal. We were a rancorous group that slowly filed out of the plane onto a metal platform, descended its shaky stairs to the tarmac, and faced a nondescript, khaki-colored terminal building that complemented the patchy gray and green, rain-filled sky.

Benno was pale around the eyes but said nothing as black cordons funneled us into a waiting area, frequently signed with *Benvenuti a Bari* and tourist posters of beaches and rustic villages in Puglia and the Gargano Peninsula. As our fellow travelers headed toward exits, only a squat man in his fifties, with a shock of black hair, in a black shirt, black trousers held up by suspenders, and black shoes, remained. Benno said, tentatively, "Gianmarco?" and took a step forward.

"Bacigalupi?" the man replied and pressed Benno to his barrel chest, all the while eyeing me over Benno's shoulder. His facial features too were large for the size of his corny face, enormous ear lobes separated from his skull, his frown was forbidding; his visage was, in a word, scary.

I was introduced by Benno and since I was not family, I merited only a handshake and suspicious black eyes as he spoke sternly to Benno in a dialect I didn't understand, his throaty voice like a retreating wave on a gravel beach. Benno listened, frowned, asked questions which needed repeating, and Gianmarco often shook his head in emphatic *no*'s.

Second hiccup.

For some reason, probably a problem with language, I was not expected. Arrangements had been made in Basilicata only for the arrival of Benno who was family. Gianmarco explained to Benno with frequent head shakes at me that my presence would either not be helpful or require a further negotiation. Benno asked Gianmarco what would happen if I simply showed up. Benno translated his reply; in such a situation, Gianmarco could not be responsible.

Although very disappointed, I was confident in Benno's investigatory prowess and agreed that if Gianmarco was not successful in obtaining permission for me to accompany them, I would return to Rome while they proceeded to meet the cousin. Benno informed Gianmarco whose face opened in a full-lipped smile as he snapped his fingers above his head.

A thin, hatchet-face man, a typecast extra in any prison movie, came forward from his perch against a rail at a coffee bar and without introduction, led us through the terminal out to an adjoining parking lot and into the rear seat of a fairly new, silvery-gray BMW 7000. Gianmarco and the driver settled in front, we in the back, and the car left the airport on a cypress dotted, limited access road into Bari. Gianmarco was voluble in his conversation, Benno's translation came in fits and pieces to me, and I understood that the village was about an hour and a half by car over the provincial border. First, however, we were invited to *pranzo*.

Through rain-spotted windows, I had the perception that I had left Italy and arrived in a third world country. Dreary looking high rise apartment blocks with cage-like balconies and discolored awnings stood like dominoes on end in the horizon. Utility wires sagged on concrete pylons along the highway, orange groves and vineyards looked ill-maintained as did ochre and pinkish houses with shuttered windows and tile roofs sprouting aerials like leafless limbs. Closer to the city, rows of billboards stood in bases of litter, commercial buildings, many with graffiti on their walls and metal security doors, were painted in grime. Activity, if not beauty, picked up as our car left the highway for a traffic congested, palm-tree lined *corso* that led to Bari's working harbor filled with freighters, ferries, and small passenger ships. We inched forward in a cacophony of car horns, brake squeals, and unmuffled Vespas; even with the windows closed and the air conditioning on full blast, I smelled day old fish.

Abruptly, as a weak sun broke through the clouds, we turned into an elegant neighborhood of church domes, stone walls holding the remnants of a fortress, pink and beige Baroque palazzi, fountains, statues, and cobbled streets. Gianmarco pointed here and there with pride and Benno, sometimes, translated.

Our destination was the Manfredi, a *trattoria* in the *citta vecchia* with a dining area that spilled out into a piazza near the Basilica di San Nicola. The *trattoria*'s ceiling beams were thick and blackened, as though boasting that they had held for centuries. The *padrone di casa* directed us to a table prepared for our arrival; the staff bowed deferentially to Gianmarco. As aromas of onion and garlic and meat sauce emanated from the kitchen, my stomach grumbled in expectation. Gianmarco, after discussion with our host, ordered a thick chickpeas soup with ribbons of pasta and mushrooms, antipasto, a risotto, filet of monkfish, *taralli* which is a local bread with a pretzel texture served with a spiced oil, and beef slices rolled in spicy tomato sauce. What, no *bracioli di asino*? Dessert was a platter of fruit, biscuits, and cream filled tarts. Our camaraderie was enhanced by red and white local wines served from large carafes.

Benno and his cousin had obviously become *amici*, their language and demeanors had relaxed, with Benno occasionally sharing tidbits. At one point, after a long, hand waving discourse from Gianmarco, Benno said to me, "Basilicata is ruled by the 'friends' so, don't be surprised by precautions."

And then, a revelation: Gianmarco understood and spoke some

English, an ability that had been hidden from us until he had a level of confidence that we were not troublemakers. As a bottle of grappa appeared and espresso was served, Gianmarco lit a Marlboro cigarette and took a call on his *telefono* at the table.

Third hiccup.

Gianmarco said that I could accompany them to Gianosa d'Acri and be present for the interview but I would not be permitted to converse directly with the cousin. He then reverted to dialect and said something that straightened Benno's shoulders which, after a nod, he translated for me.

"Gianmarco says that if you embarrass him, not only would the interview be over, but you and I will have insulted him. We don't want that."

43

WE LEFT THE *TRATTORIA* shortly thereafter. Four gigantic baskets of food and wine wrapped in yellowish plastic had been loaded into the car's trunk, gifts, I assumed, to those in the chain of protocol; a cooler of bottled water was placed on the floor of the front passenger seat.

Our seat positions in the BMW changed with Benno riding in front and Gianmarco and me in the spacious rear seat. Gianmarco, now wearing sunglasses, instructed me in a garbled English-Italian, that I must follow his lead in all things, I would not speak unless spoken to, Benno would ask any questions of the cousin through Gianmarco, who would take care of formalities as necessary. It was possible, he said, even after all of this, I might have to remain in the car while the cousin, who was named as Camilla, was interviewed. Such arrangements, Gianmarco said, were not out of disrespect but to protect me.

I thanked Gianmarco profusely for his efforts. To Benno who had turned to listen to Gianmarco, I mouthed *Protect?*

His expression said, *Don't ask.*

o O o

After fifteen minutes of driving through the humble outskirts of Bari, we came to a regional highway identified as the S96, with a signpost that pointed us west toward Basilicata. After Gianmarco's lecture, we were silent for the most part, looking out at an arid, sun-parched land with thickets of scrub trees and clusters of cypresses.

Gray clouds crowned the looming, foreboding fortress like mountains of the southern Appennines as the sun ate through a high haze that followed us from Bari. Soon, I heard, and felt, Gianmarco's snore, something like that of a bull elephant. The driver eventually said *"Basilicata,"* and pointed to a rusty stanchion holding a metal shield with four blue wavy lines, the provincial seal of Basilicata. The shield was punctured with multiple bullet holes. Not a good omen.

Nor was I braced with confidence when we pulled over to the side of the road just past the stanchion and our driver retrieved a double barreled, sawed off shotgun with a taped stock from the BMW's trunk and lodged it in a slot in the driver's door. Gianmarco, who had awoken with a start when the car stopped, grumbled something I understood to be about a *precaution.*

S96, a *strada importante,* well paved up to the border, became two narrow, ill-maintained lanes, a *strada con difficolta,* that clung to the sides of steep ravines and dipped into valleys with rock filled gullies and dry, cracked, creek beds. We encountered little traffic as the country became even more barren, a stark, chalky, denuded moonscape. I recalled that Gianmarco or the driver at lunch remarking that no one went to Basilicata without a reason, that under Mussolini, the province was known as *Lucania,* home of the wolf. That made perfect sense.

Noticing the withered vegetation for want of water and soil, Benno muttered, "What do they grow here, stones?"

Gianmarco replied, with his hands emphasizing his words, that in a few days, the autumn rains would begin, thunder, hail, gales of wind, rain that would smack against the hillsides. Water would flood through the valleys further eroding the parched, barren earth, setting the stage for spring landslides; the area's population survived until the next rainy season only because of dry farming, reservoirs, deep wells and on remittances from sons and daughters working in the North and the efforts of a male population that spent months away from home.

We continued up and down ridges, and for the first time in Italy, I saw old men driving donkeys at the sides of the road. Stray goats stood on rocky grades so steep they appeared to have upgrade legs shorter than downgrade legs. Cacti and growths of prickly pears were common wherever water might puddle long enough to let life sprout. The purplish mountains, seemingly higher and craggier, were now closer and scarred by ravines. Red-winged hawks circled slowly in updrafts of air.

The distant whitewashed villages on the hillsides were pictur-esque but were likely as dusty and decrepit and dilapidated as those through which S96 passed. As best I could, I followed my tourist map and identified Rocca Lauria, Marlina Colle, and Montesca-gliuso. Each appeared more wretched, more poverty stricken than the one just passed.

About this time, Benno, probably making conversation, told Gianmarco that Italo Palagi, the father of Vittorio Ruggieri, was the author of Caesare Forza novels. Gianmarco became animated. "Caesare Forza?" His eyes opened wide in his appreciation of Benno and me; our quest was instantaneously heightened in importance. He lit a cigarette and rambled on to Benno about Forza and being a teenager in his image. *"Sono forzaissmo,"* he said, flashing his crooked smile at me. I smiled back, braving his secondhand smoke with my own *forzaissmo.*

The BMW stopped at a crossing and a weathered signpost with a sheaf of arrows pointed to tracks toward various villages including Gianosa d'Acri. Gianmarco remarked that our destination, five ki-lometers towards a line of hills, was near a tributary of the far larger Agri River that flowed into the Gulfo di Taranto south of Bari. The car turned into a *via blanca*, an unpaved, single lane, chalky road, through acres of tilled land filled with stubbles of brown stalks, leaving a plume of dust giving fair notice of our arrival.

Gianosa d'Acri looked like it had been through its share of earthquakes and refused, stubbornly, to fall down, a place where, for some unknown historical reason, generations lived and died perched in tiers of houses above a dry, rocky valley. In the glare of the afternoon sun, its buildings were a blur of pale, scruffy, yellow with maroon tile roofs, their cracked walls showed interior bricks where stucco had fallen away. Some appeared vacant or abandoned and most had closed shutters; the only splashes of color came from brilliant flowers on second floor balconies, advertising signs of *tabacchi* with racks of newspapers, a neon green cross in the window of a *famacia,* and the lights of other tiny, shabby shops.

In the shadows of a dilapidated church, a silent crowd of plain-faced old men and black-shawled women and mangy dogs had gathered around a stone basin in the center of a cobblestone piazza with a modest, newer building identified by Italian and provincial flags as the *comune.* Where were the children playing kickball, the young adults? The only other car in the piazza, a dusty blue and white Fiat, was that of the *polizia.* We parked and instructed by Gianmarco, our driver entered the *comune,* soon returning with four old men dressed in black trousers, unpressed white shirts, and black jackets, followed by a portly cop in wrinkled police uniform.

We got out, the afternoon heat immediately pressing us, opening our skin pores, and shook hands all around. One elderly gent with a wide, tri-color sash across his chest, whom I assumed was the mayor, addressed us in a dialect that even Gianmarco seemed to have trouble understanding, but it made little difference as Gianmarco's thanks were accepted and we were invited inside the *comune* for glasses of the grappa. After a short speech in a municipal chamber of some sort, Gianmarco learned that Camilla Ruggieri would meet us at a friend's home outside of the village. At least that is what I got from Gianmarco. The *grappa*—it was a white lightning—was passed around again, our driver delivered plastic-wrapped baskets to the mayor and the policeman, and we got back into the BMW and followed a police escort around the piazza and back down the hill to another *via blanca* and into a cemetery.

"A cemetery?" I asked Benno.

"Yeah. Pay our respects to the Ruggieri family."

And we did, slowly, following the *polizia,* our vehicles sending up white dust to isolated cypresses and statues of the Madonna, past family plots all in perfect rectangles, separated from each other by rocks and whitewashed masonry. Fresh red carnations filled vases attached to headstones and held photographs of loved ones behind thick glass frames. Benno whispered, "In the winter, they use artificial flowers. And they always make sure the photographs are clean."

"Why us and now," I said as we momentarily stopped in front of a large plot with numerous monuments and flowers.

"So, you'll get a show of family and death," he said.

My mouth opened for more explanation but he shook his head

signaling silence. I thought, not exactly Swan Point.

o O o

We returned to the *via blanca* for five minutes along crumbling walls and washed-out gullies to a valley dotted with dusty scrub along the dry river bed of the "small" Acri and arrived at an oasis, an ochre *palazzo* right out of a tourist guide, except for the razor wire atop stone walls six feet high.

"What's this?" I asked Benno, who asked Gianmarco, who said it was "Okay."

At a grilled gate, the driver touched the car's horn and a lean-faced, scrawny guy in a cloth cap, a vest over a long sleeve shirt, and black trousers, cigarette dangling from his lips, left the shadows and came to the car. Maybe he had shaved three or four days ago. He didn't bother to hide the rifle slung over his shoulder. After he spoke to our driver, he opened the gate, and we drove inside the walls. Flower gardens flanked either side of the drive, mostly dusty roses, vegetables were further back under sheets of flimsy cloth, and rows of nodding sunflowers were planted along the interior walls. A small grove of olive trees was on one side of the shuttered *palazzo*; on the other side was a *loggia* by a brownish pool. In its shade, sat a man; a woman in a black skirt, white blouse, and black shawl stood behind him. So, the 'friend' of the cousin was truly a 'friend,' the local don. Which meant the 'Ndrangheta.

I exhaled. To Benno, I muttered, "You're kidding!"

"Welcome to the real Basilicata," he replied.

Gianmarco waved his hand to quiet us.

Our driver got out, placed the shotgun on his seat, opened the trunk, and delivered the two remaining baskets to the hired help and returned to lean against the front fender of the BMW appearing to be prepared to jump back in for a hasty retreat. Gianmarco stepped forward on a gravel path and greeted the seated old man with a kiss on his offered hand; he nodded to the woman, while Benno and I remained in the car. Gianmarco spoke to the old man for several minutes before he gestured to us to come forward to be introduced. "Don Primo Briguglia," he said.

My eyes adjusted slowly to the stark shade of the *loggia*. It took several seconds before I realized the Don Primo was in a wheelchair. His yellow shirt with vertical black stripes was unstarched and baggy, a straw hat covered what had to be a bald head and shadowed a wrinkled forehead and pockmarked cheeks. Tufts of white hair sprouted from his ears. His lips barely moved when he repeated our names slowly and gestured to us to sit in wicker chairs before him. An elderly stooped woman in black, wearing a black kerchief even in the heat, appeared with a tray of dark red, almost black, wine, small bottles of mineral water, sliced cheese, and a crusty loaf of bread. When she left, the don introduced the woman standing behind him as Camilla Ruggieri.

At her name being spoken, she seemed startled. She was tiny, no more than five feet tall, with parchment skin, white hair pulled back in a bun, a fog of fear on her bird-like face when she raised her worried eyes to us.

We drank the heavy tannic wine as Gianmarco, with obvious deference, informed Don Primo of our mission. This had to be more protocol because we would never have gotten this far without detailed information and *bona fides* given. The don didn't respond; all the while his sharp eyes inspected Benno and me, these *Americanos* of interest. By now, sweat beaded on my forehead, my back was clammy, the wine went through my body like a drug. When Gianmarco finished, the old man spoke in dialect, Gianmarco answered him, and they went back and forth, both somber. I heard what I thought were *paternita, patrigno, patrimonio* from the old man, all words denoting duty, protection, obligations. Eventually, the old man raised his hands, seemingly granting Gianmarco's request, and said something to Camilla Ruggieri. She sat next to the don to face us.

It was obvious she had been prepared because she began to speak before hearing Gianmarco's questions. Gianmarco translated her dialect, breaking up her narrative. Maria Ruggieri, she said sternly, grew up too smart and too wild for country life, was *testata*—stubborn—and her family scraped up enough money to send her to Rome to be a nurse. While there, she became pregnant, had her baby, left him with a Catholic orphanage, and returned to work in the provincial dispensary. Didn't tell anybody about the baby but later, somehow, the birth became known. This was a family disgrace, worse when she refused her family's demand to name the father.

Don Briguglia interrupted her to emphasize this was an *infamia*. Gianmarco made the point to explain to us that to the Ruggieris, her silence meant she was unsure of the father, that there was more than one lover. She was vilified a *punta*, a tramp, and worse, a liability who had wasted family money with her education, a cardinal sin in the poor countryside. She was destined to be a spinster when someone born in the area returned from New York looking for a full-time nurse for his ailing mother who spoke only the local dialect. The family volunteered Maria who carried her disgrace to America.

Benno asked, through Gianmarco, "Did Maria Ruggieri ever return here?"

She responded that Maria returned only once, about a year ago. She came for an afternoon with a driver from Bari, like the *"Signori."* Camilla Ruggieri was the only close family member still living in the village. When she asked about Maria's son, Maria became angry, said that she should have gotten an abortion for all the trouble the baby had caused her, that the baby ruined her life. Saying that, Camilla Ruggieri made the sign of the Cross. Within months thereafter, the cousin heard that Maria had died in New York. Again, the sign of the Cross.

Gianmarco referenced Italo Palagi in a context I did not understand. Her eyes flickered in the direction of the don before she shook her head as though she did not recognize the name. A raised eyebrow indicated that the don was better informed.

I whispered to Benno to ask if Vittorio Ruggieri had ever visited the village and Gianmarco did so. She again looked to the don before she shook her head and said *no*.

The don raised his right hand from the wheelchair's arm indicating the interview was over and began speaking in paragraphs to us, with '*paternita* and *patrimoni*' coupled with Palagi. Gianmarco shook his head several times and shrugged toward me, and the old man then directed his spiel at me with *negoziare*—to negotiate—repeated. Gianmarco nodded sympathetically and responded in dialect. The don finished his speech by saying something to me very directly that was unintelligible and then gave me a flinty smile. He picked up his glass, looked at each of us in turn, nodded to us, and we finished our wine.

Three thousand miles, a dusty two hours from Bari, for a forty-five minute interview, and now, as it was clearly time to depart, I didn't understand exactly what had happened.

We stood, and following Gianmarco's lead, nodded in respect

to Don Briguglia who offered his hand, which we each shook once. I thought my shake was longer than that of the others as he gave me that same smile. We then nodded our thanks to Camilla Ruggieri and returned to the BMW. Gianmarco tendered some euros to the guard "*per Signora.*" Our driver backed out the BMW slowly, and the gates opened and closed behind us.

44

I N THE COMFORT OF the car's air conditioning, with bottled water from the cooler all around, Gianmarco fleshed out Camilla Ruggieri's story. During her visit, Maria had not identified her lover because, according to the cousin, in her stubbornness, she insisted it was not the family's business. The baby was her mistake; the father, a student, didn't know she was pregnant when she left him. Why should he be harmed after all these years?

I asked, "Did Maria know he had become rich? Famous?"

"Yes, she boasted that he was but still wouldn't reveal his name."

Benno mused, "I bet the vendetta was forgotten until Camilla told people, like she would in a place like that where nothing happens and nothing is unknown, that Maria's lover was rich. It was too good a story not to tell, one that got back to whomever, and the vendetta was on again. Anyone who collects for the family is entitled to a cut. Maria, back in New York, must have been pressured to reveal Palagi's name before she died. That set things in motion."

"So, you think the cousin was telling the truth?"

"Yeah. Except for the part about Vittorio. They knew all about him. You could see it in their faces."

Gianmarco interrupted. The Ruggieri family was mostly in that cemetery, he said, the rest desperately poor, and they craved the debt of honor owed by Palagi but remained unpaid. Don Primo was now responsible to collect the debt. When Gianmarco told him Palagi was dead, which Gianmarco said surprised the old man, it was agreed that there could be some lessening of the amount due the family, so long as it was *'giusto'*—fair.

Gianmarco then spoke so rapidly in Italian to Benno that I couldn't follow. Benno's eyes widened and he shrugged as he translated for me. "Gianmarco promised that you would consider the situation."

"What?"

"What should he have said? Forget it? Did you want to leave there with all your fingers and toes?"

o O o

Slow-moving trucks along the narrow road back to the border caused a series of hair-raising maneuvers in the face of oncoming cars. Our driver seemed to have an innate sense to know when the car in the facing lane bearing down on us would slow to allow passage. Benno and Gianmarco began a long conversation in which I didn't participate, hesitant that Gianmarco would ask me directly for some rendering to Caesar. For my part, I considered that in Basilicata, nothing was as simple as it might appear. While we had confirmed Palagi's story of the vendetta and that his payment to the 'Ndrangheta in New York never reached Basilicata, I became aware that ascertainment of the facts led to even more uncertainty.

As we approached Bari and thunderclouds squatting over the city, Benno told me it would be impolite, and impolitic, for him to leave for Rome tonight, that he should accept Gianmarco's offer of hospitality for the evening, and that he would join me tomorrow in Rome. He would use the time to delve into Vittorio's connection to the extortion through the family, the amount of payment that had been expected from Palagi, and flesh out family connections with the Giambazzis of New York. Also, that Gianmarco had found a seat for me on the seven-thirty Alitalia flight to Rome.

Had I missed something? Was I getting the bum's rush out of town?

o O o

It was after midnight, six o'clock Providence time, when I arrived at the hotel. A few minutes later in my fifth floor suite, I logged on and attacked a cascade of e-mails. A few were easy deletes, others required short messages of excuse, and I was gratified that one from the Provost confirmed a meeting at Banco di San

Paolo at three tomorrow afternoon; another was from Father Pietro for espresso Wednesday morning. As to Columbus Day, the Provost e-mail said:

"National news is on to other things, but locally, of course, different story. On campus, tonight, a new ad hoc group, the Campus Collective Against Racism, is planning a demonstration on The Green "to support the decision of the faculty senate of Carter University to no longer honor a destroyer of native civilizations and the rights of indigenous people." We go on!

o O o

Nadie was walking home from her office on Meeting Street when I reached her on her cell phone. "I'm right on schedule," I proclaimed, described my accommodations in Rome, and asked, "Everything okay?"

"I'm staying at your mother's tonight and tomorrow. It is more convenient and I need company!"

I didn't take the bait.

"You will love Rome," I said. "It's magical. Love is expected to happen here, like in the movies."

"I miss you," she said. "Be here on Thursday."

In the comfortable bed, I quickly gave into sleep. I dreamt of lovemaking, Nadie naked, her breath warm, flowing over me. Her hair had fallen over her shoulders, she leaned forward over me and I am drenched with her scent. I lost myself in her, melting away, face on fire, feeling exhilaration and exhaustion, more and more active, faster and further ...

45 Tuesday

THE ROMAN DAWN ARRIVED with the best of intentions in a rosy light filtered by high wispy clouds.

I had slept soundly and found, as I opened the slatted shutters fully, that my suite had a view of both the dun colored roof of the Pantheon and Santa Maria sopra Minerva, one of the great Roman basilicas. In the thick comfort of a complimentary bathrobe, I tapped out a memo on my laptop as to our visit to Gianosa d'Acri.

Enzo, my host, had the Lancia outside the hotel at ten o'clock and we were driven—the uniformed driver, no surprise, was Enzo's cousin—across the Tiber to the Institute's Roman campus on the Janiculum Hill abutting the Palazzi Corsini and the Botanical Gardens. In very stop-and-go traffic, I was delivered to an imposing four story, Baroque building of pale yellow masonry, displaying American, Italian, and Carter flags. An elaborately decorated portico led into a high ceiling central hall capped by a plaster fluted dome, its marble floor was inlaid with colored circles and triangles of stone. Corridors on either side led to two semi-attached smaller, less imposing buildings which, according to my limited information, housed apartments and a library for visiting scholars.

An attractive, lustrous haired woman in her early forties, in a black business suit accented by silver crescent moon pin, looked up from the reception desk and smiled. "Ah, Signor Temple," she said in a husky voice, flashing a practiced smile, "*Buon giorno*! *Direttore* Brunotti is in his office. *Due piano*. I will escort you."

She told me, rather officiously, that she had made an appointment on Thursday morning with *Avvocato* Maurizio Musumeci,

Vittorio Ruggieri's lawyer in Rome, and led me through a mauve sitting room with a grand piano, scattered sofas, soft chairs, tables, and shelves of books to an antique elevator with accordion metal gates. As it silently lifted us, I wondered if she was another 'friend' of Brunotti. "*Permisso*," she said, opening the elevator gate, and I followed her down a hall painted maroon, with a row of landscape paintings in gold frames under discrete lighting. She knocked smartly at a door at the end of the hall, opened it, and I crossed in front of her as she announced my arrival.

Brunotti, in shirt sleeves, sat behind a huge desk at the far side of the large room. His informality I took as reflecting irritation and disrespect. Behind him, two large windows were heavily draped, allowing only slivers of light that cut through to files and newspapers on his desk; the elaborate ceiling light fixture was on dim. Brunotti did not rise from his chair nor offer his hand as I sat in the hardback chair opposite him. His fingers trembled as he portentously raised a shirt cuff to glance at his watch.

"I have deferred an interview with *Corriere Della Sera*. An important opportunity to tell our story to Italy's largest newspaper. Already, a critical editorial." He picked up a newspaper and dropped it on the desk. "Damage is done every minute the President hesitates to criticize, condemn."

Not a promising start. I glanced around the room, as though disinterested or calculating what its elegant period furnishings cost, and removed a Moleskine notebook and pen from my jacket pocket. That was purposeful, meant to be disconcerting and I had annoyance in my voice when I said, "You have been told to refer the media to the Public Information Office."

"Public ... Information ... Office?" He stood abruptly, hands on hips, his chin thrust forward, striking a pose of indignation. "In Italy, they care nothing for the Public ... Information ... Office. I must speak. I am the *Direttore*. You have no idea what trouble we're in here, how we are being vilified in the press, that our friends, donors, are horrified by this calculated insult."

I recognized an honest concern escaping his ego. He spread his hands to the width of his desk and leaned forward to me. "I ... the Institute ... have been dealt an assassin's blow. The Institute is reeling. Don't you care?"

"We all care, Cosimo. Do *you* care enough to return the Provost's e-mails, the President's call?"

"So, you are here to reprimand me?" He shook his head and turned his reddened face to a profile. "Because I travel, with events crashing around me, my ... our ... prestige plummeting, donors upset, government furious? It is *I* who bears this disgrace, *I* who must deal with the media while Danby equivocates!"

"The President understands your predicament but your comments must be guided by him."

"Is he afraid to take on those idiots? Why was I not informed that the Institute was to be insulted?" He stood and came around his desk.

"We were surprised, and embarrassed, like you, Cosimo."

"This idiocy will cost the Institute millions in support and donations. Passions have been unleashed!" And he went on in like vein, reciting his efforts to pacify angry donors and politicians as he paced back and forth, then to the window to grip the drapes in his anger. He finished his tirade standing no more than two feet in front of me, his eyes boring into mine. "It is intolerable!"

We had reached the moment of his greatest belligerence, when I had to deflate him, and not gently. Coolly, I informed him of the loss of Palagi's funds at Ravensford Capital. His face was sucked of anger, fell into disbelief, and then dismay. His right hand slapped his forehead; his left hand went to the desk to steady him. "The old fool," he moaned, "the old, stupid fool!" Then he sat, fitting his chin on laced fingers, staring at me. "How much did we lose?"

"Over six million dollars."

His right hand returned to his forehead. "Is it possible? *Dio*, is it possible? How are we to survive if we lose our donors *and* Palagi's money?" His bravado, his self-importance were gone; he was, certainly for the first time in my experience, crestfallen.

"Cosimo, I'm here because the Institute hasn't received a euro from Italy under the royalty agreement since Palagi's death. I have an appointment at Banco di San Paolo this afternoon to find out why. It could be that Palagi's son has obtained a court order against the bank doling out funds. With that and the loss of Palagi's trust, the Provost has ordered a budget review of the Institute, including an audit to be conducted here and in Providence."

His eyes widened. "What, you do not trust our accounts? My management? You do this now, while we face a crisis? You insult me ? I ..."

"Not so intended. Just good business. And one last matter. Before you left, you fired Claudia Cioffi."

He took his time to respond but he was ready. "A *strega*, a crone. Abusive. Deaf. A useless burden. There was no place for her."

"Not because she refused to serve as Palagi's executor?" My index finger went to my pursed lips as though I expected further explanation.

"Absurd!" he shouted, his hands shooting upward in exasperation as he regained his seat.

His reinflation to belligerence led me to test Benno's theory that the notebook found in Palagi's valise was an account of Brunotti's fraud against the Institute. A better investigative technique would be to let the forensic auditors use the notebook as a guide to malfeasance, and then question him, but I could not resist. "Did Palagi ever mention an entity called Montecristo'?"

"Monte ... cristo?" he repeated, reacting as though I had begun to speak in tongues. His line of sight moved from me, his louder breaths were not disguised, and he rubbed his hands together as though the gesture would help him decide his response. "I do not recall any *Monte ... cristo*," he said slowly, after allowing a hand to glide over his mouth as though in reflection.

Recall is a word of art from a practiced witness. I waited for more but he was silent.

I changed the subject back to immediate issues, "I suggest you call Danby, not e-mail him, today."

"I must be able to speak ... to Italy," he said slowly, without emotion, to no one in particular.

I took my leave. "*Arrivederci*," I said and I did not expect or receive a response.

46

LUNCH WITH ENZO AND his cousin was at Da Lucia in nearby Trastevere, a family operated *trattoria* off a moss-covered alley, offering *alici al limone*—anchovies in lemon sauce—marinated sea bass served with pasta, and a delicious white wine drained from a barrel into our carafe. My companions' conversation strayed to former Prime Minister Silvio Berlusconi. The Italian media had reported breathlessly that he still hosted *bunga-bunga* parties at his various *palazzi* with his *velines*, buxom, big-haired showgirls, who, whatever else they did with him at sleepovers, kept the party going with pole dancing and petting in lascivious soft porn settings. The *velines* had become national celebrities, known everywhere by their first names and nicknames, Monica, Bianca, Cheri, Naomi, Rozanna ...

The cousin defended him with frequent shrugs and an amused smile. "Silvio enjoys life, women, soccer, parties," the cousin said. "He adores his kids, loves his mamma, breaks some rules. Good for him. He's what we'd do if we had his money. Ah, if Bianca threw herself at me ..." He pursed his lips for a kiss and put two fingers there. "What's wrong with that? At least, he's no hypocrite like all the others."

This defense had a familiar ring; he's a rascal but he's *our* rascal. "Womanizing when the country's an economic basket case?" retorted Enzo who obviously despised Berlusconi. "He embarrasses Italy."

"Enzo, come on, you'd love to be him," the cousin rejoined.

o O o

At the sleekly modern offices of Banco di San Paolo on the Via Nazionale, I was greeted by an embodiment of an Italian banker, a man of slight stature in a dark suit that whispered discretion, gleaming shoes, and whose pale complexion, keen expression, and intelligent eyes reminded me of likenesses captured in museum portraits of sixteenth century cardinals. *Direttore* Lorenzo Carvo spoke English with a charming accent as he escorted me into a gilt-edged paneled office with a chandelier of dangling crystals. His large desk was clear of bothersome papers, a computer on a matching credenza at one side. I explained my purpose, gave him copies of Palagi's will, trust and royalty agreement, and watched his serious demeanor as he made notes with a slim silver pen on a lined pad.

He was very courteous but very firm. "I am very sorry, Signor Temple, but there can be no access to the account you refer or any remittance until every judicial requirement is met. Signor Palagi was a co-owner of the account and upon his death the bank requires instructions from both the Institute, which you clearly represent, *and* his legal representative.

"*Legi è lege*," he said, "the law is the law. I assure you, as soon as this small difficulty is satisfied, the Bank will promptly remit whatever is due."

He further explained that while all governmental contributions and private donations to the Institute were, upon receipt, immediately placed into a collection account and remitted to the University's account at Citibank, all funds attributable to *Signor* Palagi's licenses and royalties were placed in a separate account from which, after deduction of the monthly administrative fee, one-half was sent to *Signor* Palagi's personal account at Bank of America and the balance to the University's account at Citibank.

My interest was pricked by *monthly administrative fee*. 'For what? To whom?' I asked if it was a charge of his bank. He responded, "Some years ago, Signor Palagi gave written instructions to pay a fee to a third party that assisted him with his accounts."

That was news, troublesome news. I asked for a copy of the instructions but was refused for the reasons already given. Disappointed, I very pointedly told him so, but he remained resolute. I prepared to leave empty handed when with a discrete knock at the door, a young man, also in banker's attire, entered, and passed a note to his senior who read it carefully before placing it on the desk.

"I am relieved, and pleased, that a determination has been made by my superiors, after consultation with the Ministry of Finance, that since Signor Palagi was the director of an institute which is part of your university, you should be permitted to review the accounts we have faithfully managed." Did this abrupt change come through from brother Nick's efforts? "This would, of course, include our instructions from Signor Palagi as to the administrative fee. It will take some time, however, to retrieve the records. How long will you be in Rome?"

When I said until Thursday morning, he indicated the impossibility of providing all the information on such short notice but agreed to promptly send copies of the records to Providence. He added, "I should tell you that I, personally, received his instructions as to the administrative fee."

To nudge him to take the next step of divulging the circumstances, I praised his memory, his integrity, and discretion, which flattered him. "*Grazie*," he said proudly. "I have been fortunate to be of service to Signor Palagi, such a distinguished man. In my youth, I was a reader of Signor Palagi's Caesare Forza novels. All of my generation were Caesare Forza fans." His face reddened. "On one occasion, Signor Palagi was pleased to autograph one of his books. Let me show you." He left his desk to take two steps to a bookcase and pulled out a slender volume, its dust cover portraying a hairy hand clutching a revolver aimed at a blood-red bull's eye with the silhouette of a man in its center. He opened the book to the title page and a barely legible signature similar to that I had briefly seen on Palagi's letter of affirmation and the estate documents. I smiled appreciatively, and with a stroke of intuition, leaned forward in a confidential manner. "The administrative fee is paid to Montecristo, is it not?"

His eyes lightened perceptively and his face became as cherubic and as knowing as a Roman *putti*, suggesting we shared in Palagi's confidence. In Providence, under similar circumstances, there would have been a shrug or a nudge.

"I'm curious how much had been wired to Montecristo's account."

He turned to the computer on a credenza, punched keys, and his eyes flitted through columns. "The fee is ten percent of the amount we collect. Through last month, approximately ninety thousand euros. Over a many year period, of course, and, unfortunately, much diminished in recent months. The funds were wired on the tenth of each month to a correspondent bank in Genoa."

"Seems all is correct," I said to relieve his concern.

"After the funds are remitted of course, I have no further information. We are under no duty of inquiry nor do we undertake to ensure anything other than that the funds have been transmitted in accordance with our client's instructions."

"Of course," I said smoothly.

"The bank would appreciate it if it was known to the appropriate officials at the Ministry that we cooperated with you in this matter ..."

"You have been very courteous and very helpful and I shall make that known appropriately."

"That would be most satisfactory."

I thought of a final question. "Do you recall anyone from the Institute ever inquiring about the administrative fee?"

His head went back in remembrance. "Yes, just once. Last April. An inquiry from Signor Brunotti, the present director of the Institute. I am embarrassed to say that was as a result of our error. Signor Palagi was in Rome and requested an advance of funds that were collected and about to be paid over. A clerk mistakenly sent a check to the Institute instead of to Signor Palagi's hotel with an accounting showing the administrative fee as a deduction from the account. This brought a call from Signor Brunotti to me. I examined the situation, apologized for our error, and explained our instructions."

"What did he say?"

"Signor Brunotti seemed unaware of the fee arrangement, but he was very understanding for which I was appreciative, given our long relationship to the Institute and Signor Palagi."

So smooth, so calculating, so ... Brunotti.

o O o

Later, I took a flight of stairs to the hotel's rooftop terrace restaurant, crowded with early dining tourists, mostly fellow Americans. In the day's lingering warmth and the afterglow of a sunset below purple clouds, service was prompt, and the antipasto, prima patti of spinach pasta, and the veal piccata entree were well-prepared, and served efficiently.

My table had a view over tile roofs toward Castello Sant'Angelo and St. Peter's. As I ordered espresso, dusk rolled over the city and I remembered an aphorism about Rome told by my mother: when the evening hid cracks in facades, patches, holes, and missing pavers, Rome, like a woman of a certain age, used the dark to hide her blemishes, to discredit any thought of age.

I stayed longer than I expected over an aged grappa and considered Palagi and Brunotti, the former, deceitful on a grand scale, the latter, *grimy* came to mind. Both operated in the refined world of unsuspecting academia. How was the University, the Institute, to come to grips with these frauds?

o O o

My return to my suite was greeted by harsh buzzes from the room's phone. I answered, "*Pronto.*"

"*Pronto* yourself," Benno shouted at me.

Laughter and a woman's high pitched voice were in the background, placing Benno in a bar or restaurant which was confirmed as he acknowledged a greeting in Italian from a woman, and I heard a clatter of dishes, a woman's high pitched peal of laughter.

"What a day. Checking on things. Getting things straight. I see it now. How it all works." He lowered his voice slightly. "We're in a restaurant in that stone fortress you saw at the harbor. Having *cena* with Gianmarco and the family. Never knew how many relatives I had." Then, "Looks like I can't get back to Rome until tomorrow. Not sure of the time yet. No problem?"

"No problem," I answered, realizing Benno was likely having the time of his life.

o O o

I answered e-mails including a short one from Nadie that I was still very much missed and was expected on Thursday. I undressed, and lay on the bed to continue *The Leopard*. More than ever, I appreciated di Lampedusa's insights on his homeland, a land of shifting arrangements among people where nothing really changes, not only in a village like Gianosa d'Agri where its inhabitants standing in their doorways would refuse to admit they lived there to a stranger, but in a cynical city like Rome where merit was often equated with how much you could get away with.

Fatigue suddenly numbs my mind and my dreaded claustro-phobia nudges away other concerns. It is as if a spider web is across my mind, sticky, clinging. My chest tightening becomes worse, a cold sweat wets my forehead, I feel the pressure of blackness and tight space. I am not helped when my cell phone runs out of juice, leaving me with only the pencil flashlight and that eye of light also becomes dimmer and will soon be gone.

I concentrate on pain. My stomach hurts, my ribs don't enjoy breathing. I must be one big bruise. My calves and hamstrings are afflicted with muscle spasms.

Despite my efforts, the black hole deepens, my breathing becomes constrained, ragged, and I feel my heartbeat, my pulse, gain momentum. I am at the brink of a mental battle I fear to confront.

I squirm to keep circulation in my legs, only the aches keep me focused, away from the tightening closeness.

Then, I concentrate on the opening to the back seat, barely visible in the blackness. I am not entombed. There is hope.

Come on, Benno!

47 Wednesday

THE FOLLOWING MORNING, I awaited Father Pietro in the Antico Caffé della Pace near the Piazza Navona with *cornetti* and an espresso. I was five minutes early, not wanting to risk being without a table.

The day was clear, cooler, the café's Cinzano umbrellas were furled at outside tables. I sipped the superb espresso at a window to watch a parade of backpackers and obvious tourists, nuns in flowing robes and wimples, matrons clutching purses or being led by their tiny dogs, cell phone–engaged students, *fashionistas* in stiletto heels somehow avoiding the crevices between St. Peter's stones—the blackened squares of the piazza—begging gypsies, women in tight skirts with sublime behinds, slim men in sunglasses and in the dark suits of government and business. Romans dashed into the elegant bar area of blue tile floors and gilded formal mirrors to down quick espressos; tourists struggled to place orders for 'Italian toast,' cappuccinos, lattes, and bagels with distracted waiters.

I spotted the priest as he made his way across the piazza, his shoulders covered by a black *cappa*. He acknowledged my wave as he made his way to my tiny table, releasing a catch on his cloak which he placed on a chair, revealing a white habit. A diminutive waiter in black waistcoat took the priest's order for espresso.

Father Pietro handed me a large square envelope of heavy white paper with an embossed gold seal, from which I extracted two white cards printed in an elaborate Latin script. "These are confirmation of your admission to the Vatican on Thursday of your visit. We will be accompanied by an old friend, a museum curator, who speaks excellent English, and knows the Vatican as few do. He promises you shall view treasures that tourists rarely see."

"*Molto grazie*," I replied as the waiter delivered his espresso. Then, I saw that the priest's face had collapsed into melancholy.

"I welcome the opportunity to speak to you. Something has been on my mind. The letter which affirms Palagi's will and trust? Neither you nor Mr. Pine asked me to confirm the handwriting's authenticity ..."

He saw the apprehension that splashed on my face. "The handwriting may not be that of Italo Palagi. Likely, it is that of Claudia Cioffi ..."

"Father ...!"

"You remember that I told you Italo suffered from the result of Guillain–Barré Syndrome. That his illness cost Italo his once vigorous stride and the fluid use of his fingers. The permanent weakness meant he could no longer drive. He could not button his shirts or walk steadily, thus the collarless shirts he wore, the suspenders, slip-on-shoes and his walking stick. His handwriting, always poor, became nearly impossible to read, and he gave up. For anything that was written by hand, Claudia Cioffi became his amanuensis, she even signed his checks." He raised his eyes to mine. "For something as lengthy as his letter ..."

He sipped his coffee, and continued. "But, whether in his own hand or not, in every way, the letter *is* his. He appeared before a notary and told the notary it was his own. That's what the document says. Strictly speaking, I cannot and could not affirm or disaffirm that he wrote or signed the letter. Perhaps, by the grace of a merciful God, he recovered. Who is to say anything different?"

Me! If the letter was not handwritten by Palagi, Judge Cremasoli would refuse to admit it as evidence of Palagi's intent. The University's case to sustain Palagi's estate plan would suffer a staggering blow. Since Pine had submitted the letter to the Court as written by Palagi, doubt as to the letter's authenticity also weighed on my responsibility as an officer of the court. Non-disclosure risked Court sanction and humiliation.

"I am sorry to burden you. I see the letter, now, as Palagi's corrupted streak of irony. He ... perhaps ... used Claudia to write a letter that she believed would protect her legacy from the claim of the son. Consider the subtleness of Palagi to use her in his scheme. She was led to believe she had bested the son. Yet, her action, her involvement, would perhaps lose her legacy. Until the letter was challenged in court, she would not realize how he used her."

"But ...!"

His right hand rose as though he was about to bestow a blessing, his voice was low and reflective, as though speaking to himself. "He exploited me, by accusing everyone and leaving me ... us ... to cast his stones at sinners."

I wondered if Palagi did the same to me, got me involved not just because he would be using my skills, my natural inquisitiveness but to punish my antipathy toward him.

He finished his coffee in a swallow, pushed his cup and saucer away, and allowed his voice to harden. "What is the recording but excuses for his many imperfections, and accusations against those who have wounded him, in his saying, a faithless companion, a son who is a criminal, those sworn to a vendetta against his life, an untrustworthy successor. At his end, facing a godless future, he determined to make us all pay. May God have mercy on him."

"Are you suggesting that his allegations are false? I ..."

He looked over my shoulder to the busy piazza, his face empty of emotion. "Some people tell lies as gracefully as they tell the truth. Look at our politicians ..."

I told him that I knew of witnesses, albeit not very reliable witnesses, who saw Palagi go inside and leave a car, followed by someone into the fog to where he likely entered the river. And of the Beretta in his pocket. And what Benno and I had learned in Basilicata as to the vendetta and the 'Ndrangheta. He listened impassively, only the Beretta seemed to surprise him.

"Father, under the circumstances, one cannot discount murder ..."

I saw a wary disquiet rise in his face.

"Murder?" he mused. "Physical murder?"

"There's an expression in the United States: 'Follow the money.'"

"Italians have a similar phrase. *Cui bono?* 'Who will gain?' But is it that simple? Everyone he accused profited from his death?"

"I feel it is our duty to examine all possibilities. Claudia, for instance, hated him, perhaps extorted the insurance, a legacy."

"I am sorry," the priest replied, a palm raised to me. "If you are to investigate, you must proceed alone. I have done my duty." He signaled to a passing waiter for a fresh espresso. "I will not allow

Italo to further his spite against me. Perhaps he could not resist the dismal call of a final resolution. I suggest we will never know, for sure. I have decided that I do not need to know."

I recognized that the priest had a different, likely better, moral center than my own. His coffee arrived, and he finished it in a gulp, and found a wallet from inside his habit. I reminded him that he was my guest. "*Grazie*, my friend," he said. "And I have some information for you. I told you last week that Claudia would be in Rome. What I did not know then is that she is at a private clinic. She suffers from a malady which I suspect is cancer. She contacted our priory here two days ago and I was called."

"For confession?"

"An interesting question. I have spoken to my spiritual director and conclude it was not confession in a sacramental way but nevertheless a confidence. Despite her sickness, her brain burns brightly. And angrily. She felt the need to tell me what she plans to do with her legacy, with her insurance policy proceeds. And why. She seemed compelled to denounce Palagi to someone who knew him, detailing his many sins. We say in Italy *come era, dove era.* 'As it was, where it was.' I listened until she tired. Suffice to say her hatred is not satiated. She plans to vent it on his son if a lawsuit delays or prevents prompt payment of her legacy. So long as her health holds out, she will press her claims, here and in Providence. It may be that her obstinacy might help you."

"How, Father?"

"Faced with such opposition, would not Vittorio, or the 'Ndrangheta who surely back him, seek compromise, with her, with you. These people lust for money. They are impatient at delay."

I mentioned my planned visit to Vittorio's lawyer. He said, "In Rome, it is not only in the courts where arrangements are made. For better or for worse, over the centuries, Romans have learned that the organs of government are designed primarily to frustrate purpose. They have little faith in a justice system that is chaotic and are steeped in a culture of the practical, in resignation as to how things actually are. Thus, in private situations, they find it is easier to act directly. Claudia is related to the Guilias, an old family here. With a phone call here, a message there, an arrangement can be made. Given the influence of such people ..."

His comments echoed passages in the early chapters of *The Leopard*. Italians, di Lampedusa made clear, have developed a highly sophisticated sense of contacts and power, a keen understanding of whom you should say 'yes' to and to whom you can get away with saying 'no' to, and when to compromise. All the deep currents of Italian society—family, nostalgia, distrust of government, and style—reflect this truth.

○ ○ ○

The waiter arrived with our bill. Father Sacchi's eyes went to it. "An espresso at two euros? Rome is so expensive. It shouldn't be, should it?" He stood, wrapped his *cappa* over his shoulders, and closed its clasp. "Are we not both caught in Palagi's web of deception? Neither of us can wish it away nor wield a saber through it. We must let it wither away, as all spider webs eventually do." He took my hand and smiled a shy smile. "I look forward to your return to Rome and meeting your wife. Perhaps by then, all of Italo's machinations will be history."

He threaded his way among the tables into the piazza and disappeared into the crowd. Father Pietro would not have to live with a misjudgment on my part. Or any unforeseen consequences. *Que sera, sera.*

48

I DECIDED TO WALK the core of the city, giving myself the opportunity to consider Father Pietro's advice to compromise, to perhaps leave Palagi, and his murderer—if there was one—to God.

I soon came upon the stalls of Campo de'Fiori and its mountains of vegetables, hanging cured meats, tables of cheeses, varied fish on beds of ice, hawked by hoarse-voiced vendors whose hands and mouths moved with an auctioneer's rapidity. I continued and it seemed only appropriate to enter the cool precincts of the wonderfully restored San'Isidoro Basilica. Its interior's stillness was a relief from the bustle of the city; in a rear pew under a frescoed vault of ceiling, in meager lighting and the smell of old incense and candles, I realized I was in stasis, conflicted by opposing emotions and motives. Palagi was a deceiver, a fraud. He had lost a fortune that should have gone to the Institute. Did it matter if he was a good person or not if he was murdered? Wasn't the existence of a crime enough to be worth resolution and penalty for the perpetrator? What, if anything, weighed heavy in the scale of things so that I should continue? And would it amount to anything?

I left the church and found my way through a dense network of alleys, *borgos*, *largos*, and *viales*, stopping for espresso at an unpretentious bar along the Via Gulia crowded with locals, when something attracted my eye in a dusty shop window displaying vintage military uniforms, antique swords, muskets, and replicas of more modern weapons and ammunition. The shop's sign read *Antiquario Replica Arma da Fuoco*.

I stood at the window and suddenly, I had an intuition that I dismissed as absurd until my fingers rolled in the lingering memory of a tube of metal in plush carpet. The shopkeeper, a matronly woman, was surprised at my request and grumbled at the tiny sale she made after handing me a cartridge for a Beretta and answering my time-consuming questions. I left with my purchase in a plastic envelope. I felt a little silly: would it end up being a souvenir?

I returned to the hotel through throngs of tourists, many of whom were led by guides holding aloft wands draped with flags or ribbons. When I arrived at my suite, I opened the windows and shutters and stretched out on a sofa and got comfortable with *The Leopard* when a brisk rap at the door interrupted me. Benno Bacigalupi, sporting a day's beard, a straw fedora, a floral casual shirt, and pleated gray slacks, smiled jauntily and sauntered in; the dour Benno had seemingly been transformed into the relaxed Benno. He told me he liked our hotel, of his excursion into the Piazza Navona for *pranzo*; we moved to the lounge area facing the balcony, stopping for a bucket of ice, tall glasses, a San Pellegrino for me, and a premixed limoncello from the mini bar for him.

"What you got here is a *frittata*, a ... *pasticcio*, a mess. First, more on family background, what's going on. Most of this I got from Gianmarco, some of which we guessed at before, some I now can confirm. Gotta tell you, without him, we'd have gotten *nada*."

With that comment, he took a handwritten statement from his shirt pocket, an Italian version of 'For Services Rendered,' for a thousand euros from Gianmarco.

"Cheap," Benno said firmly. "He prefers cash. Can you arrange it?"

I said I supposed it could be managed.

Benno, relieved by my quick acceptance, took a long sip of limoncello and continued. "Maria Ruggieri's family were farmers, shopkeepers and minor politicians with a modest local prominence because their relatives in Matera, that's the provincial capital—where that guy Gibson filmed that movie *The Passion of the Christ*—and not far from the village, ran a cell of the 'Ndrangheta. In Basilicata, no matter who thought they were in charge and tried to make their laws hold sway, Socialists, Fascists, Christian Democrats, back to the time of the monarchy, it has always been run by the 'Ndrangheta."

After more limoncello, he continued, "In the countryside where we went, the gang is into small stuff, blackmail, protection, fixes, prostitution, payoffs, and the like, and they take care of families. Times are tough now, with people leaving, so they scratch at anything and everything that looks like it could turn a euro. In the larger towns and cities, they run drug rackets and smuggling, dump toxic waste wherever, and control the unions and they used to have it *all* until the Albanians and Arabs arrived." He looked up. "Like Providence, with the Latino and Asian gangs taking over drugs."

He finished the limoncello and barely stiffled a yawn. "They are opportunistic, take what comes along, process it through ancestry, family, those who are with you and those against. And, pardon my expression, but in Basilicata, it is 'fuck you' unless you're *la famiglia*. They speak the truth to no one except family. Their attitude towards Palagi, rich, soft because he was from the North, was to take him down and collect while doing it."

He was interrupted by a telephone call from the hotel concierge who suggested a *prenotazione* for *cena* at the nearby *LeCornacchie*, celebrated, according to the concierge, for classic Roman cuisine. Benno didn't disguise a second yawn. "You know, I could use a nap. What say we finish up with dinner?"

Benno, a nap?

He left me and I used the downtime for more notes on my laptop, then continued *The Leopard* as the serene estate life of the princely class disintegrated after Garibaldi and his cohort landed in Sicily and *new* men, mean men, corrupt men, replaced it. I came to a passage that I underlined electronically: *'The change of spots of government in the South was illusory, the concentration of power, the illegalities, and alliances, continue.'*

Benno was waiting for me in the lobby, cleanly shaven, in a black, satin finish jacket, white ruffled-front shirt, flaired trousers, and black leather shoes. The clothes, he said, were provided by Gianmarco. We walked the few blocks to the restaurant and found its décor almost too romantic for two straight guys to be having dinner there. Benno asked for a table not within listening distance of other diners, we ordered campari and sodas, and antipasti, and told the waiter we would order later from the menu. When our drinks arrived, I asked, "How could Maria Ruggieri live with the Giambazzis all these years? Disowned? Never mentioning her affair with Palagi?"

Benno took down half of his campari. "You are getting ahead of me," he said testily. That was more like the *old* Benno.

"Sorry."

"Like I said, in Basilicata, things are tough. They fight over a crust of bread, says Gianmarco, and they still avenge wrongs."

A waiter brought dishes of marinated artichokes, roast peppers, olives, and sun-dried tomatoes with toasted bread rubbed with a seasoned oil. From a multi-page menu, skipping the pasta, Benno ordered *salimbacca alla romana*, I chose a special *abbacchio al forno*, and we found a wine from Puglia to honor Gianmarco.

When the waiter left us, Benno continued. "Gianmarco figured that at some point, the family found Maria's kid and got him into the fringes of a 'Ndrangheta cell in Rome. Putting two and two together, among the cells of the gang," he raised his hands, fists out to me, "I figure the right hand—New York—didn't know what interests the left—Basilicata, and vice versa. Each is territorial, didn't know of their joint interest in Palagi, until Maria spilled the beans and then," he delved into the antipasti, spearing olives and peppers, "somebody came up with the idea for a triple score. Get a piece of whatever Vittorio could extort out of Palagi now as a destitute son, then use the threat of the vendetta for a big pay off, and lastly, pick Palagi's bones by Vittorio making a claim as to his estate."

His precise description of the extortion made it seem an ingenious plan. I wasn't so convinced; it seemed fitful and happenstance and I said so.

"Explains a lot," he snorted. "Say you're Palagi. You're threatened. You borrow the funds from Zito, the *strazzino*, the loan shark, to pay the vendetta. You return to Italy, you're told by your worthless son that the blood money didn't get to the Ruggieris, the debt of honor remains outstanding, you're still in danger. You figure the New York cell stole the money but the Giambazzis should protect you from the Basilicata gang because the A-4 account remains in your name. It is your ace in the hole against retribution. But you want to check. So you contact the investment guy who tells you 'Sorry, that account has been closed.' There goes your protection. You are out of money, maybe the Ruggieris will enforce the vendetta, you start carrying the Beretta."

My thoughts bang into one another. "So, where are we? Did the 'Ndrangheta kill him?"

"Not what I said. The 'Ndrangheta wouldn't knock him off after a payment like that. Not while there was still the opportunity to squeeze him even more."

49 Thursday

THE NEXT MORNING, ENZO'S cousin placed our carry-ons, now augmented by Benno's new clothes in a separate bag, in the trunk of the Lancia. A slightly hungover Benno, in the nondescript suit he arrived in, appeared to have abandoned his new persona.

Avvocato Maurizio Musumeci's office was not on Rome's 'lawyer row,' the Viale Castro Pretorio, but in a less than prosperous area, on the Via Galvani in a building that could have been designed by a Mussolini era modernist, a box with veneer columns in a concrete façade webbed by poorly repaired cracks.

The pokey elevator groaned its way up one floor and opened directly into an office suite and a red-eyed receptionist, her chestnut hair frizzy, who might have arrived directly from a long night of clubbing in Testaccio. Even so, she seemed aware that these *Americanos* were important enough to greet with a smile that cracked through her makeup. In Italian, she informed us that the lawyer would be with us momentarily, waved a bangled hand at some uncomfortable looking chairs under faded landscape prints, and inquired if we desired coffee. We declined and she went to her desk where she concentrated on varnishing her fingernails a bright pink from a tiny bottle.

This being Italy, it was not surprising that we were required to wait an appropriate interval of time for the sake of Musumeci's prestige. Benno stared ahead in detective mode while I used the time to refocus. Palagi's probate estate had been reduced to his Providence condominium, any personal property, a miniscule income stream from the Forza novels and license fees; his trust held title to his Italian apartments and a worthless claim against Ravensford Capital. Palagi's letter of affirmation which had fortified our case was now of questionable value because it was likely in Claudia Cioffi's handwriting. Which meant for the small potatoes, I had to put up a good fight, which in turn meant, without leverage, I had to bluff it out.

After ten minutes, we were ushered into an overheated room that smelled of yellowing paper. The lawyer's back was to two dusty windows facing south toward fog-laden hills, putting his jowly features in semi-shadow. An overhead light barely exposed a threadbare carpet, smudgy glass-fronted cabinets, newspapers, and piles of folders on his desk. He made a gesture of half rising from his chair as I introduced myself and Benno as my consultant in various aspects of the Palagi estate. The lawyer responded in passable English and pointed to two chairs in front of his desk. Somewhere in the room, a fly buzzed.

The lawyer's head was too small for a thick neck which seemed to pop out of his white shirt and green tie; dusty lenses in black frames hid his eyes. His thin lips held a cryptic smile as he clasped his hands over his stomach and sat back, apparently waiting for me to plead my case; after all, I had come to him.

I reiterated our position as to his client's claim and our determination to require a forensic affirmation of paternity through DNA testing. As I went on, Musumeci appeared to be more interested in the fly's circumnavigation of his desk; it swooped by his head several times and landed on a folder, its legs rubbing against one another. As I finished, the fly was dispatched with a well-aimed copy of *La Republica*. Satisfied with his victory, the lawyer replied, "We need no testing here. We rely on Signor Palagi's acceptance of his son in an instrument I prepared and witnessed, and which has been accepted by appropriate officials."

"In Rhode Island, our court will require a test, I assure you."

"I have been briefed extensively on these matters by eminent local counsel," he said brusquely. "I also understand that considerable assets were lost in a fraud in which the University was culpable, permitting his funds to be negligently invested, losing what should be my client's inheritance. The University is culpable." The Lucca theory. "And there are other assets, like his condominium, whatever else he owned. In any event, and particularly as to Italian assets, Italo Palagi was a citizen of Italy and the laws of Italy protect a son's interest. You know our *successione legittima*? Our *quota legittima*?"

I had been advised by Eustace Pine that under Italian estate law, a son would be entitled to not less than a fifty percent share of Italian real estate owned by his father, the *successione necessaria*.

In emphasis, he hunched forward, his eyes holding mine like magnets, sizing me up, his face screwed up in impatience. "You came all this way and you offer nothing?" he grunted. "You waste this time?" and in expressing his determination to fight the University, reminded me of a Providence lawyer noted for his blustering threats and once described to me as gas-filled, and with as many tentacles, as a Portuguese man-of-war.

After his bluster receded, I said, "The University would agree to sell the apartments here and share proceeds to the extent required by Italian law for a son, if paternity can be proven, in return for a release of any and all claims against Palagi's estate or trust, both in Italy and America."

"You offer what we own, nothing else," he growled and the lawyer twisted in his chair to stare at the shelves of books. "And you ignore our client's considerable expenses, both here and in America, including my representation of him before his father's death and the taxes that will be due, the *imposta sulle successione*."

Before I could reply "your problem," he continued, taking off his glasses, his eyes in a narrow squint that hinted at cunning. "Your proposal is totally unfair, and it will take, in any event, too much time to sell the apartments in these difficult days. And what of other claimants? Are they to be satisfied? Do you first pay them out of the remaining U.S. assets so I do not worry about their claims here?"

The *other claimants*? Father Pietro's suggestion as to a possible *Roman arrangement* came to mind. If Palagi's probate estate in Providence did not have the ability to pay Claudia Cioffi's legacy in full, the difference, she likely had let it be known, had come out of whatever Vittorio Ruggieri and the 'Ndrangheta collected from the sale of the Italian apartments. Since she was determined to come out whole, Avvocato Musumeci needed our cooperation for a prompt resolution. "All depends upon proof of paternity," I said sternly and grabbed the arms of my chair as though about to leave.

Before my bottom left my chair, he countered, "We could not

settle on such a basis. If you drop this testing idea, agree to take Palagi's acknowledgement of paternity, I might advise my client to withdraw our claim in your court, provided you acknowledge Vittorio as his son, the apartments are sold, and we are assured other claimants are paid from funds in the US. And you will need to cover my destitute client's legal expenses," and quoted a number that was outrageous.

With my elbows resting on the chair's arms, my fingers went to my chin, hopefully expressing both interest and disappointment. I said that I'd have to check the value of assets left in Palagi's probate estate after payment of debts and expenses. Purposefully, I did not mention that his debt to Heritage Finance might bankrupt the estate; that was for later. As to Musumeci's bills, I offered a fraction of his exaggerated, if not fictional, fees and expenses which he brusquely rejected, and it took more palaver to reach a tentative accord: thirty percent of his questioned fees from off the top of apartment sales proceeds, all Italian taxes, fees and expenses of the sale to be split, Lucca's and Puppy Dog's fees to come from Vittorio's net share, all subject to approval of our respective clients and execution of suitable documentation and releases. Neither one of us made the offer to conclude our negotiation with a handshake.

"We are leaving Rome later today," I said. "The University must have your client's assent within a week of my return. Or, we begin our pursuit of assets." I gave him my business card. "E-mail me at this address."

He nodded and rose from his seat. Our business having been concluded, likely profitable to him, if not his clients, I stood to leave when Benno said, "It would be useful for you to be aware of certain facts before you discuss the proposed arrangement with your client."

I was taken aback; we had discussed no such interjection.

'What is this?' Musumeci's eyes questioned, 'we have completed our business!'

I returned to my chair as Benno explained he was a former member of the Rhode Island State Police, that's like the *carabinari*, retained to investigate the circumstances of Italo Palagi's death, in Providence and in Basilicata. He said Vittorio knew of the vendetta against his father, and as a confederate of the 'Ndrangheta, tried to extort funds. The lawyer's attempts to interrupt ended at Benno's repetition of *'Ndrangheta*. "Such a criminal act would destroy his legal position here in Italy or in Providence." And he added in disgust, "Should an Italian son do *that* to his father?"

Musumeci had become physically agitated, his hands waving at me, his face contorted. He blasted Benno in Italian vernacular for his *calunnia*, spittle spraying his desk. Benno remained impassive, which further infuriated Musumeci who now appealed to me. "Your investigator. I dismiss his speculative, inflammatory allegations as provocative and threatening to our agreement. I ignore *him*." He turned away from us and I signaled Benno it was time to leave.

o O o

We left the lawyer's office with something of a swagger in our steps. Benno's unexpected intervention seemed to have locked up our deal. That more than paid for his trip. A mission accomplished, I thought, until I remembered the Heritage Finance obligation that might torpedo the deal. How was I going to deal with that?

We approached the waiting Lancia and I was about to commend Benno when he pointed to a street sign on the wall of an adjoining building. We, the representatives of Carter University, were parked at the cross street of Via Cristoforo Colombo.

50

OUR RETURN FLIGHT WAS hours late departing Rome but was otherwise smooth, lunch heavy, and uneventful. Benno had returned to his taciturn self and watched a movie before napping while I finished *The Leopard*, taking away the thought that so much of what the Prince lived through remained: a listless economic spirit, political dysfunction that grinds on, a society based on personal allegiances, one with the ability to recognize societal ills without the will to change. Italians, I concluded, still live in two linear levels, one is family, Italian culture and creativity; another fends off government, taxes, social responsibility to a united nation which squanders opportunities for the future with reliance on favoritism and tolerance for the status quo. Palagi was a poster child of that society.

Upon arrival at Logan, I checked my cell phone and noticed an e-mail from *Direttore* Carvo from the Banco di San Paolo. Palagi's letter of instruction as to the administrative fee arrangement would take longer to retrieve than expected. I smelled a rat. In the limo back to Providence, I texted Nadie that I would soon be home but didn't get a response. On Congdon Street, where I left Benno in the limo, I asked for a write-up on the information from Basilicata, thanked him for his excellent service, opened the front door to the house, and shouted triumphantly, "I'm back. On Thursday, on schedule!"

No reply. No movement heard. No rush to the head of the stairs for the loft.

Nadie was on the sofa, a *Vanity Fair* magazine was unopened on her lap. She was holding a wine glass in her right hand across her breasts, like Katherine Hepburn or Bette Davis would hold a cigarette in a late thirties movies. She said neutrally, "Your ex-wife sent us a wedding gift. Champagne glasses. Tiffany."

She finished the wine, a drop landed on her blouse, but she didn't notice, which meant it was at least a second or third glass. She placed the glass on a table, perhaps so she could berate me with both hands.

"She would," I muttered.

"Did you tell her?"

I took a deep breath, sat, struggling for the right words. "Remember, in New York, I interviewed a potential witness from Ravensford? Turned out, he's represented by Jocelyn. I had no clue she was his lawyer until I walked into the meeting. Couldn't believe it. I hadn't seen her in years and she waltzed into my life."

Nadie's eyes had a martini olive color that was at once opaque, frosty, and filled with danger. "Are you going to meet her again?"

"It's all Champlin & Burrill from now on."

"What did she say about us?"

"'Congratulations.'"

"What about her?"

"Said she was dating."

"How did you feel?"

"Ambushed. But, I was pleasant, our session with her client was businesslike."

"You didn't tell me."

"I should have."

"When I mentioned her later, on the train, you still didn't tell me."

"I was embarrassed. Sorry for ..."

"She's devious, isn't she?" Nadie mused, picking up her glass, her eyes focused somewhere behind me. "Probably knew *you* would struggle with telling me about her sudden re-appearance right before our wedding. She wanted to embarrass you into hiding something from me. So, she sent the gift to spring her trap." Nadie was buying into comments I made over time about Jocelyn's deviousness. "She's a big deal in politics, a successful lawyer, but she lost you. You are an itch that she has to scratch. She must have Googled you once she knew of your interest in her client." She finished the wine. "The bitch!"

"It's all about her ego," I suggested, pushing Nadie to conclude that Jocelyn's gift *was* meant to poison our well. I moved closer to Nadie and touched her arm. "I should have told you right away."

She looked at me, her face clouded. "I knew that the faculty senate would be asked to abolish Columbus Day. I didn't tell you. Not too much different, is it?" Sternness melted from her face. She stood and we kissed like two love-starved kids. "Let's not get ourselves into something like this again."

As I unpacked, Nadie became chatty, telling me that the wedding arrangements were settling in, her wedding dress would be delivered tomorrow to Temple House, there was a last meeting with the caterer tomorrow morning, another with the band leader, the Renaissance Hotel had to be checked to be sure that the Shoot-Out's pro tournament that began today hadn't disrupted our guests' reservations, and that all fingers were crossed for an outside ceremony on Sunday. One late entry into Nadie's panoply of concerns was the family dinner for the Gershowitzs and Temples on Saturday evening in one of the Hope Club's private dining rooms.

"I had a dream last night that the dinner was an absolute disaster. Ida, the boys, started to argue about the loan. Your brother got involved, more as a referee, but they remained loud and boisterous and unfeeling, your family could see how boorish they can be, and when I tried to get them to stop yelling at one another, and at you, they wouldn't, and that's when I woke up. A premonition?"

While I showered off three thousand miles of travel, I was hoping my timely return would negate Nadie's pledge of chastity, but when I returned to the loft wearing only shorts and a splash of musk cologne she liked, she was sleeping. Her hair was spread on a pillow gently caressing her head, framing her face, one lock created a peekaboo effect. One hand was stretched toward my side of the bed. I could not take my eyes off the blush on her high cheek bones, knowing that her skin would feel like velvet. Should I wake her? Risk a later recrimination?

A car approaches throwing up gravel in its tire treads. The slot through to the rear seat fills with the glare of headlights and blue and red strobes.

My stomach tightens as I hear the crackle of a police radio, a car door opens, footsteps.

I am screwed, here comes the publicity, the dreaded notoriety. Nevertheless, I yell, "Help!" and hear the surprised response, "What the f—!"

The driver side door opens, the interior light is on, showing the open slot in the rear seat from which my voice bellows, "Get me out of here! Keys on the front seat!"

Seconds later, the trunk lock pops and despite very sore muscles and spongy legs, I manage to angle myself out to face a blinding flashlight and a shiny police service revolver. Before I can suck in a lungful of fresh night air, the cop's young, gruff but strained, voice demands, "Spread 'em! Hands on the car! C'mon, spread 'em!"

As my sore hands flatten on the car's roof, my feet are forcefully spread apart by the flashlight as my leg muscles scream in protest. I huff, "Hey, this is my car! I was abducted! In Providence, in a parking lot, stuffed in the trunk ..."

"Car jack?" He asks.

"If that's what you call it when ..." I sound like my mental gears are not meshing.

He must have stowed away the revolver because he gives me a one hand pat down. Finally, "You can relax," he says.

'Relax?' Like No-Neck, he wants me to 'relax?'

I turn to him slowly, squeezing my aching fingers, my leg muscles trembling, I am disoriented but thoughts, excuses, alibis crowd my mind. The cop stands five five or so, is muscular, wears a gray starched shirt, is a clean cut looking twenty-five-ish, with black eyebrows. If he's got a Friday night patrol that includes the landfill, he must be the rookie of the rookies. "Are you okay?"

"Yeah. A little shook up from being bounced around." I notice he doesn't bother to look in the trunk.

"Took your money?"

Good question. I feel my back pocket. "My wallet's gone."

"How many?"

I assume he means assailants. "Two guys. Never saw the faces."

"Why bring you down here?"

"Beats me."

"Registration?"

"In the glove box."

"Get it."

I squeeze into the front seat to retrieve the car's registration and go through stuff that collects in there. "We come down here to scare off kids drinking or whatever," he says. "But a few years ago, we had that double murder, a couple who were kidnapped in Providence near the Arcade, brought out here, shot. For what, fifty bucks? Remember that?"

I do.

I hand him the registration and get out of the car. He reads aloud, "Alger Temple. Congdon Street, Providence. Got an ID?"

"In my wallet ..."

"Yeah, well, that's what they wanted, but I still don't get why they brought you here. Stay put. I'm gonna report in."

He walks back toward his patrol car just as Benno's Taurus comes bouncing up the road and stops.

51 Friday

MY CIRCADIAN RHYTHMS WERE out of sync after three nights in Italy. When I finally fell asleep, the next thing I knew, the sun was streaming through the slats of the loft's blinds, splintering the room's darkness and it was quarter to nine.

Sluggishly, I slung myself out of bed, put on my robe, went down to the kitchen, and found the morning *Journal* with a Post-It note on the breakfast counter: *I love you, left for my last class!* A double espresso provided the necessary caffeine charge to get on with the day.

At College Hall, after a brief meeting to catch up with Marcie, I closeted myself with the Provost. In my absence, his assistant had found a governance wonk in the faculty senate who filed a motion for reconsideration of the Columbus Day name change on the procedural basis I had suggested. The Provost said, "If we can get through this weekend," when a Native American teach-in was scheduled on The Green on Sunday—Columbus Day—"we might make it through until Commencement." As to negotiations on the tax treaty, he said the President was resigned to waiting it out. "We were so close, Algy, so close."

I reported my discovery of Palagi's fraudulent administration fee and that Brunotti was aware of Palagi's fraud but failed to report it as required by both University regulation and common sense. As to Palagi's accusation of Brunotti's fraud, I told him of Benno's theory as to the pages in the notebook. "Is everyone at the Institute a crook?" the Provost thundered and added that Brunotti, after a terse telephone conversation with the President on Tuesday evening, had gone to ground. "I bet he's working on Plan B right now."

I explained the proposed settlement with Palagi's son. "If the son goes away for a split of the sale proceeds of the Italian apartments in return for a complete release of any claims, it's a win," he replied. "A probate court contest isn't in our interest right now."

$$\circ \, \bigcirc \, \circ$$

Young Jimmy had called my office several times during the past two days and I returned his call. His voice was nervous and high pitched with anxiety. "I'm screwed! Zito called me to his office yesterday. This big, bald guy shows up and sits down next to me and Zito tells me to dump my match tonight. Keep it going as long as I can, and then dump."

"Who are you playing?"

"Are you ready for this? Harley Smoot. It's a huge deal. You can feel the action building. With the pros in town for the Shoot-Out, they all want to play him but he's been cute. He's been in the Club. He wins, nothing heavy on the table, he's playing good but not pushing it, not banging balls, all finesse. But the later it gets, I see him lose his edge. Thought it was a hustle at first, but it isn't. I can win! I can beat Harley Smoot! I could pay down, maybe pay off, Zito. And he wants me to dump!"

I remembered the "Love to play you sometime" from Young Jimmy to Smoot at the Gala. "How much have you bet?"

"I play Harley even for the ten grand from what I still have from the Shoot-Out, and with what I got out of beating Romero and Salazar on the side, so I've got down close to twenty."

"You need a lot more than that."

He paused, maybe swallowed, before he said, "I told Zito you are my sweater, that you could cover any bets I made, and he'll be taken out."

"What?"

"Algy, I panicked. I figured if he thought Algy Temple was backing me, win or lose, Zito might back off. You're the only guy I know who would sound legit, like I could pay off the loan if I won, take the hit and pay off my bets if I lost. Zito already has the house cut, would make plenty out of that, plus what he spreads out on Harley or me. He's just fuckin' greedy!"

Should I have been surprised that Young Jimmy would lie? No, for a hustler, lying was a condition of play. Young Jimmy had no reason to know that my backing him would be grit in a festering wound for Zito, give him an excuse to crap all over me even if he had been warned to stop his harassment. All Young Jimmy was thinking about was his restaurant, his Club, his reputation, his life and limb. I was thinking about Nadie.

"What can I do," I asked, hoping he had an answer.

"I don't know. I had to tell you."

"Where are you playing?"

"I think at En Core but I don't know for sure."

En Core would work. Lots of parking, no problem with logistics for the out-of-towners, put a table up in the third floor party room.

"Is Smoot into this?"

"No way. Doesn't know and doesn't care who has side action. He's here to play pool, win our bet."

"Does Maria Catarina know?"

"No."

"How did you leave it with Zito?"

"He thinks I'm going along. Told me not to talk to you. If I do, that big fuck goes into action. Zito seemed to like the thought you might lose plenty backing me if I fold."

"The way I see it," I said, "you have to go to Tuttle because you can't get out of Zito's sway. If you beat Smoot, you lose with Zito and Scuiglie. If you dump ..."

"Can't dump. I never have. Smoot may beat me fair and square but I'm not gonna dump."

I couldn't conceive how Young Jimmy would get out of this self-inflicted mess. "Where are you going to be in the next few hours?" I needed time to think through every possible avenue of attack.

"I'm going home to shower and then down to the Dunk for an exhibition at seven-thirty, have to stay there for some ESPN color until about ten-thirty."

"If you don't see me at the Dunk or you don't hear from me before you play Smoot, you are on your own. You'll have to make a decision right then and there to dump or not."

"Are you saying you could help? Back me if I play to win?"

I remembered Big Bill Halsey and the long ago match at Falvey's. "I'm not saying that. But I'm thinking."

"Algy, if you do this for me and I win, I could pay down Zito. I tell him right before the match that I'm gonna win so he doesn't put money on Smoot. He still has the book and get's paid."

"And if you don't win?"

"I owe you. I'll pay you back somehow, sometime. But that's all it will be. Because I'm not gonna have anything left."

I remained at my desk. Frannie Zito was a player in both the Palagi conundrum and Young Jimmy's woes. Both debtors seemingly screwed; and me, his target, a player in each dilemma. While not related to one another, nothing would work that didn't relieve both. I doodled on a yellow legal pad, lines and boxes and arrows were in parallel, then mixed together. Slowly, shadows emerged from the connections like a photographic plate immersed in a developing solution. Could I concoct a plan of action, implement an idea, one that might work out for both Young Jimmy and the estate of Italo Palagi? And me?

Joe Laretta was in his office and he assumed I was calling to catch up on last Tuesday's probate court meeting. "Cremasoli's a beauty. Started off tough, like I expected, showing off for the Luccas. He orders the trust documents to be turned over and wonders aloud about 'fairness' to the son. Pine argued that under Rhode Island law, the probate court has no jurisdiction over Palagi's trust assets and then produces the letter of affirmation from Palagi."

He chuckled. "So much for confidentially. Cremasoli already knew about the letter and recognized a legal as well as political problem he would rather not deal with. He was looking for a way out. 'Judge,' I say, 'both sides agree that the will has to be presented, even if it is only to get to the contest.' 'Anybody have a problem with that?' he asks. Nobody does. That effectively puts the case off at least three months after all the advertising and other procedural crap required. From Cremasoli's perspective, three months is a long time for something to happen that makes this go away."

I explained the prospective settlement with the son's lawyer in Rome.

He replied, "Got to say, a settlement would be good because Cremasoli is really pissed off about this Columbus Day stuff."

"There's not much I can do about that."

"They put up a *Keep Columbus In Columbus Day* banner below the *pino* hanging in the Arch on Atwells, right where the parade ends. The show at the Columbus Theatre on Saturday that the boys are producing will get tempers boiling and the parade will have a lot of anti-Carter stuff. All it's gonna take is some jerk to show up with a Native American Day banner, an Indian headdress, or a couple of insulting placards, and ka-pow! And you lost a car, I hear."

Because of what I was going to ask him to do for me, I gave him the details of the threatening phone calls, my session with Zito in his Bentley, the Mini's demise, and Young Jimmy's indebtedness to Zito. I took his long silence as sympathetic and that encouraged me to ask for a favor.

"*You* want a meet with Zito? Tonight? After you challenged him? After his goons destroy your car? After your buddy claims you are backing him against Smoot? Are you out of your f'n mind?"

"I've got something Zito would want in return for taking the pressure off Young Jimmy. He won't regret it."

"What."

"Later," I said.

"Look," Laretta said, "you are out of your league here. No insult intended. An injury on the Hill is forgiven, but not forgotten. Zito doesn't want any deal with you. He wants to spit in your face."

"He'll take a call from you but not me. For *bona fides*, I want you there. Don't worry. Nothing that could embarrass you."

"He'll never do it."

"Try."

o O o

A couple hours later Laretta called me back. "You've got a meeting at seven."

"Where?"

"At least it's gonna be convenient. Hard Core. In the office."

"Cripes, I don't want to be seen going in there!"

"What did you expect? The Hope Club? Yeah, he's rubbing your face in it. Look," Laretta said impatiently, "you asked me to get a meet, you have the meet."

"I'll go. I just didn't think it would be ..."

"And here's the other thing. It's only you. Not me."

"What?"

"I tried but it has to be one-on-one. I got to warn you. Don't do this. Don't go it alone. He's a snake."

I knew he was right.

"Tell me you won't do it and prove to me you're smart."

"No, I have to do it."

Laretta paused, "You better get your back covered."

I told him I had hired Benno.

"Sure, Bacigalupi with six others and it's even-steven. They hate him but respect him, but he's not muscle. Not going to do you any good in a one-on-one inside Hard Core." He paused. "If it doesn't work out, can I represent your estate?"

Was he kidding?

I call out to the cop who has turned on his flashlight to check out the arrival. Benno gets out and approaches, one hand shielding his eyes from the cop's flashlight, the other palm up flashing his badge. The scene is out of a movie, headlights, strobes, hands-up. "Officer, my name's Bacigalupi. Chief Romano knows me. I'd like to talk to you for a minute," Benno says confidently and moves closer to the cop. They are too far away for me to hear but Benno appears to be explaining something very deliberately, using his hands, nodding at the cop's questions. The cop puts a hand through his brush cut as though trying to decide something, then, he says, "Okay," and gets behind the wheel of the patrol car, a cell phone at his ear.

Benno comes over to me. He shrugs toward the patrol car. "Kid's father is a sergeant on the Johnston police. I know him pretty well. I asked him if we could leave now, and file a report later. He could write up his immediate report and everything would be kosher."

"Did he agree?"

"He's calling his father. I bet he'll say no problem. In Johnston, all they got is a car sitting on the side of the road where it shouldn't be. If somebody should be interested, it's where the assault took place and that's Providence. And you're a victim. And, you got your car back. The only thing missing is your wallet and who knows where that is.

I took two steps to the maw of the trunk, which remains open and has an interior light, and there it is. And my fedora. Benno takes the wallet, and empties the cash into his pocket.

The cop finishes his call, gets out of the patrol car, and walks slowly back to us. Benno shows him my empty wallet and I confirm it is mine. He checks my driver's license photograph with the face in the beam of his flashlight. "Yeah, I don't see any problems as long as you come in. All we need is a report," and he hands me the keys to the Charger. That earns him a pat on the shoulder from Benno, a reminiscence about his father, and an escort back to the patrol car. With strobe lights off, he leaves us.

Benno and I get into our respective cars and I follow Benno out onto the Plainville Pike to a McDonald's. Not for coffee or food. The restroom.

52

BENNO AGREED WITH LARETTA that a meeting with Zito under these circumstances was crazy. Worse, he said, he was sure *somebody* had talked to *somebody* to cool off Zito. All I was going to do was roil it up again, give Zito an excuse to continue harassment. Since I was adamant, we agreed that I was to let Zito know that everything I told him was also known by Laretta, and Benno who was waiting for me in the Hard Core parking lot. Benno agreed to meet me in the lot at seven.

"What about the car paint guy?"

"From a Bentley. But within a three year span. So close, but no cigar."

o O o

I knew that if I wasn't home for dinner after my trip to Italy, Nadie would be upset. I arrived on Congdon Street at the same time she returned from Temple House's wedding prep and to keep myself calm and focused, I volunteered to make dinner. She agreed, saying she was tired and had been caught in a passing shower on her walk home. "Oh, I miss the Mini!" she said, toweling her hair, and joined me in the kitchen.

A classic Caesar salad requires anchovies. Nadie hates anchovies. Under the circumstances, I deferred to her taste preference and became a receptive audience for a play-by-play of wedding dilemmas with caterers, musicians—the oboist for the ceremony called in sick—florists, and guests as I washed and chopped greens and grated parmesan cheese in front of her at the counter. We opened a bottle of Newport Vineyards Reisling, toasted ourselves, and before I realized it, I was telling her of Palagi's fraud, his years as a conspirator against the Italian government, later as a front for a criminal gang, and his cancerous pathology. Her questions indicated I had won her professional attention.

She mused aloud, wine glass in hand, comparing Palagi's duplicity to the arch schemer Sugarman. "By all accounts, Sugarman was charming, disarming, and looked the part, competent like an accountant, wise, prudent. People trusted him, pure and simple. With investors, Sugarman had won his halo."

"And?"

"Now take Palagi," she said, swirling the wine in her glass. "He fooled the University because he was an academic with the right pedigree, a generous benefactor in giving up half his royalties to the Institute, making the Institute his estate beneficiary. He had everyone's trust ... except maybe, you." She added that grudgingly. "All the while, he was living a lie, just like Sugarman, probably angry because his sordid prior life required him to act so generously to tamp down criticism and avoid uncomfortable questions. Like Sugarman, he was greedy, arrogant, dismissive of others, and, *his* victim, the University, never bothered to dig into his background or why his donors were donating, or what was going in or what he was taking out of accounts. Everybody trusted him."

Leave it to Nadie to dissect Palagi's psyche, how his mind and emotions might work. I asked what it would take for someone inured to duplicity to suddenly pack it in.

"Most of us have a tipping point. Sugarman apparently decided to confess because he couldn't handle the pressure of increased withdrawals and constant replenishment of funds. His confession was the emotional equivalent of a suicide, the end of his life of lies." She finished her wine. "For Palagi, his cancer, the threat of exposure by Brunotti, his son's extortion, all of the above?"

"But only a few days before he died, Palagi said in his recording he wouldn't commit suicide."

"But this isn't about how Palagi died," she continued. "It's how he lived. For decades, he lived a lie and expected to continue to get away with it. Sure, some niggling doubts, some questions maybe, but he believed his lies would never trip him up because he had been exempt from retribution for so long. Anyone who accused him would be at fault or not credible, or he could turn the accusation around. Even with the vendetta, he thought he could buy it off. But just in case, when the end was near, he left his recording in case he was wrong. He believed under the circumstances, you—being you—and the priest would accept his statements as the truth and go after his enemies." She paused, suspicion in her voice. "*Did* you?"

Somehow, I was able to dissemble an answer.

o O o

During dinner, I told Nadie that I wanted to watch Young Jimmy play at least one exhibition during the Shoot-Out, which was true, tonight was my last chance, and I didn't expect to be home late. Luckily, my absence didn't interfere with her plans to meet with Zelda and Ida arriving at the Renaissance Hotel tonight; she wanted to be there to get Zelda settled in. After I changed into jeans, polo shirt, sneakers, and a Carter Cats windbreaker jacket, with a yellow slicker and an old fedora from the back of the hall closet under my arm, I shouted a goodbye to Nadie and left the house for the garage.

The fedora and slicker were my half-ass attempt to disguise myself entering Hard Core, but I put on both as the wind pushed a bank of black clouds against the East Side and the rain became hard pellets. Water cascaded down the hill on East Street, carrying a slurry of leaves toward storm drains. Diamond crystals of windshield glass sparkled in the garage lights and scarred asphalt marked the demise of the Mini. As I entered the garage, my cell phone vibrated and its screen showed Fausto Tramonti's number. I let it buzz until I was in the Charger. I struggled whether to answer but did.

"What-the-fuck-are-you-doing-with Jimmy Hannigan?" he thundered.

I grit my teeth. "Nothing that concerns you."

"You, a member of the Commission, backing a deadbeat like Hannigan?"

"How do you know?" Fausto couldn't have learned this from Laretta or from Young Jimmy so it had to be Zito! What did that mean? "This has nothing to do with the Commission. Has to do with Hannigan ..."

"Fuck Hannigan! You're risking serious embarrassment for

Tony. What are you thinking getting in the middle of the action? You're a Commissioner for Christ's sake."

What I'm thinking is Fausto, goddammit, is in cahoots with Zito, warning me to back off from being Young Jimmy's sweater! The son of a bitch!

"I understand my risk ..."

"I don't give a fuck about *your* risk. I'm thinking of Tony's. So should you. Best friend? Bullshit, if you do this and fuck up Tony, if this blows up, you're never going to get within ten feet of the Mayor's office. Never!"

At that, I ended his call and slipped my phone into my windbreaker's pocket. Fausto was right; I had to admit my loyalties were at cross purposes, my course of action dangerous to both friends. But it was too late. I was, again, Young Jimmy's sweater.

53

THE RAIN HAD A relentless fervor as I parked the Charger in the puddled asphalt lot behind Hard Core. I was getting sweaty from wearing both the jacket and slicker, or from nerves, and I took off the slicker, peeled off the windbreaker, tossed it on the rear seat, and put the slicker back on.

Where was Benno? It was a minute past seven. Zito's Bentley was parked by the club's side door. What to do, continue to wait for Benno or go in now? I couldn't take the chance of standing up Zito and if I waited any longer, I would lose my mojo. With the fedora down to my ears, I left the car and walked by the Bentley, apprehensive that Sal would suddenly pop out. He didn't, and if there was a scrape on the paint of the passenger side door, rain beads covered it up.

Two heavyset bouncers in black jackets and jeans, thick arms clenched across their barrel chests, barely glanced at me from under the Club's canopy. I joined two other rained on customers at the admission window within a shocking pink and gold splashed entryway accompanied by booming bump and grind music. A wall sign over the window gave me three choices, with rising cover fees for each: the Lust Lounge—cheapest—the Show Room, and the Gentlemen's Club. I wondered what happened in the Ultimate Private Club, which an arrow indicated was on the second floor.

I asked for the office and the heavily made-up ticket seller with her boobs falling out of a halter motioned to the right, which I mistakenly took as meaning the Lust Lounge. I paid a five dollar cover and moved into a dimly lit bar where a couple of hostesses were mixing it up with customers in a row of banquettes. Guided by the bluish light from a half dozen televisions showing sports and porn above the bar, the single bartender, a Pauly D look-alike with spiked hair and silver earrings, was talking to a beer drinker watching the porn. He came over and I asked for the office. He frowned and snapped, "Go through the Show Room."

The hallway to the Show Room was adorned with photographs of nudes—in silhouette and straight on—none incredibly beautiful. I paid ten bucks to enter.

Revolving blue and white spotlights and flashing balls reflected off the moist bodies of three writhing pole dancers, two white and one black—one of the white gals probably breaking the *at least eighteen years old* law—tightly lined along a runway three feet above tables. The dancers' faces were neutral, their pelvic grinds keeping more or less in time with the heavy bass thumps, throwing their hair this way and that as they got it on with the poles, acknowledging with fake interest the cash gawkers folded into whatever held their G-strings together. Two bar girls in lacy panties worked the tables, their pasties pressed against the gawkers' shirts, steadying themselves by squeezing their buttocks against a rail behind the lines of tables. One mush-mouthed drunk grasped a thigh and got slapped. At another table, a nude black girl was in a lap dance, her crotch barely above the neck-straining patrons. Through the dust motes that rose from the floor in the revolving spotlights, leering faces looked down from the balcony over the runway. It was tawdry, and nobody was having much fun.

A blonde with a wide mouth, up to my chin in height even in spiked heels, heavily made up, her hair gelled, her breasts falling out of a Madonna bustier, made a move on me. "Hi ya, hot shot," she said stroking her breasts. "What ya need?"

"Where's the office?"

"Buy me a drink first and we'll talk about it," she said grabbing my hand and pulling me toward a table.

I shook myself loose. "Got an appointment."

The light went off in her eyes. She backed off, walked to a bar and leaned into two men in black tees and jeans who turned to check me out. No-Neck and Ditto, the Jersey Boys. Whatever she said caused No-Neck to walk ponderously over to me. "You here to see Mr. Zito?" he said with a smirk. Ditto backed him, twirling a toothpick in his lips.

"Yeah."

No-Neck puffed up and replied with mock politeness. "Well, suppose we go right over and see if he's here." He turned to Ditto for approval.

"Yeah," Ditto grunted, "let's do that," and he smiled like I was tracking in a dog turd. He took my right arm and pushed me behind No-Neck into an alcove which opened on a hallway to a scratched-up wooden door with a metal *Private* sign. Electronic pulses from the show-floor followed us. No-Neck opened the door, entered, and closed it behind him. "I seen ya before," Ditto said. His eyes brightened. "Hey, I remember. The other night, right? En Core?"

Either he was as stupid as he looked or it was an act. I smiled in acknowledgement and stared at my shoes until No-Neck opened the door and moved out of the way. Sal, Zito's bodyguard–driver, sat behind a beat-up wooden desk in a bluish shirt unbuttoned halfway down his chest to show a mat of hair and loops of gold chain. An open Ronzio pizza box and Bud Light bottle were in front of him. His eyes were gray nailheads.

"Hey, Mario Andretti!" Sal said and bit into a pizza slice.

"Where's your boss?"

Sal elaborately looked around the room. It lacked windows, its ceiling was stained by leaks. "Goodness me, he's not here," he said in false wonderment and swiped a paper napkin across his thick lips. "Last minute business. Ya know, this is Columbus Weekend. Heard of that? Lots of doin's on the Hill. Asked me to cover. What's the story?"

I remained calm enough to take the insult. Zito had sent a *cafone*, a *spacone*, the epitome of guido-ism, flashy, big, loud, stupid, and outlandish, mimicking cable show thugs and movie bad-guys.

"He said you can tell me."

"Personal," I said.

"C'mon, Frannie said it was okay."

"No." I turned to leave.

Sal belched loudly and got up. "Maybe I can get him on the phone." His gut bulged over jeans made for a man twenty pounds lighter, a bruiser gone to pot. He brushed by me. "I'll be back. Here," he said and offered a *Playboy* from the desk.

Sal would never win an Oscar. I figured Zito might be here somewhere because Sal probably did not get the Bentley often as a loaner. Unless I could make my deal with Zito, I would go home, get a stash of cash from the basement safe, and steel Young Jimmy's resolve not to dump by backing him. But why did Zito get me here and be a no-show? Just to insult me, the interfering rich East Side asshole, again?

Sal returned and remained at the opened door.

"Didn't reach him."

I flipped the magazine on the desk. "Let your boss know I had a deal for him."

"Yeah, I'm gonna do that. You can go out through the back. Closer to the parking lot."

Sal moved me along the hallway into another where I faced an exterior door with a push bar. Right about then, I remembered I hadn't mentioned Benno waiting for me; now, it seemed too late. I took a step outside, the door closed behind me. I was under an overhang, barely out of the rain. I pushed the fedora down on my head, put up my collar, fumbled in my pockets for my car keys. In the brightness of the parking lot's sodium lights, I was disoriented momentarily and then realized my car was across the lot. Where was Benno? He had to be out there someplace.

I hunched up my shoulders, my slicker creaked in its stiffness, and walked into the lot. I had gone maybe twenty feet when I heard a door open and footsteps behind me. I didn't turn, somehow I didn't want to see, and picked up my pace, not exactly running toward the Charger, but moving, the footsteps behind me matching my own, getting closer. My decision to run came too late. Powerful arms pinned my shoulders, my keys fell to the asphalt, my fedora was knocked off my head, my headbutt missed, my elbow went into a gut, and ... I took a stomach punch and fell to the asphalt.

54

IN THE MCDONALD'S RESTROOM, I found my stomach tattooed with a purple bruise the size of a large fist and my face red with carpet burn. My clothes felt like they had grown on me, I reeked of damp and sweat, I could shave my tongue.

"Match got moved at the last minute," he said. "Was going to be at En Core and maybe because Tuttle is screwing everything down tight, they changed it to Jimmy's. It's close by, everybody's been told to park at Hard Core and walk over." His face scrunched up. "Lot's of talk about a big money game. All cash, no markers, no wires. You got a member key?"

"Yes, but we won't get in."

"Don't worry."

∘ O ∘

We parked our cars in the Holy Ghost Church lot a block away from Jimmy's. My legs felt like they were filled with oatmeal as I got out of the Charger; rain dripped from my fedora's brim to slip under my jacket's collar. We stopped in the shadows one tenement away from Jimmy's. The floodlight over the outside staircase to the Billiard Club showed a guard posted at the door.

"You stay here," Benno whispered, "until he leaves. Then get up there fast. Give me your key."

Benno, with his collar up, chin tucked in, and hands in jacket, was quickly up the stairs. It was No-Neck who confronted him. Benno kept his head down as he said something to No-Neck; No-

Neck hesitated then marched down the stairs to the sidewalk and around the building to Wickenden Street. Benno opened the door and I hustled up the stairs.

The Club generated a sweaty electricity. The overhead lights over Jimmy's Table were cones of cigar and cigarette smoke. Testosterone and the odor of sweat-stained bills in clammy pockets emanated from the overheated sports. My fedora, pulled down to my ears, wasn't an orphan; there were others as well as panamas, a pork pie or two, and cockeyed caps. This was a crate of hard cases, the sweaters, railbirds, and assorted gamblers who frequent big money matches.

Young Jimmy, at the far side of the table, stared over the business end of his cue. He was tieless, his white shirt collar open, his hair oily, his brow shiny. In the stark lighting, his skin was yellowish and his piercing blue eyes were like two aquamarines. A sharp clack of balls was accompanied by a chorus of support; Harley Smoot in his classic black shirt, straightened, and beamed a gratified smile at the reaction. A classic match; you could tell that from the hush of the crowd before a shot and because the bar was open only between games. This was the match that Young Jimmy *had* to play.

Benno disappeared in the crowd as I spotted Ditto, his arms crossed, standing next to a tall, stocky guy wearing a black suede jacket over a blue shirt who scribbled furiously on a pad of paper. He was the *book* who took the bets on behalf of the house, and gave odds periodically depending on the status of the match. The numerals on the chalkboard behind them, which would indicate how many games in the match and the standings, were blocked from my view. As I got my bearings, I asked myself was I there only to witness Young Jimmy's desperate wager? Or had he gotten other backers? Or would he, disheartened by my absence and Zito's threats, dump?

The crowd shuffled around the play table to make room for the next shot. Smoot remained the shooter, and earned a collective gasp followed by rough voices of encouragement and disappointment. A bobblehead in front of me said to no one in particular that Smoot had played a safety, a shot that effectively placed balls on the table to block Young Jimmy's next shot. "Hannigan," he said, "will never pull this one off."

I squeezed closer to the table; nobody paid attention to me, just another guy with some dough on the match. Smoot brushed Young

Jimmy's shoulder and said something that made Young Jimmy smile, probably giving Young Jimmy a hustler's boost.

Benno reappeared and nudged me to follow him into the men's room next to the bar where we unzipped at the urinals. "Hannigan's behind a game, ten-nine," he whispered, "race to eleven. Started off with Hannigan winning until Smoot ran off a bunch of racks. Odds changed. Hannigan came back to one down. Smoot has a bunch of out-of-town backers here, big money. The book's got to be Zito's guy. The guy at the door and the one by the book are to make sure nobody leaves until they settle up. Your guy is going to dump ..."

We heard shouts from the tables. Maybe Young Jimmy made the shot! "He's not going to dump," I whispered back, not really sure, and went to the sink where the mirror reflected my fatigue, hurt, and a brain working too slow.

Benno joined me. "He has to. Zito's got to have it figured both ways. He's not just taking a cut on the bets, he's gotta be heavily down on this."

"If we can't help Young Jimmy, what the hell are we doing here?"

Benno checked his watch. "The match is moving too fast. It's got to last a little longer."

"Huh ...?"

The men's room's door opened. Ditto didn't check us out as he headed into a stall. Benno shrugged toward the door and we were back by the bar. "Stay here," he said.

I didn't do as I was told. I had to see the play. Benno became invisible in the crowd while I stood in the shadows of the first row of the viewing platform, looking over hats, oily hair, and bald heads. Young Jimmy had survived. Loud breathing and muttering and swearing increased the tension; money was being won or lost with each shot and pool money was never totally quiet. Then, a collective sigh of disappointment from Smoot backers at a missed shot. The play went back to Young Jimmy.

I left the gallery and pressed into the outer ring of spectators for a glimpse of the table, five balls in a wide spread, nine ball behind the six ball. Young Jimmy's wasted no time. He straightened, that glint of hard blue crystal was in his eyes, his face suddenly confident and chalked the cue tip slowly, waved the crowd back from the table, and this was the ideal opportunity for a dump, a difficult shot after a great comeback, lose, smile, shake hands. He bent from the waist, I heard the cue ball smack its target accompanied by gasps and applause. A double-chinned, red-faced man who must be the ref yelled, "Ten-ten. Shooters are gonna take a five minute break," he shouted over the noise.

The railbirds and gamblers rushed from the table to the bar, some faces grim, others smiling, all a little nervous, the book on a cell phone, Young Jimmy's great shot, maybe, wasn't on script. Benno gripped my elbow with authority. "C'mon," he grunted and I followed him to stand next to the inner staircase door between the viewing platform and the men's room. The door's dark stain blended into the woodwork. Benno looked at his watch; what was the deal on time?

Young Jimmy's head bobbed among well-wishers and back slappers, almost as many as those who surrounded Smoot. Young Jimmy handed someone his cue and walked toward the men's room as did Smoot. A couple of mean-faced guys followed—pool gamblers are suspicious of out-of-sight player chats during a match— but instead of entering of the men's room, Young Jimmy veered off to go behind the packed bar and drew a glass of water from the tap; Smoot pushed opened the men's room door.

Young Jimmy surveyed the crowd, acknowledging encouraging comments, when Benno, his head low over the bar, caught Young Jimmy's attention. Young Jimmy's head jerked up, his eyes searched the room, he saw me, and his face registered indecision. Was he playing to win, or putting on a great show just to dump? The next game, the deciding game, would tell. Across the room, No-Neck made a noisy entrance and pushed into the crowd no doubt looking for Benno. He saw Benno at the bar, took two steps in his direction, and the lights went off.

For a count to five, everything in the room, except for gasps of shortened breaths, stopped. Then, a cacophony of shouts, loud swearing, the sounds of bodies shuffling against one another. An emergency spotlight over the bar triggered, catching ghostly figures twisting away from the shaft of brilliance as the door of the interior staircase blew open in a burst of a half dozen cops. Flashlight beams like searchlights caught the crowd that shrank away as the cops fanned out, corralling those scattered around the room back toward the game table, batons and foot-long metal flashlights raised, their voices profane and threatening. Bill Tuttle, in uniform, appeared in the mix, directing a cop here or there. The book, caught in a flashlight beam, chewed mightily as he was hustled against the far wall along with complaining sports with hands in their pockets protecting their cash.

I was about to get swept up by a cop brandishing a baton when I was saved by a punch thrown by someone near the book that got the cop's attention. Benno flashed his badge to another cop in the light of his cell phone, and we were momentarily alone between the staircase door and the men's room. The commotion gave cover for Young Jimmy, in a crouch, to sneak from behind the bar, and using me as a shield, he made it into the men's room. Benno followed. The ruckus was still getting lots of cop attention, batons at chest level pushing the angry sports to line up against the wall, when Young Jimmy and Benno, with Smoot in tow, slipped out of the men's room through the door to the staircase. I joined them, bouncing off walls in the dark as we descended to a landing where Benno said something I couldn't hear. Young Jimmy nodded, opened an electrical circuit box, yanked up a lever, and the lights were back on.

Smoot appeared winded but otherwise as placid as an Arkansas fish pond in August as we moved into the restaurant. Benno pointed him to a table set with linen napkins, utensils, and glasses; Smoot sat facing Young Jimmy and began talking to him comfortably in a low voice, as Benno and I made for the kitchen. Benno quickly had the commercial refrigerator open and handed me plates of cold cuts, pickles and onions, and a pot of mustard. "You knew?" I asked.

"You can't have a national pool champion, an honoree, in the can overnight, can you?" He filled a water pitcher while I grabbed Bud Lights from the refrigerator and popped their caps.

"I guess not."

"Tuttle warned everybody, didn't he, that Providence was not going to be the Big Sleazy, not on his watch." He found two loaves of sandwich bread in a drawer and took out a handful of slices. I removed single serving bags of Wise potato chips from a carton. "So, a bust can't be a surprise to anyone. Anyway, no harm, no foul."

"What do you mean?"

"How are they going to prove there was any gaming? In the dark? No cash stash, because everybody kept their cash until the match was over and they settled up. Whatever else that could be evidence is in the book's gullet. All Tuttle's got is a crowd in a pool room. 'Who's playing?' 'Couple of guys.' Lot of suspicion but no facts. The sweaters and sports will be pissed and it'll cost 'em law-yer's fees to get out of the tank tonight but they'll be on the street in a couple of hours. No winners and no losers."

We headed back into the dining room; I brought the beer, bread and potato chips, Benno, the cold cuts. "Benno, you ..."

"Yeah. I know it's not perfect but how much time did I have? Who knew how it would turn out. Win? Lose? So, your buddy keeps all his earnings and winnings to date and whatever he bet on him-self. Smoot's gonna be okay. Reputations saved."

And I would never know if Young Jimmy was playing to win or if he was going to dump.

55

It wasn't quite over.

Two young cops, followed by Bill Tuttle, bumped down the stairs to confront four late-night snackers. We were told to stand and we did; they took our names and addresses, as a red-faced Tuttle blasted Young Jimmy, ripping him up and down, telling him that he would be charged with running a gambling nuisance at the Club, and that he was going downtown with the rest of the deadbeats. Was this tirade for the benefit of the two cops? As for me and Benno, what I hoped were theatrics heated up. "So, enjoying a couple of beers and a nice chat about pool?" Tuttle growled at me, "And you on the goddamn Commission!"

"I resigned," I responded. "Wedding on Sunday." My resignation had been dated and witnessed by Marcie this afternoon and mailed.

My response was received as smart-alecky. Disgustedly, Tuttle sent Young Jimmy upstairs with the two cops and told us three to clear out. I wanted, expected, a wink and a nod, at least a grim smile, but there wasn't any. I didn't get to ask him who let the cops into the restaurant or who hit the master electrical switch precisely at twelve thirty. Or who set the table.

o O o

I closed the garage door and stumbled up East Street and into the house. Nadie's note was on the refrigerator door: *I love you, I'm tired and I'm going to bed. Zelda and Ida are at the Renaissance.*

Everything is still on track. See you in the morning.

I poured two fingers of Jameson to puzzle out what had happened.

Police department vans were filling up with the sports as we snuck Harley Smoot into Benno's car for the champ's return to the Omni. As he got in, Smoot said, "Thanks, boys. Screwed up a great match. Next time I'm in town, you tell Jimmy I want to play again. Y'all come."

Before he left, Benno told me how, with a throw-away cell phone call on his way to the landfill, he had made the deal with Tuttle and worked out timing and logistics. Tuttle had agreed that Young Jimmy and Smoot wouldn't be swept up in the raid *if* they could make it out of the Club before the raiding cops had them lined up. As for Young Jimmy, as the Club's owner, he would go downtown like everyone else, but no tank time. Since Benno said, there was only one more night left on the event booze license, there really wasn't much that could happen to the Club. "Gambling nuisance? Sounded good," said Benno, "but ain't gonna happen."

"The lights?" I asked.

"Tuttle's idea."

"How did the cops get in? Was the door open?"

His answer was interrupted by a patrol car showing up next to the Taurus. He got into his car and I left into mine.

○ ○ ○

The whiskey was smooth and went quickly. I poured another finger, added two ice cubes and went to the den. I focused on the match: as between the two shooters, a tied or interrupted match is one never played. In other words, Harley Smoot's play lived up to his reputation as a supreme shot maker and sportsman; our local hero was to be remembered as being a game away from victory in a big money match with an all time great. Not a bad result. Not intended, but not bad. Something for Young Jimmy to hold on to, and the local pool fraternity to gossip about.

That would have made a neat ending, except for Zito and Scuiglie. Zito will call Young Jimmy's loan and I remained a target. The Mini's destruction and my abduction showed what Zito could do. This would end *mano a mano*. How? Where? How does an East Side guy challenge extortion and retribution from a Hill guy?

An idea rattled around in my brain. Pinball like, it caromed from bumpers into slides to be slapped back by flippers as I focused on Zito and the Palagi loan.

Thirty minutes later, I e-mailed Joe Laretta and left a message on his cell phone to meet me in the morning. I had a plan but I might end up catching a falling knife.

56 Saturday

NOT WANTING TO DISTURB Nadie, I had slept in my clothes in the den. I used the lavette off the hall to wash up and left a Post-It note explaining my need to catch up on work, pledging that I would be back from the campus before noon, and that I would keep my cell phone on. In fact, after a double espresso and two glazed donuts from the Dunkin' Donuts on Gano Street, I did go to my office to shave, change clothes, and wait for Laretta's call. That came at eight twenty.

"To whom does the criminal bar owe its thanks?"

"For what?"

"For the busy, lucrative night. Had a bunch of calls myself but referred them out to guys who deserve some pay back. Easy doings. Out of town guys with cash will pay anything to get out of the tank. Want to tell me?"

"No."

"Okay. I never asked. How did it go with Zito?"

My carjacking stung Laretta, eliciting a string of expletives, including a few in Italian. Being used, being part of a setup, was disrespectful to him, a black mark on his reputation. "On the Hill, an insult has to be faced down right away." He said he had to confront Zito this morning, but then he paused. "No, I got to go see somebody. You know what I got to do? You know where I'm going?"

I said I thought I did. Sunday on Columbus Weekend. The *Godfather* scene. I asked to come along.

"Are you nuts? Somebody like you offends him just by breathing. Do you have any idea what could happen?"

"Maybe," and under protection of attorney-client confidentiality, I gave him background on last night's raid at the Billiard Club without casting light on who did what to whom, Italo Palagi's debt to Heritage Finance for the vendetta money that never got to Italy, and my suspicions as to the reason why. I also told him of my willingness to guarantee Young Jimmy's loan in return for peace from Zito, that his 'somebody' might have to make the deal.

He listened, and relented. "A one-in-ten. Depends on whether he okayed the hit on you after Zito got his message to lay off. And how much credibility I've still got. And his curiosity after what I tell him. A long shot ..."

o O o

I drove the Charger—it had to be the Charger—across town, up the Hill, and parked on Dean Street at the rear of Heritage Finance, two cars behind Laretta's black Mercedes sedan. I joined Laretta as the dashboard digital clock of the Mercedes read nine forty-five. I felt compelled to put out my hand to him which he shook curtly. He was dressed informally in slacks and open collar shirt. He hadn't shaved and his face was etched in anger, but his voice was lawyer smooth. He discouraged me from trying to see Scuiglie, said he would represent me if allowed to make a case. I repeated my determination to do it myself if at all possible. He shook his head at my stubbornness and asked me questions about Palagi, the estate, and the loan from Heritage Finance, quickly assimilating facts. At ten o'clock, he said sternly, "Let's go," and we left the car.

It was a clear morning, bright and the buildings' shadows were stark. Around the corner at Atwells Avenue, familiar Italian music blared from speakers. The street was closed to traffic for the holiday weekend's events, food and souvenir vendors were busy setting up, and early shoppers gathered on flag-lined sidewalks. I could smell fresh bread from the bakeries. We passed a brick two-story with an ornate arch over its front door, its plate glass windows, with shades drawn, had gold lettering spelling out 'Heritage Finance Company' and 'Fast, Friendly Service.' An Italian tri-color hung over the door. Laretta snarled. "Hope the fuck is licking his wounds from last night."

We continued another block and came to a low-slung clapboard building with a weathered sign that read *Atwells Social Club*. Three mildewed plastic chairs leaned against dirty glass windows which had been painted black on the inside; conspicuously, no vendors had set up on its sidewalk. Laretta tried the door and it was locked. He knocked loudly and the door opened enough for a huge shaved head loudly chewing gum to peer out. A voice from the darkness said, "Joe Laretta? What are you doin' here?"

"I've got to see somebody. I've got something that has to be delivered personally."

"Who's this?"

"Somebody that's part of it."

"Wait right there, Joe," the voice rumbled.

The door closed shut and Laretta turned to me. "That's Paulie Matto. A capo. I just got him off a fraud charge on an insurance claim scam."

Two minutes later, the door opened slightly. "Joe, go around to the back." The door shut.

We retraced our steps around the corner to Dean Street, on to a crumbling concrete sidewalk to the rear of the Social Club. Waiting for us by an overflowing waste bin and a dented, paint-chipped, metal door were the Jersey Boys in full leather mode. Their eyes were red and puffy probably from a lack of sleep in the tank at the police station.

No-Neck put up a hand. "Just you, mouthpiece. "

That made me ballsy. "How you doing, fellas? Did that greaser ever get his car back? You know, that shit mobile from Broad Street?"

Ditto, a few bricks short of a load, was slow on the uptake but not No-Neck. He whipped the back of his hand to Laretta's chest. "Tell him to back the fuck off."

As Laretta braced his shoulders, I defused the moment. "I'll wait in the car, Joe."

Laretta held his tongue, nodded, gave me the keys to his car, and was patted down as I left. He followed No-Neck inside while Ditto remained posted at the door. Ten minutes later, Laretta rejoined me in the car. "You never know, do you. All my life I've tried to get inside their heads and I can't."

"What happened?"

"Told him how pissed I was, pissed enough not to represent any of his boys. I told him a whole load of shit was coming his way because Zito, using *his* guys, had stupidly carnapped the Mayor's best buddy, and that one way or the other, you would eventually get even with Zito." He rubbed his chin in thought. "I could be wrong but I don't think he authorized the move on you. Whatever else he is, Scuiglie is shrewd, doesn't take unnecessary chances. Guess he figured I wouldn't screw around with him and he had to know that Zito's ego could blind him. Anyway, I told him I came to bring a resolution between you and Zito, and you're outside in my car. Told me to wait. I think Frannie is getting a call."

We sat in silence, the boiling mad Laretta muttering an occasional expletive in Italian, until the Bentley pulled into the chain link fenced lot behind Heritage Finance. Through a side mirror, I saw Sal get out, slam the door, and check the area before Zito got out of the rear door. They stormed past the Mercedes without looking inside. Zito was a head shorter than Sal, no more than five five, his shiny black hair in a ponytail, his shoulders wide and covered by a maroon dress shirt. Ditto opened the metal door and let them in, but not before saying something that directed their attention to the Mercedes. Laretta got out and started toward them; from inside, knowing they couldn't see through the sunlight's reflection on the windshield, I shot them a middle finger salute.

They all went inside.

I hadn't seen Sal snap the fob that would lock the Bentley's doors after Zito got out. I thought, a gift, an unexpected opportunity! I left the Mercedes and approached the Bentley from the driver's side and was quickly inside. My left hand squeezed down between the console and the seat approximately to where it had been stuffed only days ago. I felt the metal tube, managed to grasp it, inspect it, and put it in my shirt pocket. My gambit would be legit! Would it work? I was excited enough to fail to check for a scratch on the paint on the passenger side door. And luckily I didn't because I barely made it back inside the Mercedes when the door to the Social Club opened and Ditto jerked his thumb at me. I had been summoned.

Having seen Laretta searched, I knew the drill. My arms were stretched against a cinder block wall, my feet spread. Ditto was rough around the crotch but since I wasn't carrying, it didn't take long, the metal door opened, and I was pushed down a dark hallway. Ditto opened another metal door, and left us, and I faced Frannie Zito. Behind him stood Sal.

The room didn't have windows and its fluorescent tubes barely perked up the lighting to dreary. Zito's eyes were bloodshot, with purple pouches below, yet, his hard face held a smirk: probably thought I came here as a humbled, humiliated, beaten man, with my lawyer pleading for mercy.

I took a step inside. Laretta was seated on a folding chair facing Gianni the Brow Scuiglie half hidden behind a huge metal desk, No-Neck standing at his side. Despite his nickname, I was not prepared for Scuiglie's appearance: Cro-Magnon forehead that held huge black eyebrows, a nose that began thickly before it flattened out over a large mouth with fleshy sensual lips, pale brown eyes with an intensity that got your attention. A white scar sliced through one eyebrow and ended at a receding hairline of cropped, jet black hair. He wore a dark blue shirt under a red cardigan sweater, a regular Mister Rogers. Unbidden, I sat on a folding chair next to Laretta. Scuiglie had a smoker's rough voice. "Joe, this better not be a fucking waste of my time."

Laretta, eyes like slits, answered stiffly. "You know I take care of my clients and I wouldn't waste your time."

Scuiglie didn't respond. He had the same flinty smile as Don Briguglia of Basilicata and I remembered I had heard a rumor about this windowless office—that it was virtually impossible to bug because a prior Hill boss had the room sheathed in lead. Became known as the *tomb* and for good reason.

"As I told you, I made an arrangement with Frannie to see my client last night. My client had a proposition." Laretta's voice crackled with anger. "The bullshit between him and my client was supposed to be over, everything supposed to be cool. Frannie made the meet at Hard Core. My client didn't like it but still went there and Frannie was a no-show. This, like I said, embarrassed me."

"Sorry about that," Zito sneered, his face wrinkled in mock surprise, "I left it to Sal. Anyway, all the guy wanted to do was apologize for being such an asshole. Right, Sal?"

Sal snickered, "Yeah, and ..."

Laretta's anger was palpable. "I got used for a goddamn setup! My client got stuffed into his car's trunk and taken out to the dump. Pretty goddamn over the top."

Zito replied flatly, "You got nothing to prove I had anything to do with that." He sat on the arm of a scruffy sofa at the right of Scuiglie's desk, his pose theatrical as he lit a cigarette, exhaled smoke, and leaned into Scuiglie who muttered to him. Zito waved off Sal, and Ditto and No-Neck were dismissed with a flit of Scuiglie's wrist. An ancient air conditioner's compressor kicked on and blew fetid air.

After they left, Scuiglie said to Laretta, "You got a beef with Frannie, I understand that. So how does it affect me?" and he pushed back in his chair as his large fingers interlaced across his thick belly.

Laretta replied that he represented the University in the estate of Italo Palagi. Scuiglie interrupted. "Only Palagi around here ran ice cream trucks around North P and Pawtucket ..."

Zito said, "An old fuck who borrowed from me. What's that got to do with—"

Laretta held up his hand. "Let my client finish this."

And I did. Like a well-rehearsed witness, I recounted Palagi's death, the Basilicata vendetta, and the saga of Maria Ruggieri who worked for the Giambazzi family on Long Island. Although Scuiglie avoided my eyes like I was the Gorgon who would enter and destroy his soul, the name Giambazzi got his attention. Laretta added, "Weeks before he died, Palagi borrowed two hundred fifty grand from Heritage that was to pay the Giambazzis."

Scuiglie's eyebrow, the one with the slice, rose a tick.

"Here's why you should know," Laretta said. "Before Palagi died, he hired Benno Bacigalupi ..."

"Bacigalupi?" Scuiglie interrupted. "That son of a bitch! Spent a career trying to nail me. He's retired and he's still a pain in my butt!"

Laretta shook his head. "Not through me. You know he's a dog with a bone when he's got a case. Palagi hired him to figure out where the money he borrowed went, because it didn't get to Italy to end the vendetta." Not exactly true, Joe, but ingenious. "Palagi died before Bacigalupi got far into it but he's got Palagi's bank statements, which didn't show the loan proceeds deposited. He figured the arrangement had to be that Palagi was never to see the money, it would never be traced to him, it would be paid out by Heritage to a front for the Giambazzis, from there to Basilicata."

Scuiglie's bulging forehead had furrowed in impatience as he followed Laretta's narrative.

"Bacigalupi confirmed that the money never reached Basilicata. Last Monday, he was there, in the family's village, with the local don through some connection he had in the Boot. Four months after the loan, according to the don, the family was still waiting for the money. Very angry."

Zito forced a smile, shaking his head as though Laretta's spiel was absurd. "Hey, it was a good loan. Not my fault if Palagi got screwed." He thrust his hands forward and cracked his knuckles as Scuiglie's steely stare left Laretta for Zito. The intelligence in his eyes confirmed everything I had heard about Scuiglie was true: he was a smart bad one.

"Either the Giambazzis didn't get the loan proceeds from Heritage," Laretta continued coolly, "or they got them and didn't turn them over to the family. Somehow, I can't see them not taking care of family. Imagine how pissed they would be if it turned out somebody used them. Which means to me, the loan proceeds weren't paid out by Heritage even though Palagi was paying interest on the loan. Over three g's a month. If the loan wasn't paid out, Heritage owes Palagi's estate the loan proceeds because he signed the note, and I've got a copy, and Palagi paid the vigorish on it. His estate has to make a demand for the proceeds. And even if the loan *was* paid out and it went to the Giambazzis, you see the problem. It's all public. The estate is in probate, Rudy and Bobby Lucca are in the case representing the Italian government and Puppy Dog represents a son in Italy, and the proceeds have to be accounted for. Who got the money? Lots of messy questions. *Journal* will be on it, the Department of Banking likely notified, maybe the AG ..."

The expected eruption from Zito didn't happen; instead, his lips were pursed like he was thinking something over.

"So, to protect people, that's why I arranged the meet between my client and this asshole who scammed Palagi. My client came with a proposition to negotiate."

"Bullshit," Zito shouted at Laretta. "He only came to plead for Hannigan."

Laretta came half out of his chair. "Are you calling me a liar, you piece of ..."

Scuiglie pounded the desk with a thick fist. "Shut the fuck up! Both of you!" But his angry stare went to Zito.

My turn. I addressed Scuiglie. "My offer was that the University as the estate beneficiary wouldn't press for Palagi's loan proceeds if he agreed Heritage wouldn't bring a claim against Palagi's estate, and that I'd personally guarantee repayment of Hannigan's loan in return for his dropping the pressure in Hannigan's match with Harley Smoot. Fair deal. After being car-jacked, that's off the table."

"You don't learn, do you?" Zito growled at me, his dark face filled with hatred. "Take your fucking guarantee and shove it up your ass! Joe, get 'im out of here before I ..."

This next part, I had not previewed for Laretta. Could I pull it off?

My right hand went to my shirt pocket. Very slowly, I took out a cartridge, not the one I had just taken out of the Bentley—that remained in Laretta's Mercedes—but the one I bought in Rome from the military antiques dealer. I had planned to spin the same story, if my courage held up, with this one from Rome. I held the cartridge in three fingers, twirling it in the dim light. Its brass casing caught the light and reflected it on the dingy walls.

"A bullet?" Zito said. "I hear it doesn't do anything without a gun." He laughed thinly, and all by himself.

Anger welled up within me. I had the absurd urge to grab Zito by the shirt to pummel him. In the emotion of the moment, my voice slipped into an archy Waspishness. "A cartridge like this was between the seat and console in your Bentley when you *invited* me into your car and pushed my fingers into the carpet. Fits a World War II Beretta, an Italian officer's side arm. Beretta stopped making the gun, and its ammo, after the war. Palagi threw a handful of Beretta cartridges inside your car the night he died. When he was fished out of the river, he had a Berretta in a trouser pocket, loaded with an identical cartridge. What's the odds on that?" I stuck out my chin. "You should fire whomever vacuums your car."

Zito's face reflected his recollection of Palagi's rage, the old man emptying his pocket, and flinging a handful of cartridges inside the Bentley. His jaw pressed into his chest, his eyes bulged as he coughed out, "Million fuckin' bullets in the world!"

"Yeah, that's true, but is there another dark green Bentley Flying Spur in Rhode Island? When Palagi was rousted out of the Bentley, he scraped its door with the knob of his walking stick. Paint got caught on its knob. Dark green paint. Been identified as paint from a Bentley."

"Who says?"

"Bacigalupi. He's got the cartridge ..." a white lie, "... and the walking stick, and he's working the case for *me*. Getting witnesses. Ever notice those fishermen, all those little Asian guys that are always there. Watching what's going on, minding their business. They get to be like background. Like the night Palagi got into your car and then was rousted out by Sal."

"Fuckin' bullshit!" Zito turned to Scuiglie. "The old fuck committed suicide!"

"You know," I said evenly, "you could be right." I sat back, like I was about to concede the point. "But Bacigalupi's relentless when he thinks he's got a case ..."

Zito began to interrupt but Scuiglie shut him up with the palm of his right hand raised to Zito's mouth. For the first time, he addressed me, "What's your deal with that fuck-off Hannigan. Lotta people spent last night in the tank." The scar pulsated faster as his voice rose. "And now I think maybe you're the fuck that caused the problem."

"No, I'm the guy hustled out of Hard Core's parking lot by two guys who came out of nowhere, who dropped me in the trunk of my car, and took me to the landfill."

Although Scuiglie's face never changed, I knew I hit home when his malevolent eyes became even more shaded and shifted to Zito.

Before Zito responded, I said, "No one wanted that match last night more than Hannigan. Against Harley Smoot? Dream match? Sure, I didn't want him to play, I tried to convince him not to, but he wanted to make enough to pay down his debt. Nothing was going to stop that match if he had his way. So, he's my friend and I agreed to be his backer, behind every wager he made, and he made a bunch. The bust screwed up a lot of people but especially him, he still owes Heritage over two hundred grand, and *you* are pissed. Think about it. Why would he bring in Tuttle?"

"Tuttle got a tip ..."

"With the number of pool junkies who knew about the match, could have come from anyone, there or not. Anyway, nobody figured on Hannigan's wife. She wasn't going to let him fall back into the action. Not rocket science for her to guess where he was going to play. She probably had no idea what or who might be involved, what danger her husband might be in."

I stood as did Laretta. Zito responded by lurching up from the sofa's arm and taking a step toward me. We were toe-to-toe, my fingers went to fists, and I braced that long jaw of mine to put it to Zito. "Cancel Palagi's note," I said, "or deliver the cash. All two hundred and fifty thousand. Hannigan gets no pressure from you before he pays off his loan. Which I guarantee he will. And, between us, you back off. We're done. I'll call off Benno when Joe tells me we have a deal."

Laretta was as terse when he spoke to Scuiglie. "You do what you think best, but I wouldn't want Bacigalupi on my ass with that bullet and walking stick and a witness or with all this shit in the probate court. And why screw around with the Giambazzi family?"

"Fuck you," Zito said and it was my turn.

To his surprise, I grabbed his hand and pressed the cartridge into it. "All or nothing."

He threw it to the floor.

57

BIG BALLS? AN OFFER he couldn't refuse? Right then, I was focused on getting out of the *tomb* alive. No-Neck, Ditto, and Sal lined the hallway as we filed past, Laretta in the lead; I half expected to be yanked aside and pummeled.

Laretta didn't say anything until we were in his Mercedes. "You blindsided me," he complained. He was angry and I couldn't blame him. I reached under my seat and picked up the cartridge.

"This is the one, Joe. I took it out of the Bentley this morning. Stroke of luck it was still there. I lied about Benno having it. He has the walking stick and it does have Bentley paint on it. The Beretta's magazine holds eight cartridges, one was in the chamber, seven for a clip, and we know that Palagi threw something into the Bentley. If Zito hadn't pushed my arm down ... if I hadn't felt it ... never would have gotten the idea that it was the rest of the clip of cartridges or to buy one like it in Rome. Still not sure why I did that. And this morning, Sal left the Bentley unlocked and I found the cartridge still there between the seats on its floor."

"Any ten-cent lawyer could blow your case away in court. You know that. So," he said slowly, "you didn't have to do this. Scuiglie never heard of Palagi and likely didn't okay the scam or your car-nap, you could have raised the defense against paying the loan at any time, *and* he doesn't need a problem with the Giambazzis and have Heritage shut down. All you did was get him pissed at Zito, make him back down. That's what this is about. Zito. You wanted that, didn't you?"

I did. Zito humbled me, threatened me, destroyed my car, stood me up when I was ready to eat humble pie, and scared the shit out of me. I had to even the score, and get some protection for Nadie. "Think it will work?"

"If Zito screwed him, or if he caused a problem or if you went through with your threats, maybe. How does he know that you will drop it?"

"Because I said I would. You know and Benno knows, that's my protection. That's got to be enough, Joe."

"So did Sal do it?"

I remembered what Benno said of the 'Ndrangheta when I asked the same question: "Not when there was still money to be had."

58 Wedding

THE PRENUPTIAL DINNER, DESPITE Nadie's apprehension, was a success, a wine-soaked affair, smiles all around and good-natured conversation, although the hugs and kisses didn't cross family lines. Some loudness from Arnie was lost in the hubbub.

As for Sunday and the wedding itself, the good Lord took a liking to us, Sylvia said. At four o'clock, the temperature was in the low seventies, the sun brilliant, the sky cloudless, with only a whisper of wind. We took our vows in the pergola in Temple House's rear garden, in front of sixty relatives and close friends. Nadie was radiantly beautiful in her Vera Wang gown. Tony Tramonti presided and kept to the sentimental script that Nadie had carefully composed.

After the ceremony, under a spacious tent, we were toasted with prosecco from Antonio's after limited but witty remarks from my brother as best man, and enjoyed the beautifully presented, sophisticated food catered by Russell Morin. As we greeted guests at their tables, I picked up bits of news and gossip. From Marco Antonio, I learned yesterday's Columbus Theatre event was crowded, the harangue against Carter University was hot and heavy, but the celebrities seemed more interested in selling books, CDs, and DVDs than defending Columbus or willing to take on Carter University. Today, at the Columbus Day parade, Italo-American girls in white party dresses and boys dressed up in what they thought were Columbus-like costumes marched with placards and banners in front of bands and floats honoring the Admiral of the Ocean Sea. The Knights of Columbus in full regalia were loudly cheered, as was a float depicting Columbus arriving in the New World being greeted by kneeling natives. Another float from the Sons of Italy was festooned with 'Go Columbus' balloons and floral arrangements; still another berated Carter University for its foolishness. Some adult placard carriers—Marco thought they were paid by the Brow—lined the parade route with anti-Carter signs and attracted media attention. Tony Tramonti took some booing and Sonny Russo, marching with the Luccas, was cheered boisterously. But no incidents, thank God.

At the Gershowitz table, Aunt Ida, Arnie, Simon, and their families—Zelda being at the head table—were overtly enthusiastic about our marriage. It went well until Arnie, incorrigibly, whispered in my ear, "Joe Tucci's really unhappy that he's going to get his money back. Maybe, we ought to ..."

I squashed his gambit with a frown.

As dishes and glassware were collected, the guests entered the Temple House's ballroom for dessert and dancing. Nadie and I were particularly pleased that some friends, as suggested, had brought along their children to eat dessert. The dancing was fun and robust, lasting for another two hours, fueled by an open bar and a platoon of waitstaff. The guests began to leave around nine, Nadie and I stood by the door with my mother and her mother, and we exchanged hugs, handshakes, goodbyes and thank-yous.

Before ten, Aunt Ida and Zelda were whisked back to the Renaissance, my mother and Sylvia supervised the staff at clean-up, and Nadie and I went upstairs to the mansion's guest suite.

Let me put it this way: she was worth waiting for.

59 Rome

W̶E LANDED AT FIUMICINO at six thirty on a sun lit morning. After immigration, luggage collection and customs, Enzo welcomed Nadie with a huge bouquet of flowers and escorted us to a longer, sleeker, black Lancia, the Italian version of 'limo.'

Nadie had slept soundly on the plane and, excitedly, was looking for anything Roman. From behind new Lacoste tortoise-shell sunglasses, she followed our course into the city with a Garmin video map as Enzo enthusiastically provided local references and corrected pronunciations through Ostiense and Trastevere, over the Tiber, into city traffic. At the Piazza Trinità dei Monti, we were greeted by two doormen in ruritanian black and gold braid uniforms and escorted into a lobby sumptuous in marble, silk hangings, paintings, gilt, and thick carpet, reminding arriving guests that *this* was the Hassler, Rome's classic five-star hotel, close by the Spanish Steps, the shops of the Via Condotti and the Via Borgonona. My parents honeymooned at the hotel more than fifty years earlier and I had been able to reserve the same spacious, top-floor suite.

In its sitting room, she opened double glass doors to a terrazzo balcony to the ancient city's panorama. The hotel had iced a bottle of our wedding prosecco; I opened it and brought two glasses to the balcony. "How many hills can we see?" she asked. "Quirinal, Palatine ..." She pointed, the colorful Judith Ripka bracelet I gave her for the trip sliding down her wrist, and said, "Saint Peter's!" She took her glass, kissed her unshaven husband, sat on a lounge, her guide book in front of her, my happy, beautiful wife. I kissed her and said, "*So mo davai tutti i bacci saranno sempre pochi,*" then translated, "If you give me all the kisses in the world, they will be too few."

o O o

The next morning, after Enzo drove Nadie to the Villa Borghese gardens for a morning jog, and a sometimes argumentative telephone call with Father Pietro, I dressed in a dark suit, white shirt and red tie, and took a ten minute cab ride to a nursing home, a *casa di cura*, hidden behind a brick wall in the upper-middle class residential area of Caracalla near the Celian Hill. A brass plate below a pull bell stated visiting hours began at eleven o'clock; nevertheless, I pulled the bell cord and the door was opened by a wizened male *portiere* accompanied by a tiny, dark-skinned woman in starched white uniform. In Italian, I asked for *Signora* Claudia Cioffi, using the polite term for an elderly Italian woman even if unmarried. The nurse pointed to the plaque but said she would inquire as to whether her superior would permit my visit. She stepped back and allowed me into a sun-filled courtyard, flowers everywhere, climbing roses in particular, providing a powerfully sweet scent in the still air. In the shade of a tiled *loggia*, three elderly women in wheelchairs, another on a bench, watched me as we crossed by them. One murmured '*Dottore*' as I walked by; I smiled and shook my head at her mistake. Inside the ochre colored main building, the nurse left me at a reception desk where the acidic smell of antiseptic wasn't completely concealed by floral spray; she disappeared down a corridor to return shortly with an imposing, wide-shouldered woman in a severe black suit. "Yes?" she asked in impatient English.

"Forgive me, *Dottoressa*," giving her the honorific she easily accepted. "I beg your indulgence at this hour." She took a step forward to inspect me as though I brought nothing but bother, taking my business card as I said that the *Instituto dell' Italia Studi* where Signora Cioffi had been employed remained interested in her well-being. The *Dottoressa* nodded reluctantly in acceptance; in Italian, she asked the nurse to take me into the visitor gallery.

I was led down a hallway, past a fleet of walkers and wheelchairs, into a spacious room with bottom windows open to the court yard, walls painted a lilac color, posters of Italian scenic landscapes, a plasma screen television, card game tables, and couches and chairs, some covered in plastic, perhaps for incontinent patients.

I sat comfortably by windows that let in a golden Roman light from the courtyard until I heard the squeak of wheelchair's wheels. Claudia Cioffi, in a dark blue smock, her lank hair cut short, wearing unattractive, oversized sunglasses, was wheeled into the room. I stood in deference as the nurse tucked the chair's arms under a small table by a window; a whispered comment from the nurse as she locked the chair's wheels in place evoked her patient's dismissive wave.

"So, it is you," she croaked.

The sunglasses hid much of her face and were likely not worn out of vanity but to avoid the glare of a morning sun. Her complexion was pale, there were sags of skin in her cheeks, loose folds under her chin. Can this be the same frenetic but healthier woman who berated me not two weeks ago?

I sat opposite to her at the table. "I insisted that Father Pietro tell me where you were convalescing. I appreciate your time, Signora."

"Well?"

"Before he died, Italo Palagi delivered to Father Pietro an affirmation of his determination to leave his trust and estate to the University, even with knowledge of his son, Vittorio Ruggieri." I removed a copy of the letter of affirmation from my jacket, unfolded it, and showed it to her. She ignored it. "Signora, I must ask you if this document is in your handwriting."

"Did he not acknowledge the document as his before a notary?" she asked flatly.

"Yes, he did," I admitted.

"Then, I have no comment," she replied with a sigh and weary shake of her head.

Her hands, which had been folded in her lap, reached for the rubber wheels at each side of the chair as though she was going to wheel herself away, but she didn't; she adjusted herself in the chair for comfort and abruptly, thrust her face toward me, expelling the acidic breath of the sick. "Have you told your mother that Palagi was duplicitous? A liar? You must know by now."

"My mother will miss his company."

"Hah," she growled, showing me a profile of her gray, drained of life face. "Fooled like all the others. Do you know how often he bragged of his connection to your family, used your family name to ingratiate himself? It was his intention, always, to identify with those who could be protective, whose status could rub off on him, to disguise, disown, his past ..."

I interrupted. "Did you send him a copy of a funeral card for Maria Ruggieri?"

"Why would I do that," she said flatly but not answering. "Is that why you are here?" She said, disappointment in her voice, and turned her head to the window.

"A portion of Palagi's royalty and license fees to be shared with the University were diverted to ..."

"Montecristo?" She coughed out a dry laugh, still facing the window. "Do you not see his attempt at humor in the name? Like the Count of Monte Cristo, Dumas' fictional count, Italo considered himself an innocent forced by society to take revenge. Montecristo, to save you time, was Italo's pleasure account. Because of your faculty's jealousy, his fear of publicity and discovery of his past, he felt browbeaten into giving up half of his royalties and license fees, and to create the trust account. He felt justified in his theft. He took advantage of your lax supervision. The funds helped maintain his Florence apartment, his Lerici apartment, pay his gambling losses, for his long trips to Europe, the ... boys ... he debased. After the funds reached Genoa, they were sent to Lugano, Switzerland. On his trips to Italy, he would cross the border, make his withdrawals. In Lugano, the account was under an alias. He had a fake passport for identification. Never once questioned by the *Guardia di Finaza* or the *Frontiere*." She turned to me as her face cracked into a dolorous grin. "The amounts he could divert each year became smaller and smaller as the royalties and other payments diminished. With his expenses so high, he was becoming a pauper."

She stopped, took a momentous breath and wiped her dry lips with the back of a mottled hand. I then breached a professional confidence for the greater good. "The Institute's accounts in Rome are being audited and ..."

"Ha!" Her hands came together weakly, as if to clap, but made no sound.

"... we know Brunotti was aware of the Montecristo fraud ..."

"Brunotti insisted I act as executor because he thought he could control any investigation by the estate or the University into Montecristo or into his own fraudulent accounts, thinking my reputation, Palagi's reputation, were important to me. As if I cared. When I refused, the idiot terminated me." Her lips formed the grim, determined smile of one who senses victory. Brunotti had been out-classed.

Her hands moved slowly, painfully to remove her sunglass-es. She blinked in the sunlight; the eye with the cataract seemed opaque, the other was gray and rheumy. Her head was thrust back and she spoke louder than before, as though addressing an audi-ence.

"Palagi portrayed himself as the victim, misled, seduced by oth-ers' lies, as when he claimed he felt compelled by poverty to join *La Lega*, the conspirators who plotted against the Republic. But I tell you he was a willing participant, an organizer, using his father's name, his uncle's contacts, all the while stealing from contributions to their cause. Yes, stealing from them! In this too, he justified it as retribution for his shame. Because the conspirators operated in cells, most did not know of one another, nobody knew how much was paid in or from whom, except Italo who opened accounts, paid bills and bribes. After the plot was smashed, he blackmailed those involved, the businessmen, those in the police and army, politi-cians, men of affairs who feared that their names might be given to the SDI. I have always wondered if Italo exposed the plot in return for protection from the SDI."

She raised her chin to me, staring down her nose. "How did his books get published so quickly? Distributed in every bookstore in Italy? Because, they were literature?" A shake of her head ended in a cackle. "Or how did he quickly become a full professor at Bo-logna while others languished on the lists? Or why he left Italy? Even years later, he blackmailed many to contribute to the Institute to influence the government's generosity. It was only his longevity that brought him down; he outlived them, their donations ceased, and the royalties, the fees, diminished. Again, he was reduced to theft, skimming off monies that belonged to the Institute, feeding his gambling, paying for his boys ..."

"And the 'Ndrangheta ...?"

"What irony. The extortionist was himself a victim. They took their pound of flesh, allowed him his reputation so long as he kept his name on their account. You need to know that he ...?" She stopped herself abruptly.

"What, Signora?"

"You said you spoke to Sacchi, the Dominican?" she asked warily.

"Yes, only to locate you."

That opaque eye searched my face to demand my complete attention. "He told me you want to know about Palagi's death," she hissed. "And I tell you it was as deceptive as the rest of his disgusting life!" She clutched her robe as though chilled.

"He telephoned me that night, demanding I come to his apartment. I arrived, I used my key, he was at the dining room table, raving that the money he borrowed had not been paid to the Ruggieri family, that they would kill him, that the 'Ndrangheta had liquidated its investment account, that his one prideful asset, the trust account for the University, was likely lost in a Ponzi scheme. On the dining table was a vial of pills, a gun, and a handful of bullets. He said the gun was his father's, kept by him all these years. He put a bullet into a magazine, slammed it into the gun, all very dramatic, very Italo, and sobbed he wanted to commit suicide but lacked the courage to pull the trigger."

A trembling hand went to her lips. "He pushed the gun into my hands, placed its muzzle to his head, demanded I put my fingers over his, and squeeze the trigger. I was tempted, but I refused," she said and turned her head back to me. "He put the gun down and picked up the pills. He shook the vial before my face, back and forth, the pills rattling inside. 'Push them down my throat,' he shouted. I refused, again, and he taunted me. 'Help me die and you win the *tontine*.' You know of the *tontine*?"

I nodded.

"My anger had built up by then and I challenged him. 'Do it, do it, coward!' I shouted. He picked up the gun, walked to the window overlooking the street below, opened it, pulled up its screen. For a moment, I thought he might actually shoot himself. But instead, he stared down at the street, and when he finally turned back to me, he seemed calmer. He pocketed the gun, took the bullets from the table and the vial of pills, put them in his trouser pockets ..."

She coughed, bringing up phlegm, holding it in her mouth until she worked a tissue from her robe's pocket and spat into it, returning the soiled tissue to her pocket.

"He went to his study, stayed there less than a minute, took his walking stick, and left the apartment." She looked over my shoulder as though remembering. "From the open window, I watched him as he exited our building, crossed the street, and approached a car in the parking lot of that striptease club by the river. I swear he looked up at me before he banged on the car's window, a door opened, and he got inside. What was he doing? Who was in the car? I left the apartment, locking the door behind me, took the stairs to the first floor, and exited, like he did. Although the *nebbia*, the fog, was gathering, I saw someone huge fling open the car's door and drag him out. Italo shouted into the car, in a rage again, and threw something, maybe the bullets, into the car. Still shouting, he swiped the side of the car with the knob of his stick, before he was pushed away."

"You followed?"

"From across the street," she said. "The fog was thick along the river. Every few seconds, it would open up and I saw Italo being pushed along. And then it was too thick. The man from the car quickly returned. Where was Italo? Minutes went by." Her voice lowered to barely audible. "I waited and waited. He did not return. There was no sound from a gun. Had he mustered the courage to swallow his pills? I left without knowing."

She coughed, a hacking cough deeper than before. I expected her to call the nurse, but instead, she pressed her face to within inches of mine. "Why did I stay with him, years and years and years, you ask. Money? I have no obsession for money. *Cupiditas radix malorum*. The root of all evil. Not for money, no, I stayed," she said in a voice cold as ice, "to insure his eternal damnation!"

She stopped abruptly and snatched a handkerchief from her sleeve to wipe her eyes, not of tears but of ooze. I used the opportunity to sit back, to move my face further away from her fetid breath.

"My father's family is Roman, but when my parents separated, I was raised by my mother in Modena. Giovanni Strozzi was my cousin, my mother's sister's son, a calm, beautiful boy, intelligent, kind, destined for great things, the pride of our family. He was like a younger brother to me and I loved him. For reasons I can't guess since he was so beautiful and attractive to girls, he decided after preparatory school to become a priest. With his family connections, his brilliance, his personality, he could have become a bishop or cardinal, maybe Pope. He was at the seminary when, at seventeen, he visited me in Rome during a summer vacation. I was then living with Italo. Giovanni thought our arrangement was shameful and he lectured me outside of Italo's presence and I lied to him, told him Italo would marry me. I didn't chaperone him as I should have, I was too busy in those days as Italo's courier, running up and down the country delivering messages, acting as his agent."

Her fingers clenched together as a strangler might grip his victim. "He became a priest five years later and five years after, he committed suicide. A priest suicide? A terrible scandal, to be hushed up. To save family embarrassment, it became an accidental overdose of sleeping pills. I never accepted that, and a year later, I went through his belongings that were finally delivered to the family, including a diary that exposed his deep despair. He had been raped by Italo! Raped! Not just once, but many times during the weeks I was away from Rome. Giovanni was intensely ashamed that it awakened in him some dark passion that he could not confess. That was why after his ordination, he devoted himself, in a kind of penance, to parish work with the poor in Reggio, far below his education and status, wearing himself out. Alone, despairing, he died." She paused, swallowed, and continued. "After that, I knew my fate was to avenge Giovanni. I contrived to meet Palagi in New York. My life would be numb, perhaps without love or family, but Italo would pay for his corruption of my beautiful cousin."

Her good eye stared at a spot above my head, as she braced herself against the back of the wheelchair. "He was only a boy!" she shouted. "Italo raped him! You see how it was. Italo was making love to me and raping my beloved cousin!" She coughed up phlegm and her voice was barely audible as she gasped, "I planned to divulge Giovanni's diary to Italo just before he died, when his soul, forever blackened, would be beyond the possibility of penance, of confession...." Then, abruptly she collected herself; slowly, her voice tightly controlled, she said, "He cheated me of my opportunity. Still, he died a suicide, forever damned."

The nurse appeared, a questioning look in her face for me at the distressed old woman before her. "Take me back to my room," the old woman demanded in Italian. The nurse released the brakes on the chair's wheels and turned Claudia Cioffi toward the corridor, a long, dark corridor, that gave finality to the scene.

One Year Later

IT HAD BEEN QUITE a year.

Sugarman: The Musical opened off Broadway, hyped as the next *The Producers*. Reviewers have been unkind.

The Shoot-Out was so successful that the promoters found a larger city venue. Happened before with the X-Games. Providence had always exported success.

Tony Tramonti remained a popular, if battle-worn, mayor, with sharpened political skills in his budget, reform, and political engagements with the Lucca faction on the City Council. He had gaffs, like being on vacation in Florida when a surprise snowstorm dumped a foot of wet, sticky snow on Providence, stranding kids on school buses.

People talk about the *good* Fausto—supportive of his brother— and the *bad* Fausto—enmeshed in the nether world of Providence politics. I didn't ask what he was doing behind the scenes during the Shoot-Out or his connection to Frannie Zito. We haven't spoken much since.

Columbus Day remained a nagging issue for Carter University but the rancorous local controversy slowly fizzled, overshadowed by the indictments of Sonny Russo and Puppy Dog for bribery and corruption. There is a God!

The Columbus Day fiasco stopped negotiations on the tax treaty. As an interim measure, the University voluntarily paid the City an amount equal to ten percent of the amount of tax that would be applied to the assessed valuation of its real estate, minus the value of services that the University, its faculty, its social service agencies, and students rendered to the city and its residents. The ten million donation soothed some members of the City Council, but not the Lucca cabal who claimed the City was being shortchanged. No one in College Hall thinks the payment will be the final tab or bring civic peace but it was a start.

The University executed a settlement agreement with Vittorio Ruggieri within weeks of my meeting with his lawyer in Rome. Puppy Dog came to Pine's office to represent Vittorio Ruggieri; neither of the Luccas showed. Later, the two Italian apartments, which we belatedly found had also been mortgaged by Palagi, were sold for close to seven hundred thousand euros; after payment of the mortgages, fees of the brokers and lawyers and taxes, the net proceeds of barely two hundred thousand were split between Vittorio and the Institute. Benno and I wondered if Vittorio squandered his share, assuming that the 'Ndrangheta left him with something to squander, and if the Ruggieris of Basilicata ever received a euro. As to the estate, his will was admitted to probate without objection, Heritage Finance did not file a claim in Italo Palagi's probate, and there was just enough left from his other assets to pay expenses and the legacies in full, leaving nothing for the Institute.

Later, I got a note from Puppy Dog, enclosing crisp new business cards, saying he was available to assist the University at any time. His chutzpah was impressive.

Frannie Zito disappeared last March. Joe Laretta told me that Zito had a falling out with *somebody* and that Zito may have contributed—bodily—to the stability of a new bridge abutment in the Barrington River.

Young Jimmy found that an influential friend could help secure a favorable loan refinancing, and with his earnings and winnings during the Shoot-Out, coupled with recovering patronage at the restaurant, he paid Heritage Finance every last penny shortly before Zito disappeared. To keep his occasional color commentary spots on ESPN's pool matches, he rid himself from any connection with the sweaters who came after him for a rematch with Harley Smoot. His ego was in good stead, as was, after weeks of penance and reconciliation, his marriage.

Cosimo Brunotti's resignation was accepted, not with regret, but with relief. During the termination negotiations, he wrapped himself in a patriotic cloak. He soon was hired as a managing director of a Fiat subsidiary in Torino and recently was placed on an election list for Parliament by *Avanti Forza*, a rightist political party. Somehow, that fit. As to his possible involvement in Italo Palagi's death, I concluded Brunotti was too smooth to involve himself, personally, in the old man's death and had neither enough time nor perhaps courage to plan or execute a murder.

The Institute never fully recovered from the Ravensford debacle and the Columbus Day fiasco, although it retained some loyal donors. An Italo-American scholar became its new executive director and reduced the scope of its activities. Ironically, only last week, the publisher of the Forza novels indicated a desire to reissue the series, maybe updating them as had been the case with the James Bond novels, even thinking of sequels in graphic novel form. Maybe Caesare Forza once again will provide the Institute with substantial royalties.

Father Pietro informed me of Claudia Cioffi's death in Rome. He sent me a funeral card of remembrance that had a picture of Blessed Virgin of Loreto, without a comment. In a subsequent e-mail, he said Claudia Cioffi left her considerable estate, augmented by Palagi's legacy and the insurance policy proceeds, to a charitable foundation for seminary scholarships in memory of her cousin, Giovanni Strozzi.

Palagi's estate filed a claim against Ravensford Capital in its bankruptcy but received little besides Champlin & Burrill legal bills. The disbursed A-4 account funds simply disappeared into the Italian banking system. From there, who knows?

Aunt Ida continued to reign in Brooklyn and was solicitous of her sister's every need. Zelda Winokur enjoyed Palm Beach last winter for six weeks at the Brazilian Court. People keep dying, allowing the Gershowitz funeral homes to pay bills, the trust fund to become balanced, the investors, mostly, paid off. The loans were current, although our accountant fought every month with Arnie for accurate information.

Algy's Autorama now has a Nissan Leaf hybrid, with a battery charger, which has survived two Nadie fender benders over the past year. For myself, a super-charged red Camaro ZL1 replaced the Charger.

Nadie is nauseous most mornings and wonders aloud if she will survive her pregnancy. The thought of pushing into my late sixties when he, it is a *he* as identified by an infinitesimal smudge on an ultrasound, will be entering Carter University, is unsettling.

o O o

As to the death of Italo Palagi, Nadie said maybe, it was all a "bit of bad business" to be gotten through and forgotten, even if a part of me remained uneasy.

That was, until ...

I have been blessed with excellent, even robust, health. I rarely, if ever, have to think about opening a childproof, tamper-proof, prescription vial. One night, Nadie, suffering with the flu, asked me to get her medication from the medicine cabinet in the bathroom, which I did, and try as I might, I couldn't open the goddamn pill vial! Only then did I remember that the prescription bottles in Palagi's medicine cabinet were all without caps. Not a one had a lid. And why? Because Palagi couldn't open them. Palagi's bout of Guillain-Barré cost him strength in his fingers. If the pill vial was shaken under Claudia Cioffi's nose, as she claimed, the vial had to have a lid. That night, Palagi didn't smash the vial open to get at his pills; the vial Benno found by the river didn't bear a crack. Someone opened the pill vial for him when he sat on the slab of granite by the river or shortly before. Who would have been there to do it?

Sal? Possibly, but he was more of a stomp, kick, and butt kind of guy. A drug-soaked resident of the shanty town interested in stealing a walking stick? No way. An agent of the 'Ndrangheta suddenly in town to complete the vendetta? Not likely. Certainly not Brunotti.

I returned to bed that night painting this scene in my mind. Claudia Cioffi watched Sal emerge from the fog, returning to the Bentley. She ventured across the street and saw Palagi on that slab of rock. Maybe he fingered his pills or the Beretta in indecision. As determined as a Harpy, she managed to get down the slope and confront Palagi. *That's* when she reviled him in his rape of her cousin Giovanni, delivered her challenge to die, goaded him to commit the deed that would damn his soul. She opened the pill vial that Palagi could not have managed, and watched him ingest his poison. Was there a last, spiteful, ironic laugh from the cancer victim as he swallowed his pills knowing his enemies would soon be suspects in a murder he designed for them? Was that, in the last analysis, why he ingested the pills, to spite them all?

o O o

What eventually settled my mind was a lunch with Father Pietro upon his return to Providence at the Carter Faculty Club. I said to me the most interesting thing about Italo Palagi was his death and told him of my theory.

"If so, my friend, we must admit he was artful? See what has happened. Brunotti, a fraud, discovered, and terminated from the Institute. The son, unworthy certainly, cheated out of his estate by his own wrongdoing. And Claudia, his agent in his final act of spite. Very Italian. And for you and to me, it was 'you have pained me, you will now be my agents to cause my enemies downfall.'"

For the first time in months, I thought of Don Fabrizio's death-bed in *The Leopard*, as his life eases away into darkness, anticipating the last journey, still wondering how he became a prisoner of his own making, at the last seeing his life as one of tragedy and disappointment, a life as bare as despair.

"We shall never know. Perhaps teaching us a valuable lesson? We are never free of temptation even to the last."

Other Algy Temple Mystery books
by J.J. Partridge

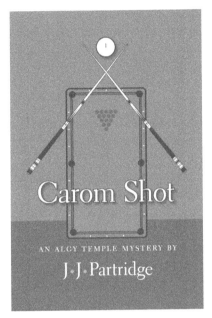

Available online in print and Ebook

Acknowledgments

First to my agent, Paula Munier, for her diligence and faith in my work, I appreciate her patience and attention.

To my manuscript readers, Norah Christianson, Jack Manning, and Jim Taricani, for their time and helpful comments.

To those patient enough to answer questions and give advice and guidance, such as Barnaby Evans, the creator and impresario of WaterFire, Father Brian Shanley, O.P., President of Providence College, and Deborah DiNardo, Esq. for legal background on American and Italian law.

To AnnMarie Pedro, a nine ball player extraordinaire and the folks at Snookers, for background on Rhode Island pool and tournament action.

To readers of *Carom Shot* and *Straight Pool* and booksellers worldwide who encouraged the continuation of the series.

Especially to Donna Beals who was so patient in working through the drafts.

To David Partridge for his sense of humor and critical eye.

To Ruth Clegg for my professional photograph.

To Joe Coccaro and Courtney Davison from Köehler Books for their valuable support.

Finally, to Regina who lost me after many dinners and weekends as I worked with Algy Temple and his friends and foes. The hours together were missed. "At least, we had Rome."

I also recommend di Lampedusa's *The Leopard* (translated by Guido Waldman, Pantheon Books) for a thoughtful, beautifully written novel on Southern Italian culture and history and *The Salamander* by Morris West for the idea of postwar conspiracy in Italy and its aftermath.

CPSIA information can be obtained
at www.ICGtesting.com
Printed in the USA
FFHW020025191119
56087286-62121FF